The Away Place

Ruth Tiger

Eloquent Books
New York, New York

Copyright © 2009

All rights reserved – Ruth Tiger

This novel is a work of fiction. Though based on the author's experiences, all names, characters, places and incidents have been changed and fictionalized. Any resemblance to individuals or events is coincidental.

Cover Art: Siri Tiger © 2009. All rights reserved.

Dedication Art: "Lou" by Lauretta Davies © 2009. All rights reserved.

No part of this book may be reproduced or transmitted in any form or by any means, graphic, electronic, or mechanical, including photocopying, recording, taping, or by any information storage retrieval system, without the permission, in writing, from the publisher.

Eloquent Books
An imprint of Writers Literary & Publishing Services, Inc.
845 Third Avenue, 6th Floor – 6016
New York, NY 10022

http://www.strategicbookpublishing.com

ISBN: 978-1-60693-577-4

Printed in the United States of America

Dedication

To Lou and the others who made it out,
and to those who didn't

Acknowledgements

The writing of this book has been a long journey, from tossing around the seeds of the idea on our back deck in Denver in the early 1980s to its fruition many years later. The funny, tragic, and even bizarre events of those with whom my husband and I have worked, and whom we knew and loved, seemed like a story that must be told. Important rights were established for those with disabilities since the 1970s yet it is vital to remember both how far we have come from the days of habitual institutionalization, and that there is still far to go in giving equal opportunities to the most vulnerable among us. This book attempts to give a snapshot into the lives of institutionalized individuals and the life-changing opportunities that occurred when they were integrated into a world they knew nothing about, in John's words, *The Away Place*.

I could not have written this book without the love and support of many people in my life; those who shared these experiences, those who encouraged me to keep writing, and those who believed I could do this. My loving thanks first goes to my husband, Alan, who put up with my early morning hours of writing for so many years and for his constant encouragement and unfailing faith in me. He lived through many of the events in the book; this story is not only mine, but his, as well. I am also thankful to my writing partners who read and reread my book and were honest with me: Connie Conally, Sandy

Johanson, Sheryl Rogel, Shari Shelton, Betsy Sherman, and my sister, Carolyn Westberg. My thanks goes to others who supported me in many ways: Lauretta Davies for her wonderful painting of "Lou," my daughter, foremost fan and painter par excellence, Siri Tiger, who translated my concept of Larkspur into the cover design, and to my late mother, Alvera Westberg, who modeled a life-long love of writing. I also want to thank Eloquent Books for working so efficiently and quickly to bring this work to publication. Most of all, I am grateful to the many individuals with significant disabilities whom I have known, none of whom can read this book. Working with these special and challenging people has been my joy, sometimes my sorrow, and one of the great privileges of my life.

Chapter 1

Larkspur

The urge to pee woke him. John thought about getting up, but what if the Mean Man was still here? He tugged the sheet down from his face and peered to his left to see if Lonnie was awake yet. The sheet-covered form in the bed next to his was still, as were all the others. A narrow window near the top of the wall was faintly gray. Any minute the wake-up call would come.

Instinctively, John fingered his ear. It was lumpy from all the pulling. The Mean Man was the worst at that. Nurse Julette called it cauliflower ear. She told John she was trying to stop the ward techs from pulling on ears, but they kept doing it anyway, especially when she wasn't there.

Soon the impulse became too powerful. John swung his bad leg over the side of the bed. He stood up slowly, testing to be sure it would bear his weight. Then he tiptoed toward the toilet room, trying not to let the flats of his feet touch the cold floor. He passed the row of beds that lined the white walls on both sides of the sleeping room, each bed containing a white wrapped figure. In the light of the bare bulbs overhead, they looked like mummies. Everyone, including John, kept the sheets over their eyes to ward off the glaring lights. The techs kept them on all night for safety, they said.

Barney-the-Giant's enormous feet poked out from the end of his bed. John resisted the temptation to tickle them. He knew that Barney-the-Giant would roar awake and that would surely bring the Mean Man running. As he passed Timmy's giant-size crib, John noticed Timmy was already awake, writhing under the covers. Hurrying past, he decided he would stop to talk to Timmy on his way back.

John held himself as he shuffled quickly toward the toilet room, mumbling softly so the Mean Man wouldn't hear, "Gotta pee. Oh, gotta pee bad."

He sat down on his favorite toilet, the one near the wall where he could hang on. The tingle of relief made him sigh. He absently glanced down the row of black-seated toilets that stood out against the white of the tile floor. Just around the corner were the showers. John didn't like them. The drain in the center of the floor sucked the water down, and when he was wet, John had trouble maneuvering this slope. He had fallen more than once and was secretly afraid he might get sucked down the drain. At least that's what the Mean Man had told him once.

John pushed the silver flusher with his foot. Water whooshed down loudly and he cringed. He hoped the Mean Man had his radio turned on loud. John stopped at the clouded mirror above one of the sinks and gazed at his reflection. His hair was getting long, curling over his ears a bit. The barber would probably come this week. John's eyes were slanted, folds of skin partly covering them. Cookie said he looked Chinese. She told him he was a Mongoloid, but John wasn't sure what that meant. He peered at his flat nose then stuck his finger up his nostril. John's tongue was thick and fell out of his mouth as he concentrated on exploring. Finding nothing, he swept his hair back from his forehead with his stubby fingers and slurped his tongue back into his mouth. He thought of the Mean Man and quickly headed back to bed to wait for Cookie, his favorite tech, to arrive and waken them. Just as he turned the corner, intently watching his bare feet, he nearly smacked right into Cookie. They both jumped.

"'S'cuse me!" she frowned. But John could tell she wasn't mad. Her brown jiggly face shook reprovingly. She had the biggest cheeks he'd ever seen and tiny black eyes with deep creases around them. Her eyes were smiling behind the frown. "You gotta watch where yer goin', Johnny boy. I was just comin' to wake ya'll."

"Sowy, Cookie." He patted her cheek and frowned empathetically. "Me sca'e you?"

She rubbed his shoulder. "Nah, I'm just jumpy."

"You hab good sweep?" he asked.

"Just dandy, Johnny boy. I always sleep like a baby. And you?"

"Me hab bad dweam." That always got her sympathy.

"Again?" She put her hands on her hips and cocked her head to one side, her eyebrows scrunching up in the middle.

"Yep. Icky hands pokin' me." John wiggled his fingers toward her face in a spooky way.

She pushed him back. "Git outa here. You know I don't like that stuff."

"Sowy." John hugged her then pushed away and looked into her smiling eyes. "Wo'k day t'day?"

"Yes sir, it's a workday all right. And it's a special day for you, I heard."

"My bi'fday?" John's eyes widened hopefully.

"No, your birthday is in October. It's only January. Some woman named Sarah something or other is comin' to talk to you about some experiment, taking kids out of here. I don't know. Anyway, your name came up and she's going to be here after lunch to see you." Cookie turned John around and patted his butt. "Time to git everybody up around here."

John followed her down the aisle between the rows of beds. He could see her dark skin right through the thin white tech dress. Her short sleeves were tight and her chubby arms bulged out from under them. John had known Cookie ever since he came to Starlight, more Christmases ago than John could count.

Cookie pulled the little bell out of her pocket and handed it to John. "Go ahead, Johnny."

He shook it hard. The mummies sprang to life.

Cookie walked down the aisle and called out the same thing she did every day, "Rise and shine! Up and at 'em you passel of sleepyheads!"

All but two boys scrambled from their sheets and trudged in their pajamas to the toilet room. Timmy lay in his crib, helpless. His arms flailed and he grunted loudly.

Cookie pulled the sheet off Timmy. "Good mornin', Mr. Tim. I'll send Marley back to help you in just a minute."

Oh, good, John thought. *The Mean Man is gone and it's just brown-toothed Marley.*

Timmy grinned up at her. His mouth was open wide and his arms drew back beside his head. He was arched backward uncomfortably, but John knew that's just how his body moved. Timmy couldn't do anything for himself. He was fairly new to their ward. Marley said he was a veggie, but he wasn't. When John talked to him, he could tell Timmy understood. He even talked, though John couldn't always understand him. Cookie didn't believe it.

"Ga man!" Timmy chewed exaggeratedly around the words.

"Him say, good mornin'," John told Cookie.

"That's what you tell me," she said. "Sounds like gibberish to me." She patted Timmy's leg and walked on down the aisle.

Timmy's smile faded as John moved away. John wished he could help him but he had to get Lonnie dressed so they wouldn't be late.

Walking on ahead, Cookie shook Lonnie's foot. He was the other figure who hadn't risen. "That means you, too, boy." Then Cookie meandered out the other door to go over to the girl's side, just like she did every morning.

John hurried to Lonnie's bed. He sat down beside the white bump and bounced it up and down. "Wake up, Yonnie. Time fo' bweakfas'."

Lonnie didn't stir beneath the sheet. John jerked the sheet down. Lonnie's smiling face peered upward.

"Oh, you," John laughed. "You 'wake. You jokin' me. Git up now!"

Lonnie's face was much like John's, slanted eyes and wide mouth, his over-sized tongue often curling out. Cookie said he had the Mongolism, too. Lonnie wiggled his fingers in a baby wave right at John's face.

"Git up," John commanded, ignoring the wave. "Me bewy hungwy! Us gotta huwy!"

Slowly, Lonnie lifted his head, then his shoulders, then his waist and hips, in one long smooth gliding motion. Shot with slug juice, that's what Cookie said Lonnie was. He moved so slowly that finally John couldn't stand it.

"You too swow." He pulled Lonnie's arms until he sat upright.

Lonnie pushed John's hands away and carefully knotted his legs like a pretzel. He was not in a hurry. He stared at John, grinning. His tongue slipped out and explored his chin. Then he tried to tickle John's neck.

John shrugged his shoulders up to cut off the tickle. "Come on, Yonnie. No ticko'. Me get dwessed. You, too."

John opened one of his two dresser drawers and pulled out his clothes—a blue pullover sweatshirt, jeans, socks and underwear. Cookie said they ought to change their underwear every day, but if he was in a hurry John didn't always do it. He looked around and saw that Marley had come in and was struggling to get Timmy dressed. John decided he better change his underwear today. He lined everything up on his bed in the order he would put it on, then stripped. He liked to dress from the bottom up, socks first. Because of his bad hip, John had to put them on from behind, slipping his hand into the sock, pulling it inside out and then rolling it up over his foot while it stretched out behind him. Underwear was easy but he had trouble with the jeans. This pair had no button at the top. John's fingers were thick and he fumbled with the tiny clasp on the zipper before working it up. He slipped on the sweatshirt then teased his loafers out from under the bed with his toes so he didn't have to bend down. Bending down hurt his hip.

Quickly John smoothed the sheet and blanket on his bed and tucked them in all around. He fluffed up his pillow. All done.

Satisfied, he glanced over at Lonnie. He hadn't moved. Lonnie sat in the center of his bed, legs crossed, finger-flicking. Tap, flick, tap, flick, tap, flick. The baby finger of his right hand flicked against the thumb of his other hand, palms open like he was fanning himself. He chewed on his massive tongue, making a squeaking noise.

"Yonnie!" John glowered, hands on his hips trying to look like Cookie. He tapped his foot impatiently. "No veggin'!" Vegging was what you did when you were not doing what you were supposed to do. Finger flicking was Lonnie's way of vegging. "You betta git up! Us be yate fo' bweakfas."

Snail-like, Lonnie finally began to move. One foot unwound itself and crept onto the floor. The other foot followed. Each painfully slow movement made John feel tighter inside. *We'll never make it*, John worried.

"Now go pee." John pointed toward the toilet room.

After one more thwarted attempt to tickle John's chin, Lonnie rose and strolled to the toilet room in no particular rush.

"Huwy back!" John admonished, shaking his head. He knew he would have to go and get Lonnie, like he did every day. First he reached into his drawer and groped around for his watch. He had found it outside along the walk. The hands never moved and it didn't buckle, but John liked it anyway. He stuck it in his pocket. Next he plucked out his wallet. Santa had given this to him for Christmas. He flipped the wallet open. Not much in there. An unused Balhalla buck, the money they earned for being good or working. They could use Balhalla bucks to buy things at the canteen. In another slot of his wallet was a picture of John, taken when he was younger, standing in front of Beacon Hall with Gretchen. He liked Gretchen. She was red-haired and skinny, and had freckles all over her arms and neck. She was his favorite tech at Beacon, but he hadn't seen her since he left. Now the Veggies, the others like Timmy who couldn't do anything for themselves, lived in Beacon, and John had moved to Starlight. He jammed the wallet into his back pocket.

Turning toward his nightstand, John kissed the tiny framed picture beside his bed. "Bye, mama. See ya yate'." Mama was beautiful, her flowing blonde hair covering her shoulders as she tipped her head to the side and smiled coyly.

John started toward the toilet room to get Lonnie. The other boys were all getting dressed as fast as they could. On workdays, they had to go down to the main cafeteria for breakfast. John passed Marley who had finished dressing Timmy and was maneuvering him into a wheelchair.

Marley growled at the boys, "Straighten out that sheet! Yer bed looks like shit, Pat. Ain't you dressed yet, David? We're leavin' in five minutes. If you ain't ready, we'll leave without ya."

John passed Marley without looking up. He didn't like the look of Marley's cigarette stained teeth and pale pimply face.

"Peter! For God's sake!" John stopped when he heard Marley yell. "Another ripped shirt? When are you gonna stop this shit?"

Marley grabbed the torn shirt and jerked it off Peter's arms. He rolled it into a ball and tossed it at the big garbage can in the corner. "You come over here and git another one. I oughta let you wear the ripped one and freeze yer butt off. In fact, you oughta go naked. That'd teach ya."

Peter stood still, staring at the ceiling. He didn't talk, he didn't look at people, and he hated to be touched by anyone.

After waiting a few moments for Peter to move and pointing to the clothes cupboard, Marley lost his patience. He grabbed Peter's ear and tugged him forward. John shook his head. Marley shouldn't have done that.

Peter screamed, a bloodthirsty scream that John knew from experience could be heard from outside. Peter jerked backward and banged his head with his fist. Wham! He screamed again and beat his temple repeatedly. Wham, wham, wham!

John flinched. "Ouch," he whispered.

Marley let go as if Peter's ear was hot. He looked around the room. Everyone was staring at him. "Shut up, Peter! Stop it!" he hollered.

Peter kept screaming and hitting himself mercilessly.

"Just shut the fuck up! What the hell am I s'pose to do with you?" Marley made two fists that trembled at his sides. Somehow he controlled himself and backed up a few steps.

Gradually, Peter's screams subsided. Silently he pounded his forehead until it turned a deep red.

Marley backed away further. Peter's hitting slowed.

Cookie stormed around the corner in a huff. "Marley, what did you do? Did you touch Peter again?"

"Just barely, the son of a bitch," he spat.

Cookie shook her finger in Marley's face. "I told you, you can't touch him, you fool. He hates that."

Marley shoved his hands into his pockets. "He ripped his shirt. What the hell am I supposed to do?"

"Just git him another one and try not to make him mad. We've tried everything and nothin' works. He's gonna hurt himself." Cookie's face looked awfully mad.

"Shit. If it was up to me ..." he said, turning his back on Cookie.

"Well, it ain't. And don't touch him again," Cookie scowled, then left.

John snickered behind his hand. Marley was so dumb. He didn't know anything about being a tech.

Marley stuck his middle finger up toward Cookie's retreating figure and threw a clean shirt at Peter. "Here," he sneered. "Put this on. You git off easy this time, but don't count on it next time. If it was up to me, I'd wallop you!"

Peter thumped his head a few more times, not so hard, and stared up at the lights. Marley turned away to help some of the other boys who had trouble with zippers and buttons.

John walked to the toilet room. It was empty except for Lonnie, who sat on the toilet bent over so far his face lay flat on his knees. He didn't move, but John could hear him humming.

"Yonnie, huwy up!" John's voice echoed against the tiles. "You done?"

Lonnie peered down between his legs. "All done," he signed, flipping his hands apart. Lonnie didn't talk much but he knew a lot of sign language.

Before John could remind him to wipe, Lonnie stood and yanked his underwear up from around his ankles. Too late. Sluggishly Lonnie lifted his foot and pressed down slowly on the silver handle until it finally flushed.

Lonnie liked to watch the swirling water but John snatched his hand and dragged him back to his bed. He pulled Lonnie's shirt and pants out of the drawer and quickly helped Lonnie into them. When he reached for Lonnie's socks, they were all tied together in knots again.

"No good, Yonnie." John threw them back into the drawer. It would take too long to untie them and John could never get them undone by himself. "You no git socks t'day."

Marley called, "Everybody in line, boys!"

The rest of the boys moved toward the doorway to line up. John's heart pounded. "Put shoes on!" he shouted at Lonnie. Lonnie slipped one foot in, working it to the end and giggling.

John's hands were trembling. "No yaugh! No funny!"

Marley called, "Why don't you jest leave him, John? No sense in you missin' out on yer cinnamon roll. Teach him a lesson." Marley wheeled Timmy out into the dayroom where they would meet the girls and walk down to the cafeteria together.

The line of boys started out through the sleeping room door into the hallway. They were putting their coats on.

"Yonnie, dem yeavin'!" Quickly, John stuck Lonnie's other shoe onto his foot and pulled him to a stand. John smoothed the covers on Lonnie's bed as best he could in three seconds. Lonnie tried to get the wrinkle out of the middle, but the sheet was crumpled underneath it. He didn't like to leave unless it was just right.

"No good, Yonnie!" John panicked. The cinnamon rolls would be gone if they were late. "Fix bed yata."

John pushed Lonnie from behind out into the dayroom. Lonnie wanted to stop and push all the chairs under the table where they belonged but John wouldn't let him. When they finally reached the outside door, the line of boys and girls was winding down the walkway, everyone holding hands. The frigid air brought instant goose-bumps to John's arms and back. In his rush, he had forgotten their coats. He plucked up Lonnie's hand and rushed to catch up with the group. Lonnie bounced stiffly after him. He hated to hurry.

John and Lonnie wound down the path past the stone and brick buildings that were spread throughout the large campus. Leafless trees loomed over them as they twisted between the ominous-looking structures with their small windows peering eerily down over the lifeless grounds. The line of workers headed for the low building with steam rising from its chimney.

Halfway down the path John and Lonnie caught up with the group. John snatched the hand of the last boy in line and they slowed to a walk, their breath puffing out like smoke. By the time they arrived at the cafeteria he was shivering with cold.

The sounds of clinking dishes and the delectable smells of bacon and cinnamon rolls greeted them as they entered. Dozens of workers were already seated at the tables eating their breakfasts.

While they stood in line, John finished buttoning Lonnie's shirt. They picked up their trays and silverware. A tech in a white hat and hair net handed them each a plate of scrambled eggs, pancakes and bacon.

John swallowed the saliva that filled his mouth in anticipation. A worker stood at the end of the line handing out cinnamon rolls. Everybody from Starlight got one today.

Mick was just ahead of John in line. After he got his cinnamon roll Mick stumbled toward the nearest table with his tray. He set it down quickly then dove for his neighbor's cinnamon roll. Luckily, one of the techs was right behind him and nabbed it before Mick could shove it into his mouth. Mick was always stealing food.

John spied a space next to Rochelle. She was a laundry worker like John, but she lived in Moonbeam. John considered her his girlfriend.

"Hi, Wocheo. How you?" He set the tray down on the table beside her.

"Okay, John." She snickered and hid her face with her hand.

"Us sit he'e?"

"Okay, John." She didn't look up. Her body quivered a little.

Lonnie slid slowly onto the bench, too close for John to squeeze in beside Rochelle.

"Move ova', Yonnie. Me sit by Wocheo." He shoved Lonnie sideways and scrunched in between them.

"Co'd outside," he commented, picking up his fork.

Rochelle didn't answer. Every time John bent over to look past her hair into her face, she turned away.

"You happy, Wocheo?"

"Yeah." She moved away a bit.

"Dat good." John cut his pancakes up with his fork, then he cut Lonnie's. "You eat, Yonnie," he commanded. In slow motion, Lonnie picked up his fork and aimed it at the plate.

John peeled his cinnamon roll apart into a long ringlet. Leaning his head back, he let the end of it fall into his mouth and bit his way up the dough. He looked to see if Rochelle noticed. She glanced up briefly, but then quickly hid her face.

"You yook pwetty," John said to her when he had swallowed his entire cinnamon roll.

"Oh, John." She put her hand over her eyes and shuddered. John stared at the back of her head. Her dark hair was matted into tight snarls, as usual. When she turned back around to take another bite John saw his chance. He kissed her bulging cheek.

She dropped her fork. "John!" Her face turned scarlet. She covered her cheeks with her hand and buried her face in the crook of her arm on the table.

John nudged Lonnie. "Me kiss Wocheo. My gewfwend!"

Lonnie's fork was poised over his eggs. He stopped, looked over at Rochelle, and shook his head. "Tsk, tsk, tsk," he scolded.

John giggled. He had done it. All tingly inside, he dug into his pancakes with gusto.

"What's your job now, John?" said Harold, a worker John sometimes saw at the canteen. He sat across the table from them and had already finished eating.

"Yaundwy. What you job?" John took a bite.

"I work outside today, doin' some rakin'. I like workin' outside." His face sagged down on one side and only the other side of his mouth moved when he talked. One eye was always half-shut, and when he walked, he dragged his leg. When John had asked him what happened to his face, he pointed to his head and said he had a stroke. John didn't know what that was, but it sounded bad.

"Pwetty co'd outside. Us wo'k inside. Wa'm in yaundwy, wight, Wocheo?" He nudged her with his elbow. She sat up and nodded without looking at him.

"What you fwend name?" John asked, pointing to a new girl sitting next to Harold. She had short brown hair that looked greasy. Her eyes were like black marbles resting in dirt holes.

"She's not my friend!" Harold scooted away from her then asked, "What's your name?"

"Sheila." Her voice was husky, more like a boy's.

"Whe'e hu fwom?" John asked.

"I don't know. Where you from?" Harold repeated.

When she lifted her eyes, they darted around the room. She talked very fast. "You know. Had to leave. They hate me. Go up the hill!" Her voice got loud and she pointed straight upward. John looked up to where she pointed. Nothing but ceiling.

"No, no, no!" she shouted. "I won't go! No, I won't! You can't make me." She paused and looked behind her, then lowered her voice. "Okay. It's okay. I'll be good. The table said to be good."

A tech approached and Sheila put her head down. She bent low over her plate and shoveled food into her mouth.

"Sheila, are you having a problem?" the tech asked.

"Nononononono!" she fired. "I'll be good. Not going back. Not Cadby."

The tech walked to the end of the table and stood guard.

Cadby! John stared at Sheila. So that's where she was from. She was crazy then. The thought of Cadby terrified him. The groping hands of his nightmare flickered before his eyes.

Sheila ate as fast as she could until her plate was empty. Then she picked up her tray and stomped away. The tech followed her.

No one spoke for a while. John concentrated on his eggs.

After a minute, Harold broke the silence, "I know someone who went to Cadby before. Let's see, who was it?" His eyebrow drew down. "You goed to Cadby, right John?"

John stuffed a forkful of eggs into his mouth so he couldn't answer, his heart pounding like a drum.

Just then a worker came over in a white apron and began washing the tables. Harold started talking to her. John sighed. He had to remember not to sit by Harold anymore.

The buzzer rang loudly, startling them. Workers from all over the cafeteria got up and took their trays to the dishwashing window. Lonnie had only eaten half a pancake, but John made him stop.

"Aw done, Yonnie. Go wo'k now." John pulled the fork out of Lonnie's hand and set it down. He made Lonnie pick up his tray. Lonnie followed John to the counter where they slipped their silverware into a large dishpan half-filled with dirty water and set their trays on a moving belt. Lonnie dangled his napkin over the trashcan until John gently slapped his hand to make him let go.

When the napkin finally dropped in, Lonnie said, "Putsch!" the sound he loved to make when something fell.

The workers congregated near the outside doors. Some techs were already there, and others soon appeared, laughing and smiling. Two of them crushed their cigarettes out on the side of the trashcan and blew a stream of blue smoke upward. John always wondered how they did that. *Did they have fire in their mouths?*

One of the techs, Erickson, shouted, "Line up!" Erickson was fat. His stomach hung down over his belt and he had big folds of skin under his chin that reached to the first button on his shirt.

"Time to get to work. No more time to stand around and look stupid." He laughed.

Linda Stern, John's work tech, waited in her usual spot with the other laundry workers. She looked tough with her man's haircut and faded jeans, but she was nicer than she looked.

John pushed Lonnie into Marley's line. "He'e. You go wo'k Sta'yight."

John pretended that Lonnie went to work in Starlight, even though Lonnie didn't have a real job yet. John could never figure out why he didn't have a job; Lonnie wasn't a dummy like Mick or Mamie, or Peter. Lonnie leaned against John's hands, resisting.

"Yep, Yonnie," John said, pushing harder. "You go."

Lonnie grunted and shook his head. He was getting into a "no" mood. A "no" mood always got Lonnie in trouble because he eventually slumped to the ground and hit or kicked someone. He even bit a tech once, which is why he had no front teeth now. Anyone who bit someone got his front teeth pulled.

Lonnie tried to sit down, but John grabbed him under the armpits and hoisted him into line. "You be good, Yonnie," he admonished.

"Come here, you little punk." Marley took Lonnie from John and held his upper arms firmly. Lonnie winced and shook his head.

"Be good, Yonnie! No 'no' mood!" John called back as he followed Stern out the door. He hoped Marley wouldn't pull Lonnie's ear.

John trailed the other workers down the paved pathway to the largest stone building on campus, Lawrence Hall. Rochelle was just ahead of John and he watched her awkward gait as she swung side to side. Every once in a while she slapped the side of her head. John wished she wouldn't do that because that reminded him of Peter, who was a dummy. At the basement door to Lawrence Hall, Stern fumbled through her fist-sized key ring until she found the right key. She held the door open for the workers to enter. A draft of warm air and the fresh smell of clean sheets swept over them. John liked work. It made him feel important, like a smart one.

Stern led them down two series of steps to the basement. The whir of motors grew louder as they descended to the laundry area. The cavernous space below was wide and open, the floors and walls of gray cement. Washers and dryers big enough for two people to crawl into lined the perimeter. Dull lights hung on chains from the ceiling high above, casting funny shadows that John liked to experiment with when he wasn't busy. In the middle of the room were worktables where sheets and towels and clothes were folded. Bins of dirty linens were already lined up ready for the washers.

"Go to your stations and get to work," Stern directed. She spent most of her time drinking coffee and smoking in a small office that faced the work area. The workers could see her through the glass window.

John grabbed a bin of dirty laundry and pushed it to the deep utility sink where he had to shake the sheets out, in case there were messes. If there were, he had to wear his special gloves and rinse them out before loading them into the washer. John reached into the bin and pulled out a balled-up bundle. Untangling it, he held it away from his body and shook it out. Nothing in the first two sheets. He stuffed them into the washer. The next one smelled bad and John slipped on his gloves. He turned on the faucet and rinsed the slippery mess down the drain, breathing only through his mouth so he wouldn't smell the accident, like Stern had taught him. Then he rolled it up and squeezed it out before stuffing it into the washer, too.

When the washer was full, he took two scoops of soap from the soap box and poured them into the spout. His favorite part was pushing the green button. John poised his finger over it for a second, thinking what an important job he had, then punched it. The machine roared. He watched the sheets tumble inside until the suds blurred his view. When all the washers were loaded and running, John could take a break. He wheeled the empty carts out to the main aisle where another worker pushed them back to the wards, then he sat on the laundry folding table to watch. The gushing sound of the water reminded him of a fishing show that the cartoon day tech, Smitty, liked to watch.

John dangled his legs off the table and pretended he was sitting on the bank of a river, fishing. He imagined that the shadows cast from above were big, silver fish lurking below the water, just waiting to be caught. He cast his imaginary fishing line and felt a tug on the end. A fish as long as his leg flipped out of the water. John wrestled it, flopping around, onto the table just like on TV.

"John!" Stern called, sliding the window open. "What the hell are you doing?"

John straightened up. The fish disappeared. "Me fish," he answered sheepishly.

She rolled her eyes. "Fish? That's a good one, John. Look. One of your washers is done. Get back to work, you screwball."

The light was off on the first washer. One by one each of the washers shut off. John unloaded the linens into two clean laundry bins and rolled them down to Barney-the-Giant, who ran the dryers. Barney-the Giant was so tall that if John looked straight at him he saw only his chest. But he was friendly, not mean like the giants he saw in the cartoons.

On his way back to the washers, John passed Rochelle. She was busy folding clothes on a worktable. He waved. She looked up through her hair and waved a finger, then hid her face with her hands. John thought about the kiss at breakfast. A rush of heat flooded his face.

From across the room, he watched Rochelle work. Rochelle's hair hid her face most of the time, but once in a while she looked up at him through the clumped strands, smiled then turned quickly away. She was silly, but John liked her. He used to have Brenda for a girlfriend, but she got mad and called him "dummy" and she started liking Gerald instead of him. He ignored Brenda now.

The room was steaming hot when the noon buzzer finally rang. Trickles of sweat eased down John's back. His stomach had been growling for a long time.

As the workers filed out and started back toward the cafeteria, Stern handed each of them their pay, five Balhalla bucks.

"Don't spend it all in one place," she said, slapping John on the butt. "And don't do anything I wouldn't do."

"Yep, Ste'n. Me be good." He folded his brightly colored paper bucks neatly into his wallet and slipped it into his hip pocket.

Lunch was served in shifts and John didn't see anyone from Starlight today besides Barney the Giant. He ate his lunch sitting by Rochelle. Rochelle ate more slowly than he did and she didn't talk to John at all. When John finished his lunch she offered him her banana.

After he ate it he said, "Tanks, Wocheo. Me kiss you?"

She shook her head. When he tried to put his arm around her, she shrugged his hand away, turning her back to him.

John was peeved. He didn't understand girls. Sometimes they let him kiss them and sometimes they didn't. He put his tray away, shaking his head. "Gew's!" he muttered. He had heard Marley say that when the girls messed up or Cookie made him do something he didn't want to do.

Suddenly, John realized how hot and tired he was. His bad hip ached from standing on the cement floor all morning.

He walked over to Stern who now sat by the outside door smoking. "Me go outside?" he asked her. "Me hot."

"Sure, John. In fact, you might as well go back to Starlight." She blew the smoke upward and cocked her jaw a couple of times. Little circles of smoke floated up.

"How you do dat?" he asked.

"Well, I practice a lot." Stern almost smiled.

Outside, the sun was gone. Winter clouds made the sky solid white. John walked up the little grass-lined path to a bench and sat down. The chilly air felt good on his hot skin. He noticed the smoke coming out of his mouth and tried snapping his jaw like Stern, but he couldn't make any circles appear. Maybe that's why there were so many clouds now. Lots of people had been outside smoking into the cold air.

Gazing across the lawns, past the lower campus buildings toward the Away Place, John could see the tops of houses between the bare trees, the circle of gray water Stern called the bay and more buildings and trees on the far side of the water. He could see some long wires swinging down from green posts. Stern said it was the Yaquina Bay Bridge and that it was far away. John squinted at the bridge, then climbed onto the bench for a better look.

He imagined he was walking across those long wires like a circus performer. John stuck his arms straight out and walked carefully along the bench. When he got to the end he jumped off, then sat back on the bench, staring at the Away Place. He had gone through town on the bus once or twice, but that was a long time ago, before Dr. Balhalla came. Cookie said Dr. Balhalla cut everything so they couldn't go on field trips anymore. All John could figure was he must have cut the tires on the bus.

Walking up the path toward him, Stern broke his spell, "John! What the hell are you doing now? You live in your own little world, don't you? Get your butt home!"

John jumped up and hurried back to Starlight wondering if Lonnie was working with the dummies or just tying socks into knots.

Chapter 2
Sarah

The top was down and the heat was on full blast as Sarah shoved her Triumph TR250 into third gear and hit the gas. Her dad had given her his beloved convertible when he moved out east with his growing family. She cranked up the radio to hear John Denver's newest, "Annie's Song," wishing she was heading down Surfside Highway instead of up Larkspur Drive to the state mental institution. The road wound sharply upward through rows of overgrown firs. Sarah loved how her dad's roadster made her feel deeply alive and free, such a contrast to her mission today. She raced against the thought that her life was about to change drastically.

As she rounded the last corner and slowed, the carved stone sign reading Larkspur State Home and Training School, loomed up on the side of the road. Downshifting, Sarah pulled into the curving driveway that led between the iron gates, thinking how much the sign looked like a tombstone. *What a joke, that name. Why did they call it a training school? No one ever got trained here and no one ever graduated, at least not yet.*

The single lane led past several brick buildings, each one four or five stories high, and each as large as a small hospital. This was the state's primary mental institution; lawmakers' answer to the question of what to do with all those retarded and insane people whom no one wanted to meet out on the streets. At the recommendation of doctors and extended families, parents had been putting their damaged children away here since the 1930s.

Passing the prison-like structures, thoughts of her brother's sad fate flashed through Sarah's mind. She wondered how she could feel both aching grief, and white rage at her mother's betrayal. The two emotions were inseparably linked now.

Sarah pushed these thoughts away and parked the car in front of Starlight Hall. Scrambling out, she deftly snapped the roof back into place, in case it started to rain. As her vaporous breath swirled around her face, she was reminded that snow was predicted later this week. John Denver's voice, still ringing in her ears, slowly died as she gazed at Starlight's ivy-covered brick. Her stomach churned and she gritted her teeth to ward off the urge to run.

Sarah had been to Larkspur several times before. Her first visit was as an undergraduate in one of the introductory special education classes. She had volunteered to go as part of an assignment to experience what it was like to have a disability. The last time, three months ago, she was with Dr. Montgomery, or William, as he recently asked her to call him. They had toured several wards and talked to the administrators about Sarah's doctoral dissertation project. Her research had already been approved by the university, and William had secured a start-up grant for her. Now that Larkspur had given her final approval, Sarah was coming to meet the patients whose files she had selected for her study.

The criteria for her subjects included only patients with immeasurably low IQ's or those lower than fifty, if they were testable; "imbeciles" was the pejorative term that thankfully was falling out of common use. Sarah's subjects had to be ambulatory and toilet trained, have no serious health problems and take no medications for behavior control. Through her study, Sarah hoped to show that even the severely disabled could make it in the community, given adequate support.

Readjusting the stocking cap tightly over her mass of dark curls Sarah strode quickly up the stone steps to the gray metal door of Starlight's entrance. She buzzed the doorbell. *How strange to hole people up like this,* she thought again. She watched through the reinforced window as a technician, a.k.a. tech, the institutional euphemism for an untrained, low paid assistant, strode down the wide corridor toward her with a large ring of keys. The tech, a thin white man with bad teeth, opened the door. Immediately the smells of disinfectant and urine accosted her. Moaning and low, repetitive thumping sounds could be heard from within.

"Hi," Sarah said, trying to sound at ease, her heartbeat rapid. She pulled out a paper from her backpack. "I'm here to see some of the residents. I have a letter of permission here from ..."

"Come on in." The tech held the door open and nodded her in without asking to see her paperwork. He led her down the tiled hallway to the dayroom.

Sarah forced herself to follow.

The dayroom, the main living area in each ward, was an open area where a dozen or so obviously disabled men and women sat on worn out furniture or lay on the tile floor. The room was bleak, like all the wards she had visited, and Sarah noticed with distaste the sickly green walls spotted with dirty smudges. A TV was mounted high on the wall and a cartoon show blared. Several residents were engaged in self-stimulating activities—one man lay flat on his back dangling a piece of shiny foil a few inches over his eyes and a woman with clouded eyes sat cross-legged on a wooden chair tossing her head back and forth in a figure-eight pattern. These were the things that had bothered Sarah most on her previous visits, people with nothing to do all day, just wasting their lives.

Without saying more, the sleazy tech pointed to the nurse's counter. Sarah presented the letter she had received from the director of Larkspur, Dr. James Balhalla, to the heavy-set black woman seated behind the counter.

"I'm Sarah Richardson from the university and I have a letter here from Dr... ."

"I'm Cookie. I heard you was comin' today," the woman interrupted. "The boys you want to talk to are here in the dayroom. I'll show you."

Cookie came out through a locked half-door and walked over to the only two residents who were actually watching *Bugs Bunny*. Both men had Down Syndrome. The bigger one had his arm slung around the shorter one. They sat cross-legged on the vinyl-covered couch, the smaller one repeatedly tapping his baby finger against the opposite thumb in a rhythmic, waving motion. They were dressed in clothing that looked a size too big, but at least they looked clean.

Cookie addressed these two loudly. "John! Lonnie! You have company." She had to amble over and tap the larger one on the shoulder to get his attention. "This is John," she told Sarah over her shoulder. "This one folded up like a pretzel is Lonnie. I'll find the others for you when you're ready."

John turned toward Sarah and slid his arm off Lonnie's shoulder. He stood up. Lonnie stared up at her, his tongue bulging into his cheek as he noisily chewed on it.

Sarah couldn't help but think of the brother she had never met. *What would he look like now, if he were alive? Down Syn-*

drome people looked like they could be related to one another. He would look pretty much like this, she thought as she extended her hand.

"Hi, John. My name is Sarah. I'm wondering if I can talk to you."

"Hi, Sawah," John said. He shook her hand enthusiastically.

"And this is your friend, Lonnie?" Sarah bent down to shake Lonnie's hand, as well. Lonnie stopped tapping long enough to shake the tips of her fingers before resuming his rhythmic tapping.

Sarah turned to Cookie. "Where can I sit down to talk to John and Lonnie, preferably away from the TV?"

"Back in the lunchroom would be okay. Down the hall and to the left." Cookie pointed. "Go with her now, Johnny. And take Lonnie with you. You boys be good."

Sarah walked with them back to a small room off the main hall. She found her heart hammering again, inexplicably. Reading the records was one thing, but thinking of actually taking these men out of the institution, where they had lived all their lives, was another. What if they didn't do well? What if this experiment didn't work? She remembered William's words that were her inspiration, "These places should never exist. People with disabilities have just as much right as anybody else to a life in a real home with people who care about them. Your work can make this happen, Sarah." That's why she was here.

She opened the door to the smallish lunchroom for John and Lonnie. Only one other resident was here, an extremely short man with misshapen arms and fingers standing with his back to them. He looked out the window and did not turn around when they came in.

Sarah motioned them to one of the three round tables and they sat down. Lonnie managed to perch cross-legged on his chair. He began to flip his fingers once again, back and forth, back and forth in a long practiced pattern.

"I have something I need to talk to you two about," Sarah said, pulling off her cap and unconsciously running her fingers through her disheveled hair to fluff it. Her voice quavered slightly. "I am starting a group home in town. It's a place where people like you and Lonnie can come and live in a house in the community. It's a home where you will have your own bedroom and you will learn to cook and clean and take care of yourselves. You'll have a job, too. I'd like you and Lonnie to come and live there. What do you think?"

"Huh?" John gave her a puzzled look. He stared at her face through his slanting eyes. Sarah noticed the flatness of his nose, his open mouth and large tongue, classic signs of Down Syndrome.

She tried again, more simply. "The group home is a house, like on TV, a home for you and Lonnie to live in and to have a normal ... have a sort of family, away from Larkspur."

"Us yive he'e, Sta'yight," John stated matter-of-factly.

"I know, John. You live here now, but this is a chance to move to a new house, a better place where you would have more ... more fun. You would get to live in a nice house in town." She knew she was repeating herself but she wasn't sure how else to explain it.

John smeared his finger in something sticky on the table and licked it off.

Sarah cringed inwardly.

"Away Pwace?" he asked, licking all sides of his finger.

"Away place? Yes, it's a place away from here. I'll be there, too. We'll work together and I'll teach you how to do new things like shop, go bowling, go to the Y ... here. Let me show you a picture."

Out of her backpack she pulled a snapshot of the stone house she had leased for her two-year project. According to her background research, nothing like this had been done before, so she told the landlord that she was renting to students. The house was spacious, with four bedrooms, and three bathrooms, one on each of the three floors. The expansive living room looked out over an ample front porch supported by pillars. Sarah loved the house from the first moment she saw it.

She scooted closer to John. "This is the living room," she pointed to one of the windows, "and the bedrooms are upstairs. You can share a room with Lonnie, if you like."

John nodded and touched the picture, showing some interest now. He handed the picture to Lonnie. "Yook, Yonnie, Away Pwace."

"I talked to Winifred Brecht, the assistant director about it. We've decided to have you and Lonnie, Mick Reimer, and Peter Brown all come to live in my new group home. And one more guy, Ricky, from another ward."

John looked at her breasts, braless beneath her tie-dyed T-shirt, and poked her breastbone with his finger. "You girl?"

"Yes, I'm a girl." She pulled her jacket over herself and reddened. "Do you know Mick and Peter?"

"Yep. Dummies."

"Oh, they're not dummies. They're, they're ... it's not polite to say dummies, John."

"Oh yeah," John rolled his eyes and nodded his head, "dem dummies!"

Sarah smiled in spite of herself and covered her mouth with her hand. What was it about these guys? She liked them already. No pretense here, no wondering what they thought.

She went on, "The house is in a quiet neighborhood and only two blocks from a park. There's a little store at the corner where you will be able to go to buy things like pop and treats."

"Buy candy?" John's face brightened.

"Yes! You'll have a job and earn real money."

"Money? Ba'hawa bucks?"

"Bahawa bucks? No, dollars. You can spend them on things you want. We'll do things together like go to the movies, swim, go to the gym ..."

John interrupted, "Mean Man de'e?"

"Mean man?" Sarah raised her eyebrows. She imagined there were a lot of mean men here, those hardened techs who had worked at Larkspur for years and treated these grown men and women like children. Or worse yet, abused them. John and Lonnie's crumpled ears were evidence of this. There were all kinds of stories about what happened in the wards of Larkspur where no one saw, and no one squealed. "No. No mean men."

"Good." John smiled. "'K. Go Away Pwace. Wif you!" He grabbed her hand and then unexpectedly leaned over and kissed her cheek.

Sarah laughed and patted his arm. "Great! You'll be fun to work with and I'm sure you'll like it there." *John is going to do well,* she thought. He was the one who could talk, so he would be her star pupil. "How about you, Lonnie?"

John held his hand up to stop her from talking. "Me do," he said, licking his lips. He poked two fingers from Lonnie's eyes to his own, signing, "Look," then he explained to Lonnie, "Yonnie, Sawah take us Away Pwace. Me go, you go." John pointed from himself to Lonnie. "'K?"

A smile crept slowly over Lonnie's face and he screeched, "Eeeeee!"

John patted his back. "Him go." He stood up and pulled Lonnie to his feet. "Come on, Yonnie. Us go Away Pwace."

"Oh, wait a minute!" Sarah gripped John's forearm. "We aren't going right now. In fact, it will be a couple of weeks before we can get the paperwork done. I'll come back and get you when it's time to move, okay?"

John's face fell. "Not go Away Pwace?"

"Yes, but not today. I'll come back." She squeezed his shoulder and smiled. "Really, I'm coming back for you."

John looked dubious. Sarah shook their hands again and thanked them. She wondered what they understood and whether they would remember this conversation when she came back to get them. John had a good chance of making progress from what she had read. He was cooperative and already held a job. Lonnie was his faithful sidekick, and though more limited, had few behavior problems. She was more worried about the other two she had picked from Starlight, the ones she needed to see next. Peter and Mick had a history of difficult behaviors and she knew they would present the biggest challenge to her and her university work study students.

Sarah followed John and Lonnie back to the dayroom where they returned to their TV show.

A little balding man with sagging red eyes hurried over to Sarah and grabbed her around the waist.

Sarah pushed him away and took his hand, instead. "Hi, I'm Sarah. I like to shake hands." His hand was sticky.

"Hi! I Jackie! I like you!" He dug in his pocket and pulled out a penny. "I have money in my pocket!" He shouted this as if it was a total surprise to him. He shook the penny in Sarah's face. "I have money in my pocket!"

"That's great, Jackie," Sarah said, taking a step backward.

Cookie rescued her. "Jackie likes girls." Then to Jackie she said, "Leave her alone. Go show Marley your penny."

Jackie stuck the penny into his pocket but wouldn't leave. He stood by Sarah staring at her breasts, his mouth hanging open.

"Don't stare, Jackie," Cookie said. Then she asked, "Who do you want to see next?"

"Peter Brown, then Mick Reimer," Sarah answered, zipping up her jacket.

Cookie led her to Peter and warned her not to touch him. Sarah knew from the records that he was extremely sensitive to being touched.

Peter's carmel-colored skin was marked with scars around his temples and forehead. He stood in the hall by the office door rocking vigorously. Sarah had heard that they called this movement the Larkspur Dip, a stereotypical behavior that she had seen in a couple of other wards. Peter leaned forward on one foot flapping his arms wildly, then leaned back briefly only to rock violently forward again, shaking his head, eyes closed. He was oblivious to the others in the room. He reminded her of a caged tiger senselessly pacing back and forth.

Sarah approached him cautiously and waited. Catching a glimpse of her during one of his head dips Peter suddenly stopped. He folded his arms, his hands tucked into his armpits, and looked away. He was tall and lanky, with thick curly hair that looked like it hadn't been cut for several months. He squeezed his eyes shut and his narrow face was pinched, as though her attention was painful to him.

"Hi, Peter. My name is Sarah. I've come to talk to you."

No response.

"Peter, I won't touch you," she said, clasping her hands behind her. "I just wanted to meet you and let you know ..."

Peter turned his back to her. She moved around to try to look into his face, to find his eyes, but each time she moved, he spun away. She knew that Peter didn't talk and probably wouldn't understand what she was going to tell him anyway. He was autistic, untestable. No one knew what he understood though his records reported that sometimes he had done unexpected things when asked.

She decided to explain anyway, more for Cookie's benefit than for Peter's, "I just wanted to let you know that I want to be your friend and I would like you to come to live in my new group home. I know you may not understand, but I think you'll like it there. I'm looking forward to working with you, Peter." She held her hand out toward him.

Without looking at her, Peter tentatively pushed his hand forward and shook her hand ever so briefly. Then his hands snapped back into place in his armpits.

"Very good, then!" Sarah smiled and turned away, thinking to herself, *We'll give you things to do besides the Larkspur Dip. Eventually, you will be glad you're out.* Of course, she knew there would be adjustments. But look how well they were responding to her, a stranger! Not nearly as hard as she had expected.

Cookie pointed out Mick next. He lay on the floor under a table rubbing the linoleum with his fingers. Sarah sat down confidently beside him. She tried to talk to him as she had the others, but each time she came close he scooted away from her.

"Mick, Mick! Come back! I just want to introduce myself." She tried to follow him along the floor but he jumped up and stumbled awkwardly toward the latrine, his hands shoved deep into his pockets. He almost tripped and Sarah caught her breath. Somehow he recovered his footing and disappeared.

Wondering whether to pursue him or not, Sarah stood up.

"Mick ain't gonna talk to you," Cookie said. "He's a wild one, he is. He's got his pockets full of pencils. God knows where he gets them all. He breaks them into tiny pieces and hoards them like they was the best thing this side of heaven. If you try to take them away from him he'll whack you. Just warning you. You should take Barney instead." She pointed to a very tall man draped over the arms of an overstuffed chair. He was so large he dwarfed the chair like Alice in wonderland.

"Thanks for the warning, but I already have clearance on these four." Sarah didn't look at Cookie. She didn't need any advice at this point.

Cookie gave her two-cents, anyway. "If I was you, I wouldn't even have any pencils around with Mick. You can't hide 'em from him. If he finds 'em, they'll be broke up into little pieces and stuck in his pockets. That's the main thing about him. Oh, and Mick likes to eat—you're gonna have to watch him. He'll eat anything, and I mean anything. It don't even have to be food. He'll stuff his mouth 'til he chokes. And he steals food from others."

Sarah nodded uninterestedly, trying not to encourage Cookie. She had read about his hoarding behaviors and had an idea of the treatments that she wanted to try. It was a matter of training and finding the right reinforcement. She would soon cure Mick of hoarding.

"Oh, and be careful how you touch Peter," Cookie continued. "Don't touch him, especially when he's not looking at you, or anytime, if you can help it. Otherwise, he'll beat the crap out of himself."

Sarah smiled absently. She had been reading about desensitization programs, exposing the subject to a variety of textures for longer and longer periods of time so he would eventually tolerate touching. "Uh huh," she murmured, watching a woman whose blouse collar hung over her bare shoulder thump her head against the wall.

Cookie finally got the hint. "Well, the rest you just got to learn for yourself, I guess." She walked away shaking her head.

Sarah felt a twinge of guilt for not listening to her, but she didn't want her plans tainted by Cookie's homespun treatments. "Thanks," she called to Cookie, too late to make her change course.

Sarah pulled on her cap and started for the door. "I have to rush off to Moonbeam to see my other client. Dr. Balhalla said the van will bring them down when the home is ready, so I guess I won't be back."

Cookie shrugged her shoulders. "Okay, whatever you say."

Sarah thought she heard Cookie whisper sarcastically, "Miss hoity toity," under her breath.

Somewhat chagrined, Sarah approached the greasy tech with the ring of keys, "I'm ready to go. Can you let me out?"

"Sure." He set aside his mop and walked with her down the hall. As he unlocked the door he said, "You sure you know what you're doin', little lady? These guys ain't easy and they ain't never been out of here."

"I know. That's why I picked them." Sarah slipped on her gloves, anxious to leave. "I've done a lot of research and I think we'll be able to help them adjust to living in the community. In fact, I think they have a right to be out there ... instead of in here. That's what I hope to prove."

"Well, good luck. It ain't no picnic in here sometimes." He opened the door for her to pass through. "Nope, it ain't no picnic, that's for sure."

"Which building is Moonbeam again?" she asked. These institutional monstrosities all looked alike.

"The third one," he said, pointing down the path to the right. He got so close Sarah could smell his tobacco breath. "Who ya lookin' for?"

Sarah stepped away from him. "Ricky Johnson. I've already met him, but I thought I'd stop in and say hi. He's my high functioning client."

The tech let out a howl of delight. "That's a good one! Ricky, high functioning! Don't know what records you saw but he's just plain trouble."

Sarah smiled faintly. "No, really. Winifred thought he would do well."

"I'd say he's gonna hurt somebody, but what do I know? I guess you'll find out, won't you!" He chuckled and shook his head, withdrawing into the ward and locking the door.

Sarah headed toward Moonbeam breathing deeply to clear her lungs of disinfectant. The icy air almost took her breath away.

I can't wait to get them out of this depressing place, she thought. She was irritated that the slimy tech had laughed. And what hadn't Winifred told her about Ricky? She tried to imagine Peter doing the Larkspur Dip in the kitchen of the grand old home, or Lonnie's thick tongue dripping saliva down his shirt at the dining room table. She thought of Mick crawling on his hands and knees, searching the newly laid carpet for pencils.

Then she thought about her brother again. Why hadn't her mother told her about him—until she was dying? Tears brimmed in her eyes. She changed her mind about visiting Ricky and broke into a run toward her car. Despite the cold, she flipped down the roof and wrenched the gearshift into reverse. Sarah careened out of the Larkspur drive letting the wind dry her tears.

Chapter 3
The Mean Man

After Sarah left, John stayed in the ward with Lonnie and watched TV. They ate supper in the small eating room where he had talked with that pretty girl, Sarah, and soon *Star Trek* came on. John decided to play *Star Trek* with Lonnie. He needed a communicator so Scotty could beam him up.

John walked nonchalantly toward the nurse's station where Kaeller, the evening tech, was on duty and talking on the phone. Kaeller had dark shoulder-length hair and heavy black eyebrows. She would have been pretty, but she never smiled. Sometimes she was nice and sometimes she screamed at them. Once she even started crying and left the ward for a while. John usually tried to stay out of her way.

"Kaewa?" John said, smiling as nicely as he could. She turned her back to him and kept talking, stretching the curly phone cord around her waist.

John reached over the counter and silently slipped the stapler off the desk. It worked well as a communicator, since by pushing the silver button underneath it flipped open. Cookie had shown him that.

Suddenly, Kaeller snapped, "Hey, John! What're you doing?"

"Need dis. Pway Sta'Twek."

She covered the phone with her hand. "You can't just ..." Then she spoke into the phone again, "Yeah, John wants the stapler to play *Star Trek* ... Well, okay, what the hell." Then to John she called, "Cookie says go ahead."

He trounced back to the sofa with his prize. Opening the stapler, he showed Lonnie again how to hold it to his ear. Then John dug his wallet out, flipping it open. "Dese ou' 'municato's, Yonnie. Us on pwanet. See da monsta?"

He pointed to Mamie, the headbanger. She stood near the wall rocking forward and back like she was riding an invisible rocking horse.

John spoke into his wallet. "Beam us up, Scotty."

Lonnie grunted. John jiggled himself all over, pretending to beam up. He swiped his forehead.

"Whew! Us safe on ship now."

Kaeller called to John from the station. She was off the phone. "John, Cookie said to tell you if you want to go to the canteen before bedtime you should go now. You have some Balhalla bucks to spend, right?"

John flipped the communicator shut. "Bye, Captain Ki'k. Me be back."

"Lord, John," Kaeller said shaking her head. "Why do you play these infantile games? Go on and then hurry back so you can help me pick up around here."

"Yonnie go?" he asked.

"I guess." She shrugged and picked up the phone again.

Going to the canteen was one of John's favorite things. He didn't wait for her to change her mind. This time he remembered to grab their coats. The air was even colder now and it was dark as a black cat in the devil's cave, as Cookie always said. He linked his arm through Lonnie's as they strolled carefully down the shadowy sidewalk. All the way down, Lonnie's mis-sized loafers smacked on the pavement. He hated to wear shoes and would only wear big ones so he could slip them off whenever he wanted.

"Me buy you tweat, Yonnie," John offered.

Lonnie reached over and patted John's cheek affectionately.

"You my fwend, Yonnie," John assured him, "bes' fwend."

John opened the door to Princeton Hall for Lonnie and followed him in. Inside was a small room set with a few tables and chairs. Behind the chest-high counter of the concession stand were shelves of candy and trinkets. John dug his Balhalla bucks out of his wallet. Five bucks were enough to get something for Lonnie and himself.

Monte the Monster stood behind the counter. He was always here. Everyone called him Monte the Monster because one side of his face was all red and puffy and misshapen. The other side was as smooth as John's. He had a habit of turning to one side and looking at people sideways so they could only see his good face.

"He'e." John slapped his bucks on the counter. "Candy fo' Yonnie and me."

"What kind do you want?" Monte asked with the nice side of his face turned toward them.

"Two cokes, Snicka's, Wed Hotties." John pointed them out.

"'Kay. Here you go." Monte was smart with money. He took four bucks and set the treats on the counter, covering his bad face with one hand.

"Tank you, Monte Monsta," John said. Lonnie signed, "Thank you," too, and bowed his head toward Monte.

John set their treats on a small table near a group of smart ones. He liked to sit close to them so he could hear them talk. They always had interesting things to say. John helped Lonnie pop open his coke and they sipped and ate their candy in silence.

"You know what?" one of the smart ones said. He worked in the kitchen serving food. "My tech says I was gittin' a new job. She says I been doin' such a damn good job, I'm ready to go out to a real restaurant."

"I knowed someone who went to a real job once," another worker said. "He never came back. They say he be doin' real good."

"You git real money out there," the kitchen worker added, "and you git to live in a real apartment. No mo' ugly techs breathing down yo' shirt, tellin' you what to do. That's what I heared."

"Yeah, I heard that, too," said a dwarfish girl whose legs barely reached past the edge of her chair. "I heard some techs saying they are gonna close Larkspur. They was saying we all gonna hafta go someplace else and live." She raised her stubby hands. "Where we all gonna go? I never lived no place else."

"It don't matter to me," said the kitchen worker, "long as we ain't here no damn more."

They were talking about the Away Place. John and Lonnie sipped their cokes and John listened to the smart ones. They talked about many things that John didn't understand. They talked about boyfriends and girlfriends, about the techs they hated and loved. The smart ones could go anywhere on campus and they had important jobs like working at the canteen and delivering supplies.

"You know Sally?" asked a worker whose eyes were all white and cloudy. Heads nodded around the table. "She had a problem last night. She ran outside without any clothes on. When they tried to get her back, she kicked a tech. They put one of those white jackets on her and took her away."

Everyone gasped. The kitchen worker clasped her hand over his mouth.

"Then guess what?" said the cloudy eyed one. "They sent her to Cadby!"

The kitchen worker shook his head fiercely. "She ain't never comin' outa that damn place, no damn way."

"We better all be careful," whispered the cloudy eyed one.

John looked at Lonnie. "Cadby!" he whispered.

Lonnie signed, "bad," and shook his head.

The smart ones never once spoke to John or Lonnie. After they slurped the last drops from the bottom of their cans and popped the last Red Hotties into their mouths, he and Lonnie ambled back up the hill toward Starlight holding hands. John was quiet, thinking about all the things the smart ones had said about the Away Place, and about Sarah's promise to take them there.

It was getting late. Lonnie had lain down on the floor a while ago gnawing his tongue until he fell asleep. Kaeller had put Timmy to bed, but her assistant still hadn't shown up for work. She muttered something about firing his ass as she walked by on her way to the nurse's station.

John could hear her cussing loudly on the phone, "No, they still haven't sent someone up here! How the hell am I supposed to work this shift alone? I have forty kids up here ... All right. Tell him to hurry."

She slammed down the receiver, stomped into the dayroom and stared at the workers. Mamie sat curled up, her back against the wall, head buried between her knees. For a change even Peter was sitting still looking sleepy. Lying on the sofa, Jackie snored loudly with his head on Susie's lap.

Kaeller planted her hands on her hips. "All right," she growled. "We're not taking showers tonight, I can tell you that. John! You help me get the boys to bed. I'll start with the girls. Come on, everyone, it's time for bed. Everybody up!" She switched off the TV. Some of the girls got up. Kaeller pulled Mamie up roughly and hauled her out of the dayroom. A few girls followed.

John wasn't sure what Kaeller wanted him to do, so he stood up with his hands on his hips like she had done and addressed the men. "Go bed now. Time fo' bed."

A few guys glanced up briefly. Mick growled at him and continued slowly running his hands along the floor, searching for something of interest to fill his pockets. George actually got up and went into the toilet room, yawning widely.

John tried again. "Go bed now. Kaewa' say!" Nobody else moved. Suddenly the back door slammed. John startled as he heard heavy footsteps tramp up the hallway. His heart began to pound. He knew that sound. Each step sent a shiver through him. It was the Mean Man! Why was the Mean Man here already? He usually didn't come until they were in bed.

Kaeller popped her head out of the girls' side. "Well, thank God!" Unlike John, she seemed glad to see him. "You can see how far I've gotten by myself."

"What do you want me to do?" His voice was deep and gruff, like there were cobwebs in his throat.

"I'll finish with the girls if you can get the boys going," Kaeller said. "They need to brush their teeth and use the toilet. Thanks for coming in early. My asshole assistant has a cold, poor baby. I hope he dies."

The Mean Man boomed, "Everybody up!" This time they all jumped. Frightened, John scurried to the toilet room. Just as he was about to sit on the toilet to pee he realized Lonnie was not with him. He hurried back to the dayroom where Lonnie was now awake and sitting cross-legged on the floor. The Mean Man leaned over him, their noses almost touching. He said something low to Lonnie that John couldn't hear. Lonnie's face looked sleepy, but John could tell he was in a "no" mood.

"Uh-oh," John muttered. Then he called to Lonnie, "Come on, Yonnie. Git up. No twoubo."

But it was too late. The Mean Man grabbed Lonnie's crumpled ears and jerked him upward. Lonnie squealed, scrambling to gain his footing. The Mean Man pulled him, ear first, into the sleeping room. John ran after them. The Mean Man threw Lonnie onto his bed. "You do what you're told, you hear?" he growled.

Lonnie's ears were bright red.

"Next time I tell you to stand up, you jump," he snarled, "or you're going to end up in Cadby. That's where little shits like you belong."

Lonnie lay on his back glaring at the Mean Man. He still had his "no" mood face on. John wanted to stop him from doing something bad. He ran toward them but before John could reach him, Lonnie spat straight up into the Mean Man's face. The spittle hit the Mean Man's cheek and dribbled down his chin and onto his collar.

John cried out in horror.

Before Lonnie could roll out of the way, the Mean Man slammed his fist down on Lonnie's nose. Lonnie screamed and clamped his hands over his face. Blood oozed between his fingers.

The Mean Man lumbered away, cursing under his breath, "Get what they deserve, little shitheads."

Rushing to Lonnie's bed, John bent over him. "Yonnie! You hu't!" He snatched a discarded shirt and held it to Lonnie's nose.

John was livid. "Me kiw dat Mean Man, Yonnie. Him bad! Bewy bad!"

Lonnie whimpered and his eyes watered. As John held the shirt tightly to Lonnie's nose, he tried to think of what he should do. He decided he had better get some help.

"Us find Kaewa'. You be okay, Yonnie." He lifted Lonnie to his feet. The other workers were putting on their nightshirts and climbing into bed as John led Lonnie out of the sleeping room, keeping an eye out for the Mean Man as they crossed the dayroom toward the girls' side. John stopped at the entry. He could hear their high voices chattering. John knew he wasn't supposed to go in. Even though it was against the rules, he had to find Kaeller. He yanked Lonnie through the forbidden door.

The girls were dressed in nightgowns, all except Mamie who sat naked on her bed. But then she was naked a lot, often stripping before anyone could stop her. When they saw John and Lonnie, a couple of them screeched and pointed.

Kaeller looked up from the pillowcase she was stuffing. "Oh my God! What happened to you, Lonnie?"

"Yonnie hu't!" John said as pathetically as he could.

She tossed the pillow on a bed and rushed toward Lonnie. "What the hell did you do to him, John?"

"Me? No, no, no! Mean Man!" John held up his fist to show her how the Mean Man had hit Lonnie, but she wasn't looking.

"Let me see." Gently, Kaeller pulled the shirt off Lonnie's face. "Looks like just a bloody nose. Come on. Let's go and clean this up. "

She yelled at the girls to get in bed as she pulled Lonnie by the arm back across the dayroom. Turning to John, she said, "You know you're not supposed to come over here, John. And you also know there's no fighting allowed. You're going to be in big trouble."

"No, no, no! Not me! Mean Man hit Yonnie. Pow!" He showed her again.

They stopped in the boy's toilet room.

"The who? Mean Man? I don't know what you're talking about."

"Mean Man. Sweep Man." John pointed toward the sleeping room. "Him hit Yonnie!"

"The sleep over man? Grady?" She paused then grabbed a towel. "Oh, sure, John. Grady walked right up to Lonnie and belted him in the nose."

"Yeah!"

She wet a towel. "I don't think so, John. Techs don't haul off and hit kids for no reason. But you've hit people before." She shook her head and dabbed the cloth on Lonnie's face. "And I thought you two were friends."

"No good! No good! Mean Man do it!" John was so angry he clenched and unclenched his fists, swaying from one foot to the other. He backed up to the corner, confused, and swallowed to fight back tears. Then he hit the wall with his fist. "Hate dat Mean Man!"

"Shut up, John. This is not what I need tonight. Now I have to write an incident report. As if I didn't have enough to do already." She glanced over at John and rolled her eyes. "Get out of here and go to bed, and maybe I'll think about not turning you in this time."

Tears rolled down John's cheeks. If Kaeller turned him in for fighting, it meant Cadby. John was too afraid to protest further. He limped out of the toilet room, slamming his other fist against the wall.

The Mean Man was not in the sleeping room. John hobbled to his bed rubbing his sore fists. The other boys were all in bed, their silent bodies lying still under the thin white blankets. John buried himself under his covers and seethed. He thought of all the things he would do to the Mean Man someday, when he grew up.

Soon Lonnie came to bed, too. Kaeller whispered to him to settle down, that he would be all right, and then she left. Lonnie's nose was packed with gauze and he breathed loudly through his mouth, lying on his back. Before long, though, Lonnie's breathing eased and he stopped rustling. The room became quiet.

After a little bit John heard Kaeller's footsteps clicking down the hall and then the outside door slammed shut. She had left them with the Mean Man. The TV in the dayroom came on and John could hear the sounds of tinny laughter and music.

Rolling over onto his bad side, he squinted out at the rows of covered boys. No one moved. John still needed to use the toilet before he could go to sleep. He lay for a long time, not wanting to get up, not wanting the Mean Man to hear him. Finally, he tiptoed into the toilet room. If the Mean Man came in, John would punch him, Cadby or no Cadby.

John sat down gingerly on the toilet. In his mind, all he could see was the Mean Man's fist crashing down on Lonnie's nose and the bright blood reddening his shirt. More television laughter came from the dayroom and John heard the Mean Man's low chuckling.

He thought about poor Lonnie's nose stuffed with gauze. Staring at the large toilet paper roll next to him, John suddenly had an idea. He stood up and yanked up his pants. Hand over hand he pulled paper from the roll in long lengths until only the cardboard roll was left. He dropped the whole lot into the toilet. Gleefully, he emptied two more rolls from the toilets next to him. The bowl was nearly filled with the soggy yellow mess. John snickered, rubbed his hands together, then flushed. He ran-skipped back to his bed as quietly as he could, his heart beating so loudly he was afraid the Mean Man might hear it. Swiftly covering himself up, he lay still, listening.

The sound of splashing water grew louder, like a cloudburst. He knew the toilet was overflowing onto the tile floor and soon would trickle out into the dayroom. John had seen the toilets overflow before.

Suddenly, the TV voices stopped. Heavy footsteps were followed by the Mean Man's curses.

Safe under his white cocoon, John snickered and whispered to himself, "Me got you, Mean Man!".

Chapter 4
William

Sarah bounced up the stairs of the Smith Building taking them two at a time and peeling off her woolen cap. The warm air made her instantly hot and she slowed on the landing to rip off her coat and scarf. Rounding the last corner at full speed she nearly smashed into another student. Excusing herself, she hurried to Dr. William Montgomery's door, which stood slightly ajar. She ruffled her hair and rapped lightly.

Dr. Montgomery, William, spun around in his chair to see who was there. The receiver of his phone was glued to his ear, but he motioned her in. His heavy dark eyebrows were furrowed, deep in thought. Sarah noticed in the diffuse light from the dusty window that his thick wavy hair was tinged with gray at the temples, and tousled, as usual. He was a strong-featured man, could have been a lumberjack, she mused. Sarah always thought he didn't quite fit here in the halls of learning. Yet behind his chiseled appearance lay a gentle soul and a brilliant mind.

William pointed from a stack of student papers on a chair to an empty corner on his desk. Sarah carefully moved the papers and sat down, feeling slightly uncomfortable to be listening in on his conversation. She wondered vaguely who might have been in his office overhearing his conversations with her when she spoke to him so often by phone.

William was deep in dialogue, apparently with a colleague, about a current research project design. Sarah guessed it must be Dr. Harry Sheffield in Minneapolis. She knew they were collaborating on a longitudinal study of the impact of drugs versus aversive consequences on self-abusive behaviors. She fidgeted with her scarf, then occupied herself by reading the spines of his voluminous library. This was the life she wanted, spending every day in intellectual pursuits, immersing herself in research, reading and knowing everything there was to know about a subject, teaching others, being the expert at something.

Finally, he hung up. Swiveling around, William leaned back and locked his hands behind his head. He smiled broadly. "So! How did it go? I'm sorry I couldn't go with you."

"No, that's fine," she answered. Why did she always feel so fluttery around him? "It went well, really. I found all the clients. They are going to be challenging, but that's what my project is about, of course. I'm a little worried about Ricky. He looks absolutely normal and seemed fine while I was there the first time, but comments from the staff made me think he might be different from what his file portrayed."

"He is the one we thought might be able to go the farthest, isn't he?" William asked. He was watching her intently. His deep-set eyes seemed to bore into her soul.

Sarah looked down, unable to keep eye contact with him as her heart flip-flopped. "Yes, from reading his file, but he's relatively new to Larkspur. He's only twenty, lived at home until he was thirteen when his parents got sick and couldn't care for him. Then he was put in the institution in California and just transferred up to Oregon six months ago. Evidently his parents passed away or there's a family member up here or something. So he's only been in an institution six and a half years compared to the other guys who have lived there from infancy. One of the techs warned me about him and seemed to think he would never make it outside of the institution. Then there is Peter. He's thirty-four, self-abusive and self-stimulatory, won't give eye contact and hates being touched. I'm not sure how we'll train him without physical cues, and without any medication to control his self-abuse, I'm worried about keeping him safe. Mick may be the toughest, though. His only interest seems to be in finding bits of things on the floor and hiding them in his pocket, oh, and eating inappropriate things. He's the oldest, forty, which may also make it harder to change his behavior. I'm not sure how to motivate him to do anything productive. John and Lonnie, though, they're really cute. They're like Bobbsey twins, sort of joined at the hip. They're around thirty. John uses Lonnie as a prop for his imaginary play, and Lonnie goes along with everything John does, supposedly. They're going to be my favorites, my stars. But I'm sure ..." She stopped, realizing she was running on breathlessly, like a nervous undergraduate.

William grinned at her and broke into a laugh. "So this might not be a vacation after all. It's a different animal when you actually see the real McCoy, to mix metaphors abominably."

Sarah blushed. William knew her background, knew she had taught special education for a couple of years, but also knew that most of her knowledge of the severely disabled was only from textbooks.

She admitted, "It's a bit intimidating, you know? I'm glad you're here to back me up."

He leaned forward and clasped his hands in front of him. "We'll figure this out. This is a wonderful project and I'm very proud of you for taking it on."

As Sarah talked about the challenges she faced, William listened attentively, asked thoughtful questions, and reassured her. They talked for forty-five minutes before his phone rang again.

"I'm afraid I have to take this," he apologized. He reached for the phone, said, "Hello," then covered the receiver with his hand. "I've been waiting for this call. You'll have to excuse me."

"Oh, no problem," Sarah said, suddenly feeling that she had taken up too much of his time. She quickly gathered her notes and shoved them into her backpack.

"Call me next week," he said, winking. He swiveled back to the phone. "Yes, Martin? Thanks for calling me back."

Sarah slung her backpack over her shoulder and quietly pulled his door shut behind her. On the way down the stairs she wondered what it was about his rugged looks that attracted her. He wasn't exactly handsome, but there was discernment in his probing eyes, and his strong jaw with its goatee spoke of inner strength. Most importantly, he cared about her project. William had encouraged her to go on for her Ph.D., ever since she had started her Master's program here at the U. four years ago. He believed in her. He had encouraged her like neither her mother nor her father ever had. Her mother had questioned her need to go on to school. "How long are you going to keep going to school, honey?" she had said when Sarah told her she'd been accepted into the Ph.D. program. "If you get too much education you'll have trouble finding a husband who's more educated than you. And what about having a family? Your clock is ticking, dear." Sarah had steamed over that conversation until a few months later when her mother found out she had cancer.

That must be why William's faith in her was so important, she told herself. He wanted her to be successful. She shook off the troubling thought that despite his reputation, if he wasn't married, she could fall in love with him.

That evening Sarah lay aside her reading and picked up the phone by her bed. She dialed her father's number in New Jersey. She had talked to him briefly on Christmas Day but it had been several months since she talked to him at any length. They had grown further and further apart since he had moved out east. And what with Sarah's graduate school studies, her mother dying, comprehensive exams, and now her dissertation, she was preoccupied. Thinking about her mother brought back a deep loneliness and she just needed to hear her dad's voice.

"Hi, Dad. How are things going?" she said when he picked up the phone. She realized she knew little about what was happening with him and his wife, Rebecca.

"Fine!" He sounded happy to hear from her. "We've had a lot of snow this month. Rebecca's been working too hard in her practice, but otherwise things are good. How are you, sweetie?"

"I'm well." Sarah tried to match his level of enthusiasm. " Busy! How are the kids?" They must have grown up quite a bit since she last saw them ... when was that? She had lost track of how old they were.

"They're fine. Busy. Chelsea is in fifth grade orchestra, and even as a third grader David has a constant entourage of friends around him. He's like a kid magnet." He was reminding her of their ages, she realized.

Sarah laughed. "Sounds like they're doing well, Dad. You must be proud of them."

"And how about you?" he asked. "You're still taking classes, right?"

"Actually, I'm finished with classes. I passed my orals in November. I thought I wrote that in my Christmas card."

"Oh, yes, you did. I'm sorry."

"I'm starting my research project this semester. I'm sure I told you about it." She didn't wait for him to try to remember. "I'm taking five severely disabled adults out of our state institution and we're going to teach them to live in the community."

"Wow!" He paused. "How are you going to do that? Sounds very ... difficult."

She was careful to keep an upbeat tone, though she was hurt that he didn't seem to remember. "I have a lot of help. There's a grant that my advisor, Dr. Montgomery, got from the state. I'll manage the project and I've hired some work-study students to do the shift work. I'll train the staff and then conduct my research on the effectiveness of community based living. Dr. Montgomery has been a big help. I'm really excited about it and we're thinking that this could be a model across the country for getting developmentally disabled people out of mental institutions."

"Getting them out? Are you sure that's a good idea? Aren't they dangerous, or a danger to themselves?" He sounded doubtful, like so many others when she explained her research project.

"No, Dad, they're not dangerous." Old feelings of being criticized returned in a rush and she felt herself getting defensive. "They're just people who aren't as smart as we are. It's 1974, Dad. Time to change our prejudices. They deserve a chance to live a fulfilling life, in a community, like the rest of us." She paused, trying to take the edge out of her voice.

"Okay, honey. I see what you mean," he said softly. "I'm sure you know what's best. You're the expert."

She thought about not saying it, but she couldn't help herself. "A chance like my brother never got."

Silence. She heard rustling, like he was covering the phone with his hand and maybe moving into another room. Finally, he said quietly, "Sarah, you can't go on blaming your mother for that forever. You're going to have to forgive her someday. She was young and there were no options in those days. She did the best she could."

"She could have at least told me before it was too late." Sarah wiped a tear away, glad her father couldn't see her.

"That was a mistake. But look. When she did tell you ..."

"On her deathbed." Sarah's throat tightened.

"I know. I wish I could fix that. But it helped you determine the direction of your career, so that's a good thing."

She couldn't keep the sob out of her voice. "Why didn't you tell me, Dad? I just don't understand that." Why had she called him? Talking to him just brought everything up again.

"I promised I wouldn't. She was only seventeen and it was such a shameful thing. You know that." There was empathy in his voice. "Sarah, you have to let it go. Your mom's gone and there's nothing we can do to remedy this. But you can use it ..."

"To build my character? Good Lord. How many times have I heard that?" She put the phone to her chest and wiped her nose on her sweatshirt sleeve for lack of a tissue. "Listen, I better go. I have a ton to do tonight. Nice talking to you, Dad."

"Sarah! I'll call you this weekend ..." she heard him say as she lay the receiver down.

Sarah flopped face-down on her bed and sobbed into her pillow. When the tears finally eased, she got up and made some tea, pushing thoughts of her family back into the farthest corner of her mind. She had no time for this now. She picked up the text, *The History of American Mental Institutions* and curled up in her bed to read herself to sleep.

Chapter 5
Sarah's House

The white Larkspur van stopped in front of a house John recognized from the picture Sarah had shown him three weeks ago. John pressed his face up against the cold van window and stared. The house was made of gray stones on the bottom but the top part was painted green. A wide porch held up with white pillars framed the red front door. Large curtained windows looked inviting. John glanced up and down the street and saw more houses with neatly trimmed lawns and large, bare-branched trees, just like the neighborhood of *The Partridge Family*. Sarah's house was the biggest and the prettiest on the block, John decided.

The bus driver, an old man John knew from Larkspur years ago came around and opened the sliding door on the side of the van. "Everybody out! This is your new home, boys."

John figured out how to unfasten his seatbelt and he helped Lonnie with his. In the seat behind them, Mick fought against his strap, as he had done the whole way, sweating profusely by now. Peter sat beside him next to the window, his arms crossed, staring silently outside. In the front seat next to the driver was Ricky. John had never seen Ricky before. He had dark curly hair and a handsome face, and at first John thought he was a tech. But the driver talked to him just like the other boys and Ricky didn't say a word all the way down the hill. John figured he must be a dummy.

John helped Lonnie crawl out of the van and the driver pulled the seat forward to let Mick and Peter get out. Before the driver could unfasten his seatbelt Mick redoubled his efforts, straining so hard it looked like he might squish in half.

"Calm down, boy," the driver said, reaching in to unclip the belt. When he did, Mick shot up like a spit wad from a rubber band and knocked his head on the roof. He flinched and rubbed the balding spot on his crown. Then he bounded out of the van so fast that the driver barely had time to grab him around the waist.

"Whoa, there now!" The driver somehow kept a hold of Mick, who squirmed wildly in his arms. He asked John to unbuckle Peter. John was surprised when Peter actually came out without a fuss. Ricky stepped out of the van on his own and stood stiffly upright. He looked strong and handsome, and John wondered again if maybe he was a tech after all. Ricky stared first at Peter, then Lonnie, then at John. Something about the way his eyes looked, deep and piercing, made John feel creepy. He was a dummy, all right, a bad dummy.

"No yook a' me!" John told Ricky, shaking his finger at Ricky and stepping back.

Just then, the red door of Sarah's house flung open and Sarah ran across the porch. Another young woman with a long swishing ponytail followed closely behind her.

"Hi, everyone!" Sarah called, waving as she hurried down the sidewalk that led from the wide porch steps to the curb.

"We're so glad you're here!" Both women smiled and John opened his arms wide for a hug as Sarah approached. Nimbly, she stepped aside and shook his hand instead.

"Welcome to your new home! In the group home, we shake hands with people instead of hugging, John. It's more polite that way,"

John shook her hand hard. She shook Lonnie's hands next, pulling it free when Lonnie brought her hand to his nose to smell.

"Do you need help with Mick?" Sarah called to the driver. By this time he had straightened Mick up and was holding him firmly by the arm. "I've got him, miss. Do you want me to bring him in for you?"

"Sure, thanks." Sarah pointed to the young woman. "By the way, guys, this is Jana. She's going to work with us, too." Jana shook hands all around like Sarah had. Jana was shorter than Sarah and thin, her petite features drawn into a cheery smile that lit her pixie-like face. Her blonde ponytail lay draped like a towel across her shoulder. John thought she looked like a movie star.

The driver unlocked the back door of the van and started unloading the suitcases. As he hauled a bag out of the van, Mick slipped out of his grasp, plunging to the pavement. The driver tried to grab Mick's arm but he twisted away and scrambled onto the lawn. The driver dropped the suitcase and stooped to catch Mick. Jana retrieved the luggage and handed one suitcase each to Lonnie and John, asking them to follow her toward the house.

"I'll get Mick," Sarah said to the driver, who was struggling with him on the grass. She pulled a pencil out of her pocket, squatted next to Mick and said, "Mick? You want this pencil? If you come in the house, I'll give this to you." She held it just out of his reach. Mick grabbed at it but missed. Sarah walked briskly toward the house with Mick stumbling after her. They disappeared inside.

John and Lonnie followed Jana with their burdens. Peter looked around fearfully, banged on his forehead, then followed haltingly behind them.

After heaving their suitcases up the porch steps, Lonnie hesitated, not wanting to step over the raised threshold. John urged him forward from behind, Lonnie shook his head.

"Me come back git you," John said. He didn't want to risk getting Lonnie into a "no" mood so soon. He set his suitcase down in the entry.

"Come on in and make yourselves at home," Sarah said, moving the suitcases out of the doorway. "Have a look around."

John's mouth hung open and his tongue played nervously with his lower lip. This was the first Away Place house he had ever been in. Near the front door, carpeted stairs led enticingly to a second story. John watched Jana lug two suitcases up the steps before she vanished around a corner.

The small entry opened into what must be the dayroom, but it was small and furnished with a soft sofa and a couple of cushy chairs. Ricky brushed by John, rudely bumping him with his shoulder as he passed. John grunted and turned to reprimand him, but Ricky headed straight for the dayroom and plopped down in the biggest, softest-looking chair. He folded his hands behind his head like he had staked a claim, as Cookie would say.

John stared at Ricky meanly, confused about who he was and irritated at his rudeness. Ricky ignored him and just leaned back, shutting his eyes.

Mick sunk onto the flowered sofa where he clutched the new pencil Sarah had given him in both hands.

John took a baby step through the archway. The windows were low and John could see right outside to the grass and trees. In front of the sofa was a table that had magazines and a bowl of flowers on it. Two more low tables were situated beside the chairs, each holding a lamp. The walls were covered with tiny flowers. John wondered if Sarah had painted them all by herself. A big picture of the ocean hung on one wall and a plant dangled from a rope near the window. The TV was down on the floor where anyone could reach it, a pretty glass jar sitting precariously on top.

At the far end of this dayroom was a long wooden table with "eleventeen" chairs around it, by John's count. On the wall behind the table were cupboards with glass doors and dishes inside. This was a nice house, a real house, for smart people. John was afraid of what Mick or Peter might do to mess it up.

He started to tell Sarah how Mick might break her things, but she said, "What do you think, guys? This is your new home!"

Just then Jana skipped down the stairs and headed outside again.

Sarah smiled and said, " Jana and I are going to bring in the rest of the things. Have a seat, everyone, and we'll be back in a minute to give you the grand tour. Mick, if you stay in your seat I'll give you another pencil when I get back."

Sarah's scent trailed her pleasantly as she bobbed past John.

"Go on in," he heard her say to Lonnie and Peter on the porch. Peter stepped in and stopped in the entry, staring up at the colored glass that covered the light.

As soon as Sarah left, Mick stood up and stumbled around the room. He groped the top of the TV with his puffy hands.

"No touch!" John said. He pushed Mick away from the TV, holding onto the glass jar so it wouldn't fall. Mick ran for the hanging plant. John hurried over to keep him from knocking it down. Mick turned his back to John, growling something John couldn't understand, snapped the new pencil in half and stuck it in his pocket. John shook his head. Dummy.

Jana thumped up the porch steps. John was startled when he saw Lonnie lurch forward through the doorway, gently prodded by Jana. Lonnie hated to be pushed and John feared the worst. But before Lonnie could protest, Jana patted him softly on the back and cooed, "Good job. Nothing to be afraid of here." To John's relief Lonnie just looked surprised and didn't hit or drop to the floor.

"Good boy, Yonnie," John said. He took Lonnie's hand and led him into the dayroom. "Yonnie, yook at Sawah's nice house. Pwetty!"

Lonnie grunted and shook his head, still a little peeved about being rushed.

Sarah and the driver followed Jana inside and placed the last of the luggage at the bottom of the stairs.

"Thank you," Sarah puffed, turning to the old man. "Nice of you to help. We'll be all right now."

"Nice lookin' place you have here." The driver craned his neck to look around inside.

"Thanks. We've been working hard to get it ready." Sarah smiled and put her hands on her hips.

The old man continued, "A regular house. You know, these boys are gonna tear it up. That's why Larkspur don't look like this."

Sarah's face flushed pink and her smile faded. "No, they'll be fine. We're going to teach them how to take care of a house."

"You sure you two girls can handle these boys? I know that one," he said, pointing at Mick. "He'll hurt somebody if you don't' watch him. He bites, you know."

"We'll manage. I know all about them and we have behavior plans all set." Sarah reached for the door handle.

The driver shrugged. "I have some papers here for you to sign." He pulled them out of his pocket and handed her a pen. "Sign right here."

When she finished writing, the driver handed her one of the papers and stuck his pen back in his shirt pocket. "Thanks, miss. If you run into trouble, you know where to find us. I expect we'll be seeing some of 'em back again before long."

"No, I don't think so," Sarah said. "They belong in the community, not locked up away from everybody else."

He shrugged again. "Whatever you say. Good luck. You're gonna need more than luck, though."

Sarah closed the door. "And stay out," she whispered, rolling her eyes.

Jana shook her head. "Yeah. They don't get it, do they?"

"They can't believe these guys can make it outside that ugly institution."

"That's why you're here," Jana said, smiling, "to prove them wrong."

Sarah smiled back at her and nodded. "Thanks, Jana. Okay, everyone, it's time for a tour. Come on, follow me."

Ricky got up right away. Mick turned his back to her, stuffing both hands into his pockets. Peter still stood in the entry and slowly began to rock. He stepped farther forward so he could get more leverage and rocked hard backward and then forward again. John knew he would soon start flapping.

Sarah kept talking, leaning on the back of the sofa with both arms. "Obviously, this is the living room. We'll spend a lot of leisure time in here."

"Daywoom," John corrected.

"Like a dayroom, John, but we'll call it the living room." She winked at him. John tried to make his eye wink back, but both eyes closed together.

Sarah moved to the long table and tapped it. "This is the dining room. We'll eat all our meals here. You'll take turns setting the table and cleaning up with Jana and me and the other counselors who will be here to help us. Everyone will have a job every day. Here's the job chart." She pointed to a large paper on the wall by a phone with words and pictures on it.

Sarah pushed open two swinging doors at the end of the eating room. These doors came together in the middle but didn't quite touch. They looked just like the saloon doors on Bonanza. They were cowboy doors!

Sarah continued, "The kitchen is in here. You can come in and look if you want." John grabbed Lonnie's hand and they followed her.

"Cowboy doo's!" he told Lonnie, pushing them back and forth to show Lonnie how they moved.

Sarah laughed. "Cowboy doors? That's right, John. They are like doors in old cowboy movies."

John liked Sarah already. He liked the way she talked to them and how she laughed easily. Her voice was gentle and her eyes were happy. He liked her unruly dark curls. John thought she was beautiful.

Ricky followed them into the kitchen, once again bumping into John.

John shoved him away. "No, bump!" he said, frowning at Ricky.

"I'm sure he didn't mean to touch you, John," Sarah said. "We'll work on personal space—don't worry about it."

The kitchen was small compared to Larkspur's. Little roosters covered the walls. *Sarah must be a good painter,* John thought.

There was only one small stove, a shallow sink, and a white refrigerator. The cupboards were yellow and each cupboard had a little picture taped on the outside. He found out later these were pictures of what was inside.

They followed Sarah down a narrow stairway off the kitchen to the basement. At the bottom was an open space with a large table that Sarah described as the rec. room. A tall cupboard held games and puzzles and art supplies. Sarah showed them her office, locking it up after she let them look inside, and telling them they couldn't go in without permission. *This is just like Cookie's station,* John thought.

When they came back to the dayroom where Jana had stayed with Peter and Mick, Jana said, "Let's take your things upstairs, guys." She called them guys, not boys, John noticed.

"Come on, Mick," Sarah said, holding up another short pencil. "You can have this when you come upstairs." Mick stumbled after her, reaching occasionally for the pencil that she kept just out of his reach.

Jana motioned Peter forward. "Let's go upstairs, Peter," she said. Then she pushed him gently from behind. As soon as she touched him, Peter began screaming and banging his head with his fist.

Jana jerked her hand back. "Oh, I'm sorry! I forgot!"

Peter pounded his head again and again, his scream changing to a high-pitched whine, his eyes squeezed shut.

"Sarah?" Jana stood with her hands up in the air like someone was holding a gun on her. "What should I do?"

"Just ignore him for now," Sarah answered. "He needs time to adjust. We'll talk about the desensitization program at our meeting."

Jana stepped away from Peter and picked up two suitcases. "I'm sorry, Peter," she said again. "From now on I'll try to remember."

Peter's head-pounding subsided, but he stayed downstairs and rocked furiously.

Lonnie wouldn't take a suitcase, so John struggled up the stairs with both of their bags. At the top was a narrow hall with several doors that stood open.

"This is Lonnie's and your room," Sarah said, pointing to the door nearest the stairs. John set the suitcases down inside. "Peter, Mick and Ricky have their own rooms. The bathroom is across the hall from you. You and Lonnie can unpack your clothes into those dressers. Can you unpack by yourselves, or do you need come help?"

"Me do." John tapped his chest.

"Good, John. We'll check on you in a few minutes to see if you need anything. Jana and I will get the other guys settled."

John surveyed the tiny sleeping room. On either side of the door was a bed, each with a table and a lamp by it and each covered with a brown spread. The walls were made of unpainted wood. At one end of the room the white ceiling slanted down toward a low window hung with orange and brown curtains. John could see trees through the window. The floor was covered with orange carpet. There were even pictures on the walls. Except for the beds, it didn't look like a sleeping room at all.

John noticed a door made of wood just like the walls. When he opened it, there was a rod and hangers and some folded blankets on a shelf. This must be the storage closet.

"What bed you want, Yonnie?" John asked.

Lonnie sat down on the one behind the door.

"Good. Me yike dis one." John flopped down on the other bed. He lay back and tested it; it was harder than his bed at Starlight, but comfortable. The ceiling light had a glass jar around it decorated with gold trim. Even the lights were pretty at Sarah's house.

Sitting up, John pointed to the dressers. "Dis mine. You hab dat one. Sawah say put cwothes he'e."

Lonnie nodded, but didn't move. John placed Lonnie's suitcase on the bed for him. Unlatching his own suitcase John set his clothes neatly into the drawers like Cookie had taught him. Lonnie sat cross-legged and watched, chewing noisily on his tongue. John emptied his treasures into the smallest drawer and placed mama's picture on the little table by his bed. He lay down with his head on the pillow to make sure he could see her from there.

"You tu'n, Yonnie."

Lonnie smiled. He didn't know how to unlatch his suitcase, so John helped him. When Lonnie still wouldn't help, John decided to put his things away for him.

"You undawea' and socks, he'e," John explained, unpacking Lonnie's things. "No tie socks, Yonnie. Sawah not yike dat."

Lonnie nodded and sat contentedly chewing his tongue and finger flicking.

John hoped Lonnie would be good and not tie up all his socks or get in a "no" mood. He was sure Sarah would send them back if they were bad.

When he finished, John lay down on his bed again. He thought about how strange everything was here. He couldn't imagine how it would feel to go to sleep or wake up in this small room, all closed in, like sleeping in a cupboard. At Starlight, everything was always the same—all the beds were lined up, the dirty clothes went in the laundry bin, Cookie rang her little bell. But she wouldn't be waking him up tomorrow. And what about Rochelle? He hadn't said goodbye to her. He wouldn't see her at work either. Who would help her if her sheets got tangled? A lump grew in John's throat and he swallowed hard.

"Us yive he'e, wif Sawah, Yonnie." he said, quickly rubbing away his tears with the back of his hand. He moved over onto

Lonnie's bed and held his hand. "You no be sad, Yonnie. Me he'e."

~

Once they were settled John and Lonnie spent the afternoon wandering around the house. They explored all the rooms, looking in cupboards and opening doors. No one stopped them.

Ricky followed them around for a while like a silent ghost, standing in John's way when he turned around and flashing strange faces at them.

John told him, "No fowow," and "Go 'way!" and finally Ricky disappeared.

Eventually they peeked into the kitchen through the cowboy doors. Sarah greeted them. "You're just in time to help me with dinner, John. You and Ricky are on duty tonight. Are you hungry?"

"Yep. Me hungwy. Yonnie, you hungwy?"

Lonnie nodded.

Sarah led them to the job chart posted in the eating room. "Here's how you can tell whose turn it is to do the household chores. Can you find your name, John?"

John recognized his "J" and pointed to his name next to a picture of a stove. Another name was also there that started with an "R". Other words were written beside pictures including a washing machine, a broom, and a toilet. Sarah told Lonnie to wait in the dayroom while she led John and Ricky into the kitchen. She asked them to wash their hands. John protested that his hands weren't dirty but Sarah said it was a rule.

Sarah set three boxes of macaroni on the counter for Ricky to open. She handed John a cooking pot. "John, would you fill this pan with water and bring it to the stove? We're going to make macaroni and cheese."

Being so close to Sarah made John feel warm inside. She was pretty and friendly and she smelled good. He set the pot in the sink and pushed the handle, but no water came out.

Sarah glanced over. "Oh, John, you have to lift up." She showed him with a gesture.

John tried it and filled the pan to the brim. It was heavy now, and water dripped over the sides as he carefully lifted it out of the sink. With his first tiny step toward the stove, a drip splashed over the rim and hit his shoe. He looked over at Sarah but she was on her knees reaching something in a low cupboard.

"We're going to have to move this colander. It's too hard to reach," she said, making little grunting noises. Pots and pans clanged noisily.

John inched his way toward the stove, the pan brimming over with water. Suddenly, Ricky jerked toward John and stuck his face right in front of John's, making an ugly sneer. John jumped. Water poured onto his shirt and down the front of his pants. The shock of the cold water made him lose his grip on the pan. Water cascaded forward as it clattered to the floor.

Sarah whooped and jumped to her feet, her back drenched. John yelled, too, and drew back against the door, instinctively covering his ears. He was in bad trouble!

"Yikes! That was cold!" Sarah said as she shook out the back of her shirt. But instead of scolding him, she laughed. "That was a surprise shower, John!" She didn't sound mad at all.

John pointed at Ricky. "Him make face, yike dis!" John tried to imitate Ricky but Sarah wasn't looking.

She tip-toed through the pool of water, grabbed some towels from a drawer and tossed them onto the floor "Come on, guys, help me." Sarah pulled Ricky's arm to come down and help her but he stood stiffly staring at her.

"Well, John, you can help me," she said. "Let's mop this up."

"Wicky bad," John said, still trembling. "Him make face."

"It's okay. It wasn't your fault. It could happen to anyone. I should have been watching." Together she and John soaked up all the water while Ricky stood by grinning evilly. John looked up a couple of times to stick his tongue out at Ricky.

Sarah tossed the wet towels downstairs. "We'll take care of those later when we do the laundry. We better change our wet clothes. Go get some dry clothes, John, and hurry back down."

John rushed up the stairs to change. *Sarah is different,* he thought as he quickly put on dry clothes. She hadn't pulled his ear or yelled at him or anything. When he returned, Sarah had changed into a man's shirt and was rolling up the sleeves.

She smiled at John as if nothing had happened, "Okay, guys, let's cook dinner before everyone starves."

Sarah had to take Ricky's hands to help him with everything. When she talked to him her voice was patient and instructive, even though Ricky didn't do anything by himself.

When the next half-filled pot of water was bubbling, Sarah asked John to pour the macaroni in and she gave him a wooden spoon to stir it with. He stirred carefully, trying hard to do exactly what she said.

The cowboy doors opened and Peter followed Jana into the kitchen. He had his arm bent over the top of his head as if he was hugging it, his elbow sticking straight up, so that he was able to cover both ears with one arm. His eyes were squeezed almost shut.

"How's it going in here?" Jana asked. She smiled at John and gave him a baby wave.

"Just fine," Sarah replied. She was helping Ricky tear open a bag of frozen corn. "John's helping me with the noodles and Ricky is going to put the corn on."

"Well, Peter's turn to set the table," Jana said. "Peter, let me show you where the plates are."

"Peto no wo'k," John told her, shaking his head and frowning. "Him dummy."

"Well, he works here," Jana said.

"We don't say dummy," Sarah reminded John. "It's not kind."

John's ears reddened in embarrassment. He must try to remember not to say dummy because Sarah didn't like it for some reason.

Jana tapped on a cupboard door with a picture of plates taped to it. Peter looked at the ceiling. Jana pulled out the plates and Sarah snuck up behind Peter and using a kitchen towel, pushed his free arm up. Jana set the plates on his hand and they both let go. John winced, visualizing the crash. Peter quivered all over and squealed, but shockingly, he held on to the plates. He hated loud noises, too.

Jana opened the cowboy doors. "Peter, you have to set the table or we don't eat."

Peter somehow managed to get to the eating table without dropping the plates. The cowboy doors swished shut behind him.

Sarah helped Ricky pour the corn into the pan and put it on the stove. A little clock on the stove dinged. Sarah directed John to carry the pan of noodles over to the sink and dump them into the strainer. She helped him scoop the macaroni into a large bowl and handed him milk and butter to pour in. John licked the margarine off his fingers.

"Oops! You have to wash your hands again, John," Sarah said. "We can't lick our hands when we're cooking."

"Oh." Another rule. John washed his hands begrudgingly.

"Now stir it up until the butter is melted. I'm going to see how Peter is doing." Sarah walked out of the kitchen.

John stirred the noodles as best he could. When some cheese sprinkled over the edge of the bowl John scooped it back in with his fingers and licked them, checking to make sure Sarah wasn't watching. He didn't want to wash his hands again.

When she came back Sarah said cheerfully, "They're not quite ready out there, but you can set the macaroni on the table, John. Ricky will bring the corn out in a minute."

John picked up the bowl and hesitated. He was worried that if he pushed through the cowboy doors with the bowl he might spill again.

"Just go through backward John," Sarah said, demonstrating for him. "Then if someone is coming through from the other side you'll be fine."

John hugged the steaming bowl to his chest and backed through the cowboy doors. It worked.

"Thanks, John," Jana said when he set the bowl of steaming macaroni on the table. "We better hurry, Peter."

On the table were colorful placemats with shapes on them, one for each chair. A plate sat on each placemat. Peter held a cup with two fingers dangling it over one of the plates.

"Peter, put the cup here," Jana said. She pointed to one of the small circles. Peter set the cup down on the edge of the table. "Good. You set it down!" Jana moved the cup to the circle. "Here's the next one. Put it on the circle."

John returned to the kitchen.

Ricky stood with his arms dangling at his sides, staring at Sarah.

"Here, John," Sarah said. "Would you set the corn and the bread on the table for me, too? Then you can take a break. I need to talk to Ricky." John backed through the cowboy doors with these items just as Peter passed him on his way back in with Jana.

"Silverware next, Peter," Jana was saying.

John sat down on the sofa by Lonnie who squealed in delight to see John back again. John tried to watch TV but he couldn't keep his eyes from Jana and Peter as he set out the silverware. Peter was actually working.

Finally, Jana called them to eat. Sarah and Jana told each boy where to sit. John sat at the end by Lonnie and Jana sat between Lonnie and Peter. Sarah scooted in between Mick and Ricky.

Sarah said, "Okay everyone. This is our first meal together. We are thankful for this food and that you all are here. Let's eat!"

She dished corn onto Mick's plate then passed the bowl to Ricky. Mick immediately grabbed a handful of corn off his plate and stuffed it into his mouth. Corn juice ran down his arm.

"That's not the way we eat here," Sarah said, catching his arm. "You have to use your fork, Mick."

Sarah forced the fork into his closed fist and helped him scoop it. "Like this," she said clenching her teeth with the effort.

"Mick is the one who likes to steal food, I take it," Jana whispered to Sarah.

Sarah nodded. "You have a hard time waiting, don't you, Mick?" Sarah guided Mick's hand with a firm grip. He growled at her impatiently until the fork finally reached his mouth. Sarah had to stand up behind him to keep him from using his other hand, which she held firmly on his lap. He struggled against her with each bite.

Jana spooned macaroni onto Peter's plate and then passed the bowl around. She told everyone to help themselves, something John had never done at Larkspur. When it was his turn, John took three heaping spoonfuls before Jana told him to pass it on. Jana took some food, too, which surprised John because he had never seen techs eat with the workers.

The macaroni was cool by now, but John barely noticed. He was hungry and he ate as fast as he could. When he finished his first plateful, he looked over at Lonnie. Lonnie had lifted a forkful of macaroni but it was still poised in front of his mouth. Lonnie was always so slow!

John nudged him. "You eat, Yonnie. Fast!"

"No hurry tonight," Sarah said, momentarily letting go of Mick's hand to reach for the bread.

Instantly, Mick's hand shot up and he snatched a fistful of bread slices, jamming them all into his mouth at once.

"Mick!" Sarah tried to pull his hand back but Mick used his other hand to stuff the food until his cheeks were bulging.

Sarah pushed Mick's hand down from his mouth. "We don't stuff our food like that, Mick! It's very impolite!"

Mick gulped visibly, trying to get the bread down before Sarah could stop him. Then his whole body stiffened. He stopped struggling and his eyes grew wide.

Sarah patted his arm. "That's better, Mick. Finish that bite before you take more."

John watched Mick's face turn red. "Him toke," he said.

"Toke?" Sarah's eyebrows scrunched up. "Toke, toke, I'm not sure ..."

Suddenly Jana sprang out of her seat and yelled, "Oh, he's choking!" She rushed around the table.

Jana and Sarah pulled Mick out of his chair and Sarah wrapped her arms around Mick's stomach, squeezing hard. Mick clasped his hands to his mouth, trying to hold the bread in, but a second squeeze by Sarah sent the bread rocketing across the table. It bounced off Lonnie's shirt and tumbled to the floor.

Mick sucked air in loudly. His face changed back from red to white.

Sarah let go. "Wow! You scared me, Mick. That's why you don't stuff your mouth!"

In a flash, Mick lunged under the table, diving toward the ejected bread chunk.

"Oh, my God!" Jana cried as she and Sarah grabbed Mick's legs and pulled him back. They plunked him into his chair, but not before he arduously swallowed the mass he had retrieved. Sarah held him into his chair by pressing down on his shoulders.

"He almost ..." Jana started to say, her face pale.

"I know," Sarah said. Her voice was husky. She leaned over and spoke into Mick's ear. "We don't eat like that! We don't stuff food, and we don't eat off the floor!"

"What are we going to do?" Jana asked.

Sarah's face reddened. "Um ... let's pull him away from the table for a time out. I don't have a plan for this yet."

With Mick still in the chair, they dragged him away from the table. He kicked at them with his feet even as they held his hands down on his lap.

He growled, "Bitechew! Kickyou!" These were his favorite words, the only ones John had ever heard him say.

Sarah danced out of his way, spinning his chair toward the corner. She squatted behind the chair and held him in a bear hug so he couldn't turn around to kick at her.

Jana backed away. " Have you got him?"

"Yeah. Luckily he's not that strong." Sarah spoke into Mick's ear again. "Mick, until you calm down, you're not going to eat. Understand? Sit still or no eating!"

"Need any help?" Jana stood behind Sarah and wiped sweat off her upper lip.

"I'm okay," Sarah struggled to hold onto Mick who writhed effortfully on his chair. "Have everybody else keep eating so he knows what he's missing." Sarah nodded her head toward the table where everyone had stopped to watch.

Jana sat down, visibly shaking. "Back to eating, guys. Mick is okay." But Jana didn't pick up her fork. Her face was still white.

For a while the only sounds were forks tinkling and Mick's growled threats. Ricky finished first and stood up. He started for the dayroom.

"Take your plate to the kitchen, Ricky," Jana said as she opened the cowboy doors for him. "Then you can relax. Since you cooked you're not on clean up crew."

Ricky's arms fell uselessly to his sides.

Sarah called over her shoulder. "Jana, you're going to have to help him. So far he has decided not to do anything without a complete physical assist."

"Okay, Ricky, I'll help you then," Jana said. She brought Ricky back to the table and held his hands around his plate, disappearing with him into the kitchen.

When she returned Jana said, "Let's see, whose turn it is to clean up the kitchen?" She checked the job chart. "Hmm. Lonnie and Mick. Somehow I don't think that combo is going to work."

"Me he'p," John offered. "Me an' Yonnie." He wanted to please them, and besides, since John could cook now, cleaning up shouldn't be a problem.

"Thanks, John." Jana patted him on the shoulder. "That would be a big help tonight."

John told Lonnie to hurry because he still had only taken a few bites. He took his own plate to the kitchen, careful to walk backward through the cowboy doors. Lonnie was still eating when John had taken most of the other dishes away, except Mick's.

Finally, Sarah let Mick scoot up to the table. Her face was damp with sweat and her limp curls fell into her eyes. With one hand, she pulled up a chair and sat directly behind Mick. She held one of his hands on his lap, and with the other, guided the fork to his mouth. Mick didn't like this, but he seemed so desperate to eat that he let her help him.

John stood in the doorway and watched Sarah patiently guide Mick's hand for each bite. He had never seen Mick let anyone help him do anything before. *Sarah is nice,* John thought, *even to Mick.* Marley or the Mean Man would have pulled his ear and strapped him to his bed for the evening.

When Lonnie was finished, Jana showed John and Lonnie how to rinse the dishes and place them in the dishwasher. Lonnie mostly tried to tickle John's neck, but he finally helped when John scolded him firmly and told him they couldn't play unless Lonnie helped.

Before long Sarah brought Mick's plate into the kitchen. "Well, he polished that off," she said to Jana. "I've never seen anyone eat like that. Did he eat that way at Starlight, John?'

"Yep. Him steo food, eat fast, toke." John pretended to stuff his mouth to show her how Mick ate.

"I'll talk to William when we have our meeting," Sarah said to Jana. She raised her eyebrows and took a deep breath. "We need to revise some of our behavior plans right away."

"We sure do. This is going to be harder than I thought," Jana agreed.

"Yeah, well I'm doing the best I can right now," Sarah's face reddened. She turned to leave the kitchen.

Jana caught Sarah's arm. "I didn't mean it like that, Sarah ... I'm just agreeing with you."

"No big deal," Sarah said swishing through the cowboy doors.

John sat on the floor, leaning against the sofa in front of the TV set watching *MASH*. At Starlight, they only got to watch *MASH* when someone had a problem and the techs were too busy to put them to bed at the usual time. Cross-legged beside him, Lonnie flicked his fingers and chewed on his tongue. When John glanced over at Ricky, he mouthed something to John that John couldn't quite catch. From the look on Ricky's face, whatever he said wasn't good.

Mick slouched down on the sofa fingering the cushions, absent-mindedly searching for scraps. Even he looked tired. Peter stood in the entryway slowly rocking and staring at the colorful light. Peter liked that light the best so far.

Sarah called this time of evening their leisure time, saying they could do whatever they wanted. No one knew what to do besides watch television. Sarah made several phone calls while Jana busied herself rearranging the job chart and vacuuming under the eating table. When Sarah hung up the phone, she came over and sat down beside Mick on the sofa.

"How are you guys doing over here?" she asked.

No one answered except John. "Us good, Sawah."

"What are you doing, Mick?" Sarah scooted close to him.

Mick slid to the far end of the couch and turned his back to her. "Mmf," he grunted, shaking his head. Mick's knotted hands moved back and forth over the arm of the couch.

"Him yook fo' penso's," John said. "Him dummy."

"Let's not call people names here, John," she reminded him gently. "So what's on TV, guys?"

"Hawkeye. Him good," John answered.

"You like *MASH*?"

"Yep. Dem he'p peopo'. Sma't."

"That's true. How about you, Ricky, do you like this show?"

Ricky grinned at her and said something under his breath that no one could hear.

"What's that, Ricky?" Sarah leaned toward him but he didn't repeat it.

Sarah was quiet for a minute, then said to John, "You've been a big help tonight, John." She placed her hand on his shoulder. "Thanks for jumping in and helping clean up the dishes when it wasn't your turn."

John reached back and tried to give her a hug. She shook his hand instead. "We shake hands, remember?"

"Okay, shake." He shook her hand firmly until she pulled it away.

She scooted closer to Mick. "What have you got in your pockets, Mick? It looks like they're full."

Mick jammed his hands deep into his pockets and squirmed up onto the armrest.

"Mick, do you have something you're not supposed to have?" Sarah tugged on his hand trying to pull it out of his pocket. Mick threw himself over the side of the sofa, but with both hands in his pockets he stumbled onto his knees. Sarah bent over the armrest and pulled hard on his elbow until his tightly closed fist popped out like a cork. A scattering of yellow splinters flew lightly onto the carpet.

"What is this?" Sarah asked in surprise.

Jana peered over Sarah's shoulder. "It looks like wood splinters. No, pencil pieces!"

"Yep, him bweak penso's," John told them. "Him bad boy."

Mick lay on the floor propping himself up with his elbow while he held whatever remained in his hand with three fingers.

Frantically, he picked up the dropped splinters with his thumb and pointer finger.

Sarah looked up at Jana. "He has a pocketful of this. I've only given him four pencils today."

"That looks like a lot more than four," Jana said.

"Where would he have found more pencils around here? I don't even know where to find any pencils," Sarah commented.

"I'll check the office supply drawer." Jana opened one of the drawers in the glass cupboard by the eating table. "Hey, they're all gone! I had a new box of pencils in here."

Sarah bent over Mick again. He was still busy picking up splinters and stuffing them back into his pocket. "Mick, in this house we don't steal pencils, and we don't break them into pieces because we need to write with them. I gave you pencils, and you can have more if you ask.

Now why don't we throw those little pieces away so you don't get a splinter?" She held her hand out in front of Mick expectantly.

John watched intently. She would never get the pencils away from Mick. Pencils were his very favorite things.

"If you give them to me, I'll give you a new one tomorrow morning when you get up." Sarah waited.

Mick rolled away from her, crawling on his knees with balled-up fists toward the eating table.

"Hm." Sarah stood up and watched Mick weasel between the chairs and settle under that table amid the chair legs.

"Should we pull him out?" Jana asked.

"This may have to be a fight for another day," Sarah answered. "Let's wait until he feels more secure and we have time to develop a plan."

"Fine with me. Whatever you think is best." Jana began to wind up the cord on the vacuum cleaner.

Sarah rolled her eyes, then glanced at the clock. "It's time for bed, guys. We have a big day tomorrow, your first day of work. John, would you take Lonnie upstairs and get your pajamas on and I'll be up to show you where to put your dirty clothes? Can you do that on your own?'

"Yep." John signed, "stand up," to Lonnie. His bad hip was stiff after sitting on the floor. He gently pushed Lonnie from behind as they climbed the stairs together, Lonnie holding onto the railing and placing both feet on each step.

John dug through their dresser drawers for the pajamas Cookie had given them and tossed Lonnie his pair. Lonnie crawled onto his bed and folded his legs. He shook both hands back and forth with his thumb and baby finger sticking out, signing "play."

"No, Yonnie, bedtime. Put on P.J.'s." John changed first, then talked Lonnie through each step. "Take off you socks—no tie up socks. Take off you shi't ..."

Occasionally, if Lonnie was in a good mood, he obeyed, like tonight. John patted him on the head. "Good boy."

Lonnie signed "play" again. John shook his head. He pointed Lonnie to the little toilet room across the hall. As John stood by the door waiting for Lonnie he could see Jana in Mick's room talking him into changing his clothes. Sarah was coaxing Peter to try on his pajamas in a different room and Ricky stood in the doorway of the room at the end of the hall stark naked, staring at John. John told him to get his P.J.'s on and turned away.

When it was John's turn to use the bathroom, he stared at the picture above the toilet. It was a picture of a doctor's office. A white-coated doctor was checking a little boy's heart with a stethoscope. John thought of how Hawkeye had helped the man on TV by sticking a needle in his arm. His needle was connected to a long tube that led to a bag of water.

John had an idea. "You been good, Yonnie," he said, flushing and searching the bathroom for props. "Us pway docto'."

"Lonnie grinned and tickled John's chin.

John took the pink cup from the counter and filled it with water. He led Lonnie back to their room, careful not to spill on Sarah's carpet. Lonnie sat down on the bed, legs crossed.

John set the cup on the stand beside Lonnie's bed, turned his own pajama top around backward and dug in his nightstand drawer for supplies. Finding a string and a spare checker among his treasures, he strung the string over his ear and down to Lonnie's chest. He placed the checker on Lonnie's chest to listen to his heart.

"You sick, boy," he said. "Stay stiw." He pushed Lonnie down on the bed. Lonnie grunted and lay back, his legs still locked together. John listened to his chest again. He heard nothing. He took the string off his ear and dipped one end into the cup.

"Need medicine." He pushed up Lonnie's pajama sleeve, turning his arm over like he had seen Hawkeye do. Then he pretended to poke a needle into Lonnie's arm.

"De'e. You feo betta soon." He patted Lonnie's head.

"What in the world are you doing, you guys?" Sarah stood in the doorway, hands on her hips like Cookie.

"Me Hawkeye. He'p Yonnie. Him sick." John bent over to listen once more to Lonnie's chest. Suddenly John was afraid he had done something bad. After all, he had taken the cup from the bathroom without asking. Marley would have shouted at him to "Stop acting so stupid!"

"Hawkeye?" Sarah asked, her eyebrows raised in a question. "You're playing *MASH*?"

"Yep. Me done now." John pulled the string out of the water, his hands shaking a bit, and drank it. "See. Aw gone."

A grin tinged the corners of Sarah's mouth. "Well, I don't want to interrupt your play, but it is time for bed. Maybe you can try it again tomorrow."

"Okay." John hurried across the hall to return the cup to the bathroom. He shrugged his shoulders up, waiting for the smack. But there was no smack, no ear pulling, and no yelling.

Instead, Sarah stepped out of his way as he rushed back to his bedroom and jumped into bed.

"See you in the morning," she said softly, shutting off the light and partially closing the door. "Good night, Lonnie. Good night, John."

He heard Sarah speak to Jana in hushed tones out in the hall. The whispers were followed by muffled laughter.

John closed his eyes pretending to sleep. Mick, Peter, and Ricky must have gone to bed, too, because John couldn't hear voices anymore. He wondered where Sarah and Jana would sleep. He always figured the techs lived somewhere at Larkspur, though he never knew where. He told himself to ask Sarah about that tomorrow.

He must have drifted into sleep, but suddenly John's eyes flew open. A swath of light from the hallway spread across Lonnie's bed. Lonnie had covered his head so that he looked like a formless lump. John could make out the dark shapes of the dressers, the slant of the ceiling as it sloped toward the gray square of window. A shiver passed through him from his scalp to his heels. He had never slept in the dark before.

John lay still, not daring to move. He heard whispering and footsteps, a door closing, more footsteps, a car starting. He heard the soft sounds of Lonnie's steady breathing. A shadow passed by their room briefly cutting off the light from the hall. John hunkered down under his blanket and covered his head.

He told himself to go to sleep and whispered the prayer that Cookie taught him. "Now I yay me down to sweep ..."

Suddenly, a scream pierced the silence. John stopped praying as another chill shot through him. Slowly, he slipped the covers off his eyes and ears.

The scream came again. This time he recognized it—Peter.

John couldn't lie still any longer. Nervously, he hobbled down the hall keeping his back pressed against the wall. His heart pounded. When he got to the lighted doorway of Peter's room, he heard Sarah's quiet voice.

"Peter, we don't tear our clothes here." Her voice was soothing. "We need to wear them. I'm going to help you take off your shirt now."

Feeling relieved that it was just Peter, John pretended he was a spy and peeked his head around the corner. Peter stood in the middle of the room, his shredded shirt exposing his chest. Without touching him, Sarah stood behind him and tugged carefully on the shirt to pull it off.

Peter screamed again and walloped his head several times.

"Okay, okay," Sarah said. "You take it off, then. Can you unbutton it?" Only the center button was still fastened.

Peter rocked and flapped.

"Peter," Sarah said. "You need to take your shirt off so you can get ready for bed. You're going to sleep right here." She patted the bed softly. "Everything is all right. Barry will be here all night if you need something."

It was then that John saw a man sitting on the floor in the corner of the room. He had a beard, and his hair was pulled back in a long ponytail. He hugged his legs and watched.

"That's right, Peter," he said, his voice deep and soothing. "I'll be downstairs all night if you need something. There's nothing to worry about."

Peter whacked his head again.

"Listen, Peter." Sarah ran her fingers through her hair and glanced at Barry. "I know this is scary being in a new place, but you'll get used to it. Soon it will feel like home. This is your new home, Peter. Everything is all right. We'll take care of you."

Peter stared at the ceiling light, flapping furiously.

"I'm going to take your shirt off now." Sarah reached up and gently pulled the shirt upward, without touching Peter's skin. This time he let her pull it over his head. She handed him the pajama top and he put it on by himself, only pounding his head once.

John crept quietly back to his dark room, hesitating at the door. He kicked it open wide so that light flooded the room, then he crawled into bed again.

Before long, the light in the hallway went out. John heard Sarah whispering to Barry as their footsteps padded down the stairs. In the morning he would have to ask Sarah about Barry. Barry must be the overnighter. John was thankful that Barry didn't look like a mean man.

Peering around the dark sleeping room, John was able to see the shapes a little better now. This room was just for Lonnie and him. He thought about learning to cook their own dinner and doing the chores on the chore chart. The best thing was not having his ear pulled when he was bad. And Sarah was pretty and kind. She seemed to like them, even liked Mick and Peter. Everything was different at Sarah's.

After awhile, his thoughts turned to Starlight. He wondered who was on duty tonight and who would say good night to Timmy without John there to tuck him in. *Who would help Cookie ring her bell tomorrow morning? And what about Rochelle? Was she still his girlfriend?*

An hour passed before John finally drifted off into the dream world.

Chapter 6
Workshop

The next morning, John dressed quickly and wandered downstairs to the sounds of dishes clanking in the kitchen. Sarah said this was their first work day and that they would get on a bus and go to a workshop. John pictured a large laundry room filled with giant washers and dryers. At the cowboy doors, John paused, listening to Sarah talk with someone John assumed to be Barry, the ponytail man from last night.

"So nobody got up in the night?" Sarah asked. John wondered again where Sarah had slept.

"Nope. All quiet," Barry answered.

"That's good. They're doing pretty well so far, don't you think?"

John heard the sound of water pouring.

"Yeah, I guess," Barry said. "To tell you the truth, though, I didn't think they'd be quite this weird."

Sarah laughed lightly. "I know this is kind of shocking at first, but how could they not be... unusual? They've lived in an institution all their lives. You can't imagine what they've lived with unless you've been there."

"True. Must be strange growing up in a place like Larkspur. Hard to believe their parents would just give them up."

"That's what the doctors used to recommend to families. 'They'll be happier with others of their kind,' and all that crap."

"Good thing you're the expert because I wouldn't have any idea what to do with them."

John pushed open the cowboy doors just a crack. Sarah was spreading peanut butter and jelly on sandwiches and Barry was wrapping them in plastic.

"I'm not an expert," Sarah said, taking a few cookies out of a package and sticking them in each of several paper bags lined up on the counter. "And I haven't worked with low functioning adults before, at least not as low as Mick and Peter. Only little kids. This is an experiment, you know, so none of us really knows how these guys will react to living in the community. They act weird because they've never been around normal people. All they've seen are other disabled folks and techs who treat them like children. So it's our job to teach them to act more normal, or at least to learn skills to function in the community. That's what my study is about."

Barry stuck the sandwiches into paper sacks as Sarah pulled apples out of the refrigerator.

Barry leaned his elbow on the counter. "Do you really think we can make these guys... better?"

"Sure," she said, plopping a small apple into each bag. "All of them can learn. They just haven't had much chance to do that."

"I'll take your word for it. How did you get Larkspur to let these guys out?" Barry set the bags together on the counter close to the cowboy doors. John drew back.

"Because the state lost a lawsuit from a parent who found out how her child was being treated, and as a result, the legislature is thinking of cutting state funding to the institutions to phase them out. William helped me apply for a state deinstitutionalization grant. I really believe the community is where they belong."

"You're the boss. I should get up there and check on them. I think I heard someone up." Barry pushed open the cowboy doors and John jumped back.

"Oh, hi!" Barry said. Barry held the doors open. "Which one are you?"

"Come on in," Sarah said, smiling brightly. "Barry, this is John."

Feeling a twinge of embarrassment at being caught listening, John stuck out his hand.

Barry took it. "Good morning, John. I'm Barry. How are you?"

"Fine." John shook Barry's hand hard until Barry finally pulled it away.

"Well, it's a good thing you're up," Sarah said, "because it's your turn to help me set the table for breakfast. Come on, John, I'll show you how to do it."

"I'll wake the others." Barry smiled as he passed John and patted him on the shoulder. "It's nice to meet you, John. You're a good helper, I hear." He headed for the stairs.

"Yell if you need any help," Sarah called after him.

"What bags fo'?" John pointed to the sacks.

"Those are your lunches for the workshop today. Remember, I told you last night you'd be going to your new job today?"

"Me know." John paused. "Go Ya'kspuh?"

Sarah rinsed out her coffee cup and stuck it in the dishwasher. "No, it's not at Larkspur. It's called Cloverdale Workshop. It's downtown."

"Oh." John was relieved. He stepped into the kitchen and leaned on the counter like he had seen Barry do. "What wo'kchop?"

"It's in a big warehouse," Sarah answered, "and lots of other clients work on different job assignments. I'm not sure what you'll be doing today, but they'll show you when you get there."

"What wa'ehouse?"

"A warehouse is a big building. It's hard to explain until you're there. I'm sure you'll like it. Okay, John. See this cupboard with the pictures of dishes on it?" Sarah tapped one of the cupboard doors.

John nodded. "Me know."

"Get out seven bowls, seven small plates and seven cups. We're having cereal this morning."

John noticed again how pretty Sarah was, especially when she smiled. From watching Peter yesterday, he knew the big round circles on the placemats were for the bowls and plates, and the little ones were for the cups. He set the table almost without help from Sarah, returning the extra dishes to the cupboard. Then he set out the boxes of cereal Sarah placed on the kitchen counter for him.

"Good job, John! You did great. You sure catch on quickly!" Sarah patted his shoulder and he patted her shoulder in return. She laughed.

When he finished the table, John went upstairs to see how Lonnie was doing. Surprisingly, Lonnie was already dressed and in the toilet room with Barry. Barry was helping him comb his hair. Lonnie's hair was thin and wispy and stuck straight up with the comb.

"Well," Barry sighed, wetting his hand and patting Lonnie's hair down with his hand, "I guess we'll have to keep working on it. Go down and eat breakfast."

Barry headed down the hall toward the others' rooms calling, "Are you dressed yet?"

Lonnie scowled as he walked by John. John guessed that he was mad about having to get dressed and comb his hair. John decided he better be extra nice to Lonnie so he wouldn't get into a "no" mood.

Just as they started down the steps, Ricky rushed past them half dressed, nearly knocking Lonnie over.

Lonnie screeched and caught himself on the banister.

"Hey, Ricky!" Barry called after him. "Come back here!"

"You stupid, Wicky!" John yelled, shaking his fist at Ricky's back.

"Ricky!" Barry called after him again, but Ricky was gone. He muttered, "I'll get him after breakfast. Okay, how about you, Peter?"

John led Lonnie slowly down the steps. Lonnie held tightly onto the railing with both hands. He was afraid of falling and John could tell Lonnie was very upset now. He tried to soothe him by patting Lonnie's back as they made their way to the eating table.

Ricky sat at one end of the table staring at them, so John and Lonnie sat on the opposite end. Every time Sarah left the room Ricky switched a bowl with a cup or turned things upside down. John reprimanded him and told him to switch them back before Sarah returned, but Ricky ignored him.

Barry brought Mick and Peter down, and handed Ricky his shirt to put on. When Sarah and Barry sat down at the table with everyone, Sarah said, "Thanks for setting the table, John. Next time just leave the dishes where you had them the first time." She smiled at John and quickly set the dishes back where they belonged.

John tried to tell her it was Ricky who switched things around, but she was hurrying everyone to eat quickly.

John talked Lonnie through breakfast reminding him to take another bite after each spoonful. He tried to ignore Mick who almost choked on his toast even while Sarah guided Mick's hand for every bite.

Just as John finished, a horn sounded outside. He jumped up to see what it was.

"Uh-oh!" Sarah glanced at front the window. "It's the bus already. I'm afraid we'll have to be finished with breakfast. Sorry about that. Tomorrow we'll get up earlier. Come and get your coats on. Barry, I'll get Mick if you'll get the others and the lunches."

She pulled Mick up, letting him grab the last piece of toast on his plate to take with him. Mick stuffed most of it into his mouth. Sarah didn't seem to notice.

"John, would you bring Lonnie and get your coats on?" she asked.

"Yep." He liked that Sarah asked him to help, but he wished he had time to explain that it was Ricky who messed up the table.

Sarah hurried Mick out the door. Barry handed Ricky his coat, then held Peter's coat open for him, careful not to touch Peter's arms.

John tugged on Lonnie's arm to get him to stand up. "You done."

Lonnie shook his head and clutched his spoon. He was still mad. John pushed Lonnie's cereal bowl out of reach.

Lonnie squealed, reached across the table for the bowl and signed, "Eat."

No time to waste. John knew what he had to do. He had seen the techs do it a hundred times. He slipped around behind Lonnie's chair, scooped him up under the armpits then swung him onto his feet. He made Lonnie walk, pushing Lonnie's legs forward with his own knees from behind. Lonnie hated to be rushed this way and shouted in protest, but John wrestled him all the way to the front door.

"That was interesting," Barry commented, coming up behind them with the lunch sacks. "Whatever works, I'd say."

Lonnie refused to put on his coat.

"He can put it on when he gets on the bus," Barry said, throwing Lonnie's coat over his shoulders. Then Barry grabbed Lonnie's hands and danced him to the bus singing, "You'll have fun, fun, fun 'til your daddy takes your T-bird away."

To John's surprise Lonnie went along without fighting. John wiped his forehead in relief like he'd seen Kaeller do.

The morning was dark and a heavy mist stung John's face. At the curb, a yellow school bus waited with its lights on and its engine running. Inside, faceless heads were silhouetted against the foggy windows. The doors swung open when they approached.

A woman in blue jeans and puffy red hair sat in the driver's seat. Her face was covered with wrinkles and freckles. "Come on in!" she said happily. "It's cold out there."

John stepped up into the bus holding Lonnie's hand. "Hi. Me Don," he said to the driver.

"Glad to meet you," she replied. "I'm Madge. First day of work, huh?"

"Nope. Me wo'k yaundwy." John paused to talk to her and started to pull out his wallet to show her his treasures.

"You better have a seat, sweetie," she said kindly. "We're kinda late today. I'll talk to you about it later."

John and Lonnie sat in the seat right behind Madge. Ricky moved to the back of the bus and sat down beside a plump girl with glasses.

Barry coaxed Peter up the steps and told him to sit down. "It's all right," Barry said. "I know it's scary, but you'll be all right. You'll get used to it."

To John's surprise, Peter sat down where Barry pointed. He banged his head a few times, flapped his hands vigorously, and rocked as best he could in such a small space.

Mick didn't want to get on the bus so Sarah held him around the chest and boosted him into an empty seat across from John.

"Now you stay there, Mick. You're fine." Mick slid up against the window then slunk down until John could only see his wild hair. His hands worked the vinyl surface of the bus seat.

"That's Mick, Madge," Sarah said. "He's the one I told you about."

"Is he my main worry today?" Madge asked.

"Could be. It's hard to say what they're going to do. This is new to all of them." Sarah ran her fingers through her hair. "Actually, I better go with him until he gets used to the bus. Can you bring me back here? I don't know why I didn't think of this before."

"Sure. Good idea," Madge agreed.

Sarah sat down by Mick, urging him to sit up straight.

Barry set the lunch bags on the floor by John's feet. "Don't forget to take these lunches in with you," he said to John. Barry hesitated before he got off the bus. "Do you want your coat, Sarah?"

"Yeah, thanks. My keys, too." Sarah smiled at Barry. John decided next time he would offer to get Sarah's coat.

As Barry jogged back to the house, Sarah said to Madge, "I better move Mick over by Peter so I can watch them both. Peter's likely to get upset."

"I could have Clarence keep an eye on one of them for you," Madge offered.

"Okay, maybe Peter. He doesn't like to be touched, though."

"Clarence!" Madge called, staring into a mirror above her head. "Sit behind that new boy, but don't touch him. He's nervous."

The fattest boy John had ever seen got up and squeezed down the aisle toward Peter. Rolls of flesh bulged over his belt rubbing the seats as he passed.

"Just be nice to him," Madge said.

Clarence filled the whole seat behind Peter. He leaned forward and spoke soothingly into Peter's ear. "Don't worry, buddy, it's okay. Nobody gonna hurt you."

In a minute, Barry returned with Sarah's things. "Good luck." He smiled at Sarah, waving as he stepped off the bus.

Madge pulled a lever and shut the bus doors.

John rubbed his sleeve on the window so he could look out. The lights were on inside the house across the street from Sarah's. The curtains were closed, but a figure stood in the big window holding them aside. John could see white hair and a blue dress. He waved. The curtains closed again.

Madge moved the ball on the long stick and the bus started off with a jolt. John turned around to look at the other people on the bus. They all looked like workers. Some gazed out the windows, others were falling asleep. Two cute girls at the back giggled and teased the boys in the next seat. They were talking to Ricky, too. They must be smart ones.

The bus curved around and then headed downhill throwing everyone forward. John wondered where this workshop was, but he couldn't see much through the foggy windows. After half a cartoon show, as Cookie would have described it, the bus slowed and pulled up in front of a large gray building. It was almost as big as a Larkspur hall but didn't have windows. The sky was lighter now, and a gray drizzle shrouded the building in mist.

Madge opened the bus doors. "Everybody out. Have a good day at work, people. I'll see you this afternoon."

"Would you take the lunches, John?" Sarah asked as she helped Mick out of the bus.

John stood up and lifted Lonnie to his feet. "Come on, Yonnie. Us go wo'k. You got job!" He gathered up their lunch sacks from the floor and handed one to Lonnie.

The workers quickly filed out and John had to pull back as Clarence's stomach brushed him on his way out. They streamed off the bus and joined other arriving workers who all went into the workshop through a bright green door.

Loaded with lunches John gently pushed Lonnie ahead of him down the steps and off the bus. Stepping onto the pavement, the windowless building reminded him of Cadby. John hesitated. *What was in there?* he wondered.

"It's okay, John." Sarah's comforting voice broke into his momentary fear. She nodded toward the door with her head as she hooked her arm through Mick's and propelled him forward. "You're going to like the workshop. There's a lot going on in there."

Inside, the workshop was warm and bright. John heard a high whirring sound he didn't recognize and a cacophony of voices assaulted him. People swarmed everywhere. Most of them looked like workers, a few were in wheelchairs, but others were clearly techs. The building was wide open and vast. Lights hung down from the high ceiling on long wires, and gigantic square posts reached from the cement floor to the ceiling. The large room they entered was filled with long tables that held boxes, envelopes, and hosts of unfamiliar objects. The far wall was lined with windows that looked into tech offices. John could see people inside the offices talking on the phone and chatting with each other. To one side of the warehouse was a smaller area with a lower ceiling where workers sat at tables drinking coffee and talking. Lining the wall by the door was a row of skinny gray closet doors.

John was overwhelmed by the sights and sounds of the workshop. He stood in the entrance clinging to Lonnie and staring at everyone around him.

Out of the din one shrill voice pierced the room. "Hi!" A tall girl with a big mouth and broken teeth suddenly wrapped her skinny arms around John's neck.

He pushed her away, startled. "No good," he mumbled. "Not you fwend."

"Hi!" she repeated, still reaching for him. "I'm Laurie, the greeter! What's your name?"

"Me Don," he answered, fending her off with his forearm.

"Hi, Don!" she sang. "You're new!"

"No, Don!"

But Laurie-the-Greeter moved on to Lonnie. "Hi! I'm Laurie, the greeter!" Lonnie raised his arms and hugged her back. A smile of delight lit Lonnie's face. Just as suddenly, Laurie-the-Greeter let go and strutted away, leaving Lonnie with his mouth hanging open and his arms outstretched.

"Hi, there, fellas." A man with brown skin like Peter's and a joyful smile extended his hand to John. "I see you've met our official greeter, Laurie. You two are ... who?"

"Me Don." John shook his strong hand.

"And who's this?" The man had white teeth and friendly eyes that crinkled when he smiled.

"Yonnie."

He shook Lonnie's hand, too. He looked down at the paper in his hands. "Hmm. I don't see you here ..."

Sarah joined them holding firmly onto Mick's arm. Ricky and Peter followed closely behind her.

"Hi, Ken! Let me introduce you." She told him their names and Ken checked them off on his paper.

"I'm glad to see you made it, Sarah. How's it going so far?" He patted Sarah's back and glanced from one to the other of the boys.

"Not bad. We have a lot to learn. You'll definitely need someone with Mick, Peter and Ricky all day, like we talked about. John can handle the line—I'm not sure about Lonnie. You could try him and see how it goes."

"Okay. These three are going to Randy's basic skills group. Let me get Millie. She'll show you where to take them and someone will stay with them there. Millie will train Lonnie." Ken wrote something else on his paper and walked away.

"He's the director," Sarah explained, "the boss. We need to wait here for Millie."

The noise and confusion grew louder as more workers came in the green door. They all seemed happy to be here. John watched them put their things away in the skinny closets and greet each other. New techs, a room full of new workers, strange sounds and smells ... Holding the lunches in one arm, John hung onto Lonnie's hand with his other hand so Lonnie wouldn't get scared.

Finally, a tech no taller than Lonnie with a long brown braid that swished down around her belt approached them. "Hi, Sarah. These your new clients?"

"Yeah." Sarah introduced them. "Which lockers are theirs?"

"Let's find some empty ones." Millie and Sarah opened several of the thin closet doors until they found two available lockers. John and the other boys all took off their coats, hung them on little hooks, and John placed the lunch sacks inside. Millie asked Sarah to help her take Mick, Peter, and Ricky over to Randy's basic skills center.

"Then I can show John and Lonnie to their stations," Millie said. "Ken told me John will work with Frank on the floor and I'll be with Lonnie at the packaging table."

"John, can you wait here with Lonnie?" Sarah asked. "We'll be right back." She held Mick's arm firmly and headed across the room with Millie.

Lonnie and John stayed put and watched Millie lead the others toward the far corner. As Millie walked away, her braid flipped back and forth like a fish on the end of a line. John wished he could touch it. Peter followed her, stopping occasionally to dip and flap. Ricky looked around nervously and stuck close to Sarah's side.

At the basic skills center, where a circle of chairs was arranged, a man took Mick from Sarah and sat him down in one of the chairs. Ricky sat down, too, but Peter wouldn't sit. He just stood nearby rocking and staring at the hanging lights. John couldn't imagine any of them doing any work. Another tech at the circle moved over to sit behind Mick and Ricky, but they let Peter remain standing. John wondered what the man was going to make them do in that circle.

When Sarah and Millie got back Sarah said, "Well, I'm going to take off. Good luck today, guys. You know where to reach me, Millie."

"Thanks, Sarah. We'll be fine." Millie waved to Sarah as she left. Then she turned to John and Lonnie. "Every morning when you come to work, put your lunches and coats in a locker. Then you can go over here to the cafeteria and relax until the bell rings. You'll have three breaks, one in the morning, a lunch break and then a short one in the afternoon. Just follow everybody else today. We'll help you if you need it."

She led them through the throngs of workers to the cafeteria. "You'll eat your lunch here. Just find a place to sit. You can buy pop and candy in the vending machines." She pointed to several brightly lit boxes with pictures of soda cans on them.

"Do you have any money?" she asked.

"Nope." John had spent all his Balhalla bucks at the canteen. He checked his wallet to make sure. "Get Ba'hawa bucks t'day?"

"Excuse me?" Millie had a puzzled look on her face.

"Ba'hawa bucks, money." John pointed to his wallet.

"You'll get a paycheck at the end of the month," Millie answered. "Sarah will put it in your bank account and I bet she'll give you some spending money."

"Okay." John didn't understand what she meant but it sounded like he wouldn't get any money today. He put his wallet away. He told himself to ask Sarah about this later.

Millie continued talking, "Those rooms with the windows are the supervisors' offices. You never go back there unless it's an emergency."

Through the glass John saw Ken with a cup of coffee in his hand, talking to a tech. Millie led them into the open expanse of the workshop. The ceiling was very high and John could see big beams criss-crossing through it. A bird flitted across the expanse and landed on a beam.

"This is the workroom floor. They call it the line. You'll be at one of these stations doing a job like you see here." She touched a stack of papers and envelopes. "Each of you will have a line supervisor who will teach you your job. I'll be Lonnie's trainer today."

Some workers already sat at their tables. A few had already started working. At the far end of the cavernous room was a wide opening to another work area. John saw someone emerge through the door pushing a cart loaded with boxes. Following this worker, a funny looking car with two pointed knives in the front whizzed by. John couldn't even imagine what those knives were for, but he pushed Lonnie back instinctively.

A teeth-rattling bell interrupted them. John and Lonnie covered their ears.

When it stopped, Millie said, "That's the buzzer. Means you have five minutes to get to your seat. When the next one sounds, you'll start work. I'll take you to your stations."

All the workers hurried toward the worktable area. Millie pointed out a chair in the middle of the room. "John, this is your seat. See? It has your name on it."

Sure enough, John's letters were printed on the back of the chair. He sat down and pointed to the chair next to him. "Yonnie, sit down."

"No, Lonnie's table is over there." Millie gestured across the room. "See you later, John. Your supervisor is Frank. He'll be here in a minute to help you."

John was disappointed because he thought for sure Lonnie would be working with him. He didn't want to be left alone without Lonnie, but he had learned the hard way not to buck a tech's orders. He said nothing.

"Let's go, Lonnie," Millie took several steps before she realized Lonnie wasn't following her.

"Yonnie, you go wo'k," John ordered. He motioned Lonnie away gruffly.

Millie marched back. "Come on, Lonnie. You work over at that table. You have a different job, but you'll see John at your break in just a little while."

Lonnie wouldn't move.

Millie tugged at his arm.

Lonnie snapped his arm way from her and set his jaw, scowling.

"Me he'p." John stood up and tenderly took Lonnie's hand. "Go wo'k now." John coaxed Lonnie forward, following Millie between the tables.

"Thanks, John," Millie said, patting his hand as she slipped Lonnie's hand from his grip. "I'll take it from here. Go on back to your seat before the bell rings."

John was afraid Lonnie would get in a "no" mood, but he didn't dare stay. He waved goodbye then signed, "work" before running back to his seat.

On his worktable sat boxes of little silver objects. John didn't know what they were, or what to do with them. He looked around. Next to him sat a worker with wisps of thin graying hair that floated around her head as if someone had just blown on it. John couldn't see her face because her head was bent so low that her chin rested on her chest. Her back was all hunched over like a turtle shell.

"Hi," John said to her. "Me Don." He stuck his hand in front of her to shake.

She didn't look up nor take his hand, but she said, "Hi. I'm Eileen. Are you my new partner?"

"Yep. Wo'k he'e now. Wo'kchop."

"That's nice. I'm blind so I can't see you."

"Oh," John said, peering down into her face. "No see? How come?"

"I was born this way," she answered without bringing her head up.

"Okay." John passed his hand in front of her face.

No reaction.

Just then Laurie-the-Greeter plopped down in the seat on his other side. "Hi!" she said joyfully and began to fill the little plastic boxes with the silver objects.

John leaned away from her, afraid she would hug him again. He knew he wasn't supposed to hug people in the Away Place.

The buzzer blared again. Everyone quieted and only paper rustling and clinking sounds were heard. John saw the funny knife car zip by again loaded with boxes. He watched Laurie-the-Greeter, her hands moving swiftly to fill the plastic boxes with silver objects. John did the same, putting as many as he could into one of the containers.

A familiar shriek echoed through the workshop. Everyone kept working. Across the room, John saw Peter standing by the circle of chairs banging his head viciously. The leader ignored Peter and spoke to the rest of the group, having them clap their hands. John saw that Mick sat on a chair facing away from the group, a tech holding him in place like Sarah had done.

"All right, John, my man, time to learn how to work!" A man's throaty voice made John jump. The man, who had been talking to Ken in the office, strolled up the aisle in front of John's table. When he got to Eileen, he tapped the table with his hand. Without looking up her hands flew into motion. She reached for her box and pulled out a handful of the silver objects, touched each one in turn and stuck some into a plastic box like Laurie-the-Greeter had done. Then she reached for more.

"Welcome to Cloverdale," the man said, stopping in front of John. "I'm Frank, your supe. You're John, right?" Frank was short with thick brown hair that curled around his collar. He had only one heavy eyebrow that stretched straight across his forehead, and an equally heavy mustache that dipped over his upper lip. This man didn't look very nice.

John replied cautiously, "Yep. Me Don."

"Ever work in a workshop before?" he asked.

John shook his head.

"Well, this is your job, packaging bolts." He dumped out the container John had just filled and held up one of the long silver things. "See these bolts? And these nuts?" He pointed to little silver circles. "You have to put ten of each of these into a plastic container and close it. Can you count to ten?" He spread some bolts on the table.

John waited, apprehensive.

"Go ahead, count them," Frank said.

"One," John began as Frank pointed to the next bolt. "Two, fwee, fo', fibe, seben ..."

"Six."

"Six, seben, nine ..."

"Okay. Stop." Frank's eyebrow moved down in the middle, shading his eyes. "So you can't count. Here. Try it with this." From a table nearby he pulled out a piece of cardboard. It had small black circles drawn on it. Frank set it down in front of John.

"You put one bolt and one nut on each circle, see? Then you'll have ten. Go ahead." Frank stood over John and watched.

John was so nervous his hands trembled. He picked up a bolt and set it on the circle, then another and another until they were filled.

"Now the nuts," Frank said.

John complied.

"Okay, now scoop them up and put them in the box." Frank shoved the plastic box toward John. John scooped them into the box and snapped it shut.

"Good! That's all there is to it! Put the ones you've done in this "finish" box. Now go ahead and get started. Just keep going until the break buzzer rings. I'll be checking on you. If you run out of anything, let me know by raising your hand."

John carefully set out more bolts and nuts, careful to fill each mark on the cardboard. At first he had trouble unsnapping the little boxes, but he finally figured out how to do it. He swept the nuts and bolts into another plastic box and set it into the "finish" box beside him. Frank watched him do this a few times then walked down the aisle, checking on others.

John kept going. It was fun to put the bolts and nuts out on the little circles. This was a real job, not like doing laundry at Larkspur. He took pride in seeing the pile of boxes mounting up. This was the kind of work smart ones did, grown-up work.

After a while, Frank came back. "Good work there, John. You're catching on real quick. The more you do, the more money you make. Did you know that?"

John smiled. "Ba'hawa bucks?"

"Cold hard cash, my friend." Frank winked without smiling and walked on.

John worked as fast as he could. He practiced counting. He didn't think he was getting it right, though, because he never came out at ten when he filled the last circle. After a while he started to think about the lunch waiting for him in the locker. When did they get to eat? There was a whole apple in his sack. At Larkspur they never got whole apples, just little pieces cut up in fruit cups.

Then he thought of Lonnie. John tried to see where Lonnie was, but all he could see were the heads of other workers. He wondered if Lonnie's "no" mood had gone away, and suddenly he became worried. What if something happened? What if Lonnie wouldn't do his work? John's stomach tightened. He stood up.

Searching the room in a panic, he finally spotted Lonnie. Millie sat beside him at a worktable pointing to something. Lonnie's cheeks bulged as he chewed his tongue rapidly. He looked mad. Millie lifted his arm from his lap and placed his hand over the object. His hand tightened around it. Millie's head nodded as she helped him place it in a box.

"Hey, John!" Frank called from the end of the row. "What are you doing?"

"Uh, see Yonnie wo'k." John instinctively sat down.

Frank approached, his eyebrows forming a V. "Well, watching him won't get your work done. When you're on the line you stay in your seat until the buzzer rings, understand?" He leaned on his hands on the table in front of John. "Listen, John. I'll tell you straight up front. I don't take any fooling around on my line. There'll be a consequence for screwing off. This is just a warning."

Frank moved to the end of the row and stood watching for a while. Warily, John picked up some bolts and started to work again. His heart sank. Frank was a mean man.

The buzzer finally blared. John jumped and plugged his ears. Eileen dropped her bolts in mid-air and they clattered to the table. She picked up a white stick that leaned against the table, stood up, and rubbed the stick along the floor as she made her way into the aisle.

Laurie-the-Greeter bounded out of her seat and ripped happily toward the cafeteria. "Come on!" she called. "Break time!"

Everyone streamed toward the cafeteria and John followed. He looked for Lonnie, but couldn't see him through the crowd. John stopped at the lighted pop machines and watched, transfixed, as workers put coins in and pop cans rolled out. He hoped he would get his Balhalla bucks at the end of the day so he could buy pop tomorrow—if they came back to the workshop.

Just then, Millie approached holding Lonnie by the arm. "Here you go, Lonnie. You can take your break with John. I'll be back in fifteen minutes." Millie walked away, her braid dangling behind her like a rope.

"Hi, Yonnie! How you?" John was so happy to see him he gave him a hug.

"Fine," Lonnie signed, thumb to his chest. But his face didn't look fine. He shifted from one foot to the other visibly agitated.

John patted Lonnie's head. "You wo'k, Yonnie. You big boy."

Lonnie gradually smiled. He tickled John's neck and they both laughed. Since they couldn't buy pop, they stood together and watched the other workers. Big Clarence waddled by with a box of candy. John saw Eileen sitting at a table by herself snacking on something, and Laurie-the-Greeter flitted from one person to another giving them break-hugs.

John looked for Peter or Ricky or Mick, but didn't find them. Before long, the buzzer rang again. The workers tossed their cans or candy wrappers away and hustled back to their tables.

Millie came to get Lonnie.

"Go wo'k now, Yonnie," John said, giving him one last head pat.

"Mmf," Lonnie grunted. He shook his head.

"Yep. You be good boy." John pointed toward Lonnie's table.

Millie led Lonnie away by the hand, Lonnie leaning back against her grasp with each step.

After walking several tables too far, John circled back and finally found his table. He was just scooting around Eileen's chair when the buzzer went off.

"You're almost late, John," Frank called, walking toward him again.

"Me not yate. Me he'e," John said, picking up some bolts and placing them on the circles.

Frank leaned his hands on the table in front of John again and pushed his face down toward John's. "You only have three minutes to get to your seat after the break, so you have to hurry.

Don't be late next time. Here's a new box. You did pretty well this morning."

Frank lifted another box of bolts and nuts onto the table beside John. The work seemed easy now, so easy that John started setting the bolts on the little circles in different ways, just for fun. But whenever he saw Frank coming he moved as fast as he could and didn't look up.

When the buzzer rang again, John moved with the rest of the workers toward the cafeteria. Lonnie was waiting for him in the same place they had met before. The other workers swarmed to the lockers to retrieve their lunches.

"Git yunch, Yonnie," John said excitedly. The lockers all looked the same. John started opening every locker looking for their lunches.

"Hi, John." It was Millie. Peter and Ricky stood beside her. "Do you need some help finding your locker? It's hard to remember the first day."

She opened a few of the lockers until she found the right one. "Let's see. How can you remember your locker next time?" Millie tapped the post next to the locker. "Here's a post with the red paint on it. It's right next to that. Can you remember that?"

John nodded.

She handed them each a lunch sack. "John, would you help find seats for everyone? I've got to go get Mick out of time out. Let me know if you need any help."

John motioned for them to follow him and found a table where no one else was sitting. Peter followed, stopping every few steps to flap. Ricky, Lonnie and John sat down, but Peter paced beside their table and banged his forehead, which was quickly turning dark. John was hungry and devoured half his sandwich before helping Lonnie unwrap his.

"Sit down, Peto." John gave Peter his sandwich. Peter grabbed it, but he wouldn't sit down. He ate his whole lunch standing up and rocking.

While Lonnie took his first slow bites, John finished off his chips and cookies. He was one of the lucky ones at Larkspur who still had his front teeth, so he crunched the apple down to the seeds. Peter wouldn't touch his apple so John ate it for him.

As Lonnie continued slowly munching, most of the workers had finished eating and were talking in groups or wandering around the cafeteria. Their voices grew louder. They were laughing and chatting, and Laurie-the-Greeter's cackle could be heard above the roar.

A few tables away, a commotion caused all activity in the cafeteria to stop.

One of the techs shouted, "You can't eat that!"

John stood up to see. Two techs held a squirming figure by the arms. When his head popped up, John saw Mick stuffing something large and yellow in his mouth with the palm of his hand. Whatever it was disappeared into Mick's bulging cheeks. One tech wrestled Mick's arms behind his back while the other pushed on Mick's cheeks, telling him to spit it out.

Just when John thought Mick might choke again, a yellow mass of banana peel shot out and splattered on the table.

The workers at the table scattered shouting, "Ooo!" and "Gross!"

The techs hauled Mick away toward the offices. He reached for someone's sandwich as he passed, but the tech knocked his hand away.

"Mick bad," John said to Lonnie. "Him dummy."

Lonnie signed, "bad."

Mick was nothing but trouble.

Lonnie was just starting on his chips when John saw a pretty girl standing alone by one of the big posts. He hadn't noticed her before. She was small with brown hair that curled up against her shoulders. She had dark eyes and the longest eyelashes he had ever seen.

"Me fwow sack away," John told Lonnie, standing up. He tossed his sack into a garbage can then swaggered over to her.

"Hi," he said, holding out his hand.

She looked up in surprise and said, "Hi." She was even prettier close up, though one eyelid sagged part-way down.

"Me Don. What you name?"

"Betsy." She spoke deliberately, one side of her mouth drooping a bit. "I new at Cloverdale." Her eyes darted away.

"Oh." John nodded knowingly. "Me, too." Not sure what to say, he pulled out his wallet and flipped it open. He showed her the picture of himself with Gretchen when he was younger. "Me baby, Moonbeam."

She gazed at the picture and smiled shyly. John dug in his pockets to see if he could find anything else to show her and brought out the broken watch.

Betsy glanced politely at it but still didn't say anything. She held one fist against her chest, curled up at the wrist. This reminded John of the way Timmy held his hands and he liked her even more.

He decided to try a different tact. Placing his foot up against the post beside her, John pulled up his pant leg and pointed to a scar on his leg.

"Yook," he said. "Me hu't. Me faw."

Betsy looked at it and frowned. "Still hurt?"

John shook his pant leg down and straightened up. He tried to look tough. "Me okay now."

Betsy glanced nervously around. Then with the hand that was bent, she used two fingers to pull up her sleeve. A broad scar nearly covered her thin forearm.

Sympathetically, John clicked his tongue and shook his head. "Bad owie! You cut?"

"Burned wif a iron." She said. She rolled the sleeve back down quickly. "Don?"

He opened his mouth to correct her, but changed his mind.

"Where your work table?"

John pointed.

"I over there." She pointed to a table at the back, nearest to the cafeteria. "You got friends here?"

"Yep. Yonnie my fwend." John pointed out Lonnie who was now the only one sitting at the table, emptying the last crumbs out of the chip bag into his hand.

"Where you live, Don?"

"Sawah's now. Yib Ya'kspuh, but move Sawah's yeste'day. Whe'e you yib?"

"Wif Jodie and Richard. They take care a me now." John noticed a little scar on her lip below her nose, and another beside the eye that sagged.

"Dat nice."

Betsy looked down, her face sad. For a moment they were quiet. Eileen hobbled by swishing her white stick back and forth against posts and worker's legs.

John glanced over at Lonnie. He was motioning John over.

"Gotta he'p Yonnie," John said. "See ya yata."

"Bye," she answered quietly, glancing up briefly.

Lonnie handed John his sack and signed, "apple," then shook his head, no. Lonnie couldn't' eat hard things without any front teeth.

"Me teo Sawah, cut appo' fo' you, Yonnie." He stuck the apple in his pocket and tossed Lonnie's sack in the trash. "Me got new fwend, Yonnie, Bessy."

John pointed to the post, but Betsy was gone.

"Yet's watch pop machine," he suggested. Lonnie followed him over and they stared wide-eyed as a worker put in her money and pop rolled out. The bright pictures of different kinds of pop mesmerized him.

As they watched, Millie came up behind them. "John, are you and Lonnie thirsty?"

"Yep," John answered.

"There's a drinking fountain over there where you can get water any time. But today..." Millie dug in her pocket. "Here. Have a coke on me."

She handed John some silver pennies. John took the money gratefully. He stared at the lighted surface. Where had he seen the other workers put their money? There were many silver buttons and levers and John wasn't sure what to do.

A worker came up behind him and told him to hurry up. John searched the machine, but he could see no round hole for his penny. Finally, he turned away. He handed Millie the money.

"No want pop," he said.

"You don't? Well, keep it for another time. I'm going to have one anyway." Millie took more pennies out of her pocket and said, "I'll just put two quarters in this little slot."

The coins jingled down inside the machine. She continued talking to no one in particular. "Then, let's see. I think I'll have a root beer." She pushed the silver button below the root beer picture and a can bumped out of the mouth of the machine. She opened the flip-top and sipped it. "Your turn, John. You can do it."

John slipped his coins into the skinny slot and they clanked down. He ran his hand across the silver buttons trying to decide. One button moved under his finger and an orange can plopped out. Lonnie squealed in delight.

Millie showed John how to open it and she laughed when his first drink fizzed into his nose. "Careful, there. One for you, too, Lonnie." She handed Lonnie two more coins, smiled and walked away.

John and Lonnie sat down happily to drink their prizes together. John felt like a grown-up working here. Before they finished, the buzzer sounded. John downed the last several gulps, but since Lonnie wasn't finished he had to toss Lonnie's nearly full can into the trash.

Millie appeared. "I've got him, John. You go on back to work. Lonnie, it's time for work. You need to stand up and follow me to your table." She signed, "Stand up."

Lonnie wouldn't stand up. He grunted and curled his legs up underneath him, somehow balancing on the narrow bench.

John didn't want to leave Lonnie this way. He was afraid Lonnie would be bad. But he was also afraid of Frank. He backed slowly toward the work area, signing to Lonnie, "Go wo'k."

Lonnie signed, "No," and grunted.

Millie motioned John away and he rushed for his work station, burping loudly as he ran. Just as he sat down, the buzzer rang. He started to work, not daring to glance around until he heard yelling.

From behind him, Ken and another tech dragged Lonnie past the circle where Peter, Mick, and Ricky were seated again with the other dummies. They lifted Lonnie by the arms toward a door with a small window and pushed Lonnie inside a tiny room.

John covered his mouth in horror. This was a time-out room, like at Cadby! John glanced nervously from Frank to the door and back to his worktable. He tried to keep working, but all he could think about was poor Lonnie.

In just a couple of minutes, Ken opened the time-out room door. This time Lonnie walked on his own back to the table with Millie.

John sighed. Lonnie looked all right. John craned his neck around to see Lonnie settle in. Between other workers' heads he picked out the dark hair of Betsy, too. She folded pages and stuffed them into envelopes. At that moment Betsy glanced up. When she saw him staring at her, they both looked away. John's heart pounded with excitement.

Before long, John began to squirm because he needed to use the toilet. He hadn't thought to ask where it was, and he wasn't sure if Frank would let him go during work time. Frank was busy across the room opening some boxes. He began working with only one hand so he could hold himself with the other.

After a few minutes Frank sauntered over to him. "What's the trouble here? Your hand hurt? Look around you. Everybody else is working with two hands."

"Gotta go pee," John answered quietly.

"Oh." Frank glanced down at John's lap. "I'll let you go this time, but you're supposed to go during your breaks and at lunch time."

John stood up and looked around desperately for the toilet room, still holding himself. He didn't know how much longer he could hold it.

"It's this way. Follow me," Frank said.

John limped hurriedly after him toward the back of the workshop. As they passed Betsy's row, John summoned all of his control and let go of his crotch. She looked up and smiled. John smiled back.

Frank pointed out two doors in the corner and John found the one with the picture of a man on it. Gratefully, he pushed his way in and made it without wetting himself.

When the afternoon break bell rang, John took Lonnie's hand and stood by the post where he had first seen Betsy. Before long she joined them.

John introduced Lonnie. Betsy nodded and smiled, one side of her mouth going up more than the other. She shook Lonnie's hand and even let him hug her. John searched Lonnie's arms and legs for a scar to show her. When he couldn't find one, he pointed out where Lonnie was working and told her he had a grown-up job now.

Just then the sound of a siren rose outside the workshop, growing closer and closer until it passed by, then fell away. A worker near John started to spin excitedly when he heard the siren. He paced back and forth, rubbing his hands along posts, walls, and people who happened to be standing in his path.

"Police car," the worker muttered rapidly, "ambulance ... go to the hospital." He covered his ears and shook his head hard. "Siren, police. Police, guns. Don't shoot!" Unexpectedly, the worker began to run. He sped along the wall all the way around the perimeter of the cafeteria shouting these same words until he came to the techs' office windows and stopped.

"Uh-oh," Laurie-the-Greeter shouted. "Crazy Henry's havin' a seizure!"

Crazy Henry put his face up to the plate glass window momentarily then banged his forehead against it so hard that the whole window shook. All the techs inside the office and from across the workshop sprinted toward Crazy Henry. Before they could reach him, though, he picked up a chair and threw it through the window. The glass broke with a startling crack and shards exploded everywhere.

Crazy Henry shouted, "Ambulance!" He stepped back to get a running start and started to throw himself toward the jagged hole. Just in time, two techs nabbed him and pulled him away from the glass daggers. He fought to get away until they finally wrestled him to the floor. Two more techs joined the fight before they could pin him down, a tech holding each of his limbs. Crazy Henry jerked around on the floor, seizing and squirming for several minutes before finally lying still.

The buzzer rang. Workers began to move, walking slowly past Crazy Henry on their way back to work. Some stopped to stare. Techs hurried to cordon off the area with the broken glass.

"Everything's all right!" Ken shouted to the onlookers. "Get back to work. Henry's going to be fine. It's under control now ... go to your stations."

John was so shocked by what Crazy Henry had done that he couldn't move. Staring at the wicked blades of glass he imagined what might have happened to Henry if he had jumped through the window. He could visualize blood dripping from Henry's face and body and making a mess on the floor. A shudder enveloped him.

The buzzer rang again. Shaking himself out of his stupor, John pointed Lonnie toward his seat and scanned the room for Frank. Sure enough, Frank stood menacingly by John's chair, hands on his hips. John scurried back to his seat and sat down. Reflexively, he covered his ears with his hands.

Frank said firmly, "Take your hands off your ears. I'm not going to hurt you."

Slowly John drew his hands down to his lap.

"This is the second time today you've been late. I know this is your first day, but there has to be a consequence so you will learn."

"Me, me see ... Cwazy Henwy ..."

"It doesn't matter what's going on." Frank pushed his face right up to John's. "When the bell rings, you come back to your seat. That's the rule. The consequence for being late is that you work ten minutes more after the final buzzer rings. If it happens again, it will be longer and I'll have to call your manager."

John let out his breath, not realizing he had been holding it. That was it? Working ten extra minutes didn't seem that bad. He pulled his box of nuts and bolts closer and started to work.

Frank stood over him for a while then moved on down the line. In the background, John heard the sounds of glass being swept, and soon pounding, as they nailed a big board over the broken window.

When the final buzzer rang, all the workers sprang up. Laurie-the-Greeter stepped over and hugged John goodbye before he could stop her. Eileen hobbled away, clicking her cane against the chair and table legs.

John stood up, but Frank called, "Keep working, John. I'll tell you when ten minutes are up." Frank checked his watch.

John sat down. He watched the other workers getting ready to leave. They got their coats, said good-bye to each other and filed out the door. He saw Millie taking Lonnie, Ricky and Peter to their lockers. Randy grappled with Mick on the floor, trying to get him to stand up. John thought he glimpsed the top of Betsy's head among the workers moving out. He wished he could say good-bye to her.

Only a few workers were left inside the workshop when Frank shouted at John from the office door, "Time's up, John. Go on home. You'll do better tomorrow."

John hurried to the post with the red paint on it and opened his locker. He slipped one arm into his coat and raced for the door.

The same yellow bus John and the others had come on this morning waited close to the workshop entrance. Down at the corner of the block a group of smart ones boarded a long, white bus that had pulled up to the street curb. Millie stood by the open bus doors talking to Madge. John could see Lonnie's head in the front seat window.

When John stepped past her, Millie turned. "Oh, John! There you are. Frank made you stay after, didn't he?"

"Yep. Me yate."

"Frank's tough at first but he's fair. He gets easier as you learn the ropes. Don't worry; you did a good job today. We'll see you in the morning." She patted his back and smiled.

Madge tisked, "Had to stay after work already? You'll figure it out, my friend." She nodded toward the aisle, inviting John to board.

Jana sat next to Mick at the back of the bus. John waved at her, then plopped down next to Lonnie. He was still mad at Frank, but he said automatically, "How you, Yonnie?"

Lonnie signed, "Fine."

Madge shut the bus doors.

"Fwank make me stay. Wo'k mo'. Me yate." John scowled.

Lonnie shook his head. He put his arm around John's shoulder and clicked his tongue in sympathy.

"You yike wo'k?" John asked him, feeling bad that Lonnie had gone to time out.

"No," Lonnie signed and shook his head.

Madge moved the long stick and the bus jerked forward.

"Me yike new job. No yike Fwank." Then John remembered they got no money for working. "Yonnie, us no git Ba'hawa bucks." They wouldn't have money for the pop machine tomorrow. John frowned, wishing he had saved some Balhalla bucks.

Lonnie shrugged and tried to tickle John's ear. John pushed his hand away. He wasn't in the mood for teasing.

Gazing out the window past Lonnie's head, John saw a white car screech around the bus and out of the parking lot. Through the backseat window, he saw Betsy. She was crying.

Chapter 7
Ivory Tower

"Welcome to my little nest in the ivory tower," William said magnanimously, leaning back in his leather chair, his fingers hooked behind his head. "I've meant to get out to the house but I've been swamped."

Sarah, Jana, and Barry sat in Dr. Montgomery's cluttered office on three stiff chairs that he had pulled into a semi-circle from amongst his piles of books and papers.

Sarah nervously opened the binder on her lap and took the cap off her pen, "Thanks for meeting with us on such short notice. We have a few questions. Shouldn't take too long."

"No problem, Sarah. Your research is our department's star project." He smiled at her warmly.

Sarah blushed and mumbled something about how she hoped she would do them proud, silently flagellating herself for such a stupid remark.

"So, I hear the first few days have been bumpy," William said, breaking the awkward moment.

Sarah crossed her legs and took a calming breath. "Yes, but overall things have gone surprisingly well ... don't you think, you guys?" She looked imploringly at Jana and Barry.

"For the first two days, I'd say yeah," Barry said. "No one has died or anything."

Sarah shot him a look of dismay.

"They sure are interesting people." Jana said brightly. *She is far too cheery*, Sarah thought. "We could use some direction, I think," Jana added.

Sarah tried not to roll her eyes. Not exactly the support she had been looking for. Sarah took over, "We do have a couple of behavior problems to bring up that we need help with, Dr. Montgomery."

He smiled again and opened a file with Sarah's name on it. "Please, it's William."

"Yes, of course," she said, kicking herself for feeling so uncomfortable around Jana and Barry. She plunged in. "For one, Peter has been ripping his clothes—we've lost ten shirts in two days. He seems to start ripping when he's really stressed or when demands are being made of him. I need to get a stack of old shirts for him while we're working on this."

"Good idea." William said. "I should donate some of mine. It would help me clean out my closet."

Sarah smiled at this. "That's okay. I'll pick some up at Goodwill. Unless you want to contribute..."

William laughed out loud. "Just kidding. What else?"

"Well, there's Mick's hoarding behavior. He finds pencils in places we didn't even know we had them, breaks them up, and keeps the pieces in his pockets. He's obsessed with pencils and spends the majority of his time searching for more."

William wrote on a notepad. "And what else?"

"Ricky," Barry interjected, tapping on his knee nervously. "There's something sneaky about that guy. Can't put my finger on it ..."

Sarah glanced at him to let him know she wanted to lead. "He does seem to bother the others, especially John, but he's a lower priority than Mick who is always stealing food and stuffing his mouth to the point of choking. We haven't caught Ricky doing anything that bad yet."

Barry shrugged. "It's coming. There's something about his eyes ..."

"Let's take them one at a time." William slipped on reading glasses and gazed at them over the rims. "What have you tried for the hoarding behavior? That's a classic result of attachment disorder due to institutionalization. We see it in the mentally ill as well as the severely retarded populations."

"And my aunt Josie," Barry interjected, in a weak attempt at humor, Sarah supposed.

"I have one of those in my family, too," William said, laughing. "They'll need a crane to clean out her house when she dies."

Sarah forced herself to smile, regretting bringing Barry. "We started giving pencils to Mick as a reinforcer because that's what the techs at Larkspur said he liked best. But he found our whole stash of pencils and broke them into tiny pieces, even pulling out the pencil leads. They're in his bed, under his pillow, in all his pockets. So when he broke them all up and had his pockets stuffed with them, we thought we should take them away. He got very upset. Did I tell you he tries to bite and kick? Luckily, he's not very strong ..."

"Or quick," Barry finished. "He hasn't connected yet, at least not with me."

Sarah ignored him. "He almost bit Jana last night."

William looked at Sarah thoughtfully. She held her breath under his gaze.

"Hmm." William scratched his beard. "Something that was successful in a research project back in the 50s was a satiation program. There was an institutionalized adult who hoarded pillows—kept stealing them off everyone's beds and sleeping on a pile of them. They decided to try satiation. Have you heard of that?" he glanced at Barry and Jana.

They shook their heads, listening wide-eyed.

"You talked about that in your Abnormal Psych course," Sarah said, trying hard to seem competent and searching her memory for details. "It involves giving them so much of what they like that they get tired of it, doesn't it?" *Why did she say 'doesn't it'?* Sarah chided herself.

"Yes—the theory is that if you give them what they hoard and keep giving it to them until they have more than they can physically manage, they will eventually lose interest in the item and stop hoarding it. That may apply here. It would be a good behavior to measure in your study, Sarah. It's never been documented outside an institution, yours being the first group home for this level of client."

William lifted his glasses and gazed at Sarah. "This is an exciting project and I want you to keep me up on all aspects of it."

Sarah reddened again, trying to decide how best to respond to William's praise without revealing her discomfort.

Barry leaned back and cracked his neck to the side with a loud pop. "So how is that supposed to work?"

Sarah wished Barry wasn't so quick to jump in ... and that she had asked the question.

William leaned forward. "Give him pencils all the time, as reinforcers for doing something you want, and even just for not getting into trouble. After a while he'll run out of places to put them. His pockets will be full, his bed will be uncomfortable, he'll get stuck with them, and they'll lose their appeal to him. Over time."

"How long do you think it will take?" Sarah asked as she wrote furiously in her notebook.

"It seems to me a couple of weeks should do it, if I'm remembering the details of the pillow study correctly. Maybe a month." William leaned forward and rested his elbows on his knees, rubbing his hands together in anticipation. "Okay, what's next?"

Sarah paused, wanting to ask more questions about the satiation program but deciding against it. William clearly wanted her to figure out how to do most of this on her own. She would look up that study in the library Saturday.

"Since we're talking about Mick, how about his food stuffing," she suggested. "That scares us because he really choked. We all need a thorough review of the Heimlich maneuver, too."

"Food stuffing until he chokes..." William stroked his beard once more. "He must have a reduced gag reflex or he wouldn't be able to keep from throwing up, which means there may be some sensory issues, as well as the behavioral components. Probably a fear that he might not get his portion of food from some time in his past, or even just a food fetish, another manifestation of the same hoarding tendencies. Is he particular about his foods at all?"

"He'll eat anything that is on the table," Jana said.

"Or under the table," Barry added.

William's eyes squinted in a brief smile before he continued intensely. "So he probably has reduced oral sensation compounded by habitual hoarding, all classic institutionalization related reactions. Fascinating. What a wonderful research opportunity this is!"

He looked at Sarah. "I can see several publications coming out of this, Sarah."

"So how should we handle it?" Sarah asked, wondering whose name would get top billing on any future publications. She knew professors typically took the credit while grad students did the work. "I have been physically prompting him through each bite while holding his left hand down, insisting that he use his fork instead of his hands. He doesn't like it, but because he likes to eat and I'm stronger, he's tolerating it. Sort of."

"He bites at her hand if she's not careful," Jana said, concerned. "And he curses and hits at us. I'm worried she'll be bitten badly."

"The price we pay for fame. Is he verbal?" William asked. "I'm forgetting which one is which."

"Well, he says just a few words, mostly threats ..." Sarah started.

"Like 'Bitechew!' and 'Kick you!'" Barry imitated Mick's gruff voice and swiped out at Sarah's arm with his head bent forward in a fair imitation of Mick.

Sarah winced, but William laughed. "So what do you think about the complete physical guidance? I'm thinking over time I can reduce the prompts."

"It sounds like your physical guidance technique has promise because you're teaching him what you want him to do. And the food is a natural reinforcer for him, so he's going to let you do it. My only concerns would be generalizing this to times when you are not there, or to other people. How are you thinking you'll reduce your prompts?"

Sarah thought back to her class notes. "Well ... I guess I can slowly move from full to partial prompts, holding his arm at the wrist, then the elbow then the upper arm, pairing the touch with verbal directions, and giving him lots of verbal praise. I'll have to come up with a negative consequence for stuffing his mouth."

"What would that be?" William watched her closely over his glasses.

Sarah felt like she was taking an exam. She began to sweat. "I could pull him away from the table for a minute or so if he tries to grab food with his hands, or if he stuffs his mouth full we would move him completely away from the table for, say, five minutes."

"Time out and removal of opportunity for reinforcement. Sounds like a plan," William said. "You'll want to record all the variables of these behavior programs as you develop them and take your baseline data over one or two weeks before beginning intervention."

"Well, I have to start some things right away ..."

"Have you conducted your data training with staff?"

"Yes," she answered, glad she had, "but that will be ongoing as things change. We have weekly meetings set up."

"Good. Otherwise your data will be skewed." He removed his reading glasses and reached forward to squeeze her hand. "You are one of my best students and if anyone can make this work, you can, Sarah."

Sarah smiled weakly. She felt the sweat drip down her sides from her armpits as she wrote heavily, wondering if her notes would be coherent when she got back to her office. Such a bad idea, bringing her staff. She had wanted them to meet William and be able to ask their questions directly to him. Never again.

Barry raised the next issue before Sarah was finished writing. "What about the shirt ripping? Sometimes Peter does it when we make demands of him, but it also happens when he's all by himself with no one around. We'll come into a room and he is standing there with his shirt torn from tail to collar."

"I would think that would be hard to do," Jana added innocently. "It's not easy to tear fabric like that. He must be very frustrated."

William twisted his beard thoughtfully. "So, you don't know what's preceding it. At least not yet."

"Right." Barry glanced at Sarah.

She ignored him and put her pen down, focusing on William.

"And what do you do afterward?" William asked Barry.

"Not much," he answered. "We can't even touch him or he goes berserk."

Sarah took over. "We've been making him change his shirt, but last night he ripped three shirts in a row. There needs to be some consequence, I know, but when we touch him he starts hitting himself." She softly demonstrated Peter's violent head pounding. "He's really hurting himself."

"This is a little tougher since we don't know the antecedent or the payoff for him. What would he get out of ripping something?" William didn't wait for a response. "Could be the sensory experience of hearing or feeling fabric tear, or could be he doesn't like the feeling of clothes on him. He's autistic, right?"

"Yes. And nonverbal," Sarah twirled her pen unconsciously. "He definitely doesn't like to be touched. It makes sense that he wouldn't like how his clothes feel, either."

Barry leaned back and crossed his arms, "But he knows how to take his clothes off and on by himself and he's not undressing, just ripping them and leaving them on."

"That's true." Sarah turned to William. "We're not sure what to do."

"And it's hard to say this early. What did his records say?" William asked.

"They described these same behaviors. The Larkspur staff tried different things, but eventually gave up. I could call the duty nurse ..." Sarah offered.

"This is such a new situation for him," William mused. "He's also probably frustrated with all the changes in his life. You'll have to experiment with different strategies and keep some data. When you analyze it you will get some clues, and of course, you'll get to know him better as time goes on. Look for triggers, even unusual triggers like a light or a sound, too much time alone, or a particular person. Note the time of day. It could be several factors working together."

"So what would you suggest we try first?" Sarah bit nervously on the end of her pen staring at a blank page she had titled "Peter".

"I'd like you to try to figure this one out on your own—there's no pat answer. Let me know what you decide to try. I'd like to see your data as you go."

Just then his phone rang and he spun around to pick it up. "Excuse me. I have to take this."

Barry leaned over and whispered into Sarah's ear. "He doesn't know, does he?"

Sarah whispered back. "Nobody knows yet because there's no research on it."

"It seems to me," Barry said softy, "if we just make him do something with it, like wash it. Yeah, wash it and all the other laundry every time he rips something, he'd get tired of that in a hurry. We know he hates to work."

"I'll have to think about it."

William hung up the phone. "So, is there anything else? I actually have another appointment in a few minutes. I'll try to get over there next week to visit."

Sarah closed her notebook and stuffed it into her backpack. "You've been very helpful. I'm sure there'll be more questions as we go ..."

William stood up, clearly cutting off the discussion. "Sarah, come in to meet with me next week and then we can talk about what you've come up with so far. We should probably meet every week for a while, and you can always call me with questions in between."

"That would be great." Sarah gathered her things and stood up along with Jana and Barry. "When can you meet?"

William glanced at his desk calendar. "How about Tuesday. It's a full day, but I have time for lunch. Let's meet at Rennie's and that way we'll kill two birds with one stone. About noon?"

"Okay, noon it is. I'll bring my data so we can go over it together." Sarah stepped toward the door.

"Very good." William gripped Sarah's shoulder reassuringly. "We'll work through all of this together, Sarah."

When the three students were down the hall and out of earshot, Barry said, "What an asshole! He's as arrogant as they come!"

"What do you mean?" Sarah was astonished. "He's knowledgeable and he was very helpful to us."

"Bullshit. He's out to jump your bones. You didn't see the way he was looking down your blouse when you were writing."

"What? That's ridiculous." Sarah blushed and slugged Barry's arm a little harder than she meant to. "He's my mentor. He's supposed to be encouraging me."

"Mentor, schmentor. Haven't you heard his reputation with doc students?" Barry asked.

"Well, yes, but he's not like that with me." Sarah had never thought of herself as being attractive to a man like William. The rumor was that he picked the buxom, flirty types.

"Jana? What do you think? " Barry asked as they downed the stairs.

"He did look at you in a provocative way, Sarah," Jana agreed. "I'd be careful if I were you."

Sarah shook her head. "I've known him for five years now and I've never had that feeling. I can tell when ... well, I can tell. Besides, he's seeing Katrina."

"Ah ha! You haven't heard!" Barry spun around and jogged down the steps backward, pointing at Sarah. "She's graduating this spring so he's looking for fresh meat."

"No, no, no! Don't even say that! He's been nothing but very professional with me," Sarah insisted. But her heart quickened, and not because they were hurrying down the steps of the Smith Building.

Sarah spent the rest of the afternoon in the university library researching obscure case histories, hoping to find the magic bullet for Peter's shirt ripping. She found articles in the area of treatment of autism that involved punishment like face slapping for flapping and squirting water on their faces for spitting. These methods were based on Pavlov's classical conditioning principles of punishment for undesirable behavior, and reinforcement for desired behavior. To Sarah, they seemed archaic and cruel, though she knew of researchers who still employed them. So little was known about autism and there were still those who thought it was caused by lack of bonding with an emotionally crippled mother, a concept rejected by behaviorists like William.

Sarah decided she would just have to try something and see how it went. That's what the doctoral degree was about, she told herself, trying to find new solutions.

A bit discouraged that she hadn't found any answers, Sarah gathered her notes together and jammed them into her backpack. She slipped the journal volumes back onto the library shelves, marking her spot in the last journal she'd looked at with a slip of pink paper. She would have to peruse all the related journal articles to make sure she wasn't missing something. By Friday, after training the weekend guy, Michael, she would have two days to search for answers.

Sarah stopped for a cup of takeout coffee at Rennie's, greeting one of her ex-roommate's former boyfriends in passing. She thought about meeting William here next week and about what Barry and Jana had said about William's lustful ways. But she concluded again that this was nonsense. He would never be attracted to Sarah with her unruly hair, funky glasses and no make up. William went for the glamorous women, like Katrina, who was finishing up her ridiculously easy research project on the reactions of mice to sensory deprivation—this romancing despite the fact that William's wife was a well-known faculty member in the Fine Arts Department. They must have some arrangement between the two of them, an open marriage, because they stayed together regardless of his philandering. Still, she made a mental note to wear something modest, including a bra when they met next week.

Sarah dropped by her apartment to leave her backpack. She had always had a roommate until this year when Julie graduated and moved back to Cincinnati. In some ways it was nice not to have to worry about keeping things neat, or having to engage in conversation when Julie came home bubbling about her latest romantic encounter. The year before, her other roommate Carl had left for his residency in Boston. Sarah had sorely missed their evenings together, even though his preferred discussion topic was tropical infectious diseases. Their roommate status had evolved into friendship and eventually into love, or so she thought. She told herself it was a blessing that Carl left. She would be extremely busy for the next two years conducting her research and writing her dissertation. When he had written last fall that he had been accepted into a prestigious intern position in Mombassa for the next three years, she saw the writing on the wall. Better to forget any social life until this is over, she admitted. She would be far too busy anyway. Still, amidst the streams of undergrads, professors, and other grad students surrounding her during the day, she often felt lonely and isolated, especially at night.

Unlocking her bike from the light pole in front of the apartment building, Sarah effortlessly rode the mile to the group home. How lucky she was to have found the perfect house so close to campus. Jana was waiting for her and opened the door when she saw Sarah coming.

"How goes the studying?" Jana asked sweetly. Sarah wanted to like Jana. She seemed mature and sensible. But Sarah also felt unsure about her own role as supervisor, being only a couple of years older than Jana, and not just a bit defensive.

"Slow." Sarah rolled her bike onto the porch.

"So you didn't find anything useful for Peter?"

Sarah wished Jana wasn't so cheery. "Not yet. There have been very few studies on this. What's on the menu tonight?"

"Corned beef hash. I could peel the potatoes ahead of time—it's Peter and Lonnie tonight. I wonder if we should rethink this and maybe have just one of them at a time assigned to help with cooking, since they need so much coaching."

Sarah pushed back her initial reaction to reject Jana's idea and forced herself to smile, "Yeah, that's a good idea. Let's talk about that at our staff meeting."

"Sounds great!" Jana was trying hard. She disappeared inside the house.

While Jana peeled potatoes, Sarah revised the written directions for Michael who would be coming over tonight at 8:00 to start the weekend shift. She had only met Michael once during the interview, and he had been her only candidate for the forty-eight-hour solo shift. He was a student in the political science department and was a bit unkempt. But his scruffy beard and Salvation Army clothing were not unusual for a poor student scraping by on work study funds and government grants. Sarah knew that most of the client training would have to go on during the week when there were two on a shift, so basically she just needed someone who would do no harm on the weekends and keep the men safe. With her limited grant money, this was the only way she could figure out how to cover all the shifts.

Jana stuck her head out through the café doors. "I found some pudding we could make for dessert—will that do?"

"Sure, sounds fine … Oh, Jana?" Sarah paused.

"Yeah?"

"I just wanted to tell you you're doing a great job. Thanks for all your help. I'm sorry if I get a little snippy sometimes."

"Completely understandable." Jana smiled. "I can't imagine taking on this project myself, Sarah. You amaze me!" She disappeared behind the café doors.

I amaze her? Sarah asked herself sardonically. *Who is this woman? If you only knew me better you wouldn't be so amazed.*

Jana was an elementary education major and newly married. *She is probably so happy because she had sex this morning,* Sarah told herself. Sex was something Sarah tried not to think about. She pushed the image of William's overly friendly smile to the back of her mind when she heard the workshop bus honk out front.

Chapter 8
Michael

John lay awake in the growing light thinking about what Sarah had told him last night. She wouldn't be here in the morning because it was her day off. John couldn't figure that out because this was Sarah's house. Where did she go? He kept forgetting to ask her where she slept, though he knew Barry slept on the couch that made into a bed. Barry and Jana wouldn't be here either, just Michael, the weekender.

Michael had come by last night to meet them and right off John didn't like him. His blonde scraggly hair hung over his ears in a way that reminded John of brown-toothed Marley, and he had light, see-through eyes that looked like clearie marbles. But Sarah had told him they were going to have a good time because Michael was in charge of recreation, which meant fun.

Suddenly John remembered—it was cartoon day! He dressed quickly and hurried down the stairs. The smells of coffee and cigarette smoke, something he hadn't smelled all week, met him in the hall. He could hear cartoon music blaring on the TV. Ricky was up already and sat in the cushy chair watching *Bugs Bunny*. When Ricky saw John, he twitched spasmodically and screwed up his face into an ugly sneer. John tried to imitate his nasty smirk, but eventually just stuck out his tongue at Ricky.

Michael sat at the eating table reading a newspaper and drinking coffee. Bluish smoke circled his head and floated up into the light above.

"Morning, John," he said. The cigarette hung from his lips and smoke swam out as he talked. "Glad you're up. It's Saturday. No work today, so you can watch TV." He tapped the cigarette on the ashtray.

John grunted hello and slumped down at the far end of the sofa. *Bugs Bunny* was funny, and John laughed out loud.

"Want some coffee, John?" Michael asked. "I just made some. Help yourself."

No one had ever offered John coffee before. That was a tech drink, and Cookie always said he wouldn't like it. Maybe Michael was nicer than he thought.

John decided to try some. He went into the kitchen and poured himself a brimming mug. Gripping the cup with both hands John walked slowly through the cowboy doors. No matter how carefully he walked, however, the sizzling liquid sloshed over the side, burning his fingers.

John didn't dare yell. Michael might make him put it back. He baby stepped to the dayroom, spilling a few drops here and there and stopping to rub them away with his foot. John felt grown-up sipping coffee, even though he burned his tongue and it tasted like dirt.

Bugs Bunny ended and *Pink Panther* came on. Lonnie loved *Pink Panther* so John ran upstairs to wake him. To his surprise, Lonnie was already sitting up tying yesterday's socks in knots. He smiled at John and squealed his hello.

"Ca'toon day, Yonnie!" John said excitedly. He snatched the socks and unknotted them.

Lonnie happily wormed his fingers toward John's chin. John shrugged to protect his neck.

"Come on, Yonnie. Pink Pantha'. You favewit!"

John took Lonnie's hand and drew him to a stand. He made Lonnie get dressed quickly and waited impatiently for him in the hallway while he used the toilet room. Lonnie had just flushed when Mick popped his head out of his sleeping room.

John stared at Mick in astonishment. As Mick stumbled toward them, buck-naked, John was shocked to see his body streaked with sparkles. Colored flecks flew off him like a trail of fairy dust and he bumped into the wall in his rush toward the toilet.

John burst into laughter. "You shiny, Mick! What you do?"

Mick didn't answer but pushed past them toward the toilet. A wave of odor followed and John realized what made the sparkles stick to Mick's body. Poop!

Lonnie grabbed his nose and uttered one of his few words, "P. U!"

"You poop you bed, Mick!" John said disgustedly. "You 'tink!"

Mick must have had the runs again. At Starlight, he got the runs when he ate something he shouldn't. John clearly remembered Marley screaming at him for eating glue as he scrubbed Mick off in the shower with a long-handled brush.

"Us teo' Miko', Yonnie," John said. There was no telling what Mick would do in the bathroom by himself.

Pulling Lonnie by the hand John tried to hurry down, but Lonnie was not in a mood to be rushed. John left him and went on ahead shouting, "Miko'! Miko'!"

"Yeah?" Michael looked up from his paper when John came around the corner.

"Mick need showa'." He pointed upstairs.

"Mick's up? You'll all have showers later today, after basketball."

"No, him need showa' now! Him shitty."

"That's not a very nice thing to say." Michael drained his coffee cup. "Where'd you learn that word?"

"No, him 'tink! Poop!" John pointed to his bottom.

"What? He shit himself?" Michael stood up.

"Yep." John held his nose and made a face.

"Good god. Where is he now?" Michael's eyes grew wide.

"Toiwet."

"Is he cleaning it up?" He crushed out his cigarette.

"Mick not cwean up." John pointed to Michael. "You cwean up."

Michael bolted up the stairs, swearing under his breath. John wanted to follow to see Mick get in trouble, but the Pink Panther was crouched and ready to jump on someone. Lonnie appeared and they both sunk onto the couch to watch.

"Oh, my god!" Michael's distressed voice drifted down from upstairs. "What the bloody hell?" A door slammed and his voice trailed off.

John heard bumping noises. The shower turned on.

"Mick in big twoubo!" John said. Lonnie giggled and tickled John's neck.

Pink Panther was over and *Underdog* was on when Michael finally brought Mick downstairs. Michael's ears were red and his T-shirt was soaking wet. Mick was dressed, his wet haired combed flat to his head, and he smelled like soap.

"Where did Mick get those sparkles?" Michael asked. "Does anybody know? John?"

John shook his head.

"Great." Michael looked mad. "He must have gotten into the art supplies. Sit down on the couch, Mick, and don't move until breakfast! There's shit everywhere up there. I'm gonna have to clean the walls, not to mention the floor, the toilet, the sink ... everybody stay down here until I'm done. Shit! Just the way I want to spend my first morning with you guys!" Michael stomped up the stairs, cursing all the way.

When Michael finally came down again, Peter followed him, halting in the entry to bang his head. Michael muttered, "Found Peter up there ripping his shirt and rocking out. Not that anybody cares. You guys hear me?"

"Yep." John didn't take his eyes off the television set.

"Anybody else hungry?" Michael asked. "I've lost my appetite. "

John raised his hand and hauled Lonnie's arm up, too. "Us hungwy!"

"All right then, you two can help me with the pancakes." Michael lit a cigarette and took a couple of quick puffs, then he disappeared into the kitchen.

John patted Lonnie's head and pulled him to a stand. "Pancakes! Us he'p Miko'."

Lonnie stopped in the eating room to push in Michael's chair. He liked things neat. John noticed Michael's cigarette smoldering in the ashtray. He touched the mouth end with his finger and it wasn't even hot.

Just then Michael stuck his head out the cowboy doors. John jerked his hand away.

"Hey, take a drag, man," Michael said. "It will make you sick and then you won't want to start. It's a nasty habit."

John's face turned red. He covered his ears, but Michael just disappeared back into the kitchen.

Relieved not to be in trouble, John pulled Lonnie through the cowboy doors. Michael helped Lonnie mix up the batter and he let John cook the sausages. Then he showed John how to flip the pancakes over on the griddle. Ricky stood behind them watching. Even though Michael asked Ricky to help, he wouldn't use his spaghetti arms at all.

John tried not to look at Ricky. Every time he accidentally caught Ricky's eye, Ricky made a face or clenched his fist at John. For some reason Michael was never looking when Ricky acted up.

When they finally had a steaming plateful of pancakes, Michael called out to Peter and Mick, "Breakfast's ready! Come in the kitchen and get your food."

Peter rocked timidly through the cowboy doors as Michael held them open for him. On his way into the kitchen, Mick shoved Peter out of his way with his elbow. Peter pounded his head.

"Cut it out, you guys," Michael said, pushing Mick out of the kitchen. "Don't act like jerks. You're at the end of the line for that, Mick."

Michael handed Lonnie, John and Ricky plates and forks. He jabbed some pancakes and sausages onto their plates, dotted on the butter and squirted on the syrup.

Peter wouldn't hold his plate, so Michael set it on the eating table for him. "You've got to learn to do these things on your own, Petey," he chided. "I'm not always going to carry your plate for you. The rest of you can take your plates into the living room if you want to watch cartoons."

"Us not eat tabo'?" John asked. He knew it was Mick's turn to set the table because he had checked the job chart.

"Naw, today is Saturday. Take a break."

"Sawah say ..." John began.

"I know, but she's not here, is she?" Michael loaded up a plate for himself.

John shrugged and led Lonnie to the dayroom walking slowly so he wouldn't slop the syrup over the side. Only a few drips spilled onto the carpet. He sat down on the sofa and balanced his plate on his lap before helping Lonnie place his on the coffee table.

John heard Michael tell Mick it was his turn. He heard Mick growl and looked up. As Mick came out through the cowboy doors holding his plate, he tripped on the edge of the carpet, flipping his plate out of his hands.

"Uh-oh!" Mick said. He dove to snatch the pancakes off the carpet.

"Mick!" Michael grabbed him by the back of the collar. "You'll have to throw those away, man. They're dirty now."

But Mick was taking no chances. He palmed the pancakes and crammed them into his mouth.

"Hey, I said, don't eat those!" Michael was on top of him squeezing his cheeks. "Spit that out!"

Michael lifted Mick up and dragged him with his bulging face into the kitchen. "If you can't eat like a human being, you're done with breakfast!"

As John began to eat, Ricky started making faces at him and Lonnie again. John stuck out his pancake-covered tongue. "You bad, Wicky!" he slurred through a mouthful of food.

Ricky flicked a piece of his pancake at John but missed. The sticky wad landed on the sofa. Ricky loaded his fork again and shook it toward John sending another chunk flying.

"Me teo' Miko'," John said, shaking his head. He didn't want to fight because his favorite cartoon was on now. He scooted closer to Lonnie. Ricky tried a couple more shots, but John just ignored him.

Michael ended up letting Mick eat pancakes at the table anyway. Mick stuffed them in as fast as he could with his hands while Michael finished his cigarette and read the paper. Michael cleaned up the kitchen by himself, even though it was Ricky's turn.

When Michael was finished, he switched off the TV.

John groaned.

"It's pretty nice outside," Michael said. "Almost feels like Spring. Let's go down to the park. We'll take the basketball and shoot around for a while."

This made John happy again—he had never gone to a park.

Michael noticed the pancake chunks on the sofa and floor near John. "Hey, man, why didn't you clean up your mess? You don't leave spilled food just sitting here. Someone could sit on it. I don't think Sarah wants sticky syrup on your pants or her carpet."

"Me not do!" John protested. "Wicky fwow pancakes. Make mess."

Michael looked at Ricky. "Did you do this?"

Ricky shook his head, his eyes staring in innocence.

"Well, I don't know, John, but they're by you, so you clean them up. Go get a paper towel and throw them away. Then everybody get ready to go."

"Me not do!" John protested, pointing at Ricky. "Wicky, him fwow. Him cwean up!"

"Sorry. You're the one this time. Next time Ricky will clean up." Michael hauled Mick upstairs. "Time to brush your teeth, sparkle-man."

John glowered. He picked the pancake pieces up reluctantly, muttering about Ricky all the way back to his room. "Not fai'. Wicky bad."

When everyone had their coats on, they started out the front door. "Now stay together," Michael said. "I don't want anybody running off from the group. Just follow me. The park is only two blocks away."

By the time they stepped out into the brisk morning, John was feeling better. The sun was shining and he was excited about going to the park. He pulled Lonnie by the hand, trying to make him walk faster while keeping their distance from Ricky.

"The basketball is in my trunk," Michael said. A pink car with paintings all over it was parked in the driveway.

"Dis you ca'?" John asked. He touched its shiny surface.

"Yeah. Do you like it?" Michael opened the trunk and pulled out the basketball.

"Yeah, pwetty ca'!" John pushed the trunk closed for Michael.

"Painted it myself," Michael said. He handed the ball to Ricky, then lit a cigarette. "Let's go."

As they started down the sidewalk, John glanced across the street to the house where he had seen someone watching them the other morning. An old woman stood in the window staring at them. John waved but she turned away.

Michael held Mick's arm all the way to the park but he wouldn't let John hold Lonnie's hand. He said men didn't do that in public. Ricky held the basketball and walked with Michael, occasionally tossing the ball in the air and catching it. Peter trailed far behind, stopping to dip and flap. Michael backtracked a couple of times to try to get Peter going, but finally they just walked on ahead of him.

The park reminded John of Larkspur with an expanse of grassy hills punctuated with thick bare-branched trees. There was a bridge over a pond where more ducks than John could count were huddled together by the shore. As they passed, the ducks waddled off the bank into the water, quacking like a burbling brook. Mick tried to chase them, but Michael held him firmly by the arm.

Beyond the duck pond was a playground with swings, a slide, and a circular toy with seats all around it. John wanted to try them, but Michael led them on, stopping at the blacktopped surface where two basketball hoops were set up on poles at either end. Three men were already playing basketball, circling each other as they danced around one of the baskets.

Michael motioned everyone over to him. "We can play at this end. Take your jackets off—you'll be hot in a few minutes." Then his voice got stern, "Nobody wander off. You could get lost. And nobody go near the water, do you hear? You'll be sitting in your room all day if you don't stay with me." He stripped off his jacket.

John tossed his coat on the ground, too, but Lonnie didn't want to take his off. Michael tried to get Mick's coat off, but Mick started kicking at him.

"Okay, be hot, then." Michael said, shrugging. "Come on. Let's shoot some hoops."

Michael took the ball and tossed it at the basket. It circled around the hoop and bounced out. The second time he threw it up, it went through.

"See? It's easy." Michael shoved the ball at Peter's chest. "Here, Peter, you shoot it."

Peter screamed and banged his head. The men playing basketball at the other end of the court stopped their game and stared.

"Come on, Peter," Michael hissed. "Don't act like a mental case."

Peter rocked hard, each step leading him away from Michael and toward the edge of the blacktop.

Michael turned back to the others. "Okay, John, you first." He handed John the ball.

John crouched, letting the ball dip momentarily between his knees. Then he thrust it upward with both hands. The ball flew past the pole and onto the grass.

Michael retrieved it. "That's okay. Good try, John. Here, Mick, you try it."

Mick wouldn't take his hands out of his pockets. "Hold the ball, Mick." Michael pulled Mick's fisted hands out of his pockets. Yellow pencil fragments spilled onto the pavement. Mick scrambled after them on hands and knees.

"Well, shit." Michael rolled his eyes. "If you'd rather have pencils than play basketball who gives a f—?" He stopped himself from saying the bad word. "How about you, Lonnie?"

Lonnie took the ball and slowly heaved it across the court. It bounced toward the other basketball players, rolling in front of the tallest one who almost tripped over it. He swore and kicked it out into the grass.

"Hey!" he yelled at Michael. "Keep your ball and your retards on your own side of the court."

John had been called a retard before—he didn't know what it meant but he knew it wasn't nice.

The other ball players laughed and continued their game.

"Up yours," Michael shouted back, showing them his middle finger. "Just ignore those assholes, you guys. You get the ball, John."

John jogged after the ball and tossed it back to Michael.

"Who else wants to try it?" Michael threw the ball underhanded at Ricky.

Unexpectedly, Ricky's spaghetti arms shot up and he caught it. He fired it at the basket. The ball rimmed the hoop and fell away, barely missing.

"Good try!" Michael brightened. He chased the ball and threw it back at Ricky. "Try again—you almost made it!"

Swish.

"Hey, good shot!" Michael danced around Ricky dribbling the ball. "Where did you learn to play basketball? Come on, John, help me out here!"

Ricky snatched the ball between bounces and tossed it up. Another basket. John ran onto the court and held his hands out. Michael threw the ball to John and it smacked him squarely in the nose. The pain brought John to his knees.

"You okay?" Michael came over and touched John's shoulder as he crouched on the ground in agony. "You gotta be tough to be a good player, Johnny. Suck it up."

John's eyes watered but there was no blood—he checked several times.

"You better take it easy for a few minutes," Michael led John onto the grass at the edge of the court where he could sit down.

John held his nose and watched Michael hop back onto the court. He and Ricky bounced the ball and chased each other around, shooting repeatedly at the basket. Sometimes they made it, sometimes they didn't, but Michael told Ricky over and over how good he was. Ricky grinned his evil grin.

Michael laughed. "You love this stuff, don't you Ricky. Somebody taught you how to play. Who was that, Ricky?"

Ricky didn't answer.

John brooded. First Michael threw the ball at John's nose and now he was treating Ricky like a friend. John was disliking Michael more and more.

When the pain subsided, John walked back onto the court. By this time, Ricky's shirt dripped with sweat and Michael's forehead glistened.

"Ready, John? Here you go." Michael handed him the ball instead of throwing it, and John shot it. He missed.

Lonnie joined in, and they all took turns shooting at the basket.

"Here, Lonnie, hold it like this." Michael helped him hold the ball right. After several practice shots that missed altogether, the ball bounced off the board behind the basket.

"Good one, Lonnie! You almost made your first basket."

Once in a while Michael gave John or Lonnie the ball, but most of the time he and Ricky played by themselves, chasing each other and shooting like they were playing a real game.

Suddenly whipping his head around, Michael shouted. "Where's Peter?"

John pointed across the court. Peter had rocked to the far end of the pavement near the other basket. He flapped his hands vigorously, coming closer and closer to the other players.

"Come on back, Peter!" Michael called. "We're playing at this basket."

Peter stopped flapping and looked up briefly. Wide-eyed, he walked straight across the court toward Michael just as the three players flew at him chasing their ball. The tall one smashed into Peter, knocking him backward onto his butt. The player stumbled, but twirled adroitly back onto his feet. Peter scrambled up, screamed piercingly and flogged his forehead with a vengeance.

Michael dashed toward him.

"What's wrong with him?" the basketball player shouted at Michael. "I didn't hit him that hard!"

"He's retarded, stupid," said the shorter one. "Is he hurt?"

Peter banged harder. His forehead turned dark and bluish.

"Can't you shut him up?" spat the tall one.

Michael shushed Peter. "Calm down! Quiet, now, Peter! For god's sake, Peter. That's enough! You don't need to do that."

He held Peter's hand back to try to stop him from hitting himself, but Peter screamed louder.

"All right, all right!" Michael pulled his hand away. "I won't touch you if you just stop screaming."

Peter stopped banging and bit his hand, something John knew he only did when he was extremely upset. Cookie used to squirt him with water to break him out of it.

"Don't bite, Peter." Michael threw his hands up and paced in a circle around Peter. "Shit! You've got to stop this!"

The other players stared open-mouthed. Peter's hand was bleeding.

"Just give him a minute here," Michael implored. "He doesn't like to be touched."

Peter backed away from the group, rocking. Frantically, he grabbed the sides of his coat and pulled them apart, unzipping it. Then he grasped his shirt with both hands and yanked, popping all the buttons off. He ripped again, tearing the front from collar to hem.

"Damn you, Peter!" Michael herded Peter off the pavement with his arms outstretched. "Not here."

The tall player yelled after them, "You should lock him up where he belongs. All of them belong in the looney bin." He spit on the pavement and turned away.

Michael's face grew red. "You asshole. You don't know anything. One bump on the head and this is you!"

The player turned toward Michael with clenched fists and tightened his jaw. John thought, *They are going to fight!*

"Forget it, Russ," the short guy said. He held Russ's arm at the elbow. "Give it a rest."

"Let's get the hell out of here." Russ spat again and struck the air with his fist, just like Mick did when he was mad.

As they walked off the court, the short one called over his shoulder, "Sorry, man. He has a hot temper."

Peter calmed down slowly and followed Michael back to their end of the basketball court. Mick lay on the grass searching out tiny sticks and stuffing them in his pocket. Michael pointed to the grass beside Mick and Peter stayed close this time, rocking slowly and occasionally biting his injured hand.

Ricky, John and Lonnie shot a few more baskets with Michael until he said, "Okay, one more each. Peter is probably getting cold by now with that bare chest. We should go home."

Michael bounced the ball to John. "Eyes on the basket, not too hard."

John concentrated on the orange circle. He shot. The ball soared upward, heading right for the basket. John closed his eyes. He heard it hit the circle. One eye peeked open, just far enough to see the ball spiral down through the net. He squealed and jumped up and down ecstatically.

"Right on!" Michael shouted. He held his hand up in the air. "Give me five, man."

John grabbed his hand.

"No, hit it like this." Michael slapped John's hand pretty hard. It stung, but John smiled. All the way home, John showed Lonnie how to give him five and pretended to shoot the basketball into the hoop again.

After lunch, Michael said they could all relax. He took Peter upstairs with him and locked him in his room as punishment for ripping his shirt. Then Michael went down to the basement to do the laundry, including Mick' poopy sheets.

John sat on the sofa with Lonnie going through his wallet. He found the stick of gum Betsy had given him at work and popped it in his mouth. He wished he had Betsy's picture. She was prettier than Rochelle and she always combed her hair. Maybe he would bring Betsy something special on the next work day. He tried to think of something she might like. Maybe

Michael would know what girls liked. He decided to ask Michael about that when he came back up.

Just then, they heard a knock at the front door. Ricky jumped up first and opened it. John came up right behind him and peered curiously over Ricky's shoulder.

On the porch stood a man with a black mustache. His hair was flecked with gray and he wore a white shirt and tie.

"Hello!" The man smiled and extended his hand to Ricky. "I'm Pastor Ron Conley, minister of First Baptist Church down on Sea Perch. May I come in?"

Ricky opened the door wide for him. The man stepped inside.

John stuck out his hand. "Me Don."

"Nice to meet you, Don."

Pastor Conley spoke directly to Ricky like he was a tech. "One of my parishioners told me, that is, I heard that you have a home for adults who are disabled. A group home, is that right?"

Ricky grinned and nodded slightly.

"That's excellent. Very good idea to get these folks out into the community, I think. I used to work in a mental hospital, so I've been around them lots. Just unique individuals no different from you and me in most ways."

Ricky smiled and glanced uneasily at John.

Pastor Conley continued, "Well, we, uh, I was wondering if you would like to send your ... guests to church? They could benefit from God's word just like the rest of us. In fact, we have a new program we've started recently for retarded children, and we'd be glad to include your adults. Not with the children, of course, but in their own class. We even have a church bus that could provide transportation."

"Mmm." Ricky nodded again. John looked at Ricky curiously. He looked like he understood what Pastor Conley was saying.

"Are you interested? We could at least try it and see how it goes."

Ricky shrugged and smiled.

Pastor Conley smiled, too. "All right then. It's all settled. We'll start tomorrow. Around 9:15?"

"Us go chu'ch?" John asked.

"Sounds like the answer is yes," Pastor Conley said cheerily. "A man named Joe will be driving the bus, so he'll see you first thing in the morning."

He took Ricky's hand with both of his and shook it firmly. "See you tomorrow, then."

Ricky nodded and shut the door.

"Us go chu'ch, Wicky?" John asked again. Ricky seemed to have agreed to this even though he wasn't a tech.

Ricky shrugged again and walked toward the kitchen.

"You teo Miko'?" John called after him.

Ricky grinned, then spasmodically jerked in a full body shiver. John tried to remember to tell Michael, but by the time Michael returned from the basement he had forgotten.

The next morning John woke to the pounding bass of rock and roll music. When he opened his eyes, he saw Lonnie sitting up cross-legged, staring at him and concentrating on flicking his fingers.

"Ahhh!" Lonnie squealed when he saw that John was awake. He smiled and wiggled his fingers toward John to say hello.

"Hi, Yonnie. You up ea'wy."

The pounding beat of the music vibrated the floor as John padded to the toilet room. The other bedrooms were empty. John had the uncomfortable feeling that he had missed something. He liked to be the first one up.

Lonnie followed John downstairs without prompting. Everybody else was dressed. Michael sat reading the paper and smoking, just like yesterday. He tapped his feet to the music and appeared to be singing along, though John couldn't hear his voice over the noise.

"Hi!" John called.

"Mornin' lazy bones." Michael shouted. He picked up his cigarette and sucked. "Would you mind turning that down? Mick turned it up, but we can't hear ourselves think!"

John happened on the right button on his second try. When the music suddenly quieted, Michael was saying,"... not that all of us are thinking that hard. Lonnie, it's your turn to work in the kitchen this morning."

"Me hungwy!" John said, tapping Lonnie on the shoulder. "You fix bweakfas', Yonnie."

"Let's boogie, then," Michael folded up his newspaper. "You can help, too, John."

John set the table while Michael helped Lonnie make oatmeal. John decided to get dressed before breakfast. As he made his bed he caught sight of mama's picture on his nightstand. He sat down on the bed for a moment. He had been busy. A couple of days had passed since he had talked to her.

Her smile was pretty, as always. John stroked the glass. "You good mama. Pwetty hai', pwetty eyes."

An ache of loneliness stirred in his stomach. Lying back John stared at the flowers that adorned the ceiling light. The ceiling of Sarah's house disappeared and the bare bulb of Starlight took its place. He could see Cookie's face smiling at him. When would he see her again? He thought about Nurse Julette and how she would sit and talk to him and the other boys. Sometimes she gave him candy and told him not to tell Cookie. John missed them. And Timmy ... who was helping him? Nobody else could understand him except John. Marley treated Timmy like a baby. Then there was Jackie. John was glad Jackie wasn't here because he always hung around the girls. Jackie would be telling Sarah about Mrs. Baker every day. John's mind drifted through the dayroom at Starlight from one worker's face to another.

Startlingly, the Mean Man's face appeared before John's glazed eyes. His face was creased and his black eyes were buried deep under his shaggy eyebrows. John heard him yelling at Lonnie, "We oughta send you to Cadby where you belong!"

Cadby. The thought chilled him. A bare cement wall smeared with shit. A scream. John's heart began to pound wildly and he fended off the hands with his arms.

"John?"

John snapped his eyes open.

Michael stood in the doorway. "Breakfast's ready."

"Okay." John took a deep breath, relieved to be at Sarah's instead of Cadby.

John ate breakfast in silence, still spooked by the disturbing images of the inside world.

When breakfast was nearly over, Michael said, "I think we're going to hang around here today. We can have a picnic out back if it doesn't rain. And we can clean up the house. I need to write stuff down for Sarah."

"Go chu'ch?" John asked him.

"Church? No. I don't have any way to get you to church, and Sarah didn't say anything about that."

"Bus?"

"I don't have a bus, John. I only have my car. You saw it—it's tiny."

John was disappointed. He wanted to go with Pastor Conley because he seemed so nice.

When breakfast dishes were cleaned up, Michael said, "I gotta run to the corner store for some cigarettes, guys. I'll be gone ten minutes, tops." He put on his jacket. "John, keep an eye on Mick and don't let him go in the kitchen. Don't let anyone go downstairs. And don't let Ricky out of your sight. You're in charge."

"Okay," John said uncertainly. He stepped out on the porch to watch Michael go. Yellow flowers were blooming at the neighbor's house across the street where John had seen the old woman working. The window stood empty and dark today.

Michael called, "I'll be right back. Go inside and shut the door. Don't let anybody come out while I'm gone, okay, pal?"

"Okay." John waved.

John watched Michael until he disappeared around the corner. As he turned to go inside, John caught sight of a yellow bus coming around the corner where Michael had just disappeared. The bus slowed down and stopped right in front of Sarah's house. On the side of the bus were painted some words and a cross.

A man with a big red beard jumped out of the door.

"Morning!" he called to John. " I'm supposed to pick up some guys for church. I bet you're one of them, right?"

"Yeah," John said tentatively.

"I'm Joe, from the church." He waved John toward the bus. "Go ahead and get in. I'll get the others."

John was confused. Michael said they weren't going to church.

"Okay us go chu'ch?" John asked, just to be sure.

"It's okay," Joe said, squeezing John's shoulder as he passed him on the porch. "Pastor Conley cleared it all with your manager yesterday."

Joe was so cheerful and kindly that John's doubts melted. Michael must have forgotten about church.

Joe knocked on the partly opened front door and stepped in. "Hellooo!" he called. "The church bus is here! We're kind of late so we better hurry."

John heard Joe talking to the other boys inside and soon he reappeared holding Lonnie and Mick by the arms. Mick's hands were stuck in his pockets to protect his treasures, and Lonnie looked perturbed until he saw John outside. Ricky bolted after them and Peter followed, not to be left alone.

"Let's go, fellas." Joe led them confidently toward the bus. John shut the front door and followed.

"Ever been to church?" Joe asked as they climbed into the yellow bus.

"Nope," John answered, taking his place behind the driver's seat like he did on Madge's bus.

"You'll like our church," Joe said, sitting down and closing the door. "We have a special Sunday School class for you."

Peter and Mick sat across the aisle from John and Lonnie, and Ricky wound his way to the back, as usual. A few other people, who looked like workers, were scattered throughout the seats behind them, but John didn't recognize them.

Then he saw her.

Betsy! She sat half-way back, staring out the window. She looked pretty in a flowered dress, her hair neatly combed.

John nudged Lonnie. "Bessy go chu'ch!" He twisted around and waved, calling her name.

Betsy glanced up, covering one eye with her hand. When she smiled and waved back, John could see that she had a black eye. She quickly covered it again.

He mouthed the words, "What happen you eye?" but she shrugged and turned away.

The engine roared and the bus jerked forward. Joe whistled a tune and switched on the radio.

John watched Sarah's house grow smaller behind them. Suddenly, he saw Michael sprinting down the sidewalk after them, waving his arms at the bus and yelling. John couldn't hear him and figured he wanted to say goodbye. He waved back at Michael until the bus turned the corner and Michael disappeared.

Chapter 9
Church

Sarah sweated through her morning run, gliding along the tree-lined streets surrounding the university, their vintage homes recessed behind expansive lawns. At the edge of the bluff overlooking the mist-shrouded bay she dropped down the three levels of steps leading to the waterfront, deserted at this early hour except for the gulls. The salty sea air stung her nostrils and filled her with both exhilaration and a deep nostalgia as she padded past rows of souvenir shops to the boardwalk that led along the wharf. She wondered again how she could feel several emotions at once. How many times had she and her mother mused that no experience in life seemed pure? Great joy was always tinged with loss, and even tragedy was accompanied by redemption.

Sarah tried to push thoughts of her mother back into the lake of sorrow where they lived, but the last moments of her mother's life flooded back with a vengeance ... her pale face clinging to life, her struggle to speak through the oxygen mask, the grip of her blue-veined hand as she told Sarah about her firstborn son, swiftly pirated away. He was sickly and Mongoloid, a curse shamefully visited upon an unwed teenage mother. He was undoubtedly long dead by now since he had the hole in his heart that was so common to Down Syndrome babies. Sarah's mother had regretted never telling Sarah before this; the pain of the long-kept secret had driven her to confess her deepest sorrow before she died. Her mother's unburdening had become Sarah's double loss.

There were days Sarah wished she did not know about this mysterious brother at all, then others when she wished she knew everything. How long had he lived? Did he learn to talk? What had his life been like, wallowing his short life away in a state institution. Sarah regretted not having a family that welcomed her brother as a cherished family member, remembered his birthday, talked about him fondly at family gatherings. Where had she read that even your losses help to form who you become, help make you who you are? Without knowing about her brother would she be starting a group home? Given a choice, she would never have chosen the pain it took to get where she was now. She let the wind dry the tears that streaked her cheeks.

Returning to her cluttered apartment, Sarah stripped and decided once again to forego church. She had sworn to start going again in grad school, but studying and catching up on much-needed sleep had taken precedence. She would go back when she got settled somewhere in her first professorship. Sarah stood beneath the spray of the steaming shower for several minutes allowing the damp heat to ease her fatigued muscles. Her shoulders were knotting up again—she needed a massage but her stipend barely paid the rent. For the thousandth time she missed Carl's strong hands adeptly massaging away the stress. At first, they had agreed to stay together even when he accepted the residency in Boston. But the strain of separation, having little money for cross-country travel, and the distraction of their respective studies had caused them to drift apart. Now he was in Mombassa.

She must be premenstrual, thinking such melancholy thoughts this morning. Sarah needed to get a few groceries to get her through the coming week, and then she would stop by the group home to see how Michael was doing with the guys. When she had called a couple of times Saturday, Michael said everything was fine. But she had worried from the outset how he would be able to handle the weekend shift alone. The budget for her project was tight and she had to cut corners where she could.

Sarah toweled off, threw on jeans and a sweatshirt, and leaned forward with her head upside down, separating her curls with both hands. This short ritual was her only concession to beautification these days. Maybe that's why she wasn't meeting anyone. Didn't matter. She had no time for a relationship anyway, she mused again, inspecting her image only fleetingly in the mirror.

Toasting two leftover bread crusts and downing a cup of instant coffee, Sarah drove to the neighborhood grocery store. The car was running a little rough this morning. It needed an oil change and a tune-up, but that would have to wait.

After returning home to put away her few groceries, she sat down for five minutes with her prayer book to assuage her guilt over not going to church. Her mother would be so disappointed in her. She prayed for her new clients, her research study, and her inexperienced counselors, for the wisdom and patience to make this project work. Her momentary sense of peace dissipated, however, as her prayer lapsed into anxious thoughts and worries. Who did she think she was taking on something like this? Her mother's words echoed painfully through her heart, "Why do you want to get so much education? Be a high school teacher like your aunt Rita. Then you can meet some nice man, have a family, have your summers off ..."

She shut her journal and decided to phone Michael again. Maybe she wouldn't need to go over today and she could finish her library research.

Michael picked up after six rings, breathless. He said everything was fine. Ricky had a bad night, getting up several times and bothering Mick in the next room. Then Michael mentioned again Ricky's newly discovered basketball prowess. Sarah told him that all those years at home before being admitted to Larkspur must have given Ricky some athletic skills. Maybe he had brothers.

"But he won't do a lick of work," Michael told her. "Just stands there like his arms don't function."

"I know. But he has potential, I think," Sarah said. "He just isn't showing us yet. Maybe basketball will be a good reinforcer for him."

"Maybe," Michael's voice was unreadable.

"I was thinking of stopping by," she said, probing.

"Everything is fine. Don't worry about us," Michael said quickly. "It's all under control."

Something in his voice made Sarah decide she better go.

An hour and a half later, John met her at the door. "Us go chu'ch!" He held up his hand to give her a high-five.

"Hi, John. You want to go to church? I'll have to look into that." She slapped his hand and brushed past him, calling to the others who sat watching television, "Hi, everybody. Looks like you're all relaxing and enjoying your Sunday afternoon. Where's Michael?"

John followed her into the living room. "Miko' do yaundwy wif Mick, downstai's."

"Oh, good. I'll wait for them to come up." She sat down on the arm of the sofa and patted Ricky on the back. "What's up, buddy? Having a good day? Wish you could tell me what's going on inside that head of yours. Michael said you didn't sleep very well." Sarah wondered absently what it must have been like for Ricky to grow up in a real home and then to be ripped from his family and everyone he knew.

"Him not hab good day," John said. "Him say bad wo'ds at chu'ch."

"He said bad words? We haven't even heard him talk, John. And what's this about church?" Maybe John had seen church on television this morning.

Just then Michael and Mick burst through the café doors. Mick was growling at Michael and taking swipes at him with his fists.

"That's the last load, buckaroo," Michael said, ducking to avoid the jab. "You gotta take your turn like everybody else, man."

Mick escaped Michael's grasp and dove under the dining room table.

"Hi, Michael," Sarah said. "How's it going? I take it Mick didn't like doing laundry."

"That's an understatement. But the last load is in the dryer. Most of the laundry was his fault anyway, as you know."

Sarah laughed. "If it wasn't so disgusting, the sparkle incident would be pretty funny, you have to admit."

"To you, maybe. You didn't have to wash sparkly shit off a forty year old man's butt."

Sarah laughed again. "Adventures are what keep life interesting. So what's this John's telling me about Ricky swearing? Have you heard him say words?"

"No, but John says he did." Michael looked at John with a sidelong glance.

"I hope he can say more than swear words," Sarah said. "John said Ricky swore at church. Were they watching church on TV? Maybe it brought back memories for Ricky."

Michael rolled his eyes. "Oh, that. Yeah. Well, we had a little misunderstanding. Nothing to worry about. I found them."

"Found them?" Sarah's smile faded. "What do you mean?"

The phone rang and Michael picked up the receiver. "Hello? Yeah, that's me ... Oh, hi, Reverend ... I don't know. My boss is here. Why don't you talk to her?" He held the receiver toward Sarah on its ten-foot spiral cord.

"Who is it, Michael? Tell me what happened first." Sarah's heart leaped to her throat.

"The guys accidentally went to church. This is the pastor on the phone." Michael thrust the phone toward her urgently.

"Accidentally?" Sarah took the receiver and covered it with her hand.

Michael twisted away uncomfortably. "Yeah, a bus came and picked them up while I was... downstairs ..."

"Him go sto'e!" John chimed in, "buy cigawettes."

Sarah glanced over at John, then stared numbly at Michael for the explanation.

Michael explained quickly, "I guess some guy from the church came by yesterday when I was upstairs and talked to Ricky and thought he was one of us. Ricky gave them permission to go. So this bus shows up and the guys get on it, and by the time I see it, they're half-way down the street."

Sarah was rattled but tried to maintain her composure as she took her hand off the receiver. "Sorry to keep you waiting. This is Sarah, the manager. How can I help you?"

She listened, then told the pastor she would call him back when she had a chance to think it over. She wrote down his number and hung up.

Motioning for Michael to follow her, she said, "We need to talk." As Sarah led him down the stairs to her office she felt the blood rising up her neck and overheating her face. By the time she unlocked the office door and shut it behind them, she was livid.

"Start over and tell me everything," Sarah sat down, afraid her shaking legs would give her away.

Michael explained, admitting that he had run to the corner store to get cigarettes "just for two minutes."

Sarah could not keep the sarcasm from dripping through. "So you left five severely retarded men in this house by themselves, men who have been out of the institution for seven days." She stared at Michael in disbelief.

"They were fine!" Michael raised his voice defensively. "They were watching TV, doing nothing. If it hadn't been for Ricky ..."

She interrupted him, her pitch rising, "You're blaming Ricky? He doesn't even talk, Michael!"

Michael lowered his eyes, "I know, I know. It was a mistake, okay? I'm sorry."

"Sorry doesn't do it." Sarah ruthlessly tore at a loose hangnail. "It's about being responsible for five guys who can't take care of themselves. What if something happened while you were gone, or while they were at church? We are liable. *I* am liable!" She hated showing her emotions this way and took a deep breath.

Michael looked at the calendar that hung over the desk. Sarah could see his teeth were clenched. "I said I'm sorry. You don't need to lecture me. There's nothing I can do about it now."

"And it won't happen again, right?"

"Of course."

"Good." She took a slow breath to calm herself.

Michael remained silent.

Finally, to normalize the conversation she asked, "So, what else is going on? How is the chore chart working?"

"Fine." Michael didn't look at her.

"Everyone is doing their jobs then?"

"Sure. We're doing what you say, boss."

Sarah flinched at that remark. "No need to get defensive. It's my job to keep these guys safe."

"I know," he said tersely.

"Okay, then. We better go back upstairs and check on the guys. Who knows where they might go next?" Sarah stomped out, still fuming.

The buzzer on the dryer went off and she heard Michael open the dryer door. She was glad she didn't have to face him for a few minutes. She went upstairs to check on the guys and found John, listening at the basement door.

"Hi, John," she said, trying to cool off. She stopped in the dining room and flipped through the data sheet that hung next to the chore chart. Michael was supposed to mark who did their jobs and with what kind of assistance, but he hadn't marked anything. *Figures*, she thought. When she met Michael at the interview she had appreciated his casual attitude and self-assurance. But now she realized he was just irresponsible. *His* neck wasn't on the line. This was just a work study job for him. Administering employee discipline was something she had never bargained for. Sarah would have to get some advice from William.

John sidled up next to her with Lonnie in tow. He softly laid his hand on her shoulder. "You mad, Sawah?"

"No, John, I'm fine," she lied. She squeezed his hand. "So you liked church?"

"Yep! Me yike!" John prompted Lonnie, "Yonnie, you yike chu'ch?"

Lonnie nodded and smiled.

"That's good. I'll talk to Pastor Conley and see about you going to church every Sunday." If the guys were gone for a couple of hours on Sunday morning it would give Michael a break and he would have a chance to keep the data she needed.

John rubbed his hands together joyfully and giggled. Lonnie copied him.

They all looked up when they heard a loud thump from upstairs. She noticed that Ricky was missing.

As Michael appeared through the café doors with a basket of laundry, Sarah commented, "I heard something upstairs. I think we better check on Ricky."

Michael set the basket on the dining room table and followed her up the steps. John and Lonnie trailed after them.

Sarah pushed open the door to Ricky's room and stopped cold. Ricky stood in the center of his room on top of his bare mattress, a pile of linens nearby. He was naked.

Ricky grinned at them and jerked his body in a shivery spasm.

"Ricky!" Michael shouted.. "What the fuck are you doing?" He grabbed Ricky's arms and jerked him off the mattress.

Sarah was paralyzed. Physically manhandling a nude client was something else she had not anticipated. She was suddenly thankful Michael was here.

"You've got to put this mattress back on the bed and then make it, you big shit, I mean jerk." Michael wrapped his arms around Ricky from behind, grasped his hands and forced them to close around the mattress. Together they hauled the mattress back onto the bed frame.

"Now the sheets," Michael moved Ricky's arms around the pile of bed coverings.

Sarah found herself helping to separate the sheets from the blankets, but then stopped and shook her head. "He has to get dressed first. I just can't do this when he's naked, Michael. Would you help him?" Her voice was conciliatory.

They found Ricky's clothes in a pile in the corner. Michael tried to get Ricky to put his underwear on by himself, but Ricky wouldn't take them. They knew he could do it because he had dressed himself every morning so far. Michael hooked the underwear over Ricky's dangling hand.

Instead of putting them on, Ricky thrust his hips forward slightly and started to pee. A high-pressure stream arched outward toward Sarah and instantly began to form a puddle on the hardwood floor.

Sarah jumped back. "Oh my God! Stop that, Ricky!" she yelled.

Ricky kept peeing. The river ran toward the hallway carpet.

Panicked, Sarah snatched the sheet and threw it onto the little lake before it reached the doorway.

Ricky continued to pee.

"Michael, do something!"

"Me?" Michael threw his hands up in exasperation. "Hell, do what?"

"Make him stop!" she cried, "Ricky, stop that!"

On impulse, Michael reached out and grabbed Ricky's penis, clamping off the flow.

"Uh, well ..." Sarah hesitated but couldn't think of anything else to suggest. "Okay, let's take him to the bathroom." She ran down the hall, opened the bathroom door and flipped up the toilet seat.

Michael led Ricky, penis first and wide-eyed, down the hall into the bathroom.

"Oh, my gosh," Sarah groaned. "I can't believe we're doing this!"

"We?" Michael shot. He positioned Ricky in front of the toilet, side-stepped and let go. The build-up of pressure sent a blast whizzing across the wall like a loose fire hose.

"Fuck!" Michael held his wet hand in the air in disgust.

The stream gradually abated. Ricky mumbled something unintelligible then turned around and stared at Sarah. No smile this time. He was trembling.

Sarah yelled at Ricky, fighting back tears of rage. "Why would you do that? That's bad! Very bad, Ricky!"

"He did it on purpose because we were making him work," Michael said, washing his hands repeatedly.

"That's probably it," Sarah agreed. "We have to consequate him."

"Say, what?"

"Consequate ... .give him a consequence. He can't get out of work and he can't just pee everywhere."

"Sure, but how are we going to make him do anything? He's got being an asshole down to a fine art. What next, boss?"

"Well, he needs to get dressed first. Then he has to clean everything up." Sarah grabbed a bath towel. Hand-over-hand they forced Ricky to wipe off the bathroom wall and the floor. Clutching several more towels she and Michael made Ricky mop up the bedroom floor, get dressed, and make his bed. When they had finished, Ricky stood with his back to them and stared out the bedroom window. Sarah slumped to the floor against the wall and Michael fell back on the bed. They were both sweating.

Michael looked as drained and frustrated as Sarah felt. She had a twinge of sympathy for him. His first weekend had been a disaster so far.

"So, what are we going to do, boss?" Michael asked. He closed his eyes and leaned his head against the wall.

"I don't know, Michael. I'm new at this, too," Sarah admitted, forcing down the fear of failure that rose in her throat. "I didn't know he was capable of this kind of thing. I'm going to have to work out a more detailed behavior program for him. Until then, you'll have to keep him within sight all the time. We all will."

"Yeah, I figured that part out. I need a smoke. Okay if I take a break, boss?"

"Please don't call me boss ... I don't have all the answers, you know. It's an experiment."

"Sure is." Michael scooted off the bed and disappeared down the hallway.

She had handled that badly. What if Michael quit? She'd be here on her own. "Shit!" she whispered, running her hands through her hair in frustration.

"Shit," Ricky murmured, still staring out the window.

Sarah was startled. "What did you say?"

Silence.

"Did you say something, Ricky?"

Silence.

"So you *can* talk. What do you understand then?" She stared at Ricky's unmoving back. "I think you know exactly what you're doing. You can say swear words, you tear up your room when you're bored and you pee to avoid work. What am I going to do with you?"

She covered her eyes with both hands. *What am I going to do?* she wondered. Self-doubt washed over her. Tears sprang momentarily to her eyes, unbidden. She quickly wiped them away with her sleeve and rose to her feet. This would never do. She had to get a hold of herself.

Gently, Sarah took Ricky by the hand and led him downstairs to the living room where John and Lonnie were watching television. She could hear Michael banging dishes around in the kitchen and she smelled his cigarette smoke.

"John, would you make sure Ricky stays down here?" she asked, fighting back the tears that still threatened to flow.

"Yep," John answered, pointing to Ricky's favorite chair. "Sit down, Wicky!"

Ricky sat and peered innocently up at Sarah. Was that worry in his eyes?

"You be good, Ricky." Sarah said, dabbing the corners of her eyes.

Calling goodbye to Michael, Sarah slipped out of the house. She drove to her favorite beach, walking for over an hour while the tears flowed unhindered down her cheeks. She talked to herself about Michael and her own incompetence, then sent some prayers up, wondering as she did why God should listen to her, the prodigal. She walked, ran, sat, and picked up shells until her tears were spent and she finally formed a plan.

～

Monday morning after the workshop bus pulled away, Sarah, Jana, Barry, and Michael sat around the dining room table. Sarah's planning notebook lay open in front of her.

"Thanks for coming in early, you guys," she said to Jana and Barry. "And thanks for waiting, Michael. I know you're tired."

She glanced at Michael uncomfortably. He sat at the far end of the table, slumped down in his chair. His arms were crossed and he stared blankly at the table surface.

Sarah continued, trying to sound up-beat, "I think we're going to need weekly meetings for a while, at least until we have a better idea of how things are going."

Barry and Jana nodded.

"So ... here's what we're going to do with Ricky when he acts out." She laid out a detailed plan of how to physically guide him into a chair facing the corner for time-out, and how to use his favorite food as reinforcement if and when he followed directions. She explained her data chart. They wouldn't change anything for the first week, just take baseline data. Then they all had to be 100 percent consistent in consequating him according to the plan.

"I know this is going to be challenging for all of us, and we may have to let other things go. Especially Michael, since he's working alone."

She glanced at Michael again. He looked up briefly and met her eyes. She hoped he could see that she was trying to make amends.

"Any questions? I'll model it when we get started, and I'll handle it the first few times until you feel comfortable."

No one had questions.

Sarah swallowed, then continued, "This week we start the satiation program with Mick. We're trying to give him so many pencils that eventually he will get tired of them. It may take awhile, but we have to keep it up for a month at least to see if it's going to work."

Sarah opened a box that sat on the table. "I got the pro shop to donate these golf pencils, so we have plenty. We'll keep them locked up, but you'll need to carry some with you all the time so you can hand them out. For now, we give him pencils to reinforce him, every fifteen minutes if he's not doing something wrong and for sure when he follows directions. When in doubt, give him a pencil."

"Follow directions? That would be a first," Barry remarked.

Jana giggled.

Sarah smiled, encouraged. "Give them to him throughout the day. He can put them in his pockets or stash them in his bedroom—we'll have to pick them up off the furniture, but don't ever take them away from him. Just keep giving him more."

Barry nodded. "Should be interesting."

"Any questions about satiation? I know it sounds counter-intuitive, but it's supposed to work, eventually."

"I think we've got it," Jana said.

"Then for Mick's food stuffing," Sarah continued. "We have to guide his hand in using the fork or spoon while he eats and not let him eat with this hands. He needs to take one bite at a time and put his fork down between bites. Someone will have to be one-on-one with him during meals. As he starts to do more himself, back off the physical prompts. Go from holding his whole hand in yours, to holding his wrist, then his forearm, like that. Hopefully it won't take long."

"Easy for you all," Michael said, "but what about me? I'm supposed to feed him?"

"You're not feeding him." Sarah tried not to sound exasperated. "You're guiding his hand so he doesn't stuff his mouth and choke, and teaching him how to eat appropriately.

"We'll see," Michael said noncommittally.

Sarah's nostril's flared. She felt sweat dampening her armpits. "It's important, Michael, it's part of your job. Now about Peter's shirt ripping."

Barry groaned. "How many shirts has he gone through this week?"

"A lot!" Jana answered. "Maybe twenty?"

"I know," Sarah nodded. "None of us know why he's doing this so we have to experiment. I'd like to try a sensory approach first because he's also so sensitive to being touched. I read that occupational therapists are using brushing to help touch-sensitive people get used to the feel of different textures."

"Brushing?" Jana looked at Sarah quizzically. "Like brushing his hair? It's pretty curly …"

"No, brushing his arms, hands, face, places like that with a soft brush or cloth. I have an appointment with an occupational therapist at the hospital Wednesday to see how they do that. For now, just make him change his shirt."

Sarah explained the data system she had developed to track what happens just before and after shirt ripping. Jana and Barry asked questions to make sure they understood. Michael leaned back in his chair without saying anything.

When Sarah closed her notebook to signal the end of the meeting, Michael finally said, "I don't see how I can do all this by myself on the weekends. I couldn't even keep them in the house."

At least he was talking. Sarah responded, "I know, Michael. I don't think you're going to be able to do everything. Just keeping them safe and occupied is going to have to suffice for now, but that does include helping Mick eat safely. I'm looking for more money to hire someone to help you. It's just that my budget is really tight. First Ricky, then Mick are your top priorities, if that helps."

Michael stretched his arms back, yawning. "Just so you know what not to expect."

Without meaning to, she snapped, "I get it."

He stood up. "So, is that it? I have class in an hour and I'd like to go home and shower. Haven't slept much this weekend."

"Sure," Sarah answered, peeved but trying not to show it. "I'll catch you up Friday night."

Michael picked up his backpack and walked out. Barry and Jana were quiet until they heard the sound of his car engine start up.

"What's up with him?" Barry asked.

"Oh, he's mad at me," Sarah answered sullenly. "We had an issue yesterday. He messed up."

"We're all going to mess up sometimes," Jana said. "Seems to me you're the expert and we need you to tell us if we're doing it right or not."

"I'm no expert," Sarah repeated, appreciating Jana's acquiescence. "Maybe I came down too hard on him." She told them about the church incident.

Barry and Jana laughed in astonishment. Hearing herself retell the story, Sarah couldn't help but join them. "I guess it is pretty funny, now that it's over."

"Never a dull moment around here," Barry said, still chuckling. "That's why I like this job."

"No one would believe us if we told them, would they?" Jana added.

The meeting broke up and Barry and Jana left. Sarah walked around the empty house. She put the new data sheets on the clipboard and checked the journal to see if Michael had written anything. He hadn't. He was going to be a tough one. She wanted to like Michael, to make this work, but there was an edge to him that rubbed her the wrong way. Resolving again to talk to William about him, Sarah thought about their upcoming lunch. Involuntarily, she warmed at this thought.

Chapter 10
Ricky

After the first few days at the workshop, John fell easily into the routine. Every day he put Lonnie's and his backpacks in their locker, then walked Lonnie to his work station. Within two weeks Lonnie was folding paper on Betsy's row. Because he liked everything perfect, he was good at making just the right folds and putting them carefully into the envelopes. He refused to lick the edges so he used a wet sponge. Lonnie wasn't very fast, finishing only a small box every day, but at least he was working. John was proud of him.

The workshop supes were nicer to the workers than the techs had been at Larkspur. John always made it to his worktable before the buzzer now. Each day he filled more boxes than the day before. Frank seemed pleased and left him alone for the most part. When Frank walked by, John tensed up, afraid that he might get in trouble again. Then he would remember that even if he got in trouble, all he had to do was stay a little late. He began to relax more each day.

The little time-out room by the dummy circle was the only scary place in the workshop—with its small window and heavy door it reminded John of his nightmares of Cadby. At first, even though all Mick had to do was follow directions at the dummy circle, he went to the time-out room many times a day. But now Mick could do a real job, emptying containers of electrical wires that needed stripping. He was learning to pull the wires apart, too. When John saw him working, he shook his head in disbelief.

Ricky and Peter were mostly at the dummy circle learning to follow directions, but sometimes the supes tried to get them to do work. Ricky's arms had to be moved for him as the supes tried to get him to put bolts and nuts into a container, like John did. Peter was working on not hitting himself, sitting, standing, clapping, and raising his hands when the tech told him to. John figured he would never be able to have a real job.

Within two days, John had convinced Betsy to sit by him and Lonnie at lunch. Now he worked up enough gumption to ask Betsy, "You hab boyfwend'?"

"No. I never got a boyfriend," she said, still chewing. "You have a girlfriend?"

"Uh ..." Momentarily he thought about Rochelle, but she seemed far away now. "Not now. You be my gewfwend?" John reached over and covered her hand with his.

She looked at him and smiled shyly. "Okay. I guess so."

"Fa' out!" John shouted, leaning over to give her a hug. He nudged Lonnie and they gave each other a high-five. "Me got gewfwend, Yonnie!"

The warning bell rang. John kissed Betsy's cheek before jumping up to rush back to work. She didn't kiss him back, but she smiled again and didn't wipe her cheek off.

That afternoon, as John's hands automatically filled the plastic boxes with bolts, he noticed Ricky acting up at the dummy table. Ricky had kept silent at the workshop until now, and though he didn't do any work on his own, he hadn't done anything bad, either. But this afternoon he must have gotten tired of having someone move his arms for him. Ricky had grabbed Mick, holding his arms twisted behind his back like a cop nabbing a robber. Mick's face was contorted in pain.

One supe tried to pull Ricky's hands off Mick while another grabbed Ricky around the chest. When Ricky let loose, Mick collapsed on the floor, a spray of pencils and pencil splinters sprinkling around him. He scrambled swiftly to pick them up and tried to bite Ricky's leg before two supes dragged Ricky to the time out room and slammed the door.

As the heavy door banged shut John, who had stood up to watch, quickly sat down. Beside him, Laurie-the-Greeter sat, too. They both glanced around for Frank but he must have been on a break.

Blind Eileen asked John, "What's happening," her fingers still counting and filling boxes as if they worked on their own. John knew by now that she really couldn't see, because he had watched her eyes and waved his hand under her nose with no reaction many times. She sure could hear well, though. She could hear what people were saying across the room and noises outside that John didn't notice, and she had heard the scuffle at the dummy circle.

"Wicky, him bad. Him hu't Mick," John answered, dumping a handful of bolts onto his table.

"Who's Ricky?" she asked.

"Him yive at Sawah's, yike me. Him bad." John set the bolts on the little circles.

"That's too bad," she said.

Frank strolled by John's work station and stopped in front of him. John's heart began to beat faster and he worked swiftly without looking up.

"John, you're doing a good job," Frank said quietly.

John glanced up briefly. Frank wasn't smiling, but somehow John could tell he was happy anyway. "You've improved a lot and I'm thinking of advancing you to another job, one that will be more challenging for you. What do you think?"

"Okay." John was afraid to ask any questions and just kept working.

"Maybe the carburetor assembly," Frank said, talking more to himself than to John. He tapped John's table absently with his pencil. "That has twelve steps and takes some precision. With training, I think you could handle that."

John didn't respond. He didn't know what a carburetor was, but it sounded hard.

"We'll see how you do over the next couple of weeks. Keep up the good work." Frank walked on, tapping each worker's table with his pencil as he passed.

The final bell rang and everyone jumped up. John got his and Lonnie's things from the locker, then found Betsy. He helped her put on her jacket and walked with her outside.

"You hab good day?" he asked, petting her shoulder softly.

"Yep. You?" She smiled up at him and held his hand.

With this, John's heart felt warm and mushy. To keep the conversation going, he said, "Yep. Wicky got in twoubo'. Go time out. Him bad." He shook his head and looked around to see if Ricky was out yet.

"I know. I saw him. You don't like Ricky, John?"

"Nope. Him bad." John frowned. "Me yike you, Bessy!"

She grinned, her mouth a little crooked. John thought it was cute. "I know. I like you, too."

A car pulled up to the curb and honked. "Gotta go." Betsy opened the door and climbed into the backseat. John saw a scruffy looking man and a skinny woman in the front seat. They yelled something at Betsy that John couldn't catch as she shut the door. Betsy turned and waved at him through the window.

John waved back. "Me yove you, Bessy," he whispered as the car sped away.

John loved staying at Sarah's house. At first he was afraid that if he made a mistake or if Lonnie was in his "no" mood or tied up his socks, they might have to go back to Larkspur. But as the weeks passed, he began to feel at home at Sarah's. He liked how he could go anywhere in the house without asking and how Sarah and Jana treated him like a grown-up. He liked sharing a room just with Lonnie. They both got used to the dark bedroom in just a few days, though John kept the door open so Lonnie wouldn't be scared. In their free time John helped Lonnie act out their favorite TV shows, dressing up and using household items for props. They never got yelled at for borrowing things from other rooms. These were John's favorite times, moments of abandoning himself to his imagination. Thoughts of Larkspur came less and less often.

Sarah taught him new household chores, such as vacuuming the carpets and mopping the kitchen floor. If John didn't do the work just right, she took his hands and showed him how, encouraging him until he got it right. He liked her touch and her sweet girl-smells, and sometimes he pretended to forget so she would show him again.

Some chores were hard, like separating the laundry. At Larkspur, he threw everything Mark gave him into the washer.

But here, Sarah wanted him to separate whites from colors, only some things with colors on them she called white, while other things with white on them she called colored. He just couldn't get it right. Like at Larkspur, his favorite part of laundry was turning the washer on and hearing the gush of water rush in.

After supper each evening, all the guys—they weren't called boys anymore—worked on what Sarah called grooming and leisure skills. It turned out that grooming meant taking a shower, brushing their teeth, and combing their hair every night. John didn't mind, but some of the other guys had trouble. Sarah often waited for Barry to come for the sleepover shift before tackling Ricky's shower. She told Jana she needed a witness, whatever that meant.

When Lonnie got in a "no" mood, all they did was tell him to take a break and cool down. Lonnie was especially good at some chores like pushing in all the chairs at the eating table and straightening things up, but other chores he just didn't like. When he balked, Sarah would gently pull him by the hand and show him the candy he would get when he finished. Lonnie got used to doing what she asked and hardly ever had "no" moods.

Peter, meanwhile, spent his free time pacing back and forth in front of the big front window in the dayroom. He would stop and look outside, rock and flap his hands, then pace some more. When it was his turn to do a chore he rocked his way over to where he was supposed to go. Jana or Sarah had to coax him through every step of the job without touching him. The one job Peter was good at, after he got used to working, was matching the plates and cups to the circles on the placemats. He did that perfectly. But when he finished, he often stole out into the front entry or upstairs and ripped a shirt apart. At first, Sarah and Jana made him put on a new shirt, but one night when he ripped three shirts in a row, they just left the ripped shirt on him until bedtime. They put a box in his room for all the ripped shirts. Jana said her mother-in-law was going to fix them. They started rubbing his arms with different things every night, like a soft plastic brush, a toy that vibrated, and pieces of different kinds of fabric. This was supposed to make him stop ripping his shirts.

Mick loved the pencils, but they didn't help him work. Sarah and Jana gave him pencils for every little thing, but all Mick did was fill his pockets, his bed, even the waist band on his underwear. He kept searching for more, and now that there were so many around the house, he could usually find them under the sofa cushions, on the floor, almost anywhere. When Jana asked Sarah how many pencils it would take until he got tired of them. Sarah just shrugged and said they'd have to give it a couple more weeks.

Mick was learning to eat better, though. He hadn't choked in a while and now all Sarah had to do was sit beside him and touch his forearm between bites. He growled a little at her, but he chewed and swallowed each bite before taking the next. Sarah and Jana had to help him do his chores, of course, but he was starting to do part of the work by himself.

Ricky, however, just got worse. He was sneaky and did bad things when no one was looking. At first, he did harmless but irritating things like bumping into John or Lonnie when they walked by. But soon he started being mean, hitting or sticking his foot out to trip them. He touched and slapped Peter and made him scream, and tried to steal Mick's pencils, darting away so that Mick got blamed for spilling them on the floor. He sneaked upstairs and body-slammed the walls, shaking the house. Sarah and Jana seemed very upset when Ricky acted up and they spent a lot of time holding his arms behind him and pushing him into a chair for time-out. He was supposed to get candy for being good, but he hardly ever got any. John tried to stay far away from Ricky.

By now, the weather had turned a bit warmer, and John and Lonnie liked to go out into the fenced backyard after dinner to sit at the picnic table and pretend they were camping out. One evening when they came back in, they found Sarah at the eating table writing numbers in a big book.

"Hi, you guys," Sarah said without looking up. "How is it out there? Nice evening, isn't it? I think spring is coming."

"Yep," John said. "Us go campin', catch bear."

"Wow! I didn't know we had bears in the back yard." She kept working.

"What you do, Sawah?" he asked.

"Just finishing the budget."

John pulled out chairs at the table and they sat down. "What budget mean?" Lonnie sat down slowly and wrapped his legs into a pretzel shape, balancing on the chair. He chewed noisily on his tongue.

"It's the money we need to buy groceries and pay our bills." She kept punching numbers into a little machine and then writing them down.

The thought of money reminded John that he had not received his pay for working at Cloverdale. "Sawah, us no git Ba'hawa bucks." He signed, "money," and pretended to stuff it in his pocket.

Sarah finally looked up, twisting the tiny pencil in her fingers. "Oh, money. No, you don't get Balhalla bucks anymore. You get a paycheck every month. We've been putting it in the bank for you, but pretty soon we're going to start giving you pocket money. In fact, I was going to start a money program with you, John. I'll teach you how to buy things at the corner store."

"Sto'e? Buy candy?" John's eyes got wide.

"Sure, whatever you want. We can do that this evening since we need milk for breakfast anyway. Oh, that reminds me," she set down her pencil and reached into a drawer behind her, pulling out a shoebox. "Since you're here I'd like you to do something for me. This is a counting box."

The counting box contained many sets of objects fastened together with rubber bands and grouped into plastic bags. Sarah poured a bag of buttons onto the table.

"Let's see how high you can count," she said, pointing to the buttons.

"One, two fwee ..." He only got to five before he made a mistake.

Sarah stopped him and they started over. Sarah pointed to each button and counted as John followed. They counted together many times in a row until John finally said all ten by himself. He felt proud. Cookie had tried to work with him on his numbers but most often she would have to stop and go help someone. John never did learn to count very far.

"Okay, thanks, John," Sarah said, giving him a friendly pat. "We're done for now. Relax for about half an hour and then we'll go to the store."

She picked up her pencil again and punched more numbers into the little machine. "Jana's in the kitchen. You can have a cookie if you want."

He and Lonnie got their cookies and settled onto the sofa. John asked Jana if they could listen to Barry's records. The Beatles were Barry's favorite group. John loved to stare at the pictures on the album cover. The Beatles had long hair and funny clothes.

Jana put a record on for them and John pulled Lonnie to his feet to dance. After two songs, John had an idea. "Yet's do show." He grabbed Lonnie by the hand. "Us pway Beato's. Come on."

Leading Lonnie by one hand and tucking the album cover under his arm, they tromped upstairs. When they came downstairs with their suitcases, Sarah was just shoving her number book into a drawer.

"What's this?" she asked. "What are you guys up to?"

"Do show," John announced. "Come on!" He pointed to the sofa and handed Sarah the album cover. "Sit."

Jana emerged from the kitchen with Ricky in tow, wiping her hands on a dishtowel. "Am I missing something?" she asked.

Mick, who was lurking around Sarah eyeing her pencil pocket, followed and sat down on the floor. Peter sped up his flapping and backed into the entry, away from everyone else.

"Us Beato's. Wock 'n Wo'." John sat Lonnie down on a chair with the guitar and reminded him about strumming. He cleared his throat and nodded toward the record player. Jana jumped up and put the needle on the record.

When the music started John sang loudly, his voice warbling up and down the scale as he tried to mouth the words. He strummed his suitcase in a frenetic rhythm while Lonnie slowly moved his hands in imitation of John. When the song was over, he and Lonnie bowed.

Jana and Sarah laughed and applauded. Mick clapped briefly before sliding away along the floor. Even Ricky clapped momentarily, a strange sneer marring his face.

"I'm not sure how much of this we should encourage," Sarah whispered to Jana. They both shrugged and Sarah said, "What the heck. That was very creative, John."

"Good show," Jana agreed.

John bowed again, a joyful grin on his face.

Just then there was a knock at the front door. Everyone turned to look.

"I wonder who that is." Sarah bounced up and opened the door. John set down his suitcase guitar and followed.

On the porch two white-haired women stood close together clutching their purses. One of them held a clipboard under her arm.

"Hi! Can I help you?" Sarah asked.

"Yes, you can," said the heavy-set woman. She didn't smile.

"I am Mrs. Hanover. I live across the street." She pointed to the house where John had seen someone standing in the window several times. "And this is Mrs. Rockmont, also from the neighborhood."

"Nice to meet you. I'm Sarah Richardson." Sarah shook their hands.

"Hi!" John said. "Me Don." He extended his hand toward them.

Mrs. Hanover cleared her throat and pulled out her clipboard, pretending not to see John's hand. He lowered it and moved behind Sarah to watch over her shoulder. Something was wrong. They didn't look happy.

"Would you like to come in?" Sarah offered, opening the door wider and moving aside. "You're our first neighborhood guests."

"No, thank you," Mrs. Hanover replied sharply. "I saw you moving in and I just want to know what's going on here. Is this your family?"

"Well, actually, I don't live here myself. But I'm the manager. This is a group home."

"Group home? What does that mean?" asked Mrs. Hanover, glancing at Sarah over her glasses.

Mrs. Rockmont peered past John trying to look inside the house. Behind them Peter had resumed his flapping and Jana quickly moved to shoo him out to the kitchen.

"Well, this is a University research project. We have five men living here in a supervised home setting."

"What's wrong with them?" Mrs. Hanover's face was turning scarlet.

Sarah's voice changed. "Um... I can't disclose that information, but as you can see they have developmental disabilities."

"You mean they're retarded," Mrs. Hanover said curtly. "I've seen them leaving on that bus and I was afraid that's what was going on."

Sarah stiffened and reached back to hold onto John's arm. Now he knew something was wrong.

"You know, this is a very respectable neighborhood," Mrs. Hanover continued. "Up until now, all the neighbors have gotten along just fine. Something like this has never happened around here. I have to tell you we are not happy about it."

"We?" Sarah's voice was no longer friendly.

"The whole neighborhood!" Mrs. Hanover held out her clipboard and showed it to Sarah. "Most of the neighbors have signed this petition. I've checked the city code and this is an R-1 zone, which means ..." she flipped to the next page on her clipboard and read, "single family dwellings only. Individuals who are not related to each other are not allowed to live in the same residence."

"I'm sorry you feel that way," Sarah retorted. "These men have no family. They are supervised around the clock. You and your ... neighbors have nothing to worry about."

Ricky came up behind Sarah, though she didn't see him. He stood beside John staring at the women on the porch. He jerked his body and made a terrible face at her.

Mrs. Hanover's eyes widened as she caught his expression, "And I say we do have something to worry about!" She was almost shouting now. "I've lived here for thirty-two years and my property value has increased every year. You can't just move in a bunch of ... of ... imbeciles and ruin our neighborhood. You have no right!"

Sarah's jaw tensed. Her voice sounded funny to John. "These men have just as much right as you to live in the community. You would probably like for them to be locked away in institutions where you don't have to see them or even know they exist. Well, they do exist. They are people, too!"

Mrs. Hanover stepped back and gasped. "Well!"

Ricky stuck his tongue out at her. John knew this wasn't helping Sarah and he pushed Ricky away from the doorway.

Mrs. Rockmont stammered, "What, what we mean to say is, we, we have many older people living around here and, and we need to feel safe. You understand." She seemed nicer than Mrs. Hanover.

Sarah's voice quieted, "You are in no danger, if that's what you're worried about."

Ricky tried to get back to the door but John pushed him farther into the living room and held him there. Ricky socked him in the chest. John grunted but held his ground.

"No danger?" Mrs. Hanover squeaked. "Who knows what these types will do? Why, every day in the paper there are reports of perverts and strange people doing all kinds of things. We simply won't have it here, that's all."

"They're not perverts, Mrs. Hanover, and we're here to stay. We would like to be good neighbors, but you have to give us a chance."

"I don't have to give you a chance ..."

"I'm afraid you just have to accept it." Sarah began to shut the door. "There's nothing you can do."

"I can do something about it and I will!" Mrs. Hanover shouted. "I will contact my lawyer."

John heard the women's footsteps march off the porch.

Sarah shut the door and turned to Jana who stood behind her. "Can you believe that?" Sarah's face was contorted into a frown.

"You mad, Sawah?" John asked, letting go of Ricky and moving close to put his arm over Sarah's shoulder. "Sawah, you okay?"

"It's all right, John," Sarah squeezed his hand. "Nothing to worry about."

Lines creased Jana's forehead, too. "I can't imagine why they would say those things. What's wrong with them?"

Sarah's eyes were watering, "They want their neat little lives in their neat little neighborhood. What a..." She paused.

"Bitch?" Jana glanced around at the guys. "Can they really do anything, to, you know, make us ...?"

"No." Sarah cleared her throat and sniffed. "No, I don't think so. I'll call William tomorrow and we'll figure this out."

"Or we could kill them with kindness, bake some cookies, pull some weeds," Jana suggested following Sarah into the living room. "Maybe after awhile they'll just realize we're all right."

"Maybe. We'll see." Sarah leaned her hands on the back of the armchair. "Okay, it's time for grooming. After grooming we have a new counselor coming over. He's going to work weekends with Michael, all day Saturday and Sunday afternoons."

"New tech?" John asked.

"Yes, but we call ourselves counselors, remember? His name is Todd."

"Todd," John repeated. Sounded nice.

Sarah clapped her hands. "Jana is going to start with Mick and then Peter."

Jana corralled Mick and led him toward the stairs. He growled at her even though she gave him a pencil for coming with her. He had so many in his pockets and hands that she had to squeeze the new pencil in between his thumb and forefinger.

John shook his head. Dummy.

Sarah called up to Jana, "Will you be okay here for a few minutes while I take John and Lonnie to the store? We won't be long."

"Sure," Jana called from the top of the stairs. "Just send Ricky up here so I can watch him."

After shutting Ricky safely in his room, Sarah came down, put on her jacket, and said, "Come on John and Lonnie. We're going to walk to the neighborhood market. It's only a couple of blocks."

They donned their coats and stepped onto the porch. John's heart beat fast with excitement. He glanced across the street at Mrs. Hanover's house, but the shades were pulled tight.

The sky was a greenish blue changing to a red glow where the sun had disappeared beyond the trees at the end of their street. John and Sarah walked side by side down the sidewalk, slowing to match Lonnie's lagging pace.

"John," Sarah said, clutching her jacket around her chest, "we're going to keep working on counting and I'm going to teach you to handle money so you can go to the store by yourself and buy things we need. How does that sound?"

John straightened up, feeling as if Sarah had made him more grown up by what she said. He licked his lips to get ready to say something, but mixed up feelings tumbled around in his brain so that he couldn't think of what to say. He didn't know how to tell Sarah how happy he felt. He snuck a peek at her face, all golden and soft in the waning light. The sweet smell of her fragrance floated around them. John's heart thumped with pleasure.

She chatted lightly as they strolled. "You're here to learn to be more independent, and I think this is something you can do, don't you?"

"Yep."

"I'm also thinking I'll teach you to ride the city bus to work," she continued.

"Uh huh!" John thought about the big, white buses the smart ones at work rode home.

"We probably won't start that until later this summer, but I think you can do it on your own. I'm very proud of how well you're doing, John. And Lonnie. He's doing very well, too."

John had never felt this contented. He slung his arm over Lonnie's neck and hugged him. "Us good, Yonnie!"

Sarah laughed. "You are good!"

When they arrived at the Neighborhood Market, Sarah stopped outside and gave John several dollar bills, real money.

"Go in and find the milk. Take one gallon and then you and Lonnie can each pick out a candy bar. Give them to the woman at the counter. She'll give you some change back. I'll be close by if you need me. Go on."

Nervously, John motioned for Lonnie to follow him inside. A little bell dinged as the door opened. Sarah stayed near the entrance. There were two other customers in the store. John resisted the urge to talk to them. He walked through the aisles until he came to glass doors with milk, butter and beer behind them. He made Lonnie hold the glass door open while he pulled out a gallon of milk. Walking to the front of the store, he and Lonnie picked out some candy. They stood behind a man buying baby diapers and cigarettes.

John glanced at Sarah. She nodded and pointed to her pocket. John pulled out the dollars. When it was their turn,

John set the milk and candy down and slapped the money onto the counter beside it.

The clerk was an older woman with curly hair and a big bosom. She looked at them and then glanced at Sarah. "Did you find everything all right?" she asked. She smiled pleasantly.

"Yep. Us need milk." John tried to think of something else to say, but nothing came to him.

"Very good, then," said the friendly clerk, taking the money, punching some buttons, and giving John some coins. "Do you need a bag?"

John looked back at Sarah. She shook her head.

"Nope."

"Thank you. See you next time." The clerk smiled and pushed the milk toward him.

John picked up the jug, handed Lonnie his candy, and stuck his own into his pocket. He walked nonchalantly out of the door, Lonnie trailing close behind.

"Good job, guys," Sarah laughed. "You did great!"

John gave her a high-five and so did Lonnie.

The sky was a deep blue now and streetlights had come on. Light from the store shone out onto the sidewalk.

Sarah picked up the pace. "We better hurry because Todd will probably be waiting for us. He's going to meet everyone tonight and then he'll be back tomorrow to be with you all and Michael for the weekend."

"Him nice?" John asked.

"Yes, you'll like him."

John swung the milk back and forth as they walked briskly, feeling the cool weight of it in his hand. Lonnie followed behind, hurrying as much as he could in the growing darkness.

"Sawah?" John asked, hesitating because he was afraid he might not like the answer to his question. "Me stay you house?"

"Yes, John, you're staying. Are you worried about that?"

John shrugged. He had never been sure how long he was going to stay at Sarah's.

"You're not going back to Larkspur," Sarah said firmly. "You both live here from now on."

They walked the rest of the distance without talking. The only sounds were the call of a seagull overhead and the shuffling of Lonnie's feet behind them on the sidewalk.

A loud thump woke John with a jolt. He opened his eyes and pulled the covers off his face. The house was dark. A faint light outlined the partially closed door to his room. Maybe the noise came from the inside world. John closed his eyes.

There it was again, a heavy "whomp" followed by a deep groan. Someone must be sick or hurt. John sat up. He looked at the dark lump that was Lonnie in the bed across from him. It was still. John rose. He had to pee, anyway.

From Mick's room, he heard the moan again.

John heard footsteps on the stairs, and turned to see Michael ascending in his T-shirt and boxers. His eyes were bloodshot. "What the hell's going on?" he whispered.

"Me not know."

"Who's moaning?" Michael rubbed his face vigorously with both hands.

John pointed to Mick's room. He watched over Michael's shoulder as he pushed open the door slowly. Unable to see anything in the dark room, Michael switched on the light. John recoiled at the sudden brightness.

A few moments passed before John could make out the figure standing in the middle of the room. It was Ricky. Mick's mattress had been pulled onto the floor and Ricky stood naked atop it. From underneath, Mick's arms flailed and he muttered, "Bitechew! Kick you!"

"Ricky, what the fuck?" Michael croaked, "Get off there!"

Michael snatched Ricky's arm and jerked him off the mattress. He lifted the corner and Mick crawled out panting and mumbling something unintelligible. Mick stumbled off toward the bathroom, holding his crotch.

"Ricky, you bastard!" Michael jerked Ricky to the corner and pressed his face against the wall. "What do you think you're doing? You were hurting Mick! You are such an asshole!"

Ricky's face was mashed against the wall but he managed to croak, "Muthafucka."

"Him say bad wo'd!" John said, remembering that Michael had said that bad word, too.

Michael pressed Ricky harder, twisting his arm behind his back. "Shut up, Ricky! Sometimes I feel like I'm babysitting a bunch of little…"

John could see the muscles in Michael's jaw tighten. His face turned crimson as he held Ricky against the wall for several minutes without saying more. Finally, he took a deep breath and loosened his grip. His voice was thick and flat when he spoke. "Pick up the goddamn mattress, Ricky, you son of a bitch."

Ricky's arms went limp. He grinned unapologetically.

"Pick it up, you fucking idiot!"

Ricky turned his back on Michael.

"Well, shit. It's too late for games." Michael pulled the mattress onto the bed. Mick's sheets and blankets were balled up on the floor. Michael made the bed himself, hastily throwing the sheets over the bed and casting the blanket on top. Tiny pencils were scattered everywhere.

Mick stumbled back into the room, punching at Ricky before bee-lining it for his bed. He noticed the scattered pencils and dove to the floor, desperately picking them up and shoving them into his bed.

Michael turned Ricky around. "See what you've done? You should be cleaning up this whole room... where the hell are your clothes?" Michael kicked through the pile of Mick's clothes that Ricky had dumped onto the floor. "They must be in your room."

He dragged Ricky to the bathroom first to pee, then down the hall to his own room where he switched on the light. Ricky's room was clean and cold, in fact there was hardly anything in the room except his furniture. Even the mattress was bare but no bedding was in sight. John and Michael looked left and right and peered behind the door, finding nothing more.

At the same time, they noticed the wide open window.

"Yook!" John said, pointing. A cool breeze floated in, bringing with it the fresh smell of night sea air.

Michael held Ricky's arm firmly as they approached the window. Leaning over the sill, they looked down together. The streetlight at the corner shed just enough light for them to make out Ricky's clothes and blankets piled in a heap in the yard below the window. His lamp lay on top of the pile, cock-eyed and broken.

John stepped back and gasped. "You bad, Wicky! You big twoubo'!" He shook his finger in Ricky's face. "You bewy bad boy!"

Michael just stared into the yard in silence. Finally, Michael drew his head in. Sweat appeared on his forehead despite the cool breeze flowing through the window. He wiped it off with his free hand. Seething, Michael yanked Ricky into Peter's room and brought him back with some of Peter's clothes. He made Ricky dress in Peter's pants and a ripped shirt.

"John, you can go back to bed." He zipped up Ricky's pants, his hands shaking. "This isn't your problem."

"What you do?" John asked.

"Ricky's going to take care of this mess."

"Me he'p," John said. He wasn't sleepy any more. He wanted to see Ricky get in big trouble.

Together Michael and John hauled up load after load of Ricky's things from the yard. Since Ricky wouldn't actually help, Michael tied Ricky to his waist with two belts hooked together. He made Ricky follow him up and down the stairs, dragging him behind like a reluctant puppy. John and Michael were both panting and sweaty by the time they dumped the last load onto a pile on Ricky's floor.

Michael untied Ricky, threw a blanket on the bed and pushed Ricky onto it without a word. He told John to wait with Ricky while he ran down the stairs. In a few minutes, Michael returned with a hammer and two nails.

John covered his mouth in horror. This was going to be worse than he thought—Michael was going to nail Ricky to the bed!

Instead of nailing Ricky, Michael closed the window and nailed it shut. He nodded for John to follow him out of the room and he shut the door. Michael retrieved a dining room chair and hooked it under the doorknob so Ricky couldn't get out.

"Let's try to get some sleep," he said, his voice gravelly. "Thanks for your help, John. You're my man." He gave John a sleepy high-five and trudged downstairs.

John felt like his legs were made of concrete. He snuck quietly into his room and slipped under the sheet, staring into darkness above. Laying awake, he couldn't stop visualizing the scene again and again, Mick under the mattress, Ricky's empty room, the piles of clothes, the repeated trips up and down the stairs. He was disappointed that Michael hadn't punished Ricky. Ricky deserved to have his ear pulled and to be tied to his bed for the night. That's what the Mean Man would have done, if he didn't outright punch Ricky in the face like he had done to Lonnie.

John closed his eyes and tried to stop thinking about Ricky. Just as he was getting sleepy, a strange smoky smell drifted into his semi-consciousness. John realized he still had to go to the bathroom, so he got up, heavy with fatigue. On his way back to his room, the pungent smoke was even stronger. John crept quietly down the stairs and peeked around the corner into the living room.

Michael sat on the sofa amongst his rumpled sheets watching TV. The volume was turned down low, and Michael's face was faintly lit by the florescent glow. He picked up his cigarette from the ashtray and held it carefully with what looked like tweezers. Holding it to his lips, he sucked deeply. Then he leaned his head back, held his breath for many seconds, and let the smoke drift slowly out of his mouth.

John had never seen that kind of cigarette before. He wanted to ask Michael about it, but he was too tired. Turning back up the stairs, he tip-toed to his room, reminding himself to ask Michael about these funny cigarettes in the morning.

꿈

The ropes pulled tightly against his wrists. John felt the icy cement wall against his cheeks, his face smashed into the corner. Dark fingerprints of dried feces were just inches from his eyes. Hands pushed on his back and shoulders, other hands probed his legs, sending shivers through his frame. He tried to kick and cry out, but he couldn't make a sound. His body began to sink into the cement floor, deeper and deeper. John's heart beat like a drummer gone wild.

"Get away from him!" a woman's voice growled. "It's my turn."

The hands stopped. Heavy footsteps approached. John's breath came in shallow gulps. He grimaced and twisted his head up from the corner of the floor to see who spoke.

It was her! The witch of Cadby! She stood close behind him, feet apart, pounding her club against her hand. Whack, whack, whack. John's heartbeat fell into rhythm with the sound of the thumping club.

"Hey, hey! John! Wake up." A familiar voice and a gentle hand on his shoulder melted the inside world away.

Michael, silhouetted against the hall light, bent over him. "It's okay, man. You were just having a bad dream."

John took a deep breath. He was safe, safe at Sarah's.

Michael crouched beside the bed and whispered, "Ricky probably disturbed you. I just put him back to bed. Again. Why don't you go back to sleep. You still have a couple of hours yet."

Michael left. John shut his eyes. *Bad Ricky,* he thought. *Too bad Ricky didn't live in the inside world instead of here at Sarah's.*

Chapter 11
Barry

The house was quiet by the time Jana donned her backpack to leave for the evening. She covered a yawn with her hand as she said goodnight to Sarah and Barry and slipped out the door.

Lucky her, Sarah thought, she was going to the warm bed of her husband. Sitting at the dining room table Sarah fought back her own yawn. The daily journal lay open in front of her. Barry sat across from her, his head lying on his folded arms.

"Sometimes I can't believe what we do here," he said. "I start to tell my family or other friends about the guys and the weird things they do, and people sort of laugh uncomfortably, or worse, they ask me if I have any funny stories to tell. And then it feels like I'm making fun of them, which isn't what I meant to do, you know?"

"I do know what you mean," Sarah replied. She twirled the pen in her fingers and stared at the half-written page. "I try to explain my dissertation to someone and they stare at me like I'm out of my mind, like why would I bother with something like this? I'm learning to pretty much keep it to myself, except with William, of course."

Barry set his chin on his hands and looked up at her. "So how's it going with your William? Has he put any moves on you yet?"

Sarah scrunched up her face uncomfortably. "He's not my William. I've been meeting with him every week, first at his office, now at Rennie's. We talk about the project and he's very encouraging ... he really believes that what I'm doing is important."

"Oh, I'm sure he does. He'll get his name on your research when you publish." Barry sat up and leaned his chair back on two legs. "That's the way it works, doesn't it?"

Sarah shrugged. "Sometimes. But it's not just that. He honestly wants to see people with disabilities get out of institutions and into the community. It was his philosophy that led me to this project, after all."

"We have to give him credit for that." Barry clasped his hands behind his head. "So why hasn't he come to visit yet?"

"I don't know why, but he will. He's very busy." She paused. "You just don't like him, do you?"

Barry shrugged.

Sarah found herself getting defensive. "Have you ever taken a class from him? He's brilliant."

"No, I've just heard the rumors. And I've seen the way he looks at you." Barry raised one eyebrow provocatively and winked, mocking William. "He's attracted to you and you're ignoring it."

"Of course I'm ignoring it, if it's true, which it's probably not. I don't want to..." She hesitated, tugging at a loose hangnail.

"Be his woman on the side?" Barry supplied.

"Well, yes. Definitely not that." Sarah pushed the curls that hung limply across her cheeks behind her ears. Just talking about William like this caused her breathing to become shallow and she chided herself for being so emotional. He was nothing to her except a mentor. At least that's what she kept telling herself.

"I don't blame you for caring what he thinks of you." Barry's gaze was caring. "But he's still a letch. Power corrupts."

Sarah's heart quickened. She looked away. "I can't talk badly about him, Barry. He's my mentor. He's the head of my dissertation committee. He basically holds my career in his hands."

"I know. That's what makes his womanizing so despicable."

Sarah paused, then admitted sheepishly, "It kind of scares me. I don't want it to get to the point where ..." She stopped.

"What?"

"Where I can't refuse."

"Did he say something overt?" Barry tipped his chair back down to the floor and leaned forward, clearly wanting to hear the dirt.

Sarah wrestled with herself before she spoke. Barry was her employee, yet he was also a fellow graduate student. He didn't run in her circle of Department of Education majors, taking all his classes on the far end of campus.

She took a breath. She needed to tell someone. "You have to promise not to say anything."

"Sure. Who would I tell?" Barry looked steadily into her eyes.

She bit her lip. "The last time we met at Rennie's I was telling him about Michael and Ricky and asking for advice. I was so frustrated and unsure what to do, and I couldn't help but tear up a little. That makes me so mad! It's terribly unprofessional and demeaning."

"And he just hates to see a woman cry, I bet." Barry mimicked a sympathetic pose.

"Well, yes. I don't have anybody to talk to about this stuff so it just spilled out. He took my hand and told me I could call him anytime I was upset."

"And let me guess, he will rush right over to your apartment to make you feel better." Barry indignantly drummed the table with his fingers.

"Not exactly." She hesitated, unsure if she should tell him everything. These last couple of months she had grown to trust Barry. He always seemed to have her good at heart. His brown eyes melted her resolve. "But he did give me his home number and suggested he meet me at my apartment this weekend and talk about everything over a glass of wine."

"I knew it! What a creep!" Barry slapped the table and shook his head disgustedly.

"Then when I came to leave he gave me a big hug. It was too long, you know? I tried to pull away, but it was awkward. I didn't want to offend him. He has been so supportive."

"He's good at supportive." Barry smirked. "What a schmuck! You don't have any more doubts, do you?"

"I told myself he was just empathetic and caring ... but I don't believe myself anymore."

"Good instincts, Sarah, though kind of slow." Barry leaned forward on the table and said seriously. "So he's made his move. What are you going to do?"

"I don't know what to do!" Sarah fought back tears. "I feel trapped. If I push him away, he could pull back his support, if not fully, at least subtly. But I also can't just capitulate, either. I'm not like that. What should I do?"

"Run, Sarah, run away fast. He's schmoozing you into his bed, just like the umpteen other beautiful grad students. And you're right, you're not like them. You don't need to achieve that way."

Beautiful? Sarah filed that away. "This just isn't fair." Unwittingly, tears stung her eyes. She dabbed at the corners with her sleeve, trying to make the gesture look like she was just tired.

Barry picked up on it and his voice softened. "Sarah? I didn't mean to make you upset."

"It's not you," she said, sniffing. "It's ... it's just that I need his support. I need his advice. I can't walk away from him now but I also don't want to get involved with him. This is all so crappy!" She covered her eyes as the tears flowed.

"Sarah?" Her name flowed like silk from his mouth, "I'm really sorry about William. You're working hard here and doing a great job, and he is taking advantage of your position. These are tough cookies you've got and nobody has the answers on how to handle them. Not even Lord William. And then you also have to deal with Jana and me—and then there's Michael. I couldn't do what you're doing but I admire you for it. I have confidence in you. You're going to make the right decisions, with or without the great doctor."

"Do you think so?" She wiped her eyes and sat up straight, composing herself. "Sometimes I wonder if I'm just looking for fame, or trying to rescue people... my greatest fear is that I'm just trying to take revenge on my mother for not saving my brother."

Barry held up both hands in a gesture to stop her. "Whoa, there. You just took a turn I can't follow. Save your brother? Take revenge on your mother?"

"I'm sorry. I shouldn't drag you into my family problems. It has nothing to do with the guys, or you." Sarah shook her head. "I'm just confused right now."

Barry shifted in his chair and was silent for a moment. "Do you want to talk about it? I'm not going anyplace. In fact, I have all night."

She glanced at him, "Ha ha."

"We all have our own family issues," he said encouragingly.

Sarah debated with herself again. How much should she tell Barry? Where were the lines between boss and friendship? She didn't think about it for long. The words began to pour out.

"Okay. My mom died four years ago of cancer ..."

"Oh, I'm very sorry," he said quietly.

She shrugged it off. "We didn't get along that well. Always irritating each other. Maybe we were too much alike... stubborn. Shortly before she died, she said she had to tell me something, just like in the movies. I thought, oh, she's going to tell me I'm adopted or that she had an affair, or that I came from a long line of child molesters or something. But instead, she told me I had a brother. A half-brother, that is. She had a son when she was seventeen, long before she met my dad. Can you imagine her never telling me this before?"

"Wow! Maybe she was scared to tell you."

"I know. It was a shock. A brother I never knew. My only brother. My only sibling, actually, besides my dad's new family." Her hands were unsteady. She slipped them under the table so Barry wouldn't see, and tried to calm her voice as she continued. "But sadly, the baby was Mongoloid, as she put it, an 'imbecile,' is what the doctor called him. He told her the baby would be hopelessly retarded and would never be able to care for himself. He recommended that she put him away in an institution and forget about the whole mess of being an unwed mother—a terrible shame to her family."

Barry raised his eyebrows in surprise. "Geez, they really used to do that?"

Sarah took a ragged breath, sensing the release. "Some still do that. That's why we have so many people hidden in state institutions like Larkspur. That's why I want to get them out of there." She stopped, having said the words out loud that she had been afraid to admit. "I guess that is why I want to get them out of there."

"Where is your brother now? Have you seen him?"

"He passed away." She steeled herself against the words. "He had a heart murmur, like so many Down Syndrome babies do, and back then they never considered any kind of surgery or anything. She left him there in California, moved to Oregon, met my dad. She never saw him again. And then he passed away." Sarah felt a surge of relief, as if she had plucked a dagger from her chest.

Barry blew his breath out in a low whistle. "Whew! I can see why you have such mixed feelings about all this. And why you would want to rescue some of them. Nothing wrong with that, you know, rescuing people who need to be rescued."

She met his eyes. "Really? I feel like I might be doing this just to get back at my mother, or in some weird way to make it up to my brother. I can't stop thinking about him. It seems like I should have a better reason to put myself and you all through this, not to mention these poor guys who are my guinea pigs."

"Tell me a better reason! It's a good thing to do, for them and for us. Would you feel better if you were just doing it to get published, like William, there?"

Sarah paused. She couldn't hold his gaze. "I suppose you're right. Maybe it doesn't matter so much why we do what we do, as long as it's a worthwhile effort."

They were both silent for a moment.

"I better get going." Sarah pushed back her chair. "You're probably tired and I have some reading to do."

"Sure." Barry stood up with her. "Anything in particular I need to do tonight?"

"Would you mind transferring today's data to the graphs for me? That would save me some time." She looked at him, forcing a smile.

"No problem. I never go to bed before Johnny Carson anyway."

"Okay, thanks." Sarah walked to the entry where her coat and backpack hung from the hall tree. "Thanks for listening, Barry—I didn't mean to burden you with my personal issues."

"Don't worry, Sarah." He squeezed her elbow. "Everybody needs to talk. Some time I'll tell you my warped family history."

Sarah smiled again, his touch a welcome reassurance. "It's a deal. Are you sure you're not in the counseling department?"

Barry laughed. "No one ever accused me of that before!"

She gathered her things and hurried out the door to her car, cursing the tears that flowed from her eyes once again. All the way home she struggled to sort out her feelings—the upsurge of grief over her mother's pain and death, the unforgiveness she knew she harbored, the sense of injustice at never being allowed to know her brother, the relief of sharing her feelings with Barry. And now she had to acknowledge yet another emotion brewing in her chest. There was something about a man who was interested in a girl's feelings. Something very attractive, damn it.

Chapter 12
Shelby's

John hopped off the workshop bus one Friday afternoon in early May and was greeted by Sarah.

"No wo'k tomowow? Ca'toon day?"

"That's right, John. It's Friday. No work tomorrow." Sarah snagged Mick as he came off the bus and steered him toward the house, letting him go up the sidewalk by himself. She said to John, "Take Lonnie inside because we need to hurry with dinner tonight. We're going shopping at the mall."

"Shopping?" John slowed to match Lonnie's sloth-like pace as he lumbered down the sidewalk. "Us go shopping, Yonnie. Buy somepin!"

Lonnie gave John a high-five. Lonnie's shoes slapped noisily on the sidewalk. They were a little too loose now that all his socks had been taken away because he knotted them up hopelessly.

Mick made it to the porch and John heard Jana say to him, "Nice job, Mick, you came straight in." She gave him a tiny piece of paper that he shoved into his pocket as he grunted past her. The pencils had gotten out of hand, Sarah said, when one became embedded in his skin and she had to pull it out with tweezers. A couple of week ago Sarah found out that paper scraps worked just as well.

Ricky stomped down the bus steps and whooshed by John and Lonnie, bumping John with his shoulder again as he passed. John yelled at him, but tried hard to ignore him like Sarah said, which meant not do anything.

Lonnie was so slow today that even Peter rocked by them. Lonnie stopped every few steps to tickle John and say a couple of nondescript words and sign something. By the time John and Lonnie got into the house, Peter stood in his favorite spot by the front window, rocking and flapping madly. John hung up their coats and wandered into the kitchen where Jana was already getting dinner ready. Ricky stood beside her staring at her hands as she cut open a package of hotdogs.

"Hotdogs fo' dinna'?" John asked.

"That's right, John. It's not your turn to help so you can just relax." Jana touched Ricky's elbow and he picked up the package with two fingers, sloppily dumping the hotdogs into a pan of water. He was doing a little bit of work these days.

John retreated to the living room and turned on a record. It was Mick's turn to set the table, and because he wanted the paper scraps, he tried to help. John watched as Mick burst through the cowboy doors with one plate at a time and set it randomly on the table. He swished in and back out with another plate before the cowboy doors even stopped swinging. Mick set each plate right on top of the other one in the center of the table and Sarah handed him a piece of paper each time, even though he wasn't getting it right.

"Mick, now put one plate here," Sarah said, pointing to the large circle on the placemat. She called to John. "Would you help us set the table? We're in a hurry. Ask Jana what food needs to come out."

"Yep." John left Lonnie on the couch and hurried to the kitchen.

"Do you want to start setting the condiments on the table?" Jana asked John as she helped Ricky open a bag of hotdog buns.

"Candy mints?" John asked. He licked his lips, suddenly realizing how hungry he was.

"Condiments are things like mustard, relish, ketchup—things that go with hotdogs. Check the refrigerator door." Jana held Ricky's arms as he took the buns out and set them on a plate.

"Yep. Me do." John took an armful of candy mints to the table, wondering why Jana called them candy when they weren't even sweet.

Sarah was giving Mick cups and pointing to the little circles on the placemats now. Mick seemed to be getting tired of this job. He set the cup on a plate and immediately reached for another paper. Sarah held the paper scrap by the little circle and wouldn't give it to him until he moved the cup to the right place. Mick growled at her under his breath, stuffing the paper into his pocket with the many others. They didn't take up as much space so he could get a lot more in his pockets.

John looked up as the front door opened and Barry slapped his backpack onto the sofa. "Hi everybody!" he called.

"Glad you made it!" Sarah replied, smiling. "Thanks for coming in early again. I wish I could pay you overtime ..."

"Don't worry about it." Barry said cheerfully.

"Barry's going with us to the mall." Sarah explained. "He just can't stay away from you guys, I guess."

"What else would a chemistry student do on a Friday night?" Barry asked. "Well, except drugs, of course."

"Drugs, chemistry, I get it." Sarah laughed. John laughed, too, though he didn't know what was so funny. He noticed that Barry spent a lot of time looking at Sarah lately and he didn't like it. Whenever Barry started chatting with her, John asked Sarah a question. Sometimes she paid attention to John, but other times she just kept talking to Barry. This made John frustrated.

They ate dinner quickly. When they were finished, John and Lonnie cleared the table and Jana stuck the dishes in the dishwasher. They put their jackets back on and hurried out to Jana's and Sarah's cars. John and Lonnie got to ride with Sarah. When Sarah opened the door for John she unexpectedly slugged him in the shoulder.

"Punch buggy," she said.

John rubbed his arm, though it didn't hurt. "Punch buggy?" he repeated.

"Yeah, punch buggy. This is a Volkswagen bug. It's a game. Whenever you see a car like this, whoever notices it first gets to say 'punch buggy.'" Sarah grinned.

Even though he had ridden in her car several times, she had never played this game before. John smiled and tried to punch her back.

She stopped him, "Oh, no! You can only say it if you see the car first!" She pulled the backseat forward and Lonnie and John crawled in. John had to back in, butt-first, and then pull his bad leg with both hands. Barry rode in the front seat.

Sarah and Barry talked the whole way. John tried to butt in, but it was hard to hear from the backseat. Finally, he leaned back and gave up, taking Lonnie's hand for comfort.

After a short drive, they arrived at a big parking lot with more cars than John had ever seen parked together. The mall turned out to be a long string of shops all inside a big building, even bigger than one of Larkspur's wards or Cloverdale workshop.

The shops were lit up brightly and the windows were filled with colorful things for sale. John and Lonnie stared in wonder.

"Stay together, now," Sarah warned, as they gathered just inside the entrance. "If you're good, we will get some ice cream before we leave."

She handed Mick another paper. His pockets were fat with paper and he covered them with his hands to prevent the papers from falling out. Jana looped her arm through Mick's and Sarah led the way.

Walking down the wide center aisle there was so much to look at that Sarah had trouble keeping the guys walking. To keep Lonnie moving, Barry cast his arm over Lonnie's shoulder. Peter trailed so far behind that they often had to stop and wait for him to catch up. He looked at the lights hanging high above and flapped his arms furiously. He didn't look where he was going. Jana had to coach him so he didn't run into the trash cans and benches.

Only Ricky walked confidently beside Sarah as if he had been here before.

"He looks like he's in his element," Barry said, letting go of Lonnie and striding up to walk beside Sarah.

"Amazing, isn't it?" she answered. "You'd swear he was normal ..."

"Whatever that is," they said together, and laughed. John didn't like that they were walking together and he called Barry to come back and hurry Lonnie along. But Barry told John to do that himself and he stayed next to Sarah.

They sauntered past shop windows filled with clothes, shoes, records, and jewelry. John and Lonnie wanted to stop at every window to peer at the thousands of tempting items, but Sarah urged them forward.

"Yook, Yonnie," John said repeatedly, pointing to windows full of photographs or funny looking dolls without heads wearing only their underwear. These were just like the stores on TV.

Jana kept a hand on Mick's arm and gave him a steady stream of paper scraps that he tucked into every available niche, occasionally dropping one and scrambling to the floor to retrieve it.

John tried to get close to Sarah and Barry so he could capture Sarah's attention, but Lonnie was too slow. From several paces back he heard her say, "We got a Cease and Desist order today from the zoning board. The neighbors have turned in their complaint and are challenging our presence in the neighborhood. Wednesday I got a letter from their lawyer saying they would sue us if we didn't leave. How's that for neighborliness?"

"Dammit!" Barry said. He sounded mad. "Those nosey neighbors actually turned us in? What jerks! We can beat them, can't we?"

"I didn't think they were serious," Jana commented, pulling Mick back from a stationary store window. "Here's *your* paper, Mick," she told him and handed him a large piece.

"I don't know. I have a call in to William to see if the university can help us. I don't know anything about zoning laws." Sarah looked around to make sure everyone was with them.

"My uncle is a lawyer," Barry said. "I could ask him."

"That would be helpful ... whatever you can find out."

John moved forward and squished in between Sarah and Barry. "Me yike dis mao," he said to Sarah. "Us buy somepin'?"

"I don't know, John, we'll have to see."

Barry fell back and waited for Peter to catch up. John's ploy had worked! He kept pace with Sarah by dragging Lonnie along behind them. Lonnie wasn't happy about being rushed.

As they meandered down the long corridor, some people paused and to stare at them. John waved back. He tried to talk to some of them, but usually they just looked away. A few children tugged at their mother's sleeves with questions like, "What's wrong with them, mommy?" Barry told John he shouldn't talk to the children because little kids weren't supposed to talk to strangers.

Eventually they came to a big store at the far end of the mall that Sarah called Shelby's. This time they got to go inside and walk among the racks of items on display. When they came to an area full of clothing hanging on circles and stacked on shelves, Lonnie paused by one of the life-sized dolls and shook its hand.

"Hi," he signed and looked carefully at its oddly staring face.

"Not weo, Yonnie," John said, tugging Lonnie away. "Big doll."

They wandered through racks of shirts. Sarah and Jana stopped to hold a couple of shirts up to Mick to see if they fit. While they were busy, a pretty young woman with frizzy hair approached and spoke directly to Ricky, "May I help you?" She smiled sweetly.

Ricky stared at her and grinned.

"Are you looking for something in particular?" she asked. "We have a sale on spring shirts, over there." She pointed to a large rack by a stairway that moved up continually all by itself.

Ricky whispered something and she leaned forward, scrunching her eyebrows together. "I'm sorry, I didn't hear you."

Sarah stepped in. "Um, miss, he doesn't really talk, but thank you for asking. We're just browsing today."

The young woman's face flushed and she stammered, "Oh, I'm, I'm sorry … I thought …" She didn't finish her thought, scurrying swiftly away.

Sarah took Ricky's arm. "You better stick with me, big guy. We don't want someone asking you out on a date."

"Then again, it would be better for us if she took him," Barry said, coming alongside Sarah again.

Sarah laughed. "That poor girl. She was so embarrassed."

"I bet she won't be telling her friends she flirted with a retarded guy," Barry commented.

Jana tried to keep a hold on Mick's arm as they moved through the pants section, but finally he tugged away and slipped to the floor under a rack of jeans.

Jana bent down and said quietly, "Stand up or you get no papers, Mick."

Sarah came up beside her. "This is going to be a problem with this paper thing. It's our only reinforcement and he already has hundreds of them."

"I know. I think it's starting to wear off already," Jana said.

"He likes them but they're not really contingent on the behavior we want, since he gets them for everything." Sarah ran her fingers through her hair. "Let's just pull him out."

"I'll do it," Barry offered. "He squatted and quickly pulled Mick out from under the rack, lifting him to his feet. "We can't do that, Mick," he said firmly.

"Should I give him a paper?" Jana asked Sarah.

"No, not when he doesn't comply with directions," Sarah answered. "I'll have to think this through later. He seems to be satiated on the satiation program."

Just then, Mick lunged for Jana's purse where he knew the papers were kept. He bumped into Peter who had tread too close to them, and Peter fell against the rack of slacks. Awkwardly he twisted back onto his feet, screaming and pounding his head painfully.

Shoppers nearby stopped and stared.

"It's okay, Peter," Sarah said softly, searching in her bag for something. "You're not hurt. It was just an accident." She pulled out a square of terrycloth they had been using to rub his arms with and handed it to him.

Peter hit himself a few more times then took the cloth, flapping it near his eyes. His screaming stopped. He stared up at the lights and began to rock, holding the terrycloth to his face. Miraculously he didn't rip his shirt. Sarah had been making him haul all his ripped shirts to the basement and hang them up every time he ripped one.

"Peter," Sarah said, moving close to him but not touching him. "No rocking here. We rock at home."

After a few more rocks and a couple of head poundings, Peter calmed down and stopped.

A woman, with skin as dark as Peter's and a friendly look of concern on her face, came over to them. "Can I help you at all? Do you need something?"

"Oh, no thanks," Sarah said. "He'll be all right. He just fell and he got upset. Thanks for asking."

The woman smiled in a sad way. John wanted to give her a hug. She reminded him of Cookie, but not as puffy.

"Let's go, guys," Sarah said. She led them away from the pants section, walking slowly so Peter would keep up. He hung onto the square of cloth and followed a few paces behind them, stopping once in a while to hit his head and stare up into the lights.

"Maybe we should head home," Sarah said to Jana and Barry. "This is probably long enough for the first trip. They're starting to lose it."

"I thought of something we need while we're here, though," Barry said. "I can put a new chain and float in the tank of that toilet that keeps running. Shelby's has a hardware section downstairs. Let me pick that up and then we can go."

"Good idea," Sarah agreed. "That will give us a chance to try out the escalator, too." She led them toward the moving stairs.

Lonnie tapped John's shoulder and signed, "Toilet."

"Sawah!" John called loudly, "Yonnie go toiwet."

Sarah winced. "Oh, no. Does anyone know where the restrooms are?"

"They're on the lower floor somewhere," Jana said. "Back by home improvements, I think."

"That's good. That's where we're going anyway. Barry can take a couple of guys and you or I can take Lonnie to the restroom."

Lonnie signed toilet again and grabbed his crotch. Sarah squeezed his shoulder and said, "Hang on, Lonnie."

When they arrived at the moving stairs, John exclaimed, "Yook! Stai's go down by se'f!"

Lonnie scowled.

Sarah warned, "Now be careful. Just step on it, then hold the railing. You won't fall."

Ricky stepped right on like he had done this a hundred times. John followed, fascinated that each stair emerged from under the floor, one after the other. The movement threw him off balance for a second, but he caught hold of the rail and motioned for Lonnie to follow. Lonnie sat down on the floor and shook his head.

"Uh oh," John said. Lonnie was getting in a "no" mood.

"Not now, Lonnie," Sarah said. "You have to go. This is the way to the bathroom." Sarah tried to get Lonnie up as John and Ricky moved steadily downward on the escalator.

"John! Ricky!" Barry called. "When you get to the bottom, just stay where you are. We'll be down in a minute! I'll help you." Barry and Sarah lifted Lonnie to his feet and carried him to the stairs.

Ricky reached the bottom first and easily stepped off. The step John stood on disappeared under the threshold and John's foot caught on it, throwing him forward. He almost fell, but regained his footing by grabbing a sign that stood next to the stairway.

"Whew!" John said, turning to tell Ricky he made it. But Ricky was just disappearing down the aisle past the refrigerators.

"Wicky!" John called after him. "Come back! No wun!"

It was too late. Ricky was gone.

In a panic, John looked up the moving stairs. He called to Sarah and pointed to where Ricky had gone, but she and Barry were busy picking Lonnie up under the arms and carrying him onto the moving stairs. Lonnie was yelling in protest. They let Lonnie sit down as the stairs descended. His face was frozen in fear.

Sarah called back up to Jana, "Do you want to wait there with Mick and Peter?"

"Yes. I'll wait right here," Jana answered, pulling Mick back from the stairs by the arm. As they approached the bottom, Sarah and Barry lifted Lonnie to his feet and hiked him over the threshold.

Lonnie was shaking. John gave him a hug.

"Hey, where's Ricky?" Barry asked.

"Him wun dat way." John pointed.

"What?" Sarah's eyes widened. "Barry ..."

"I'll get him," Barry took off running.

Lonnie held himself and signed, "toilet," again, a pained look on his face.

"Oh, geez," Sarah breathed. "We better get you to the bathroom."

They hurried past lines of washers and dryers, dishwashers, and finally tubs and sinks of many different colors arranged together like many small bathrooms without walls. Down the middle of the bathroom section was a long corridor and Sarah pointed to some doors at the far end.

"There's the restroom, John. See the door with the picture of a little man on it? Take Lonnie to the bathroom and I will wait here in the main aisle so Barry can find us. Hurry!"

"Okay," John said. "Come on, Yonnie. Go toiwet."

John had never seen so many bathtubs, sinks, and toilets. They were blue, pink, gray, and red. Half-way down the hall he stopped to look in a full-length mirror that was next to a black tub big enough for two or three people.

"Go toiwet!" he commanded, pointing Lonnie down the hall.

Hesitantly, Lonnie stepped forward, still clutching his crotch, and motioned for John to come with him.

"No! You big boy. You go you'se'f!" John wanted to see the colored bathtubs and mirrors.

Lonnie side-stepped slowly down the hall.

John studied himself curiously in the long mirror. He looked different than he had at Larkspur. He wore clothes that fit just right, not like at Larkspur where he sometimes had clothes that were too tight or too long. His hair had grown much longer, hanging down to his eyebrows and curling below his ears. John dug in his back pocket for his comb. Barry was teaching him to comb his hair and he ran the comb straight back from his forehead. The hair flopped back down immediately. John reached for the faucet on the black sink and turned it to wet his comb, just like Barry showed him, but no water came out. He tried a couple of other sinks, but there was no water anywhere. He stuck the comb in his pocket and smoothed his hair down with his hand.

Then he remembered Lonnie. He better check on him. John hurried down the hall to the boy's toilet room door. One stall door was closed. A stranger stood at the tall toilet by the wall peeing standing up.

"Yonnie?" John called.

The man looked back. "Nobody in here but me," he said.

John knocked on the stall door. It creaked open. Empty.

"Whe'e Yonnie?" John said to himself as he ran out. He wandered through the many toilet rooms calling for Lonnie. Maybe he had finished and was playing hide and seek. Sometimes he liked to hide and jump out at John, saying, "Boo!"

John searched until he heard a faint response. He followed the grunting sounds through the maze of toilet rooms until he came to a bright red toilet. There sat Lonnie, his pants circling his ankles.

"No good, Yonnie. Toiwet ova' de'e!" John pointed back to the real toilet room. "Dis pwetend. No watuh. No fwush."

Lonnie looked up and smiled. He signed, "All done."

Suddenly, John could smell it. Lonnie had already done his big job here in the pretend toilets.

"No, Yonnie. No good! Pwetend toiwet!"

Lonnie stood up and pulled up his pants. The stench grew worse.

"You bad, Yonnie! Sawah be mad!" John tried the handle on the toilet just in case, but nothing happened. He closed the lid.

"P.U.!" Lonnie said, holding his nose.

John helped Lonnie zip his pants, grabbed him by the hand and rushed out to find Sarah. She was still waiting in the main aisle, chewing a fingernail, her face furrowed in worry.

"Oh, there you are!" she said, her forehead relaxing. "I haven't seen Barry yet so we better go look for him and Ricky."

"Yonnie poop in toiwet," John said, pointing toward the toilet rooms.

"That's good," she said. "We knew he had to go."

"No," John protested loudly. "Him go in pwetend toiwet. Wed one!"

Sarah's face looked puzzled. "What do you mean, John?" she asked. She followed him back to the red bathroom. They could smell it before they got there.

She stopped suddenly. "What? You didn't, Lonnie!" Sarah opened the toilet seat just enough to see inside then clasped her hands over her mouth, "Oh, my God! Lonnie! What were you thinking?"

"P.U.!" Lonnie said again proudly.

John hung his head. "Yonnie bad! Me sowy, Sawah."

Sarah's face turned scarlet. "Lonnie, this isn't a real toilet! It doesn't flush!" She bit her lip. "What am I going to do?" She glanced around. No one else was nearby.

"I can't believe I'm doing this," she whispered more to herself than to John. She jerked Lonnie away by the hand. "Come on. Let's find Barry."

John had to run to keep up with her. They hurried through the store, past the refrigerators and televisions to the furniture. When they had gone half-way around the store, they saw Barry and Ricky waiting by the moving stairs that led up.

"I found him by the beds," Barry said hanging tightly to Ricky's arm. "He was trying to lift a mattress off a bed frame when I caught him. I put him in time-out on a chair for two minutes like we decided. He was ..." Barry paused when he saw Sarah's face. "What's wrong? What happened?"

"Oh, Barry!" Sarah was pale. "I can't believe what just happened. I'm so embarrassed."

"What?"

"Let's go. I'll tell you on the way." They lifted Lonnie onto the moving stairs. even though he kicked and yelled in protest.

Barry held onto Ricky with his other hand. John followed, this time prepared for the jolt forward.

As they ascended together, Sarah cupped her hand around her mouth and said quietly to Barry, "Lonnie used one of the display toilets."

"He what?" Barry lowered his voice. "He peed in a display toilet?"

"Worse," she said.

"Him poop," John said, leaning forward. "Him gotta go bad!"

"He shit in a toilet on the showroom floor?"

Sarah nodded and glanced around nervously.

Barry shook his head. "Oh, wow. That's the worst yet. This is getting weirder every day."

Sarah slugged his arm and said, "It isn't funny!" They gripped Lonnie by the arms again as they approached the top of the moving stairs. "I thought he could make it fifty feet down the hall by himself. I showed him the door and everything!"

"They're going to know it was us," Barry said as they lifted Lonnie over the threshold. "The clerks saw us walking around. They all stared at us like we were freaks."

Sarah held onto Lonnie and Barry got a firmer grip on Ricky's arm. They speed-walked through the clothes racks. John had to jog to keep up.

"Maybe we should report it to someone," Sarah said to Barry over her shoulder. "We could apologize. Offer to clean it up."

"What would you say?" Barry said, dragging Ricky with him. "'Excuse me sir, one of these retarded guys, who by the way, belong here in the community just like everyone else, crapped in your display toilet?'"

Sarah glanced over her shoulder. "Thanks, Barry. That clinches it."

They found Jana leaning against a large pillar. Peter was rocking and flapping vigorously in the aisle. Jana nodded to where Mick was lying under one of the circles of clothing. He lay on his stomach tearing paper pieces into tiny fragments. Jana reached down and pulled him out by his legs.

"This is the best I could do," she said apologetically. "I couldn't keep them busy any longer."

"Don't worry about it," Sarah said. "You couldn't possibly do worse than we did. Come on, let's get out of here."

"What happened?" Jana asked. She hauled Mick forward, catching up with Sarah as they walked swiftly toward the exit.

"I guess we're not going to report it, then," Barry said from behind them.

"I guess not," Sarah answered. "I'm too mortified."

"What?" Jana asked. "Not report what?"

"I'll tell you in the parking lot," Sarah whispered. Without another word, they rushed through the store and out the doors. They didn't stop until they got to the cars at the far end of the parking lot.

Sarah punched John's arm again when her car came into sight. "Punch buggy!" she said.

"Punch buggy!" John said and tried to punch her back.

"No, John, only if you say it first."

Frustrated, John tried to respond but Jana interrupted. "Tell me!" She unlocked her car and pushed Mick into the backseat. Ricky and Peter crawled in, anxious to leave.

"Lonnie crapped in the display toilet," Barry said. He opened the car door for Lonnie and John.

"He what?" Jana's mouth dropped open.

"Yeah, just another exciting day in the life of a group home." Barry shrugged and shook his head.

"You've got to be kidding!" Jana was aghast.

"Nope! And we're not coming back for a very long time! Maybe never." Sarah said as she climbed into her car and started the engine.

As they zipped through the parking lot, Barry tapped his fingers on Sarah's dashboard like a piano keyboard.

After a few minutes of silence he said, "I know! An anonymous phone call." He put his hand to his ear like he was holding a phone. "'Hello. I was just in your store and I noticed one of your display toilets wasn't working. Could it be clogged?'"

Sarah stared at Barry for a moment, then burst out laughing. They both laughed so hard that John began to laugh, too. He nudged Lonnie, who joined in, giggling and squealing. They laughed so long that Sarah was soon panting for breath and wiping tears away from her eyes, and Barry was holding his stomach and groaning. No one said anything more, but they snickered in sudden spurts, off and on all the way home.

John nudged Lonnie in relief. "You not in twoubo, Yonnie, you funny!"

Chapter 13
Baseball

After the guys came home from work one warm June evening, Sarah waved a handful of tickets in the air and announced, "Someone at the A.R.C. donated baseball tickets for us. They're for tonight. We'll eat early so we can be there by 7:00."

John said excitedly, "Yippee! Baseba' game?" He clapped his hands and gave Lonnie five. Lonnie giggled in glee. John pretended to hold a bat and swing it, chanting, "Hey, batta-batta-batta, swing!"

"Where did you learn that?" Sarah laughed.

"Bawy show me," John demonstrated his batting stance once more.

"Do you think we can handle them by ourselves?" Jana asked as she helped Mick fold towels on the dining room table. "What if they have to go to the bathroom?"

"Barry will meet us there," Sarah answered trying to sound matter-of-fact. She checked the job chart to see who was cooking tonight. "He said he could take the bus straight from class." Sarah realized Barry had started coming over more often before his night shift, often arriving early enough to watch a baseball game, help with household tasks, or just to visit.

"I suppose he's only coming because he loves baseball." Jana smiled, lifting one eyebrow.

Sarah was slightly chagrinned that Jana so easily saw through Barry's intentions, something she had been suspecting for a while now and was trying to ignore. "You know he loves baseball. Stop thinking evil thoughts."

"He loves baseball, yeah, that's got to be the reason he'd give up an evening to spend with the likes of us." Jana chuckled and motioned for John to help her in the kitchen.

As Sarah and Jana hustled the guys out the door, John dashed upstairs and returned with the glove and baseball cap Barry had given him. Sarah smiled to herself, seeing how happy he was.

When they stepped out into the warm June evening, Sarah punched John in the arm again and said, "Punch buggy!" Even though she had been playing Punch Buggy with him for several weeks, he never thought to punch her first.

John chased her around the car trying to punch her back as she taunted, "You have to be first, John!"

Finally, she let him catch her and she gave him a hug, "Maybe next time. You have to be fast to beat me!"

As John and Lonnie climbed into the car Sarah glanced across the street. Mrs. Hanover was working in her flower garden but she didn't look up.

That woman! Sarah thought. *How could she be so nasty?* They hadn't done anything to her or anyone else in the neighborhood. Things could have been so different if they had just tried to get to know the guys. What an old curmudgeon.

Sarah was musing yet again on what to do about the pending lawsuit, when John shouted over to Mrs. Hanover, "Go baseba' game!" He waved enthusiastically.

Sarah cringed. Mrs. Hanover glanced up briefly but quickly resumed her work, thrusting her trowel forcefully into the flowerbed.

"She doesn't like us, John," Sarah said and gently pushed him into the back seat.

"But it's okay to be friendly anyway," Jana added, climbing into her own car.

Sarah rolled her eyes at that remark, pulling Ricky into the front seat. "See you there," she said waving Jana off. Sometimes Jana could be so ... Pollyannaish.

As they drove away, Mrs. Hanover stood up to stretch her back. She put her hands on her hips and watched them go.

"Take a good look, you old ..." Sarah's whisper trailed off.

"Hu o'd witch?" John finished.

Sarah shifted and sped up. "We shouldn't say things like that, but that's actually a good word for her."

"Hu witch," she heard John tell Lonnie.

Sarah silently reprimanded herself.

Parking next to each other at the ballpark Sarah and Jana could hear the organ music playing as soon as they stepped out of their cars. They herded the guys toward the entrance where they saw Barry leaning against a pole waiting for them.

Damn, Sarah thought, *but he looks handsome tonight.* His dark ponytail lay appealingly across his shoulder and his angular face was princely in profile. She pulled the tickets out of her bag.

Barry lit up when he saw them. Wearing a peace symbol shirt and cut-off jean shorts he greeted them with open arms, a baseball glove on his left hand.

"Baseball! The game of the gods!" The guys gave him high-fives and he guided Sarah toward the entrance with his hand on her back.

Despite her reservations, Sarah's stomach flip-flopped at his touch.

The guys all gaped at the many new sights and sounds inside the stadium. They had to be prodded to keep going. The smells of popcorn and grilling hot dogs reminded Sarah of her childhood, of attending games with her dad. Organ music played the National Anthem.

"It's starting. Let's hurry," Barry said.

Sarah and Jana each held the arms of two men and hurried on. Peter ran flapping after them. Their seats were near the very top on the third base side. Sarah sat between Mick and Ricky, then Barry scooted in followed by John, Lonnie, Peter and finally Jana.

"Sorry we're in the nosebleed section," Sarah apologized.

"Hey, I'll never scoff at free tickets. Thanks for letting me come." Barry's face was vibrant.

Sarah forced herself not to stare at him.

People crawled to and from their seats, wisps of smoke drifted lazily up from cigarettes, and venders shouted, "Ice cold Coca Cola!" and "Get your peanuts here!" Nostalgia swept over Sarah. How many times had she and her dad come to baseball games? Her mom didn't like baseball and always let them go alone for some father-daughter time. Sarah had treasured these rare moments just with him. They seemed like a lifetime ago.

John, Lonnie and Ricky looked around, sometimes with mouths open, staring at the colorful stadium scene. Mick studied the floor, frequently reaching down to feel for interesting tidbits. Peter stared upward at the gigantic stadium lights that would later light up the field.

Barry took out some gum and offered it to John, Lonnie, Ricky and then Sarah.

"Mick will just swallow it," she said when Barry extended the pack toward Mick.

"Oh, that's right." He stuck it in his pocket. "Hey, how do you think the guys are doing lately?" Barry asked, folding several pieces of gum into his mouth at once. "Seems like things are going a little more smoothly lately."

"Yeah, I've gotten Ricky to do a little work using candy as a reward, and Mick, too, though the paper thing is getting to be a pain. I find paper everywhere."

"Me, too," he said, chewing with difficulty.

"Things seem to be going better on the weekends with Todd being there." Todd and Michael had been taking the guys swimming on Saturdays, another sport at which Ricky excelled. Todd also came on Sunday afternoons to help take them to the community gym.

"Todd seems like a nice kid," Barry said. "At least he's friendly and personable. I don't know what Michael's problem is. He's pretty surly."

"I don't know either, but he seems to be handling things all right at the moment." Sarah wondered about Michael's attitude; it hadn't improved much, but she hadn't heard any complaints. In fact, he didn't communicate much at all. Still, the data was always in the book. She couldn't help but question his honesty in recording data—it seemed too good to be true. She would probably end up disregarding it. She needed to talk to William about that.

The home team jogged out onto the field to the announcer's booming voice. A batter warmed up in the on-deck circle. Jana dug in her purse and gave Peter a small square of velvet, his current favorite for soothing himself. Barry helped John put his glove on his left hand then thumped his other fist into it. John imitated him, hitting his glove in the same way.

Sarah asked Barry, "How's Peter doing in the mornings?"

"He does fine getting dressed and all. But he's still ripping plenty of shirts." Barry chewed his wad of gum like a tobacco chaw and studied the field.

"I know. I need to do something different about that." She realized he was enraptured by the game and told herself to stop talking shop.

But Barry remarked off-handedly, "I think he should have to take his ripped shirt off and on about twenty times every time he does that."

She hadn't thought of overcorrection, but it was a good idea. "Hmm. Maybe you're right. That just might work." Sarah caught herself nervously picking at a nail and slipped her hands under her thighs.

"But these guys are doing great," Barry said, patting John's and Lonnie's knees. John slapped Barry's hand and all three of them turned their caps backward.

"They sure are." Sarah smiled to herself.

The teams were in position. The umpire yelled, "Play ball!" Barry began talking to John like a father would talk to a son. "Our team is in the white jerseys. They're out in the field first. When they are up to bat, if they hit it, you can cheer. If they're out there in the field, you want them to get the batter out. Got that?"

A batter stepped up to the plate. John yelled, "Hey, batta-batta-batta, swing!"

The batter hit the ball John jumped up and yelled, "Yea!"

"Not yet," Barry admonished. The couple sitting in front of them turned around. The man said crossly, "You rooting for the other team?" He looked at John and Lonnie, then over at Barry and said, "Sorry, man." He turned around again and whispered something into his companion's ear. A few seconds later she glanced back at them, too. Sarah still hated it when people stared at the guys like that. She told herself it didn't matter. The guys were doing fine.

John waved at her and smiled.

"Just watch me and cheer when I do," Barry said, patting John on the knee again.

The next batter hit the ball. John started to jump up, but Barry pulled him by the shirt and he sat back down. When the left fielder caught the ball Barry whistled and yelled.

John cheered and nudged Lonnie. "Him catch it! Dat good!"

Sarah watched how patient Barry was with John, diligently explaining the game, though they both knew the rules were too complex for John to comprehend. She put her feet up on the back of the seat in front of her and hugged her legs, trying to put thoughts of her research behind her for a few hours. She needed to learn to enjoy the moment. That had always been hard for her. She'd looked ahead all her life to the next step, the next project, the next accomplishment. When would she ever feel like she had made it and could relax? That was something she needed to work on—when her dissertation was done. And after she had tenure in her professorship. It would be awhile.

After a few more plays, Barry asked nonchalantly, still chewing his gum like a wad of Skoal. "So how's Lord William?"

Sarah shifted in her seat. "Oh, I decided to stop meeting him at Rennie's." She tried to sound dispassionate. "So I've been stopping by his office during his office hours, instead. I always tell him I have to get over to the house to plot data or something."

"What does he say?" Barry kept his eyes on the game.

"He hasn't said anything else, nothing inappropriate, that is. Just acts very professional."

"That's good. Maybe he's getting the picture."

"Yeah, maybe." She thought about what he had said when she called him at home to tell him she couldn't meet him at her apartment that night. She told him there was an emergency at the group home and she would get in touch with him the next week. He had seemed cool after that, which was both a relief and rather painful.

The batter hit a grounder. The man in front of them stood up and shouted, "Throw him out!"

John did the same. "Fwow 'im out!"

The right fielder picked up the ball and threw it to first base.

"You got him!" the man yelled and struck the air with his fist.

John imitated him. "Got him!"

Barry smiled and held out his hand for John to slap. "Right on! Give me five, man. There's nothing like baseball, is there John?"

"Wight on!" John repeated, his face flushing with excitement.

Ricky twitched each time Barry and John yelled out. Peter covered his ears at the loud noises, hugging his head with one arm to plug both ears. Jana had to keep straightening Mick up in his seat so he wouldn't scrounge on the floor.

Sarah looked from one of her charges to another and watched how Barry and Jana interacted with them. A wash of satisfaction poured over her. This was what her project was all about, getting these men out into the community and teaching them appropriate behavior. Since the Shelby's incident they had taken a few shorter outings, making sure everyone went to the bathroom before they left and always keeping a hand on Ricky. They'd had no incidents so Sarah had gladly accepted the free baseball tickets, feeling they were ready for a longer excursion. Sarah imagined how she would write this anecdote into the introduction of her dissertation and perhaps detail tonight's events in a journal article on the benefits of community integration. Maybe this was all going to work after all. Her shoulders relaxed.

Three innings went by before Mick stood up and grabbed his crotch. He looked around frantically and muttered "toilet."

"I'll take him," Barry offered.

"Thanks. Barry." Sarah wondered what she and Jana would have done if they had been alone with all five men in a public place, and she decided they should never try that.

"Anybody else have to go?" Barry asked. No one did. Barry tugged Mick's hand away from his crotch and led him down the steps.

While they were gone, the home team hit a home run. The crowd jumped to its feet, screaming. Sarah stood up to see. John and Lonnie shrieked and slapped each other's hands. When they all sat back down, Ricky had moved into Barry's, seat next to John.

"Dat Bawy's seat, Wicky," John reprimanded, shoving Ricky's shoulder. "Move!"

Ricky just stared at John and quivered spasmodically.

Sarah leaned forward to catch John's eye. "That's okay, John. It doesn't matter which seat he's in."

"Dummy," John grumbled, giving Ricky another shove with his elbow.

After a few minutes Barry came back with Mick. "What happened?" he asked Jana as he and Mick climbed over everyone's legs. "How did we score?"

"A home run," Jana answered. "There was a guy on base, too."

"Dang!" Barry stopped when he got to where Ricky was sitting. "Hey, man, you're in my seat." He patted Ricky on the head. "But that's okay. I guess I'll have to sit by Sarah, then." He pushed Mick past Sarah toward his seat and stepped over Ricky's legs.

Sarah warmed at Barry's obvious ploy to sit by her and tried not to smile.

Barry sat down then instantly sprang up again. "Ricky!" he yelled glaring at him. He lowered his voice and hissed, "You sat right here and peed?" The back of Barry's shorts were soaked.

The kids behind them giggled.

"Oh, my gosh!" Sarah felt the blood rising to her face and she covered her mouth in dismay. "Ricky! How could you do that?" she scolded.

Barry squeezed Ricky's face and stared directly into his defiant eyes. "You wet in this seat! And I just took Mick to the bathroom. Why didn't you tell me you needed to go?"

Ricky twisted his head out of Barry's grip.

John shook his finger at Ricky. "You bad, Wicky!"

"Oh, Barry, I'm so sorry!" Sarah looked around for something to wipe the seat with and finally pulled some tissue out of her backpack. "I didn't notice or I would have warned you!"

Barry tried to wipe the back of his shorts using her whole pack of tissues but it was no help. Sarah moved Mick over one so Barry could have a dry seat.

"What a jerk he is," Barry said, steaming. "Why would he do that? It's like he did it intentionally."

"I know, I'm really sorry ... I don't know what's wrong with him." Sarah felt somehow responsible. With an attempt at humor, she said quietly, "Well, come to think of it, I do know what's wrong with him. They don't call them disabled for nothing."

Barry laughed in spite of himself. "Can I quote you on that?"

"Please don't!"

Should I take him to the bathroom?"

"I guess you better in case he's not finished." She thought of offering to go with them, but hated to leave Jana alone.

Barry took his sweatshirt out of his pack and wrapped it around his waist. He yanked Ricky out of his seat to go to the bathroom. When they returned they sat at the far end of the row by Jana rather than climbing over everyone again.

The game seemed to go slowly for Sarah after that. With Barry farther away, John and Lonnie stopped cheering and played a clapping game on their laps. Mick kept wiggling off his seat and down onto the floor. Jana finally stopped trying to make him sit up. Peter rocked back and forth, rubbing the velvet on his face in a trance. Before long, he began to hand-flap and the velvet no longer worked. Ricky started making faces at people behind them and Barry took him out several times for breaks, missing much of the game. Sarah felt guilty and kicked herself for thinking that a baseball game was a good idea. So much for the anecdotal introduction to her publication.

When Mick stood up and grabbed his crotch again, Sarah called over to Jana and Barry, "Let's go. The game is almost over anyway, and everyone is tired."

"Yeah, we should beat the rush," Jana replied. She looked as harried as Sarah felt. "We don't want to lose anyone in the crowd."

"There's only one more inning!" Barry said, clearly frustrated that he hadn't seen much of the game.

But Jana and Peter were already standing up and John had pulled Lonnie to his feet. They sidestepped into the aisle and headed down the stairs together.

At the nearest toilet sign, Barry sent Mick inside. "Hurry up. We're all waiting for you." Barry looked peeved, but he smiled tolerantly at Sarah. She didn't speak to him, feeling guilty for ruining Barry's evening, but not knowing what to say.

John tapped Sarah on the shoulder. "Yonnie go toiwet," he said. Lonnie twisted his fist in the air, signing.

"Okay, John," Sarah answered. "Would you take him? Anybody else have to go?" Sarah glared at Ricky. He ignored her, watching the crowd.

"How about you, Peter?" Sarah motioned him toward the bathroom entrance but he wouldn't go in.

"Oh! I almost forgot," Barry said. "I promised my nephew I would get him a pennant. I'll be right back." He pointed to a nearby souvenir stand and hurried away.

"Since we're waiting, I think I'll make a trip to the ladies' room, too," Jana said. "It's right around the corner. Will you be all right, Sarah?"

"Sure." Sarah positioned herself between Peter and Ricky, keeping them within arms length. After a couple of minutes she heard a banging sound coming from inside the bathroom. It sounded like a garbage can falling over.

She heard John shout, "No, Mick. Bad boy!"

Mick stumbled out, growling and chewing on something.

"Oh geez, Mick," Sarah said, disgusted by the thought of what he might be eating. "That is so gross!" Sarah held her hand in front of his mouth to get him to spit it out but he swallowed instead. Sarah fought down the urge to gag.

John poked his head out of the bathroom and told Sarah that Lonnie had to poop. Sarah nodded assent. She took ahold of Mick's arm and looked around nervously. Barry still hadn't returned. In the stands, the cheering and clapping swelled. Loud music accompanied the rumbling of feet. The game was over. She began to panic.

Keeping a grip on Mick, Sarah stepped into the entrance of the bathroom and called, "Lonnie! You have to hurry! The game is over and we need to go!"

A man walked past her into the bathroom and Sarah said, "Excuse me," withdrawing back into the corridor.

Swarms of people spilled out of the stairs and crowded past them. Peter had turned to face the wall now and was flapping furiously. Sarah looked both ways. Ricky was gone.

Her heart sprang into her throat. "Ricky!" she screamed. "Ricky! Where are you?"

Panicked, she scanned the throng of moving bodies for Ricky's black hair and red T-shirt.

Just then Jana returned, walking briskly against the stream of patrons. "Sorry! The bathroom was being cleaned and the other one was clear around on the other side."

"I can't find Ricky!" Sarah shouted frantically. "Stay here and I'll go find him. John and Lonnie are still in the bathroom and there's Peter." She handed Mick to Jana and took off jogging.

Truly frightened, Sarah zigzagged through the crowd. What if Ricky ran out into the parking lot and got hit by a car? Or what if he was seduced by some crazed molester? Anything could happen to someone like Ricky, and Sarah would be responsible.

At the men's restroom on the far side of the stadium Sarah stopped and asked someone to check the stalls for Ricky. No luck.

After going all the way around she ran up to a uniformed security guard. "Excuse me! I've lost someone. Can you help me?" She wiped sweat from her forehead and upper lip.

"Boy or girl," he said dryly.

"It's a man, but he's disabled and doesn't talk. He could be anywhere and he could get hurt if he ran in front of a car or something." She described Ricky.

"We'll find him," the guard reassured her. "We've never lost anyone yet." He radioed the description of Ricky to other guards.

Sarah walked the floor with him looking in every doorway and stairwell. The crowd was thinning now and only a few stragglers hustled toward the exits. Sarah and the guard walked swiftly down the stairs to the next level, searching that floor and the one beneath it. When they got to the bottom floor, they met up with three other guards who all shrugged their shoulders.

"Would he have gone into the parking lot?" one of them asked.

"Possibly—I just don't know." Sarah said, fighting back tears. She pictured him lying in the parking lot in a pool of blood or hidden in the backseat of some rapist's car. "He could be anywhere and he wouldn't protest if someone picked him up."

They looked at her as if to question why she would bring him to a baseball game and Sarah felt pangs of remorse. What was she thinking placing these vulnerable people in danger?

The guards discussed their search plan and Sarah followed one around the perimeter of the stadium. He shone his light into corners and checked behind closed doors.

In the parking lot, a stream of slow moving red lights crept toward the main boulevard. Sarah stared into the darkness looking for Ricky's silhouette in the odd chance that he was searching for her car.

Suddenly Sarah wondered about the others. She suspected that by now Barry and Jana probably would be waiting at their cars rather than inside the stadium.

"I better find my friends and tell them to go on home without me," she said to the guard. "I'll meet you back at the main entrance in a few minutes."

"Okay. I'll check the concession entrance," he said, sweeping the area with his flashlight.

Streetlights lit circles on the otherwise dark pavement. Sarah couldn't stop the tears now as she wound her way between the thinning lines of cars. She choked back a sob and stopped in a shadow to regain her composure. Wiping her face, she prayed desperately for help, at the same time questioning why God should help her at all.

Their cars were now alone in the middle of the parking lot and Sarah spied several figures standing beside them. She ran toward the group.

"Sawah! Dat Sawah!" John shouted first. He limped forward and slugged her arm.

"Punch buggy!" He laughed and clapped his hands joyfully.

"You've been waiting all this time to do this, haven't you," Sarah said. She definitely wasn't in the mood for games, but she had started it. She patted John's shoulder. "Good job. You remembered."

Barry asked, "Where's Ricky? You didn't find him?"

"Not yet," Her voice cracked in spite of her efforts to sound calm. "The guards are helping me search. I wanted to let you know so you could take the rest of the guys home."

"We're not going to leave you, Sarah," Barry said gripping her arm. "Let me help you search. Jana can take the rest of the guys home, right Jana?"

"Sure. Don't worry. I'll call my husband to come over and help." Mick, Peter, and Lonnie already sat in the backseat of her car.

"That's great, Jana," Sarah said, opening the passenger door for John. "John, you help get everyone to bed, okay?"

"Yep. Me he'p," he said confidently, tapping his chest. Then he asked, "Wicky gone?"

"Yes, but we'll find him ..." Sarah answered more assuredly than she felt.

"No, no find Wicky. Him gone now."

Sarah ignored him, refusing to acknowledge this possibility or John's dislike of Ricky.

Jana stalled, "I could wait ..."

"No, you should go. Thanks, Jana. We'll be back as soon as we find him."

Jana got in and rolled down her window. "He's got to be here somewhere. I'm sure he's all right."

"See you in a little while." Sarah waved.

Barry and Sarah jogged back to the stadium. They heard guards calling out and saw the flashes of light as they searched the dimmed stadium corridors.

"If you were Ricky where would you be?" Sarah asked, winded.

"You mean if I was sneaky and liked to get other people in trouble?"

"Yeah. What would you be dying to get into?"

They thought silently as they rounded the far end of the stadium, passing a guard who shook her head.

They passed another women's restroom and Sarah jetted inside. "I need to go. Be right back."

She opened a stall door and unzipped her jeans. Just then she heard a scraping metallic sound. It seemed to be coming from a neighboring stall. Stories of stalkers hiding in bathrooms pushed their way into her thoughts. Her throat tightened. Every muscle tensed and she tried to recall the moves from her self-defense class.

Something dropped to the floor and rolled across the tile. Sarah quickly zipped up her pants and peeked out of the stall door, ready to run. An empty can of soda rolled under the sinks and stopped against the wall. She heard another "pop" and then a fizz, followed by the glug glug splashing of liquid as it hit the floor. Another can then clanked and rolled out, spilling brown soda as it spun toward the wall.

"Ricky," Sarah whispered. The far stall door was slightly ajar. Sarah tiptoed forward and peered inside. Ricky sat on the toilet fully dressed, a pile of soda cans on his lap. He was working intently on opening the next can, his shirt and pants dripping wet.

"Ricky!" Sarah screamed in both joy and exasperation.

Ricky jumped and dropped the can.

"What are you doing in here?" Her pitch rose uncontrollably. "You ran away from us, Ricky! Do you know how panicked we've been! I am so mad at you!" Sarah stamped her foot in utter frustration.

Ricky's arms went limp and the last three soda cans fell onto the floor, rolling past Sarah's feet. His face went blank.

Having heard the ruckus Barry ran up beside her. "What the ...? Here you are, Ricky, you trickster! We were worried sick about you!"

"Stand up!" Sarah's teeth were clenched in fury. She yanked him to a stand and shouted, "We're going home. Then you're going to time-out forever."

Barry snatched Ricky's other arm and they marched him out of the restroom. As they hurried toward the parking lot, Sarah waved to a security guard who called off the search on his walkie-talkie.

They were panting by the time they reached Sarah's car. She fumbled in her pocket for the keys.

"What are you going to do, Sarah?" Barry asked, wiping sweat from his face.

"I don't know." She unlocked the door, shoved Ricky into the backseat and leaned wearily against the car. "I don't know what to do with him. We can't go anyplace if he's going to pull this kind of crap."

"We need one of those child leashes. And maybe a man-diaper." Barry turned to walk around to the passenger side of the car.

Sarah caught his arm. "Barry?"

"Yeah?" He turned back.

"Thank you for staying with me. I ... I don't know what I would have done without you tonight." She blinked back the tears that once more tinged her eyes.

"Any excuse to be with you." Barry took her in his arms and they held one another tightly. When Sarah finally let go, Barry smoothed the hair back from her face. "You're going to figure this out. You're so smart and so beautiful." He kissed her cheek.

Just then they heard a trickling sound. Glancing behind them they saw that Ricky sat halfway out of the open car door, his pants unzipped. The streetlight reflected off the pavement where a large puddle was forming around their feet.

Chapter 14
The Party

The weather turned warm and sunny, and everyone got to wear shorts and new sandals. Sarah told John the Fourth of July was coming and that the workshop was going to have a party at a restaurant. They were supposed to wear red, white and blue clothes and late in the evening they would hear some loud explosions called fireworks. But they shouldn't be afraid because these were to celebrate the country's birthday. John was excited about the party and he picked out Lonnie's and his clothes several days ahead.

When the night of the party arrived, John put on his white shirt, blue shorts and red baseball cap from Barry. He and Lonnie helped Sarah, Todd, and Michael carry blankets and boxes of cookies that they were bringing to the party to the cars. John liked Todd better than Michael. He was tall and skinny with reddish hair and a sparse, curly beard that never seemed to get any longer. He was always smiling and telling the guys how good and funny they were. And he never got mad. When he had to put Ricky in the time-out chair he apologized over and over, saying, "Sorry I have to do this, Ricky. It's for your own good."

John and Lonnie got to ride in Michael's painted hippy-mobile, as Sarah called it. As soon as they jumped out of the car at the restaurant John could hear the rock 'n roll music. He clapped his hands and gave Lonnie a hug. "Us go pa'ty!" he shouted excitedly.

A gray-haired woman, dressed in a tall hat with stripes and stars on it, directed them downstairs. At the bottom of the steps John and Lonnie stared in amazement. The large room was alive with gyrating bodies, twinkling lights and brightly colored decorations. The wild mass of dancers took his breath away. Streamers of red and blue hung like spider webs from the ceiling ready to catch the dancers if they jumped too high. Tiny stars and shiny balloons floated on strings above them. John began to tremble with excitement. A real party, like on TV!

He recognized most of the dancers: Laurie-the-Greeter spun haphazardly in the middle of the floor, Clarence waddled back and forth, dancing with two girls at once, and even blind Eileen held Ken's hands and swayed in rhythm. Sally-the paper-eater was being twirled around in her wheelchair by Millie, a red, white and blue striped blanket over her lap. Those who weren't dancing were smiling and chatting happily.

Lonnie's mouth hung wide open as he stared at the melee. A drip of saliva fell onto his shirt.

"No swobbo, Yonnie." John shouted above the music. He wiped Lonnie's chin with his hand and rubbed the slobber onto his shorts.

The song ended. On a small stage at one end of the dance floor two men dressed in black fiddled with some big black boxes.

One of them shouted into a microphone. "Get ready for the number-one biggest hit of all time. Heeeere's 'Louie, Louie!'"

Everyone cheered and the music roared again.

"Go on, dance—just have fun!" Sarah said, giving them a gentle push onto the dance floor. She motioned Michael and Todd over to the food tables where they set out the boxes of cookies they had brought.

Mick trailed after them with his eyes ogling the huge variety of treats spread out on the table.

"Just one, Mick," Sarah shouted. Then she strolled over to talk to some other counselors.

Peter followed close behind her, nervously flapping his hands and staring up at the floating stars. But Ricky stepped right onto the dance floor and began to dance like he was on American Bandstand. He was good at basketball, he knew how to swim and now John noted with disgust, Ricky was an excellent dancer, too. John scowled, secretly wishing Ricky would die.

Someone tapped John on the shoulder and he spun around. "Hi, Bessy!" he yelled above the noise. She had said she wasn't sure if Jodie and Richard would let her come.

Betsy wore a hat with a red, white and blue ribbon around it and a red shirt that was too big, so the sleeves had been rolled up. John was glad to see her. Timidly, she kissed his cheek. He gave her a big hug and danced her in a circle, almost lifting her off the ground.

"Us dance!" He took her hand and pulled her into the crowd. They twisted back and forth, bouncing with the beat as best they could. Betsy wiggled her rear end in a way John liked. He laughed out loud.

When the music stopped, he noticed Lonnie watching them from the edge of the dance floor. He called, "You dance, Yonnie!" and gestured for him to join them.

Lonnie meandered toward them, his cheek bulging as he chewed on his enormous tongue.

The music man wrenched the mic almost into his mouth. "Here's one that will bring back memories," he crooned, "so find your baby and hold her tight."

A slow, rolling rhythm oozed from the speakers. Partners held each other and swayed. John's heart leapt. He pressed Betsy to him like they never got to do at the workshop, and they rocked gently back and forth. The singer drawled, "Love me tender, love me true ..."

Beside them Lonnie shuffled his feet from side to side, awkwardly flicking his fingers. Betsy lay her head on John's shoulder. He could feel her breasts against his chest. That funny feeling tweaked his groin. He knew that this had something to do with having babies but he couldn't quite understand how it worked. He told himself to ask Sarah when they got home.

The song ended. Betsy slipped out of his arms.

"Betsy?" he asked shyly.

"What?"

"You hab baby?"

"No." She shook her head. "I had a operation. Can't have no babies."

"Oh."

A fast song started. The threesome, John, Betsy, and Lonnie, danced until they were panting and sweaty. Ricky whirled nearby with Todd, twisting and jumping, and spinning in amazing ways. John tried to copy the way Ricky danced when he was sure Ricky wasn't watching.

"We're going to take a break so you all can catch your breath," the music man announced. "Have yourselves a drink and we'll be back in ten."

The dancers broke up and mobbed the refreshment table. Before following the crowd toward the food, John had an idea.

He strode to the edge of the stage and motioned to the music man.

"We're taking a break," the man said without looking up.

"Me know."

"Do you have a request?"

John shook his head. "Me ... me sing. You pway music, me sing?" He tapped his chest.

"You want to sing?" He looked back at the other music man who shrugged and nodded. "What song do you want?"

"Wanna ho'd you hand," John answered excitedly.

"Okay, man. I'll call you up when we're ready."

"Yippee!" John grinned and sandpapered his hands. He knew he could sing better than Ricky, since Ricky couldn't even talk. Betsy would be proud of him.

John, Lonnie and Betsy waited in line until it was their turn to sample the colorful cookies, cakes and candy. John stuck a star cookie in his mouth and three more in his pocket before picking up his pop and cupcake. They sat down at a table where Todd and Sarah were visiting with other counselors.

"How do you like the party?" Todd asked. He patted John on the back affectionately. "You guys looked great out there."

"Good!" John answered. He patted Todd in return.

"You haven't introduced me to your girlfriend, John." Todd reached over to shake Betsy's hand.

"Dis Bessy," John said. He kissed her cheek.

"Nice to meet you, Betsy. I've heard a lot about you." Todd smiled. He liked everybody.

"Well, I have to run. I'll see you guys tomorrow after church. Have fun tonight." Todd waved at everyone as he left.

Sarah was busy talking to other workers at the table, but she paused to wave at Todd as he walked out. "Thanks, Todd. I appreciate you coming over with us."

"Whe'e Todd go?" John asked.

"His shift is over. He'll be back tomorrow." John wondered why he didn't want to stay for the party. He looked around for Michael and spied him in the back of the room sitting by a woman John didn't know. They were both leaning back in their chairs against the far wall and smoking.

As he waited for Betsy and Lonnie to eat their snacks, John noticed Mick under a table eating crumbs off the floor. Sarah had taken Ricky with her to talk to Ken, so John decided not to bother with Mick. Peter had found a corner by himself and was busy with the Larkspur dip. Behind the food table, Crazy Henry paced the room, dragging his hand along the wall. He was talking to himself, as usual.

Betsy pointed to some people a few tables over. "That's my Jodie and Richard," she said. Before this John had only glimpsed them in the car. Richard had dark greasy hair and eyes that sank into his face like a skeleton. Jodie's face was pointy, her nose turned up at the tip. She had a chipped tooth. Her hair hung to her shoulder with her ears poking through. They looked mad and seemed to be arguing with each other. Immediately, John didn't like them. From what Betsy had told him, they were mean. He felt bad that Betsy had to live with them. Once he had asked Sarah if Betsy could come and live with them at Sarah's house. She said she was sorry, but her house was just for men.

The music men returned to the stage and one of them drawled, "By request, an all-time favorite ..." Music blasted from the black boxes and tugged at John like a rope. Betsy and Lonnie were not finished eating, but John was anxious to get up and dance.

He watched as Sarah pulled Peter by the sleeve to the dance floor. She began to dance around him, motioning for him to turn in a circle. He actually let her pick up his hands and swing them briefly before they snapped back into place across his chest. After a couple of minutes, he slung his arm over his head to cover his ears and side-stepped away toward the wall.

John turned to Betsy. "Me dance Sawah?"

"Yeah. I'm tired," Betsy said. She was looking a little pasty.

John caught Sarah by the arm on her way off the floor. "Us dance?"

"Sure, John!" she smiled.

This time John tried every move he could think of. He twisted and shimmied and swung Sarah under his arm. He danced until the sweat ran from his forehead into his eyes. Sarah laughed out loud. They danced to several songs before Sarah told him she needed a break. Still chuckling, she gave him a hug. John kissed her cheek. He loved Sarah, but not the same way he loved Betsy.

John coaxed Betsy back to the dance floor for the next song, but before the song was over she said she wasn't feeling well. She sat down again and put her head on the table, looking pale.

John patted her shoulder sympathetically. She was sick again. She had been feeling sick more and more often at work, even needing to lie down in the nurse's office. Almost every day she showed him a new bruise. John told her to go to the doctor, but she said Richard gave her medicine and she would be all right. He said she didn't need to go to the doctor.

John and Lonnie wandered up to the stage and watched the music men pushing buttons and turning dials. John caught their attention.

"Me sing now?" he asked.

"Oh, that's right. Let me find it. 'I Wanna Hold Your Hand,' right?"

"Yeah, Ho'd You Hand. Me know dat."

"You're on. Right after this song." The music man searched through a stack of records and picked out the same album Barry had. He slid the black disk carefully out of its jacket and set it on a record player.

When the room quieted the man purred into the microphone, "I have a treat for you. Your friend has offered to sing for you. A little live entertainment for your dancing pleasure." He motioned John up on the stage and handed him the mic.

John scrambled up and cleared his throat. He looked out over the crowd. The dancers turned to him expectantly.

Laurie-the-Greeter waved. "I know him! That's John! He's my friend!"

John's legs began to shake. There was a hissing sound, then music started. John pulled the mic to his mouth and his voice boomed through the speakers. He couldn't remember all the words, so he just mouthed them and followed the tune up and down. When he got to the chorus, he roared the words out. "I wanna hold you hand! I wanna hold you haaaand ..."

The dancers bounced and bubbled like a wildly boiling pot. Encouraged, John sang louder. He wiggled his hips and pretended to play a guitar. He bent down low and twirled in a circle, shouting the words he knew in abandonment, ending the song in semi-splits on the floor. The crowd cheered.

John bowed low and boomed, "Tank you! Tank you bewy much!" like Elvis. Todd had shown him that.

Someone yelled, "More!" but the music man took the mic back and said, "Thanks, my man. And now for a slow number ..."

John clambered off the stage and bee-lined it to Betsy. He couldn't wait to hear her tell him what a good singer he was. When John got to Betsy, though, she still had her head down on the table.

She glanced up briefly at him and said wearily, "Good singing." She didn't sit up.

"Tank you. Tank you bewy much! You yike me sing Beato's?" he asked.

Betsy smiled weakly, then her eyes slowly blinked shut.

"You tiyed?" he asked, patting her on the back.

"Yeah." Her eyes stayed closed.

John saw Jodie approaching from across the room. "He'e come Dodie."

Betsy sat up looking paler than ever.

"What's wrong?" Jodie asked her. Her voice sounded irritated, like Betsy had done something bad.

"Nothin'." Betsy looked up at Jodie fearfully.

"You don't look too good, girl. We better go home." Jodie crushed her cigarette into a nearby ashtray and waved to Richard.

"No, please! I don't wanna go home," Betsy pleaded. "I'm okay."

"I don't think so. You must have that flu that's going around," Jodie said loudly, glancing at the other adults standing nearby. She pulled Betsy to her feet. "It's almost 9:00 anyway. You should get some extra rest when you're sick."

John wanted to protest, but he was afraid Betsy would get in trouble. He waved sadly and said, "Bye."

Betsy's hand wavered as she waved back. "Bye, John. Had fun dancin'."

After they left, John sat alone for a few minutes thinking about Betsy. She looked pretty sick. Somehow John felt it was Jodie and Richard's fault for being so mean to her. Maybe he would ask Sarah again about Betsy living with them.

Sarah wandered over and sat next to John. "I liked your song, John. Why aren't you dancing?"

He shrugged.

"Where did Betsy go?" she asked.

"Go home. Sick."

"Again? Hmm." Sarah looked worried. "She doesn't seem well lately. That's too bad. Her foster parents should take her in for a physical to see what's wrong."

"Dem mean."

"I'm sure they took her home so she could rest. That's not mean."

John shook his head. "Dem mean. Make hu sick."

"Well, I'm sure they are looking out for her, John."

"Sawah? Bessy yive you house?" John made a puppy-dog face at Sarah.

"You would like that, wouldn't you, John? That would be nice, but she already has a place to live. Come on. Let's dance."

Dancing with Sarah helped John forget Betsy's problems. Sarah was pretty and danced enthusiastically, laughing with John and making him feel loved.

As the evening wore on John danced with Lonnie, then a few other girls from the workshop, even Laurie-the-Greeter. He danced until his feet were sore and his bad hip ached.

Finally, he flopped into a chair and wiped his forehead. A slow song started. Through the crowd he glimpsed Sarah dancing with Barry. He was surprised to see Barry there. Sarah leaned her head on Barry's shoulder and closed her eyes while they danced. Even though John liked Barry, he didn't like Sarah being so close to him. He got up and tapped Barry on the shoulder to cut in.

Barry said, "Bug off. I just got here. It's my turn."

Sarah smiled at John and shrugged.

The music stopped. Ken announced that the dance was over and it was almost time for the fireworks. He said everyone should move to the lawn outside the restaurant where they would be able to watch the fireworks together.

Laurie-the-Greeter jumped around hugging several people and shouting in excitement. John grabbed Lonnie's hand, leading him up the stairs and outside onto a wide lawn that stretched along the waterfront. Michael brought out the blankets from his trunk and they all sat down on the grass.

The night was warm and the air smelled salty and fresh. Lights from the restaurant reflected in long white streaks across the shimmering water. A flat boat drifted in the middle of the bay, lit only by small lights trimming its perimeter. John could see black figures walking back and forth across the deck.

He and Lonnie lay back on the blanket staring at the night sky, now a deep indigo, dotted with tiny stars. John had rarely been outside this late at night before. He felt grown-up—he was doing what kids at Larkspur weren't allowed to do. Surrounding the restaurant and lawn were black trees and shrubbery. Who knows what could be hiding in those dark places? He felt a little bit scared and squeezed Lonnie's hand, in case Lonnie was scared, too.

Soon they heard a sharp whining sound and John sat up in time to see a streak of white shoot across the sky. It burst into a million white lights coming straight for them. John gasped, jerked back from the hurling sparks and then screamed as a huge boom made them both jump.

Everyone cheered. Lonnie covered his ears and shook his head. He didn't like loud noises. He started to stand up but John pulled him down again.

"Fi'ewo'ks, Yonnie! Dis fun! You be okay." He slung his arm over Lonnie's shoulder just as another streak shot up high into the air and shattered into red, white and blue lights that showered down on their heads. They ducked together. Another booming sound shook the ground and a fountain of sparks sizzled on the water. Several rockets of light followed by successive bright bursts thundered in John's chest. He watched in utter amazement, clinging to Lonnie to comfort him. Lonnie was trembling and covering his ears. The astonishing display continued for a long time until, by John's count, "thirty-eleven" shells burst wildly over their heads all at once in a shocking final flurry.

When the last sparks fizzled out on the water and the boat became dark, the spectators clapped and cheered. John glanced around. Party-goers and families with sleepy children gathered up their blankets and chairs and lumbered up the hill toward the parking lot.

As he and Lonnie folded their blanket and followed the crowd, John noticed a clutch of people standing up on the road above them. He heard a buzz of worried voices.

Someone shouted down the hill, "We can't find Henry. Has anyone seen Henry Jacobson?"

"I did," said Clarence. "He was talkin' 'bout ambliances and p'lice cars again."

"A seizure!" cried Laurie-the-Greeter, running awkwardly up the hill toward the supes.

Ken's voice rose above the rest, "Now calm down. Millie, you and I will go look for him. Everybody else stay put. We'll find him."

John and the others hurried up the hill toward the road. John was limping badly after all the dancing. Above them on the street, screeching tires and a blaring horn silenced the crowd. Laurie-the-Greeter screamed.

As John rose over the hill to the road, he saw Millie silhouetted against car lights, running toward the scene. She shouted, "Oh, my God! Somebody call an ambulance, quick!"

Everyone swarmed toward the car. Supes and parents shouted, "Stop! Stay back!" but the crowd pushed around them, spilling onto the road.

John noticed Michael taking Mick and Peter back toward the parking lot. Ricky stood alone on the side of the road, quivering all over. John ignored him and held tightly to Lonnie's hand, dragging him toward the car. His heart beat up in his throat.

The crowd jostled to see over one another's heads. John couldn't see anything. He crouched down and tugged on Lonnie, trying to pull him through the bystanders, but Lonnie jerked his hand away shaking his head. John signaled him to wait there and squeezed under elbows and around shoulders until he came to the edge of the crowd.

Lit by the car's headlights Sarah, Barry, Millie and a few others knelt around a figure lying on the street. All John could see was a pair of feet. His mind flashed back to Larkspur when Old Cyrus got hit by the train. They said his legs went one way and his body another.

John gulped.

Sarah shouted over her shoulder, "Have they called an ambulance?"

"They're on their way," someone behind John answered.

Sarah shifted her feet and glanced behind her, pushing a strand of hair back from her face. John saw that her hands were covered with blood. She spied John, and twisted toward him to speak, opening a space between her and Barry.

John saw that the legs belonged to Crazy Henry; his eyes were rolled back, his head rested in a dark pool. John gagged.

"Go find Ricky," Sarah ordered, reaching back to grip John's arm. "I'm afraid he'll take off."

Ken yelled, "Go back, everyone. Go on home. We're taking care of Henry." He and the other adults started to corral them back toward the restaurant.

John scrambled out of the crowd, trying to brush the bloody handprint from his sleeve. He found Lonnie, took him by the hand and retreated with the others. Ricky still stood off to the side of the road, jerking his body convulsively.

John pushed Lonnie toward the restaurant and turned to Ricky. "Come, Wicky! Come he'e! Sawah say you come!"

Ken stepped into John's path and pushed him back.

John reached forward through Ken's arms, and shouted, "Me go, get Wicky," but Ken kept forcing him backward, not listening to John.

Ricky made a few halting steps toward them. John motioned again for him to follow. Instead, Ricky spun around and dashed into a dark thicket at the side of the road.

John yelled, "Wicky! Come back!" He tried to force his way past Ken but Ken was stronger than John and was shouting directions to the crowd.

John tried to tell Ken that Ricky was getting away, but Ken snapped, "Not now, John!"

The rising wail of a siren silenced them. Flashing lights appeared and reflected spookily off the faces in the crowd. John found Lonnie and hugged him to his chest. They watched in silence as men in dark uniforms gathered around Crazy Henry. The medics worked on him for several minutes, then drew back and shook their heads. They brought out a stretcher and laid it on the pavement. Carefully, on the count of three, they lifted Crazy Henry onto the stretcher and covered him with a blanket, even his face. Silently, they slid Henry into the ambulance and shut the doors.

As Barry, Sarah, and Millie walked arm-in-arm toward him, John scanned the edge of the road for Ricky's tall form. Sarah would be mad that John hadn't kept him from running away. The red flashing lights from the ambulance lit the trees along the roadway where he had disappeared. But there was no sign of Ricky at all.

Chapter 15
Lost

Sarah watched the paramedics shift Henry's covered body onto the stretcher. They heaved him upward in synchrony and slid him into the ambulance. Red and white lights flashed across the faces of the silent bystanders. Tears rolled down Sarah's cheeks as the ambulance drove off without turning on the siren. No hurry now.

Millie wrapped her arm around Darla, the foster parent with whom Henry lived. Darla sobbed onto Millie's shoulder, "I should have seen it coming. I wasn't paying attention. I was just enjoying the fireworks while he was seizing."

"Accidents happen, Darla," Millie said sympathetically, "You couldn't have known ..."

"No, I should have known the noise would upset him," she choked.

Stunned, Sarah stepped over the blood that had spread across the pavement and trickled into the gravel on the shoulder of the road. She wiped her eyes and whispered to Barry, "It could've been one of ours. It's so senseless."

"Yeah, I know. Makes you think, doesn't it." Barry put his arm around her and gently pressed her to him. "But it wasn't. Our guys are safe."

"Yes, thankfully."

They walked slowly toward the restaurant. "We better get them home," he whispered into Sarah's ear.

Sarah nodded. She felt there was a stone in her chest, the same familiar stone she'd sensed when she watched her mother die. Something had happened that could never be undone. Death changed things, changed people. Death had changed her.

They found John and Lonnie waiting for them and headed toward the parking lot where Michael would be waiting with the other guys.

When Barry moved ahead, John hung back and slung his arm around Sarah's shoulder as he had seen Barry do. "No cwy, Sawah," he soothed.

"I'm okay, John. You're a sweetheart." She hugged him back.

"Cwazy Henwy dead?" he whispered.

"Yes, John, I'm afraid he is." She sniffed.

"Him come back wo'kchop?"

"No, John, he won't be coming back to the workshop." She wondered what John understood about death.

John was quiet after this.

They walked together silently, Sarah fighting back the tears that continued to well up in her eyes. She could see Michael and other silhouettes sitting in his car as they approached. Music blared when he opened the door.

"There you are!" Michael called. "What took ya?"

"We waited for the ambulance, obviously," Barry shot back. "Why didn't you go on home?"

"Forgot my keys to the house," Michael answered. "So where's Ricky? I've got Peter and Mick."

"I assumed he was with you," Sarah answered in alarm. "You don't have Ricky?"

"No. I thought he was with you."

"John?" Sarah spun around and took him by the sleeve, her pitch rising in fear. "I told you to get Ricky. Do you know where he is?"

John shrugged. "Him wun," he said looking down at his feet.

"He ran?" Sarah found herself shouting. "You were supposed to get him!"

John spoke softly into his chest. "Him sca'ed. Go 'way."

"Where?" Barry asked. "Which way did he run?"

John pointed toward the woods where Ricky had disappeared. "Dat way."

A cold wave rushed through Sarah's body, the kind of fear one experienced after a close call on the freeway. Her voice cracked as she yelled, "John! Why didn't you tell me before this? Why didn't you stop him like I told you to?"

John shrank back against the car and covered his ears. She had frightened him.

"It's not your fault, John," Barry interceded, moving between Sarah and John. "All of us should have been watching him." Meaning Michael.

Unexpected anger rose into Sarah's limbs and she intentionally turned away, realizing she really wanted to strike John. She clenched and unclenched her fists, telling herself she had to be the one in control. She was the boss, which she wished to God she wasn't right now. She had to think of what to do.

Furiously, she lashed out at Michael, trying to find someone to blame but John. "Why didn't you get him, Michael? You knew we were with Henry and couldn't possibly be watching everyone."

Michael shrugged, feigning innocence. "Sorry. I had these two."

"It's no one's fault," Barry repeated.

"Well, it doesn't matter now, does it? We just have to find him." Sarah was shocked at how her voice reflected the anger boiling inside her chest. She'd meant to sound calm.

"Let's spread out," Barry said, springing into action. "He's probably right around here, hiding like at the ballpark."

Taking a breath, wishing she had said that, Sarah agreed, "Yeah, maybe he's just frightened of the fireworks or the ambulance. Michael, you stay with the others. In fact, here are the keys ... take them home." Sarah tossed the house key at Michael and she and Barry dashed back to the restaurant.

She conscripted Millie and Ken, who were just leaving, to help them look for Ricky. Spreading out in four directions they searched the perimeter of the restaurant grounds. Meeting up again in the now darkened lawn, they stood in a circle staring at each other, worry evident on all of their faces.

Sarah took a staccatoed breath and fought down the panic that threatened to paralyze her. "We'll get some flashlights and start looking in those woods where John saw him heading. He probably just ducked behind a tree and is waiting for us to find him."

"I have a flashlight in my car," Ken said, hurrying away.

"Me, too," Sarah remembered.

"I'm sorry," Millie said, "but I need to get home. I'm already late for the babysitter."

"That's okay—thanks for your help." Sarah ran to her car.

When they returned with flashlights in hand, Barry suggested, "How about I take the woods? Sarah, do you want to do the waterfront and Ken can backtrack toward town. Let's meet back here in thirty minutes, okay?"

"If we don't find him we'll call the police," Ken added.

"Sounds good," Sarah said. Having a plan helped calm her. They would find him and then they could all go home and sleep. Tomorrow they would laugh about this.

Everyone moved off. Sarah strolled along the sea wall shining her flashlight beam into the dark water. Shallow waves lapped against the stones and she could hear Barry and Ken calling Ricky's name in the distance. Her mind began to see images of Ricky's floating body. What if she saw him? Would she be able to jump in after him? She had always been afraid of water, ever since her childhood friend drowned in a rip tide. Dark water held a special terror for her. Sarah walked south along the seawall, then backtracked to search north. Nothing.

They met on the road under the lone streetlight.

"We better call the police," Ken said. "I'll drive to the nearest phone booth and call."

"Thanks." Sarah tried not to let on how terrified she was. "We'll take it from here, Ken. I appreciate your help."

After Ken drove off, Barry and Sarah turned their flashlights off and stole along the edge of the thick brush on the other side of the road. They peered silently into the pockets of darkness, listening for movement. Sarah snapped on her light and pointed it toward a rustling noise. A scampering shadow disappeared under a rhododendron.

"What if he is intentionally hiding from us," Sarah whispered.

"He may just have to spend the night outside then," Barry answered. "That might be a good lesson for him."

They wandered along the shoulder, listening. The only sound was the crunching of gravel beneath their feet.

"I don't know if he'll learn from this," Sarah finally said, having mulled over his progress in her head. After the baseball game she had fastened a bell to the top of Ricky's door. If it went off at night, Barry or Michael would come right up and hold Ricky in a chair for five minutes. In the morning everyone else but Ricky would get Ricky's favorite treat, marshmallows. When Ricky occasionally stayed in his room all night, he got a marshmallow, too. If he hit or bumped someone, he was locked in the bathroom for fifteen minutes. Many evenings he didn't come out at all. The data had only shown a small drop in frequency of these behaviors.

Sarah stopped. "You better go home, Barry. It's late. I'll be all right here until the police come. They'll help me search."

He turned to face her. "What? I'm sure! I'm not going to leave you out here alone at night. What kind of creep do you think I am? Besides, what else does a chemistry student have to do on a Saturday night?"

Sarah recognized the joke, "Yeah, drugs. But really, you can go. I'll wait by the restaurant until they come. It's my fault ..."

"It's not your fault, you've got to believe that." Barry placed his hand on her shoulder and squeezed. " And where was Michael, anyway? That son of a bitch doesn't do squat."

"The bare minimum, that's for sure." Sarah calmed beneath his touch. "Well, I'm ultimately responsible. You know what I mean."

Within minutes the red lights of a patrol car flashed over the trees. Sarah was thankful they hadn't turned on their siren. The car pulled over beside them and two officers with huge flashlights got out. After a brief explanation, and description of Ricky, they split up. The officers sent Barry and Sarah down the main street toward town, thinking he might go toward the lights.

The waterfront businesses were dark and shuttered. Sarah and Barry peered down alleyways and into recessed entryways, illuminating dark corners and calling softly so Ricky wouldn't think they were mad. They searched the ten blocks of the waterfront business section until they came to the quaint white houses of the residential area. Barry and Sarah shone their weakening flashlights into the darkened yards, exposing driftwood sculptures, gardens lined with shells, and Japanese glass floats. No Ricky.

After an hour, they headed back. They met the officers cruising toward them in their squad car, lights off.

"No luck?" asked the officer who was driving.

"No. What do we do?" Barry asked. "Do we organize a search party?"

"So you say he is retarded, and he doesn't talk ..."

"Not much," Sarah said.

"And he's run away before?" the officer queried.

"Yes, at a baseball game."

"How long was he gone?"

"Well, an hour ..."

"He'll probably come back on his own. Most do, you know."

Sarah hesitated. "I don't know. We had to go and find him last time."

"What was he doing when you found him?" The officer tapped the steering wheel impatiently.

"He was hiding in the women's bathroom." Sarah suddenly felt foolish. "Drinking stolen sodas." Maybe he would come back on his own. She had no way of knowing.

The other officer leaned forward and said, "Does he have family in town? Maybe they would know what he's likely to do."

"No, he doesn't have family. My fear is that he'll get lost somewhere in the woods or fall into the bay or somehow get hurt."

"Can he swim?"

"Yes, actually he's a good swimmer," Barry answered.

The officers talked quietly to each other for a minute then the driver said, "It's not going to be cold tonight. Maybe you should come back in the morning. My guess is he might show up hungry."

"Well ..." Sarah paused. Maybe they were right.

"The other option is to put in a missing person's report. But he has to be gone for twenty-four hours, or there has to be a reason to suspect foul play. I don't think you're there yet." The car started to roll forward.

"Okay, thank you officers." Barry drew Sarah away from the road. The cops shone their spotlight into the nearby shrubbery as they crept forward.

"I think they're right," Barry said, sounding confident. "He'll come back when he's good and hungry. Tomorrow I'll hang around here all day in case he shows up. What do you think?"

"I don't know, Barry. I think we should keep looking." Sarah was shivering now. The evening had cooled considerably. "What if something happens to him? I'll never forgive myself."

"Maybe we should at least get in your car. You're cold."

Sarah turned up the heat in her bug and they cruised the area again, crawling along the dark roads with their lights out. When she began to get sleepy, they decided to wait in the parking lot in case Ricky came back looking for them. Within minutes they both fell asleep.

The sound of a car door slamming woke Sarah. The sky was light blue. She blinked, trying to remember where she was.

The car windows were fogged up and her neck was stiff. Wiping the wet window with her hand she saw that the restaurant crew was arriving for the Sunday breakfast shift. Sarah rubbed her eyes to wake herself and nudged Barry. He took a deep breath and shook his head vigorously.

Sarah got out of the car and called to a restaurant worker. She wrote down her phone number on a gum wrapper, asking them to call if they spotted Ricky. The worker nodded and stuck the scrap of paper in her pocket, telling Sarah she would let the others know.

"I'll take you home so you can get some sleep," she said to Barry, sliding back into the driver's seat, "Then I'll call around to get some help." She started the engine, chilled and shivering.

"I can still help," Barry offered. "I have a test tomorrow, but I'm pretty much ready for it. Just need a couple of hours to review."

"We'll see. You get some rest and I'll call William …"

Barry groaned, "Oh, yeah, he'll be a big help."

Sarah was too tired to argue. True, he hadn't yet come to visit, but he had university resources he could tap. "And I'll call Ken. It would be best if they were people Ricky recognized. But hopefully, he'll show up soon and the restaurant will call us."

Sarah dropped Barry off at his apartment. She squeezed his hand before he got out. "Barry, thank you, again. I appreciated you staying with me."

"No problem." Barry squeezed back. "Glad I could help. Call me later if you need me."

Driving to her apartment, Sarah tried to stave off visions of Henry's bloody face. Wearily, she unlocked the door and threw her backpack on the table. She downed a glass of milk and tumbled onto her bed without getting undressed. She was asleep within seconds.

She found herself once again exploring the water's edge, shining a flashlight into the black water. A dark shape stirred from the depths. She fixed her light on it, her heart slapping the inside of her chest in rhythm with the waves. Ricky's face rose to the surface, his eyes empty and staring, his dead mouth agape.

Sarah jerked awake gasping for breath. Jarred into reality, she glanced at the clock radio. 10:00 A.M. She had slept for over three hours.

Even so, she felt like there was gravel in her eyes. Pulling herself out of bed, she washed her face, rinsed her hair in the sink and toweled off. She shook out her unruly curls to do what they would. Spreading jam on a piece of bread, she folded it over so it wouldn't drip then dashed out the door.

When she arrived at the group home, Michael sat at the dining room table with a cup of coffee and a smoldering cigarette in the ashtray. He was reading the paper.

"Are the guys at church?" she asked, immediately realizing what a stupid question this was.

"Yeah," he said, blowing smoke upward. "Weren't they supposed to go to church today?"

"Of course." Sarah glanced around the disheveled living room. "No Ricky, obviously. We waited all night."

"What are you going to do?" Michael took another drag.

"I'm going to make some calls, get some volunteers to help us look."

"What do you want me to do?" He crushed out his cigarette.

"Stay with the guys. Someone needs to be home in case the restaurant calls."

"Todd can handle them this afternoon if you want me to help search." Michael seemed unusually cooperative this morning.

"Good idea, thanks." She smiled feebly at Michael. He was a puzzle. "I'll call Ken. Maybe a couple workshop people can help. And maybe William can get someone from the U to help, security or something."

"Sounds like a plan. Why don't I go now while you're making calls? Todd should be here about 11:30." Michael stood up and downed his coffee.

"Thanks, Michael." Her smile was genuine this time. "Take some food to lure him out, that bag of marshmallows. And keep checking in with the restaurant. They're watching for him, too."

Michael snatched the marshmallows and stuck an apple in his pocket. Sarah heard his engine sputter to a start. She picked up the phone and called Ken. He was disappointed that Ricky hadn't shown up and agreed to call some staff members to help with the search. He suggested she call the county Search and Rescue. Sarah called William's home number instead.

"Good morning." William's deep voice sent a stab of longing through her.

"Hi. It's Sarah. We've got a problem, William." Sarah explained what happened as William punctuated the conversation with an occasional "Uh huh."

"So what are you going to do?" he asked when she finished.

Sarah hesitated. "Well, the workshop staff is going to help, and my staff and I will be out there today. The police will keep an eye out for him, but they're not going to send out a search and rescue team. Not yet."

"Sounds like you have it covered then," William said coolly. He covered the phone and spoke to someone else. His words were muffled but she caught them. "It's my doc student, sweetheart. I won't be a minute." Then he said to Sarah, "Do you need anything else?"

"I guess not." Sarah was taken aback. "Can you think of anything else we, I can do?"

"No, that sounds like a good plan. Call me when you find him." William hung up.

Sarah was stunned. Slowly, she placed the receiver back on the wall phone. He hadn't offered any help nor even lent his usual empathetic ear to her plight. She sat down and stared blankly across the room for several minutes as the message sunk in. William had abandoned her. She had rejected him and he had moved on.

Michael and two Cloverdale staff members searched for Ricky all afternoon. Todd took the rest of the guys to the rec center to play basketball. Sarah called the hospital and the police to see if any John Does had turned up, but thankfully no bodies had been found.

At 4:30, Sarah picked Barry up and they met Jana and her husband at the restaurant. Together with Michael, they ate a quick dinner and marked out a search pattern on a city map, drawing ever-widening arcs through residential areas and out to the rural perimeter. They decided to meet again at dusk.

Sarah and Barry revisited the nearby woods. They stayed within voice distance of one another as they picked their way through the thick undergrowth that grew in every untended lot in town. Barry was optimistic, reassuring Sarah that Ricky would tire of this game and come back whimpering unintelligible apologies. Sarah silently scoffed at this thought, feeling more and more forlorn.

Each time the searchers came within sight of each other they looked more disheveled. Sarah tried to smooth her hair, picking leaves and sticks from among her tangles. It was no use. She and Barry combed the waterfront until they ran out of walkway, then picked their way along the rocky shoreline toward the bluff that separated the bay from the open ocean. When they could go no further because of the incoming tide, they stopped to rest on a boulder.

"So where do you think he is?" Sarah asked, watching a sailboat round the point and head toward the marina. The light was turning golden as the shadows lengthened.

"I thought he'd have shown up by now," Barry said, his enthusiasm waning. "I mean, wouldn't he be tired and starving?"

"Of course!" Sarah propped her elbows on her knees. "He's probably thirsty and desperate. He doesn't have any survival skills."

"Survival skills? Hell, he can't even put on his shoes without someone telling him how."

"I know. Why doesn't he come to us? You'd think he would come running by now."

"You'd think. Or maybe he's tired of being in time-out and getting locked in the bathroom and he saw this as his chance to get out of jail free."

Sarah leaned her chin on her hands. "Geez, when you put it that way, maybe he is just trying to get away. But I don't know what else to do to help him live in the community! The whole idea was to get him out of the institution so he could have a better life. This isn't it."

"Weird, huh?" Barry tossed a rock into the low waves.

"Yeah, it's strange. You think you're doing the right thing. We can't ever know what he's really thinking, I guess."

"If he is thinking beyond, 'Who can I bother?' and 'What can I get away with?'" Barry stood up and tossed another stone, sending it skimming across the wavy surface.

They were silent for a few moments, listening to the rattle of the waves rolling over the pebbles. Yellow sunlight streaked over the bluff, glinting off the sailboat's mast, almost too bright to look at.

Barry offered Sarah his hand. "Where to, boss?"

She took his hand and pulled herself up to her feet. Her muscles were sore and a sharp pain made her examine at her forearm. A six-inch scratch oozed blood.

"Ouch! Are you okay?" Barry asked.

"It's just a scratch." Sarah licked her finger before realizing how dirty it was, then wiped away the blood. "I'll be okay. Let's cut back up to meet the road. We can dip into the forest from there to reach the areas we haven't covered."

They headed up the beach, and Barry offered her his hand again when they came to the steep outcropping that abutted the stone-laden beach. Sarah let him pull her up and they held onto one another until the tangle of brambles forced them to separate.

By the time they made it back to the rendezvous point, darkness had set in. Everyone was exhausted. Sarah suggested they go back to the house to debrief, eat, and regroup. Michael, Jana, and her husband followed Sarah in their cars, looking equally frayed.

When she pulled into the driveway, the brightly lit group home beckoned her like a harbor to a ship. Deep weariness settled into Sarah's bones as they climbed the porch steps together.

When they opened the door, Todd asked, "Any luck?"

Sarah dug in her coat pocket, pulled out a piece of Ricky's ripped shirttail and waved it at Todd.

"You're kidding?" Todd took the soiled fabric from her. "That's it? Where could he have gone?"

"Beats the hell out of us." Michael lit a cigarette and dropped into the overstuffed chair.

"At least we know he was around that area at some point," Sarah said, plopping onto the sofa. "No one has turned up at the morgue or the hospital, so that's something."

"I hadn't even thought of that," Todd frowned. "What a depressing thought."

Sarah noticed how battered they all looked. Jana had a bruise on her forehead and her husband's face was smeared with dirt. Bits of leaves stuck to Barry's hair and Michael looked even more bedraggled than usual.

"That area around Seacrest is rough," Barry said, shaking his head to loosen the debris. "Ricky could hide anywhere."

"And that cliff," Jana added, picking leaves off her husband's back. "I'm worried that he'll stumble off and ..." She trailed away.

Sarah interrupted, "He could even be hiding somewhere close by, hearing us but afraid to come back." She rubbed her calves. "My legs feel like lead."

Todd turned down the television. Lonnie grunted in protest. John shushed him and sat down on the couch between Lonnie and Sarah. Mick had been sitting there, too, but he twisted off the arm of the couch, his hands stuck in his pockets protecting his treasured papers.

"Maybe someone took him in," Todd said hopefully.

"If he won't come to us, why would he come to a stranger?" Sarah asked. She curled her feet under her.

"Because he hates us," Michael said, tapping his cigarette on the side of a plant pot. "All we do is torture him."

Sarah ignored this remark but gritted her teeth in silent protest.

"Are you going back out tonight?" Todd asked.

"Not us," Sarah said. "We're dead. The police said if we hadn't found him by tonight they would send out a search and rescue team. I need to call them."

Barry lay out flat on the floor. "I have to sleep now." He closed his eyes.

Sarah mumbled, "We never should have gone to that party."

"There's no way you could have guessed he'd do this," Jana soothed.

Michael got up to get an ashtray. "Well, he did run away before, so it's not out of character. He's a jerk. Maybe he'll learn his lesson or we'll luck out and never find him."

"Oh, that helps, Michael," Sarah snapped.

"Hey, I'm just telling it like it is. Nobody else does." Michael moved to the dining room to smoke.

Barry rescued her. "So what do we do now, boss?"

Sarah lay her head on John's shoulder. "Well, first we all need some sleep. I can hardly focus my eyes. And for now, we just need to keep it out of the papers so nobody in the community panics. It wouldn't help our lawsuit to get negative publicity." She closed her eyes in a vain attempt to shut out this disaster.

John tapped Sarah on the shoulder. "Sawah?"

"What?" She didn't open her eyes, thinking John was going to tell her about their day.

"Pape' guy come. Take pictu'es."

"What?" Sarah's eyes flew open and she stared at John open-mouthed. Did he just say, a newspaper reporter had already been here?

Todd grimaced. "Uh, yeah … I'm afraid the paper already knows about this. I don't know who told them, but they came by and took some pictures of the guys." Todd studied his feet.

"Todd?" Sarah bolted upright. "You talked to them? You let them take pictures?"

"Sorry," Todd said, glancing up at her briefly. "I didn't know I shouldn't. I thought it might help."

"Oh great!" Sarah rubbed her forehead in angst. This was her worst nightmare. Now she would lose the lawsuit and maybe the group home. Her dissertation would be side-lined and she would never graduate.

She spoke as calmly as she could, realizing Todd didn't understand the situation in the neighborhood. "Todd, that's fodder for Mrs. Hanover and her persnickety neighbors. We told her there wouldn't be any trouble." Sarah clenched her teeth, holding back the swear words that popped into her head.

"Sorry," was all Todd said.

Everyone was silent. Jana shifted uneasily by the doorway, pulling on her husband's arm. She clearly wanted to leave. Barry sat up and leaned against the television screen. Lonnie growled so Barry moved to the side.

As the news sunk in, Sarah groaned and ran her hands absently through her tangled hair. She picked out a stick and set it on the coffee table. "It's not your fault, Todd," she said finally. "You had no way of knowing. It just complicates everything."

Barry reached up and grabbed John's ankle. "Hey, buddy, how about fixing us some popcorn. I bet Todd will help you."

Todd took the hint and motioned John into the kitchen.

"I think we're going to get going," Jana said. She took hold of her husband's over-sized hand and turned to the door. "I'll call you in the morning, Sarah."

"Good luck," her husband said, escorting Jana out the door.

"Thanks for your help," Sarah called after them. She lay her head down on the sofa pillow. Barry lay back on the floor and looked up at her. Their faces were within a foot of each other and she could clearly see the dirt lining his eyebrows. Barry reached up and squeezed her forearm supportively. His touch was like a balm. Sarah heard the sounds of clinking dishes in the kitchen and soon they smelled the popcorn. She closed her eyes. Her breath slowed. In a few seconds she was asleep.

Sarah startled awake, her heart racing. Light poured through the bedroom window of her apartment. She barely remembered making the police report and returning home last night. What was she doing sleeping when she should be out looking for Ricky? She needed to call the hospital again, and check with the police about her missing person's report. "Please let us find him today," she prayed. Her stomach knotted as she showered and quickly dressed.

Stopping by Rennie's for coffee, she noticed a discarded newspaper that lay on a deserted table. She grabbed it and sat down, sipping carefully from the steaming cup. As she spread it out on the table, she saw John and Todd's smiling faces peering back at her from the front page. Sarah caught her breath, self-consciously glancing around the coffee shop.

The headline read, "One Dead, One Lost at 4th of July Outing for Disabled." A small picture of Henry was in the bottom corner, with the caption, "Accident victim," and another one of Ricky was labeled, "Lost group home resident."

Quickly, she scanned the article. Todd had given clients' names and had mentioned Sarah as the director. To his credit, he had tried to put a positive spin on it, saying nothing like this had happened before and he was sure Ricky would return safely. But the reporter's final speculation was about whether these "severely handicapped adults" were safe in the community.

Sarah set the paper down and stared out the window. This was the last thing she needed, bad publicity. She could just imagine Mrs. Hanover's glee at seeing their troubles splashed in the paper. And what would William say? Surely he would be upset. What if he pulled her funding? There would be follow-up articles, that was certain, maybe even television news reports. Now the whole community would be peering over their shoulders, watching their every move, assessing her every mistake. These thoughts were tempered by her mental image of Ricky struggling through thick undergrowth, scratched and starving. The important thing now was finding him safe, she told herself. She'd have to deal with the aftermath later.

Sarah finished her coffee, purchased a muffin and stuck the paper under her arm. She decided to stop by the group home to check on things, as well as to make calls and solicit help. She needed time to decide how to handle the media.

Pausing at her car, she turned instead toward the Smith Building. She would try William one more time. Surely this time he would be compelled to help.

Sarah ran up the steps two at a time to William's office and rapped urgently on his closed door. William opened the door and motioned her in. His face was serious. Sarah swallowed hard, trying to stay calm.

"So what's with this?" William asked, tapping the morning paper spread out on his desktop. "Whose idea was it to go to the news media?"

"I'm so sorry," Sarah said. "My new employee, Todd. He didn't know. I should have thought to tell him, but I was out all night …"

"Any news of Ricky?" Sarah thought she detected anger in his eyes.

"Not yet. We've all been out looking for him, but so far, nothing. I filed a missing person's report and they're sending out a search party."

"That should do it." William's voice was cold.

Sarah summoned courage from somewhere deep within and asked, "I, uh, wondered if the university has funds to help us look for him, like an emergency fund or something." She shifted uncomfortably from one foot to the other, trying to maintain her professionalism while nearly hysterical inside.

"No, there's no other money I can access. You know the grant's budget. You're already going over."

"Well, could we get some volunteers? Maybe some of your students? I could come and talk to your classes ..."

"I can't ask students to do that. Summer quarter is rushed, as you know, and they're in the middle of writing their term papers. Midterms are next week. I'm sure the police will find him."

William sat down in his swivel chair and picked up a pen, tapping it impatiently against his desk.

Sarah stood awkwardly in the doorway. "William, I need some advice on how to handle the publicity. I'm afraid it's going to hurt us, with the lawsuit and everything."

His tone softened a bit. "I'd like to help, but I don't have any advice, now that the story's already out. Just keep me out of it."

"Of course! I'll take full responsibility." Sarah bit back tears.

"Sarah, you have to keep your objectivity. This is an experiment. Sometimes experiments fail."

She reddened. "This one can't fail. These are human beings. You told us how important it was that they get out of the institution. You said they deserved to live in the community and have meaningful lives. You ..."

"I know what I said." He cut her off. "All theoretical. That's what your project is about. We'll have to see, won't we?"

He was distancing himself so he wouldn't be implicated. Bastard! Tears sprang into Sarah's eyes and she looked down. "Yeah, we'll have to see."

"Sorry I can't help more." His chair squeaked, rocking back and forth.

"Yeah, me too." Sarah ran down the hall, letting the tears of anger run freely down her cheeks. Self-serving, egotistical letch!

When she pulled into the driveway at the group home, Michael's car was already gone. Of course. It was Monday and the guys were at the workshop. The house was neat and smelled of old cigarette smoke. She wished Michael wouldn't smoke in the house, but she couldn't ask him to go outside and leave the men alone.

Sarah checked the refrigerator and the menu. They needed a few groceries to get them through the week. Maybe Jana would do that for her. Sarah phoned her.

"How are you holding up?" Jana asked when Sarah got her on the phone.

"I'm okay," Sarah lied, "but I have a headache."

"I bet you do. I can hardly sleep. I wake up every hour or two worrying."

"We just have to focus on finding him."

"What's the plan?"

"I'm going to call the police this morning. It's just ridiculous that they haven't helped us more!"

"I agree. Do you want me to come out today to help? I could skip my afternoon class."

"I hate for you to do that."

"I could ask my mom to come over. She loves the guys."

"Well, check with her if you want to and let me know. It would be really helpful if you could pick up some food." Sarah read her the list of meals for the week and Jana agreed to go.

When they hung up, Sarah checked the log. Michael had not written anything about the weekend. She silently cursed him.

The phone rang.

"This is the sheriff's office. Is this Sarah Richardson?"

"Yes."

"There's been a sighting of the missing person you reported."

"What? Where?" Sarah's heart jumped.

The dispatcher gave her the address. "He was seen in a resident's backyard, but he ran away when the homeowner tried to talk to him. He recognized your man from the picture in the paper."

Sarah wrote the address on her palm. "I'll be right there." Maybe Todd had saved the day after all.

Chapter 16

The Search

Monday, when John arrived home from work, instead of finding Sarah or Jana at the house, Jana's mother was there to welcome them at the door. She had come over once or twice to help them with art projects and had fixed Peter's shirts. Her light hair was streaked with gray and she had creases around her eyes and mouth that tripled when she smiled. John liked her.

The house smelled like meat and bread and other delicious things, and the table was all set when they walked in. John's mouth watered.

"Hello, boys," she said. "Do you remember me? I'm Mrs. Dickson, Jana's mother. But you can call me Helen. Dinner's almost ready. I thought you'd like a good hearty meal."

"Whe'e Sawah?" John asked.

"Sarah and Jana are out looking for Ricky. They asked me to fill in for them today." She smiled, her face wrinkling up at the corners. "Just relax and I'll call you for dinner."

Mrs. Dickson was nice, but John wished Sarah and Jana were here. After a bit, he peeked in the kitchen but she shooed him out, clucking her tongue like a chicken. "Not now, dear. It's a surprise. You boys don't have to do any work tonight. I'm taking care of you."

Since John had no chores, he took Lonnie upstairs to their room where they could play and forget about Ricky and Sarah and Jana being gone. John mumbled to himself on the way up, "Dat Wicky. Him bad. Get yost, make Sawah be gone ..."

Lonnie patted John's cheek sympathetically.

They didn't find Ricky that day. Sarah and Jana came home looking exhausted just before the guys went to bed. Mrs. Dickson fed them the leftovers of the roast beef she had prepared. Sarah told the guys to go up to bed, but John squatted around the corner by the stairs to listen to them talk about the search. He wanted to be close to Sarah a little longer.

"So how did it go, dearies," Mrs. Dickson asked kindly.

"Ricky already was gone when I got to where he was sighted this afternoon. He had tried to snatch a bag of groceries out of someone's trunk while this man was unloading them. The man called to him, recognizing him from the paper, but Ricky ran and disappeared down into a gulley. The man said he looked pretty bad, ripped clothes, dirty."

"Did he get any food?" Mrs. Dickson asked.

"No, Mom," Jana answered. "He dropped it when they guy yelled at him. But we're encouraged because he's starting to come out of hiding."

"Sooner or later he'll come back," Mrs. Dickson said. "What's the plan for tomorrow, girls?"

Sarah's voice was raspy. John wondered if she was getting sick. "The sheriff has a crew out looking for him tonight. They said they would look tonight, but they're considering him a runaway now, not a high priority."

"Well, that's terrible!" Mrs. Dickson replied. "They know he's retarded."

"Developmentally disabled," Jana corrected.

"Yes, and they can't just leave him out there to fend for himself!" her mother exclaimed.

"I agree." It sounded like Sarah was chewing. "But that's what they do when someone escapes from the institution. Apparently they usually come back on their own."

"My, oh my," Mrs. Dickson said breathily.

Sarah continued, still chewing, "So we're on our own during the day. How long can you help us out, Helen? I really appreciate you filling in at last minute like this."

"I can be here as long as you need me, dearie. Your boys are so sweet and lovable ..."

"Mom! They're adults and we've got to treat them like men, not children," Jana chided.

"Oh, yes, of course. I'll do my best."

"How did it go this evening?" Sarah asked.

"Just fine. Everyone loved the roast. Mick needed some help, like you said. He did try to steal Lonnie's food. But when I sat next to him he was fine. I don't understand that paper thing, though. Why does Mick have all those papers again?"

John began to nod off. His chin touched his chest and woke him. He crawled out to get a pillow from the sofa, but this caught Sarah's attention,

"John?" she called. "Is that you?"

He grunted.

"He likes to listen in to conversations," Sarah explained to Helen. To John she said, "Why don't you go on up to bed. You have to work tomorrow."

John stood up. "Sawah?"

She turned around in her chair at the dining room table, setting her fork down on her nearly empty plate. "What do you need, John?"

"Sawah, Bessy not at wo'kchop t'day."

"She wasn't there? Is she sick again?"

"Yep. Hu' sick." He shook his head sadly.

"I'm so sorry, John. I bet she'll be back tomorrow." She turned to Jana, "We need to call adult foster services. I'm worried about her."

John nodded and walked sleepily upstairs. "Night, Sawah."

"Goodnight, John."

They didn't find Ricky the next day or the next. John didn't want them to find Ricky, but he did want Sarah back. Sarah and Jana spent every evening that week out searching for Ricky while Helen made meals for them and let them watch television. Every evening Sarah and Jana returned at dark, tired and discouraged.

John tried to talk to Sarah before Jana shooed them upstairs to get ready for bed, but Sarah was usually on the phone or writing in her book. Sometimes she didn't answer him, even when he told her that Betsy hadn't returned to work or that Mick had choked on his dinner. She wasn't listening. Sometimes she even waved him away and turned her back, covering her ear with her hand so she could talk on the phone. She didn't have time for John. John was very sad.

During the next week there were other sightings. Sarah would rush out to try to catch Ricky where he was sighted, but each time she came back without him. She told Jana he had been seen rummaging through someone's garbage can or stealing cookies off a plate in someone's backyard while the children were playing. People were starting to get nervous and keeping their doors locked and their children inside.

Every couple of days reporters called, and Sarah had to tell them more about Ricky. They came over to the group home again and took more pictures. They talked to Sarah and Jana and tried to talk to Peter, but he just banged his head and rocked away from them. When they stuck the microphone in front of John he started to tell them that Ricky was a bad boy, but Sarah jerked him back and stepped in. She told them he would be found any day now. John kicked the chair in the dining room when he walked by. Everything was about Ricky.

The next day the newspaper had Ricky's picture in it again. Sarah read John the headline, "Missing Man Sighted Again, Retarded Resident Still Alive."

"I don't know if this is helping or hurting," Sarah said, covering her forehead with her hand.

John patted her back in sympathy. Sarah barely noticed him.

One evening both Sarah and Jana were home when John and the others arrived on the bus. The house smelled good. John followed Sarah into the kitchen where Jana was checking something in the oven.

"Hi, John," she said. "I'm making your favorite. Macaroni casserole."

John sandpapered his hands. Finally. Things were returning to normal.

"Did you get any calls today?" Jana asked Sarah.

"Not since yesterday. But we've had six sightings, the last two in the same area, so we're narrowing it down. The flyers helped. That was a good idea, Jana."

"Why do you suppose he's not coming to us? He must be starving." Jana put on the padded glove and pulled the casserole out of the oven.

"I wish I knew," Sarah answered.

"You'd think he'd want a soft bed, if nothing else." Jana put the casserole on a trivet.

"Sawah?" John said, tapping her on the shoulder.

"Just a minute, John. Don't interrupt. Did I tell you I called William again?" Sarah asked Jana.

Jana rolled her eyes. "What did he say?"

"He asked how it was going. Said he had meant to call but had a project to finish. He didn't even offer to help."

"Jerk." Jana handed John the casserole in a special basket so it wouldn't burn his hands, and waved him out toward the dining room.

"Sawah?" John said again. "Bessy at wo'kchop t'day. Hu betta'."

Sarah sighed. "That's nice, John. I'm glad she's better."

The phone rang. Sarah rushed past him to answer it.

John set the casserole on the table, eying the phone and considering whether it would flush down the toilet. He didn't think it would fit.

"Hello?" Sarah said. "Yes, it is. Where? Okay. I'll be right there." She hung up.

"Who was it?" Jana called from the kitchen.

"Another sighting. Over by Hill Street. Same area. I better go."

"Oh, Sarah, call someone else. Maybe Barry would go."

"I can't wait. He might disappear."

"At least eat a bite first," Jana said, shoving a roll into Sarah's hand.

"I'll be back soon." She was gone.

After dinner John took Lonnie upstairs. He made Lonnie pretend he was Ricky and told him to hide while John waited outside the bedroom door. Then John searched for him, calling his name and telling him he better come back or else. When John found him under the bed he pulled him out, tied his hands up and put him in the closet.

"You stay Cabby. You bad, bad, bad, Wicky!" he said, shutting the door.

Lonnie pushed the door open and shook his head, grunting "No." He didn't like that.

John gave up on the Ricky game.

Almost every day someone called in with a sighting, yet by the time Sarah or Barry drove there, he was not to be found. The police had long since given up their search. Barry said Ricky didn't want to be found. They would just have to surprise him to catch him.

As each day passed, John felt happier that Ricky wasn't there. No one woke them up at night bumping around in his room, no one hit, pushed or swore at them. No one had to do Ricky's work while he stood nearby dangling his spaghetti arms. If only Sarah would stop looking for him, John would have her back, too.

Cartoon day came again. Ricky had been gone two whole weeks. John relaxed in the soft chair Ricky usually sat in to watch television. Michael and Todd were both there. They were planning to go to the gym today.

The front door opened. "Good morning!" Sarah called cheerfully.

"Hi Sawah!" John was glad to see her looking happy for a change.

"Hi John." She patted him on the shoulder as he sat watching *Roadrunner* with Lonnie.

"Did you get some rest?" Todd asked. He and Michael were gathering the gym bags to get ready to go.

"Yes. I feel better. I just wanted to check in before I head out to search that neighborhood. Any calls last night?"

"No. Nothing." Michael set the newspaper down and pointed to it. "Did you see this?"

"What?" She read the newspaper for a few minutes, then shook her head. "Great. Where did they get all that trash?"

"Some jerk at Larkspur," Michael said disgustedly. "Just proves their point. Institution's the safest place, you know."

"Like no one ever ran away from Larkspur," Sarah said. "Any more coffee?"

"Help yourself." Michael nodded toward the kitchen.

Sarah brought her coffee to the living room and sat down on the sofa by John. "How are you guys holding up?"

"Us go gym," John answered, slinging his arm around Sarah's shoulders.

"I know. I bet you're happy about that."

"Yep." John patted Sarah's arm with his hand, glad to have her beside him.

"Are you doing okay? Seems like I haven't talked to you for a while." she nudged him with her elbow.

"Yep. Me okay now. You back."

"Are you worried about Ricky like I am?"

"Nope." John shook his head adamantly. He was about to say "Wicky bad" when the doorbell rang. Sarah sprang up and John followed her to the door.

It was Mrs. Rockmont, the neighbor who had been most friendly, or at least, not mean. John hid behind Sarah wondering what she would say this time. Mrs. Rockmont had a plate of cookies in her hands. "I've been reading the articles in the paper ..."

"Don't worry," Sarah shot, "we'll find Ricky any day now. He hasn't hurt anyone. There's nothing to worry about."

Mrs. Rockmont looked down at her feet. "I came to tell you how sorry I am that your man is lost. I know not everyone in the neighborhood agrees with me, but I hope you find him, and I hope he's all right."

Sarah paused. "Why thank you, Mrs. Rockmont," Her voice softened as she took the plate of cookies. "We're working hard to find him. We're getting close, I think."

Mrs. Rockmont's voice quavered, "When I think of him out there all by himself with no food..." There were tears in her eyes. "He reminds me of my nephew. He had that autism, mind you, he could talk and everything, but he flapped his hands like that one there."

She pointed to Peter who was Larkspur-dipping by the front window. "He got lost on a camping trip a few years back. They didn't find him for three weeks. He had fallen into a ravine and... they were too late."

"I'm sorry to hear that," Sarah said. "Ricky seems to have good survival instincts. He's being sighted almost every day. I think we're going to catch him very soon. Thank you for the cookies."

Mrs. Rockmont shifted her feet uncomfortably. "I, I wanted to offer to help if there's anything I can do."

"How nice of you!" Sarah handed John the plate of cookies. He shoved one into his mouth. "The thing that would help the most would be to drop the lawsuit. Maybe you can talk to Mrs. Hanover and the others."

"I'll try. She's a stubborn old woman, but maybe after this she'll feel differently."

"I appreciate that. Thanks again." They shook hands and Mrs. Rockmont hurried off the porch.

"What came over her?" Michael asked. "Guilty conscience?"

"I don't know, but it's a good sign." Sarah helped them stack the gym bags by the front door. "I have to call Barry. He's going to help me search that neighborhood again. We're going door-to-door to ask if anyone has seen Ricky, and to check around under porches and in garages if they'll let us."

"This is getting old," Michael said. "Aren't you sick of it?"

"Yeah, but what choice do we have? I keep hoping he'll get so hungry and tired he'll want to get caught."

"I bet he will," Todd added cheerfully. "Do you want one of us to help? Once we get them to the gym, one could handle them alone."

"Thanks for offering, but I think we can cover it." Sarah pulled Mick to his feet, gave him a little piece of paper and headed him toward the door.

As Michael handed each of them a gym bag, he said to Sarah, "I remember hearing about a guy at Larkspur who was a runner. About once a year he took off for a few weeks, but he always showed up eventually. No one knew how he survived, but he had a knack for it. The last time he ran away, it was winter. When they found him he had frostbite so bad they had to amputate his feet."

"Oh, thanks a lot, Michael," Sarah said. "You really know how to cheer me up."

"It's true."

"Go on. Give the guys some fun." Sarah waved at them from the porch as they squeezed into Michael's hippie-mobile, Lonnie sitting on Todd's lap.

Two more weeks passed. Sightings of Ricky had slowed to a trickle. On a hot Tuesday evening in August, Jana set up a fan at each open door and opened all the windows, trying to get some circulation through the house. Everyone was wearing shorts and tank tops, and still John felt hot and sticky. Jana fixed sandwiches for dinner because she said she couldn't stand to cook in this heat.

John could tell Sarah was sad because she was quiet and she didn't smile. He heard her tell Jana that it had been five days since a sighting. Jana wondered if they shouldn't call off the search. Sarah said, not yet, but she didn't go out that evening. She stayed home for the first time in over a month. John was glad to have her there even though she didn't act like she used to. He tried to cheer her up by tickling her sides, but she brushed him off, saying it was too hot for that.

Before dinner Sarah sat down to read the books and charts everyone wrote in and she announced to Jana that it was time to make some changes around here. John perked up and listened, curious to see what she would do.

"For one thing," she said, pointing to the paper scraps all over the floor, "I'm sick of this mess. Mick's not stealing food and is pretty compliant, isn't he? The data shows he's at 70 percent and holding."

"He is, with prompting," Jana said. "He did snatch Peter's biscuit this morning. I don't think the paper means anything to him anymore. Sometimes he won't even take it when I offer it to him."

"Geez! We should have changed this a long time ago. I haven't had any time to work on my research with all this going on. Let's drop the paper thing and just use verbals for now. How's Peter doing on shirt ripping?"

"Only two last week. T-shirts are much harder to rip. The necks are all stretched out, though. He's still trying."

"Hmm. I'll have to think about that one." Sarah rubbed her head as if she had a headache.

John came up behind her and put his hand on her shoulder. "Sawah?"

She turned to look at him. "Yes, John? What is it?"

"Me yike you, Sawah." He patted her head gently.

Sarah grabbed his hand and squeezed it tightly. She didn't talk for a minute, and when she did her voice was husky. "Thanks, John. I like you, too. In fact, I love you guys."

The backyard was cooler than the house, so they ate a picnic dinner outside. After dinner Jana and Sarah started picking up paper bits all over the house. John helped. They vacuumed the rug, dug beneath the sofa cushions, and went upstairs and flipped over Mick's mattress. Paper was everywhere.

When they finally cleaned up all the paper scraps, Sarah went to Mick and stuck out her hand. "Give me the paper, Mick. We're done with that now."

Mick stuck his hands deep in his pockets and spun away.

Sarah talked with Jana and they decided they would clean out Mick's pockets when he went to bed. Then Sarah said that Lonnie needed a new program to move faster. He was always the last one finished, always walked behind everyone and had to be pulled or pushed along. She and Jana made a special chart for Lonnie to help him go faster. They told him that they were going to set a timer. If he wasn't done when the timer went off, he went to time-out. If he finished before the timer went off, he got points. If he got five points a day, he got a strawberry milkshake before bed.

Lonnie shook his head "no" while they explained it to him, but when they showed him the picture of the milkshake they had cut out of a magazine to put on his chart, he rubbed his tummy and said, "Ummm!"

Peter was also going to do something different, Sarah said. When he ripped a shirt he was going to have to carry it down to the basement, get a clean shirt from down there, carry it up and put it on, each time he ripped one, no matter how many times in a row. He was also going to have to wear a glove if he hit himself. Sarah wrote all these things down in the notebook and explained them to Jana. John sat at the table with them and listened in fascination. He couldn't wait to see what everyone would do with these changes.

As it grew dark outside, Jana turned the fans around to point inside, trying to "suck in the cool evening air," she said. John sat down in front of a fan and let the wind dry his sweat.

Sarah pulled up a chair beside him in the doorway. "Your new job is going to be helping Jana with meal planning," she said. "Every week you're going to help her think of meals to cook. You can look for pictures of things you want to make in these magazines."

She held a stack of magazines on her lap "You'll help Jana figure out what food to buy and go grocery shopping with her. How does that sound?"

John's face lit up. "Yeah! Me he'p Jana! Me gwown-up!"

"That's right, John, you are a grown-up." Sarah smiled happily for the first time in weeks, it seemed.

Friday evening they sat at the picnic table outside celebrating Peter's thirty-fifth birthday. Barry had come over to join them. Jana brought out a cake she and John had baked, lit the candles, and they sang Happy Birthday. Peter shied away from the lit candles so John and Lonnie helped blow them out.

Peter flapped his arms excitedly while Jana cut the cake. She served him first. Sarah dipped ice cream onto each plate and John sat back down, his mouth watering. He couldn't wait for Peter to open his gifts. He and Lonnie had bought Peter's favorite candy at the little store with their own spending money and wrapped it themselves. There was a lot of extra tape on it, but at least Peter couldn't see what was inside.

Everyone started eating their cake and ice cream. Peter loved the cake and had a second piece. Lonnie beat the timer and got his last point for the day to earn a strawberry milkshake, too.

Sarah licked the frosting off her fingers and said to Jana and Barry, "A week from Saturday the Division for Developmental Disabilities is coming to survey our program. I'll spend some time with them Friday going over the paperwork, then Saturday morning they want to do a site visit. We have to make sure everything's in good shape by then. I'll need your help."

"Saturday? That's unusual, isn't it?" Jana asked.

"A bit," Sarah answered. "They are flying in Friday to look at the workshop so they decided to take a look at us while they're in town."

"I didn't realize it was coming up so fast," Barry said. "Don't they know what we've been through the last few weeks?" He scraped his plate with his fork tines to get the last few crumbs.

"Yes. Apparently all our publicity made them want to come sooner rather than later. They said they'll take our circumstances into account. This is just an initial survey, since we're new, and then they'll come back next year for a full inspection, if we're still here."

"Timing's bad," Barry said, shaking his head.

"It sure is," Jana agreed.

"Who comin'?" John asked. They hadn't had many visitors.

"They're state program surveyors," Sarah explained. "They're coming to see how well our group home is doing."

"Oh." John didn't know what that meant. "Me yike?"

"Yes, you'll like them, John. They'll probably just look around and ask a few questions. I don't exactly know what they're looking for."

Sarah kept talking to Jana and Barry. "We already put them off so long, William says we can't change it. He's going to come over, too."

"Finally!" Jana said. "You'd think he would have come by during all this mess with Ricky. Or at least helped us out somehow."

Sarah rolled her eyes. "You'd think."

"You know what *I* think of him," Barry said glancing at Sarah. He stacked up the empty plates.

John held his plate tightly, hoping for seconds.

"A Saturday. That means Michael is working," Jana said quietly, pausing for a second. "Do you want me to work that Saturday?"

"No." Sarah gathered up discarded napkins. "They want everything to run as usual. I'll talk to Michael and make sure he understands how important this is. I have to come by anyway."

"I vote for Jana to work," Barry said. "Who knows what Michael and Todd might say to them? We know they can't be trusted."

"It'll be all right," Sarah assured them. "I'll coach them ahead of time on what to say and not to say."

Just then the phone rang inside the house.

"Who would dare call us during Peter's birthday party?" Barry asked, smiling at Peter. "Maybe it's Mrs. Hanover wanting to bring you a gift."

Sarah laughed and ran in to answer the phone. A few seconds later she flung open the screen door and called, "A sighting. Near Seacrest Road again. This time someone saw him go into an abandoned shack. I'm going."

Barry stood up. "I'll go with you. Don't anyone touch my plate! I plan to have another piece of cake."

He dashed after Sarah and soon John heard Sarah's punch buggy zoom away.

After the cake and plates were cleared away Peter opened his gifts; some new shirts with no buttons, a radio for his room, a game called Sorry, and the candy from John and Lonnie.

The evening was nice and cool and they stayed outside until it was almost dark.

Jana tried to teach them Peter's new game. Peter didn't seem very interested. He moved his game piece to where Jana pointed then flapped and watched the leaves in the trees above them. Jana showed John how to count out the number of squares he could move, and how to put his red game piece there. John was explaining it to Lonnie when the screen door flew open.

Everyone turned to look. Barry poked his head out and held the door open. He had a funny look on his face.

From inside the house, Sarah's soft voice coaxed, "Go on. It's okay."

Out stepped a man caked in grime. His hair was matted, accented with sticks and bits of leaves. He wore a scraggly beard. His faded clothes were tattered and filthy. He stepped out of the door then stopped, staring at them with spaghetti arms dangling at his sides.

Jana dropped her game piece and gasped. "Ricky!"

A grin disfigured his filthy face then his body was wracked by a spasm. It was Ricky all right.

Jana began to cry and ran over to hug Ricky over and over again. Sarah and Barry were smiling now, tears rolling down Sarah's face.

John felt like crying, too. He hated seeing Ricky home and getting so much attention. Why couldn't he have just stayed lost? He threw his game piece onto the table and kicked at the table leg. No one noticed.

The distinct smell of garbage drifted toward them. Lonnie held his nose and said, "P.U!"

Ricky pointed back to the kitchen and said, "Eat. Food," the first time John had heard him say anything but swear words. Jana screamed, "He can talk!" and ran inside to get him some food.

Sarah said he was too dirty to be in the house until they cleaned him up so they put his food on the picnic table. He ate three plates full of food while John and Lonnie watched in amazement, standing back because of the smell.

Sarah and Jana kept wiping away tears as they watched him eat, saying, "I can't believe it! You're back, Ricky! We're so glad to see you!"

After he finally slowed down and dropped his fork, Barry led him up to the bathroom where he scrubbed Ricky for a long time. From outside the bathroom door John could hear groans, water splashing and the tub refilling several times. Barry called for Sarah to run to the store for special shampoo because Ricky's hair had bugs in it.

After she got back, Sarah helped Barry shave off Ricky's beard and cut off most of his ragged hair. Ricky went to bed without complaining and didn't wake up all night. In fact, he slept until afternoon the next day.

The newspaper men came back and asked Jana and Sarah a lot of questions. The one with the camera wanted to take some pictures of Ricky, but Sarah wouldn't let them. She said he needed rest. John tried to get the cameraman to take his picture, but he wasn't interested in John at all.

Ricky was good for several days, though he didn't have to do any chores. He didn't hit or bump them, didn't say anything bad, and stayed close to the kitchen, even helping to bring the food out at mealtimes.

It was almost a week before John heard Ricky say something again. After not being asked to do any chores, Sarah made him help set the table.

Under his breath Ricky whispered, "Bitch." Sarah acted like she didn't hear him. John knew he was back to his old tricks.

That Friday night, after Sarah and Jana left, Ricky started acting up again. He stuck his foot out to trip Lonnie on their way up to bed and pushed a chair over, almost hitting Peter.

Michael grabbed him and pushed him up against the wall. "Ricky, you little turd. We're not going to start this again." Ricky was awake most of the night, banging things around in his room.

The next morning, the Saturday of the survey, John got dressed and hurried downstairs.

Michael was still asleep on his sofa bed. He groaned. "Is it time to get up? Shit. I was up all night with Ricky. Did you hear him last night?"

John nodded. He had heard bumps and grunts several times.

Michael rolled out of bed and stumbled into the kitchen to make some coffee. John switched on the TV and sat on Michael's rumpled sofa-bed. It was still warm.

Bugs Bunny was on. John laughed out loud when Elmer Fudd blasted Bugs Bunny with his gun. In a few minutes, Mick stumbled downstairs, too, and sat beside John. Lately, Mick had started to like watching television. Even though he didn't get pencils or paper scraps anymore, he still fingered the cushions out of habit, occasionally finding something that he stuck in his pocket. But he also glanced up at the screen through his eyebrows. He even snickered at some of the cartoon antics. Mick didn't seem so bad, especially compared to Ricky.

Michael brought a cup of coffee out of the kitchen.

"Hey, guys. You're on my bed!"

John grinned. "Me he'e fi'st."

"You hog all the good seats," Michael said.

John could tell he wasn't mad. Michael didn't like to watch cartoons anyway. He picked up the ashtray from the coffee table and sat in the dining room to smoke.

The phone rang and Michael answered it. "Shit!" he said when he hung up. He called over to John, "You have to help me clean up the house this morning because those hot shots from the state are coming to look us over. And Todd just called and said he's sick, so he won't be here. It's you and me, buddy."

"Okay," John said absently.

"That means you can only watch one show."

"Okay." John didn't mind. He felt grown-up when he helped.

Bugs Bunny had just hidden himself safely in his hole when a crash came from upstairs. Breaking glass could only mean one thing. Ricky.

Michael sprang up, crushed out his cigarette and rushed upstairs. John sprinted after him. He hoped Ricky would get in big trouble.

When they got to Ricky's room, Ricky stood buck naked on a pile of bedding knee high. Behind him, the wind blew the curtains through the shattered window. Shards of glass lay all over the floor.

Ricky grinned at them and said, "Muthafucka."

Michael swore until his face was red and he ran out of bad words. He grabbed Ricky and twisted his arms behind his back. "I oughta break your arms, you fucking imbecile! You'd think you'd appreciate having a roof over your head, you ungrateful shithead!"

"Wicky bad!" John exclaimed. "Ooo, bewy bad!"

"And we're having inspectors this morning. Fuck! I'm going to time you out for the rest of your short, pathetic life!" Michael hustled Ricky out of the bedroom and into the bathroom. John stepped out of the way in case Ricky started peeing again.

As they struggled down the hall, Michael muttered, "And here we thought you had stopped this shit. Wasn't a month in the wild enough to cure you? We should have left you out there to eat garbage."

"Muthafucka," Ricky replied. He strained against Michael's hold. Michael lost his grip on Ricky's arms and scrambled to grab him again. Ricky swung his fist at Michael and clipped his head with his fist. Michael fell back and cried out in pain.

John flinched. "Uh-oh."

"Shit, shit, shit!" Michael snarled. He snatched Ricky's arms, wrenched them behind his back, shoved him forcefully into the bathroom. "You bastard! I can hit, too, you know."

John peeked into the toilet room. Michael pressed Ricky against the wall hard. Ricky's face squished up and his eyes looked scared.

"Hit Wicky!" John shouted at Michael. "Him bad!"

"Get out of here, John! Go back downstairs!" Michael shoved the door shut with his foot. There was a thump, then a groan, then silence.

John clapped in glee. "Yea!" Ricky finally got what he deserved.

John stopped suddenly, thinking. Maybe it was Michael who got hurt. He remembered that tech who got thrown against the wall by Big Fatty. Broke his back, they said. He never came back.

John listened at the door. Nothing. He tapped, half-afraid Ricky would come flying out swinging Michael over his head.

"What?" Michael's voice was calm.

"You okay?"

"Yes, we're fine. Go downstairs and start cleaning up."

"Okay." John hurried downstairs. *Bugs Bunny* was already over. John started putting things away in the living room and emptied Michael's ashtray.

In a little bit Michael came down alone. "Let's eat breakfast," he said. His forehead was sweaty. He lit another cigarette.

John switched off the TV. He and Lonnie helped set the table for cereal. No pancakes this morning. During breakfast they heard banging upstairs. The thumps grew louder and more frequent as they ate. Michael ignored the sounds until he finished his food.

"Peter, your turn to clear the table," he said. "I'll be right back."

Michael's footsteps sounded heavy on the stairs. Peter could clear the table by himself now, one bowl at a time, though somebody had to hold the cowboy doors open for him because he refused to touch them. John held the doors for Peter each time he passed through.

Upstairs a door slammed. The banging stopped. Michael yelled something John couldn't understand. When Michael came down with Ricky in tow the table was cleared except for Lonnie's place. Lonnie was still eating.

Ricky looked around like nothing had happened. Michael pulled a dining room chair into the corner of the living room and shoved Ricky onto it facing the wall. "Sit right here and don't move." Michael rubbed his upper arm as if it hurt.

Peter stood near Lonnie, waiting for him to finish eating. Each time Lonnie set his spoon down, Peter reached for Lonnie's bowl. Lonnie squealed and pushed Peter's hand away. Peter banged his head and waited again.

"That's good enough, Peter," Michael said. "You're done. Lonnie, bring your bowl to the kitchen when you're finished. And hurry up." He tapped Lonnie's new chart on his way into the kitchen. He kept forgetting to set the timer.

John heard the water running in the kitchen sink.

Peter rocked to the front window to "keep watch," as Sarah called it, pacing back and forth and flapping. John couldn't figure out why she said he was keeping watch because Peter didn't have one.

As he waited for Lonnie to finish eating, John glanced over at Ricky who sat on the chair staring at John. His stony glare sent a shiver through John. John scooted his chair around so his back was to Ricky.

"Yonnie, you done? Yet's pway." John stood up and walked to the living room, motioning for Lonnie to follow.

That's when Ricky made his move. He bounded out of his seat like a pogo stick, covering the distance to Lonnie in one stride. Ricky shoved Lonnie sideways, grabbed his nearly empty bowl and tipped it up to his mouth. Lonnie's head bounced off the edge of the table before he landed in a heap on the carpet. He didn't move

John screeched. He dropped to his knees beside Lonnie gently shaking him. "You okay? You okay?" Carefully, he turned Lonnie's head around so he could see his face. It felt sticky. When he pulled his hand back, his fingers were red.

John screamed again. The image of Crazy Henry sprawled on the street flashed through his mind. The room started to go dark.

Michael burst through the cowboy doors. "What's wrong?"

"Yonnie dead!"

"What? What happened?"

"Wicky push him!" John began to cry, hot tears stinging his face.

Michael crouched beside Lonnie and put his ear next to Lonnie's mouth. "He's breathing, John. I think he just got knocked out. Lonnie? Wake up, Lonnie."

Michael lifted Lonnie's head and rubbed his face. Lonnie moaned, then opened one eye. John wiped the tears from his cheeks as the room came into focus again.

Ricky threw Lonnie's bowl onto the table and it shattered.

Michael jumped. "Ricky, you asshole! I swear I'll ..." but he turned back to Lonnie. "I'll get a towel. You'll be all right, big guy. Stay with him, John." Michael set Lonnie's head down gently and hurried to the kitchen.

Now that he knew Lonnie was alive, John steamed with anger. His eyes blurred. Ricky still stood by the table smiling evilly and jerking his arms around.

"You hu't Yonnie!" John growled at him and stood up. "Me kiw you!" He raised his fist to bash Ricky in the face.

Just then Michael swished through the cowboy doors.

"None of that, John. That's my job."

John lowered his hand reluctantly, trembling all over.

Michael pressed the paper towel to Lonnie's head and helped him sit up. "Are you okay?"

Lonnie moaned.

"John, hold this on Lonnie's head for awhile until the bleeding stops."

Michael stood up and faced Ricky, his hands clenched. "What the hell were you doing? I told you no breakfast. And now you hurt Lonnie! I've had it with you!"

In a movement quick as lightening Ricky grabbed Lonnie's butter knife from the table and waved it at Michael menacingly.

"Oh, sure, you twerp." Michael easily knocked the knife out of Ricky's hand.

Ricky swung his other fist up and caught Michael in the neck. Michael gulped and grabbed his neck, taking a strangled breath.

Before he could recover Ricky tackled him. They tumbled to the floor, legs flying, bumping against the dining room chairs.

"Fight!" John yelled, pulling Lonnie under the table and out of the way.

Michael and Ricky rolled into the living room. Mick stopped groping the sofa bed and growled at them, lifting his feet out of their way.

Michael tried to hold Ricky down, but he slipped out and scrambled away, knocking over the coffee table. Michael grabbed Ricky's foot, then jumped on top of him. Ricky twisted onto his back, flailing at Michael with his fists. When Michael managed to get a hold of his wrists, Ricky tried to bite him.

Puffing and red-faced, Michael finally pinned Ricky's hands to the floor and sat on his chest. "You goddamn bastard!" Michael's arms shook, but he managed to hold Ricky down.

John cowered under the table with Lonnie. He didn't know what to do. At Starlight, another tech would help. They would put one of those white jackets on the worker and take him to Cadby. For the first time since he left Starlight, John wished brown-toothed Marley was here, or even the Mean Man. Anybody!

"Hey, guys, I need help here," Michael said, breathing heavily. "John?"

"Yeah?"

"Help me out."

"What me do?" John climbed slowly out from under the table.

"Can you use the phone?" Michael asked.

"Uh..." Sarah had worked with John on dialing numbers, but he had only made one real phone call to Barry's house.

"Call Sarah."

At that, Ricky bucked up. Michael lost his grip and Ricky twisted over onto his stomach. He tried to crawl away. Michael snatched his arms and wrenched them behind his back, sitting hard on Ricky's butt.

John picked up the phone. "What numba'?"

Michael puffed, "Dial two."

John cranked the dial around.

"Now six."

John dialed each number in turn. "It wingin'," he told Michael.

"Good." Michael adjusted his grip on Ricky's hands.

"Wingin' mo'e," John said.

"Okay. She's probably on her way over already. You can hang up."

Everyone fell quiet. The only sound was Michael's labored breathing.

"Sarah will be here any minute. Until then, who has a belt?" Michael asked.

John did. "Me got bewt."

"I need it. Now!"

"Pants faw' down," John said, hesitating.

"Just give me the damn belt!"

John slipped it off and tossed it to Michael. He wrapped the belt tightly around Ricky's wrists and cinched it. Then he slid off Ricky's butt, keeping his legs slung sideways over Ricky's back. Michael's shirt was damp with sweat.

The doorbell rang.

Michael sighed. "Let her in, John!"

John ran to the door, anxious to be the first to tell Sarah that Ricky was in big trouble.

But instead of Sarah, two men and a woman stood on the porch, all dressed up in suits.

Chapter 17
The Survey

William sat on his front porch waiting for Sarah to pick him up. When Sarah pulled into the driveway, a middle-aged woman with graying hair tied up loosely on the back of her head stood up from the Adirondack next to William, kissed him on the cheek and disappeared inside the house.

Sarah instantly kicked herself for feeling a stab of what? Jealousy? Of his wife on whom he was constantly cheating? Pity maybe. *Don't be stupid,* she scolded herself.

William sauntered off the porch, leather folder under his arm, and climbed into her car. Sarah smiled briefly, her heart jumping like a schoolgirl. She hoped her face mimicked nonchalance.

"Hi," she said. "Thanks for coming."

"No problem. I appreciate you picking me up," William set his folder on the floor beneath his legs and reached for the seatbelt. "My car was supposed to be ready yesterday but they had to order a part for it that didn't arrive. Jags are notorious for needing repairs."

Then why did you buy one? Sarah thought sarcastically. But all she said was, "Bummer," and shifted into first gear. The car jerked forward a little harder than she meant it to.

"I used to have a Volkswagen," he said casually. "In those days, I loved it. They don't make 'em like this anymore." He patted the dusty dash, then unobtrusively wiped his hand on his pants.

Sarah winced. She couldn't remember the last time she had cleaned the interior. "No, they don't. Even if it doesn't always work it's easy to push-start."

"Their claim to fame," William laughed lightly.

Sarah assumed her professional voice. "I'm glad you're here because I know the surveyors will have some questions for you about the grant—stability of funding, that kind of thing. They gave me a list yesterday." She rummaged in the backseat with one hand, finding the stapled packet and handing it to William.

He flipped through the pages. "I'm not worried about this. They know it's an experiment and that there are bound to be kinks to work out. The state is happy that someone is trying it because they're eventually going to have to close that decrepit institution."

Sarah turned onto the main highway and sped up. "You really think so?"

"Well, most of it, anyway. Of course, there will be a few who won't be able to leave, the crib cases, those who are dangerous or delusional ..." William paused.

Lost in thoughts of why she was still weak-kneed around William, Sarah quickly replayed in her head what he had just said. "I suppose so ..." she said.

"So, Sarah, how do you feel about the survey? The whole project ... how is everything going, really?" He sounded like he used to, supportive, caring.

Damn! Why did he have to say things like that? She forced herself not to succumb and open up. "I'm okay with the survey. They know we're a new facility, and they've certainly read about what we've been going through with Ricky. I think they must be realistic about what to expect, don't you?"

"I'm sure they are." He put his hand on the back of her seat and tapped it with his fingers. "How are things with Ricky since he came back?"

"Not bad. Ricky's readjusting to civilization."

William cleared his throat. "Sorry I haven't been more available. I've been finishing up two articles and editing a book for Miles and Jones."

It's all about you, Sarah thought, *and advancing your career*. She said, "It worked out. I had lots of volunteer help."

"That's good. I knew you could handle it. You're so competent, so responsible."

It was a compliment but it felt like an insult. Sarah was confused about William. She cared desperately what he thought of her, yet she had learned there were limits to his commitment to her. She struggled to sort through her feelings before responding. At last she managed, "Well, we found him and he's okay. That's the important thing."

Sarah pulled into the driveway of the group home behind a rental already parked there. She frowned. "They're here," she said. "They weren't supposed to come until 9:00."

"We'll get this over faster then," William said cheerfully.

But Sarah was worried. She had intended to make sure Michael had everything ready before they arrived. "I hope everybody's up. Michael's a bit of a wild card."

"I'm sure it's fine."

As they walked up the steps onto the porch, they saw that the door was ajar. They could hear voices from within.

"But why is he tied up?" a woman's tense voice was saying. "Surely there's a different plan for violent outbursts."

Sarah's heart leaped into the hollow of her neck and she instinctively brought her hand up to her throat. Tied up? What had Michael done now?

Michael's reply was strained. "I had to control him while I called for help. He was dangerous..."

William pushed the door open for Sarah and she stepped in, barely able to breathe. The three surveyors were crowded into the entryway, blocking Sarah's view of Michael and whatever was going on.

"This is a major safety concern, " said the woman, "We'll need to see your protocol."

"Hi," Sarah said behind them. "Sorry I'm late. I thought we said 9:00."

The three suit-clad inspectors turned around. Sarah introduced them to William and everyone shook hands. Yesterday, Sarah had pegged Miss Shelby, the squeezed-faced woman, as the compliance Nazi. Chris Bothel, the team leader, was tall and lean with huge hands—he reminded Sarah of a mountain climber. Sarah breathed a bit easier when he smiled pleasantly. Len Zarno, a quiet, heavily browed man in his fifties only nodded politely.

Sarah peered beyond them to where Michael sat astride Ricky feverishly trying to undo a belt wrapped securely around his wrists.

Miss Shelby gave Sarah a serious look of disapproval and pointed at them. "Miss Richardson, this client has been tied up with a belt. Did you know this type of treatment was going on?"

Sarah stared wide-eyed. "Uh, no ... what happened, Michael?"

"Ricky went off on me. He pushed Lonnie over, threatened me with a knife and went crazy, hitting and kicking and trying to bite. I had to put him down. Without help here, what could I do?" He flipped the belt across the room and wiped sweat from his face.

"Where's Todd?" Sarah asked, shouldering past the visitors into the chaotic living room. She spied John in the dining room dabbing at Lonnie's head with a bloody paper towel.

"He called in sick. We tried to call you ..."

"What happened to Lonnie?" Sarah cried.

"I told you." Michael patted Ricky's back as if he liked him. "Ricky knocked him over and he hit his head on the table. He'll be all right."

Chris chimed in, "This must be the famous Ricky, then. We were glad to hear that you finally found him."

"So were we," Sarah said. "He's still recovering, though, so that's probably why he's acting out." She was hyper-aware of William's silent presence beside her. She wondered what he thought, seriously regretting that this was his first glimpse of the group home.

Miss Shelby adjusted her oversized glasses. "Clearly, some decision needs to be made about maintaining him in this type of facility, for his own safety. The use of restraints is prohibited, you know," she added perfunctorily, her lips pursing in a fish-like pucker.

"This isn't our normal procedure," Sarah said, trying to sound calm. "I'm sure it was an emergency, otherwise Michael wouldn't have done it." She found herself intentionally defending Michael even though she was enraged.

"It *was* an emergency," Michael said, pulling Ricky to his feet and sitting him on the sofa. "Just a one-time deal. Usually, we put him in time out when he ... he ... has these fits ..."

Michael stopped, glancing at Sarah. He slung his arm around Ricky affectionately.

Ricky gazed at the visitors, blinking innocently. "Muthafucka," he stated.

"Charming, Ricky." Michael rolled his eyes.

For several seconds no one spoke, then Sarah blurted, "Michael, why don't you take him to his room."

"Glad to." Michael yanked Ricky past them and they disappeared up the stairs.

Sarah turned the coffee table upright, shoved the sofa bed back into place, and replaced the cushions, her hands shaking slightly. Her face was hot and she knew it was scarlet. "Sorry you had to come in on such a mess. Come and sit down. I need to check on Lonnie and then we can talk."

The visitors sat down in the living room. Mick scrambled away, growling. Peter backed into the entry and began the Larkspur Dip.

Sarah bent over Lonnie. "John, would you go and talk with our visitors while I take care of Lonnie?" John left him reluctantly. Sarah was amazed once again at John's loyalty to Lonnie.

Sarah helped Lonnie stand up and led him into the kitchen. Examining his head, she rinsed off the blood, and put a Band-Aid over it. The wound was superficial and had almost stopped bleeding. She sat him down on a dining room chair before returning to her visitors.

"How do you like living here?" Chris asked John.

"Me yike. Yike Sawah," John said, pointing to her.

"What do you do around here?" Chris asked.

"Us wo'k. Cho'es. Wide big bus to wo'kchop." John pulled out his wallet and showed Chris his bus pass. "Dis me."

Len said, "Do you like working at the workshop?"

"Yep. Me git money. Weo money!"

Sarah glanced at William as she tiptoed back. He sat in the overstuffed chair watching John intently and smiling. Sarah's tension eased somewhat. She wondered when the last time was that William had worked with someone with developmental disabilities, if ever. Was all his knowledge just academic? She realized she didn't know.

"John was just telling us about riding the bus to work," Chris said, inviting Sarah into the conversation.

Sarah smiled. "Yes, he and Lonnie have learned to ride the city bus. He's a good worker and can do all the chores around the house. John's becoming very independent. He's our star, I'd say."

John beamed and tapped his chest. "Me good!"

Everyone laughed.

"Well, let me give you a tour of the house." Sarah put on her most professional demeanor, squashing down the angst in her chest. Of all days, why did Ricky act out like this today? Why did Michael tie Ricky up—today? Was it Michael or was Ricky taking a turn for the worse? She imagined a stiff wind scattering the pages of her dissertation across a vast ocean, ungraspable, all because of Ricky.

Sarah led them through the house, checking in briefly with Michael who had Ricky sitting quietly on his bed. She sighed imperceptibly, and took the visitors to her office in the basement.

They talked for almost an hour, going over the questions on the survey in detail. William spoke up in support of what Sarah was doing, explaining in scholarly terms the methods of her research, the behavior programs she was implementing (he was listening after all ... or at least reading her drafts, she realized), and the data they were gathering. He made the program shine, despite the fiasco with Ricky.

By the time they left, everyone was smiling except Miss Shelby. As they walked onto the front porch Miss Shelby said, "I think your program has potential, but you will need to tighten up on your staff training in regards to allowable procedures. I still have some doubts about having such low-functioning clients, especially volatile clients like Ricky, living in the community. I'm not sure it's safe for them or for the staff and other residents."

"That's one thing we hope to show in our research," William said, unexpectedly including himself in Sarah's project. "We need to determine which clients are best suited for the community and which are not."

This is something he had never discussed with Sarah. She kept her mouth shut.

"We'll send you our results within three weeks," Chris said shaking their hands. "Now we have to get going so we can catch our flight to Salem."

After they left, William and Sarah sat down on the porch steps.

"What do you think?" Sarah asked, grateful for his support and justifiably expecting an affirmative response.

William sobered. "You have to send Ricky back, Sarah. He can't stay in the group home. Too much of a liability."

Sarah cocked her head at William, assuming he was joking. No hint of humor laced his eyes.

"What? You mean it?" She couldn't believe he was saying this. He was the guru of community placement. His lectures and unwavering stance regarding integration were the cutting edge of severe disability thinking.

"I'm serious." He clasped his hands in front of him and looked into Sarah's eyes. "He's dangerous and getting worse, not better. He could hurt someone, Sarah, and that would blow your chances for keeping the group home going, and possibly of finishing your research."

"But, but you were the one who said that all clients deserve a chance to learn to live and function in society, to be accepted and find a place out here." Sarah couldn't keep the astonishment out of her voice.

"I know I said that in class. That's theory. There's a difference between ideology and reality. This guy is not going to make it."

"What makes you say that? We haven't tried everything yet. I have several more ideas that should work …"

"In theory," William interrupted. "These theories are new and untried in this type of situation. In formal studies everything is controlled, but here you are in a real neighborhood. Something more tragic could happen and turn the tide against us."

Sarah's eyes welled with tears. "You're giving up on him. You think I'll fail."

"It's not about you failing." William put his hand on her back. She turned her face away so he wouldn't see the tears. "It's about your project succeeding. There may be some individuals who are too destructive or violent to make it out here. At least right now. Maybe they're just beyond our behavioral technology at this point. Maybe they have co-morbid conditions and need medication controls, as well, which you're not equipped to handle. It's about your career, Sarah. Think of your future."

Sarah wiped her eyes with her hand. "My future will be fine. But what about Ricky's? We haven't tried everything."

William smoothed the back of her hair making her cringe involuntarily. "You have to face the fact that it may not work out for this one subject. That gives us information for future endeavors."

Sarah fought to regain control. "I'd like to give it another month and see what happens. I'll rework my plan tonight."

William patted her back once more and withdrew his hand. "Okay, another month. Maybe you'll hit on the right solution after all. But you have to fire Michael. You know that, right? He's not stable—a fly in the ointment for you and the university."

Sarah didn't respond at first. *Fire Michael?* The thought hadn't crossed her mind. She glanced at William. "What would be my reason for letting him go?"

"You don't have to have a reason. He's not union and he can't file a grievance; he's work study. The university will find another job for him."

Sarah suddenly knew William was right. Michael had to go. The surveyors would see that as a positive move, along with her new plan for Ricky. Michael had been a headache ever since he started.

"I guess you're right," she said tentatively, wishing childishly that William would do it for her.

"Would you do it?" She smiled, knowing what his answer would be.

He laughed. "I'm not his boss."

"I've never fired anyone before. What should I say?"

"Just tell him it's not working out. He's probably expecting it." William stood up. "I better get back. I have to pick up my car from the shop and then I'm going golfing this afternoon."

"Sure." Sarah drove him home. William chattered about her future publication opportunities, university positions he knew might be coming up in the next year or two, how they would collaborate on future research projects. All Sarah could think of was how she was going to tell Michael he was fired. Doubts flooded in. Michael would probably cuss her out,

Ricky would maim someone in the neighborhood, probably Mrs. Hanover, and Sarah would be ABD forever; the dreaded "All But Dissertation." Her mother would be right. She should never have tried any of this. She was going to fail.

When Sarah got back to the group home, she walked in quietly and closed the door behind her. Peter, rocking in the entry, stepped out of her way without giving her eye contact. John and Lonnie were playing Beatles music and John was pretending to strum his suitcase guitar. Mick was watching them from the dining room where he ran his fingers along the table, occasionally stuffing a crumb into his mouth.

"Where's Michael?" Sarah asked John.

"Up'tai's wif Wicky."

Sarah sank down onto the sofa and stared absently at the black TV screen. She ran over and over in her mind how she would tell Michael he was through. She imagined William driving over in his slick Jaguar, bursting in the door, sword in hand, to save the day. She reproached herself. There was no escape, no one else to do it.

Before long, Michael came down the stairs and sat down across from her in the overstuffed chair. "So what's the word?" He looked nervous. He must have expected a reprimand. "Are they going to close us down?"

"I don't think so," she answered. Silently, she whispered, God help me. "Michael, I've got to talk to you."

"Shoot." Michael lit a cigarette. She noticed he had a bluish spot on his cheekbone.

"I mean downstairs. Will Ricky be okay for a minute?"

"Who knows?" He took a drag and blew the smoke out slowly.

Sarah said to John, "Hey, buddy, if Ricky comes down or you hear any noise, come to my office and get us, okay?"

"Okay, Sawah. Me come?" John asked.

"No. I need to talk to Michael alone." She stood up and started for the basement.

"Dum, dee dum dum." Michael hummed a dirge and crushed his cigarette in the dining room ashtray before following her downstairs.

As soon as she closed the door, he preempted her. "Look, I'm sorry. I overslept because Ricky kept me up all night, and things got out of hand. I didn't mean for it to turn out like that. I know I screwed it up."

"You did screw it up!" Sarah raised her voice, wishing he hadn't apologized. "I come over with state surveyors and my sponsoring professor on his first-ever visit, and the house is a wreck, Lonnie is bleeding, and Ricky is tied up—how do you think I feel?"

"I know you're pretty upset with me, but if Todd wasn't home sick, none of this would have happened. I didn't have any help and Ricky went crazy. What else could I do?"

Her voice rose. "Call me or Jana …"

"I tried to call you but you were gone."

"Put Ricky in his room! Anything but tie him up! You just don't think, Michael. You don't follow the rules." She leaned back in her chair and crossed her arms to ward off his arguments.

Michael moved to the edge of his seat and yelled, "Ricky had a knife. I had to do something!"

"What knife?"

"Well, it was a table knife, but still …"

"A butter knife? Come on, Michael," Sarah scoffed.

"Could've been a sharp knife. Might be next time. And he hit me!" He pointed to his face.

"And you got mad. Who's the adult here? He wasn't threatening the other guys, was he? You lost your temper."

Michael's face was crimson. "And you wouldn't, Miss Holier-Than-Thou?"

"Maybe. But I wouldn't have tied him up."

"You're not strong enough to tie him up ... he would have beat the hell out of you."

"I wouldn't have provoked him."

"Well, aren't you the perfect one. Bitch." Michael spat the last word.

Silence. This made it easy. When Sarah spoke again, her voice was low and even. "Ever since you got here you've pushed the limits. You don't follow the programs. You make up your own way of handling things ..."

"I was alone."

"Excuse me. Can I finish?" She stared him down.

Michael's eyes were slits. He said nothing.

Sarah felt stronger, knowing she was right. "You don't follow the chore chart, you don't follow the behavior management programs, the guys watch way too much TV ..."

"It's the weekend, for god's sake!" He threw his hands up in the air.

"And you are a poor model."

"Oh, shit. That's not what you hired me for, is it? You want me to cut my hair, wear preppy sweaters, and say 'gee, golly gosh?'"

"I want you not to teach the clients bad habits, to not smoke pot in this house ..."

"What?"

"Don't deny it. I've smelled it."

"You're such a prima-donna."

"And you hurt the guys! Ricky's wrists are red, Michael. That's abuse. I could get sued, and so could you!"

"Well, I didn't mean to hurt the little bastard. I was just trying to save my skin, all of our skins. And I'm hurt, too!"

"I'm sorry you're hurt, but what am I supposed to tell the state? We're sorry?"

"Tell them whatever you goddamn please."

Sarah battled to stay in control. Finally she said evenly, "It's just not working out, Michael."

"What? Are you firing me?" He stood up, fists clenched.

"Yes, you're fired." Sarah's chest tightened. Her breath came in short gulps.

"Great! Fine! Who the hell could work for a demanding, self-righteous chunk of ice like you, anyway?" Michael jerked the door open and stormed up the stairs. His footsteps pounded above Sarah's head until the front door slammed.

Sarah closed her eyes and put her head in her hands. "Shit," she whispered. That was terrible! How could she possibly have handled it worse? She wasn't meant for firing people. She never wanted to do that again. Michael was a pain, but he wasn't horrible. He cared about the guys and she had fired him. She was pressured into doing something by William just to save her own skin. And his reputation, such as it was. Startled, she realized she was now alone with five disabled men who were doing God knows what. What had she done? Sarah bolted up the stairs.

Mick was in the kitchen pulling things out of the cupboards. His mouth was full, his hand was deep in a cracker box.

"Mick! You can't eat now!" she yelled and ripped the box out of his hands.

John met her in the dining room. "Miko' yeave, Sawah. Whe'e Miko' go?"

"He doesn't work here anymore, John."

"Him fiyed?"

"Yes. You're going to have to put up with me now for the weekend."

"What him do?"

"It just didn't work out," she answered. "Where's Ricky?"

"Him up'tai's." John pointed.

With John hot on her heels, Sarah darted upstairs and stopped at the door to Ricky's room. He sat innocently on his bed staring at the broken window. A pile of clothes and the sheets from his bed was heaped in the middle of the room.

Sarah took a deep breath and bent forward, resting her hands on her knees so she wouldn't faint. "Come on, Ricky," she said. "Let's clean this up."

She cleaned up the glass and taped a piece of cardboard over the window. Then she pointed to each piece of clothing and Ricky gingerly picked it up with two fingers. He only placed them into a dresser drawer with multiple prompts from Sarah and the promise of a treat. After thirty minutes of this, John offered to help Sarah make Ricky's bed.

As she led Ricky downstairs John asked, "Sawah, who take us swimmin'?"

"I will, John."

"Who make dinna'?"

"I will, with your help."

"Who be he'e t'night? Us go bed?"

"I will, John. I'll be doing everything this weekend." She patted him on the shoulder and forced a smile. So much for the library research she had planned for today, and the quiet evening at home. So much for getting any rest.

⁓

"Thank you so much for helping, Barry," Sarah gushed happily when, an hour later, Barry slapped his backpack on the sofa. "This is definitely beyond the call of duty."

"No problem!" Barry seemed glad to be there. "You could never handle all those naked guys at the pool by yourself. Besides, I get to see you in a bathing suit."

She blushed. "Men have one-track minds."

Barry shrugged, "We're men. That goes without saying."

Sarah playfully pushed him backward with both hands. "That's the trouble with all of you. You're all nothing but a lot of trouble."

"But that's why women love us," he teased.

"That's your fantasy, isn't it? You think women love you ..."

"You love me?" Barry said, adeptly twisting out of her reach.

"You're delusional ..." she laughed. "And I will get you back. Do you mind staying here for a few minutes while I run home and get a few things? Then we can go to the Y."

"Okay, boss. I'll get everyone ready." Barry grabbed John and Lonnie and headed for the stairs. "Come on, guys, let's get your suits."

They took the city bus to the YMCA downtown. When they got there, Barry helped the guys change while Sarah slipped into her suit in the women's locker room. She was instantly glad she hadn't tried to bring them to the pool by herself. She could never have brought herself to take them into the men's locker room, and she couldn't take them into the women's side. What was she thinking, that she might do this by herself?

Barry emerged holding a growling Mick by the arm. Once Mick got into the pool, though, he beamed. He walked through the water wearing water wings on his arms with a huge grin on his face. Sarah had never seen him smile like this.

To her surprise, Peter liked the water, too. He took his time getting in, whining as the water rose on his legs and torso. When he was finally submerged, he edged along the side of the pool flapping and screaming in delight.

Lonnie was more tentative. Even though Barry beckoned him from the shallow end, promising not to let go, Lonnie wouldn't do anything but sit on the edge and dangle his feet in the water. John, however, could now put his face underwater and blow bubbles, and could kick his feet while holding onto a little floating board.

Michael had told Sarah that Ricky could swim, and in keeping with his athletic prowess, Ricky jumped into the water and swam across the pool by himself.

The swimming teacher, Carrie, a sassy blonde with a perky ponytail and deep cleavage, praised Ricky coquettishly. She showed Sarah how to work with Ricky on the backstroke, leaning over with her chest nearly covering Ricky's face. Sarah was astounded at her brazenness. Ricky practically drooled.

When the lesson was over and everyone was cold and tired, they wrapped up in their towels and shivered their way back to the locker room. Sarah offered to help Barry get the guys dressed, but he said he really didn't mind. Sarah waited in the lobby for them for forty-five minutes before John and Lonnie came trudging out.

John hurried up to Sarah. "Wicky say bad wo'd."

"Well, John," Sarah sighed, "we're just going to ignore him today. There's nothing I can do about that right now."

John pouted and grumbled to Lonnie as he led him to a bench to wait for the others.

When Ricky came shooting out of the locker room Sarah jumped up to head him off before he reached the door. "Hey, there, Ricky. Where are you going?"

"Muthafucka," Ricky said, bumping her with his shoulder.

Sarah grabbed him by the arms and led him to a bench, pushing down firmly on his shoulders until Barry brought Peter and Mick out.

"Just in the knick of time," she said, her arms aching from holding Ricky in place.

Almost everyone fell asleep on the bus on their way home.

Later, as Barry was helping Mick set the table, he told Sarah about his friend and fellow student, Gordy, who was looking for a work study job. Sarah was interested, and after dinner Barry called him. Gordy hurried over before the dishes were done.

Sarah liked Gordy immediately. He was tall, with a huge afro that touched the doorframe when he walked into the house. He seemed comfortable right away, joking with Sarah and complimenting Barry on his good taste in women. Gordy was graduating in December and saving for travel in Europe, so he was happy to take the job. He told Sarah he had a retarded brother who still lived with his parents, so nothing would phase him. Sarah thanked Gordy for rescuing them, shook his large hand, and said goodbye. He would start the next weekend.

Barry stayed until everyone was in bed. He and Sarah snuck softly down the steps after making sure everyone was asleep.

"I'll be all right now, Barry," Sarah said, leaning again the doorway between the living room and entry. "You should get going. I've taken up your whole day and I'm sure you have work to do. Thank you so much!"

"No problem," Barry said. He stuck his hands in his pockets and shifted his feet. "Do you want me to sleep over?"

"No, that's all right. I need to do it. It's my penance for firing Michael."

"Well, I could stay, too," he offered, glancing at her sidelong.

"Oh, I see! Sleep over with me!" Sarah laughed. "Thanks for the offer, Barry, but I'm on duty. It's tempting though." She hoped her smile conveyed the right amount of playfulness without encouraging him too much. She knew Barry wanted more from their relationship but she just wasn't ready. Even so, it felt good to be desired. Sarah didn't want to drive him away.

He decided to stay to watch TV a while, and they sat on the couch shoulder to shoulder. Sarah made some popcorn and they chatted easily about the day, the men, and about Michael. Barry was easy to talk to and Sarah relaxed for the first time in weeks, it seemed. He gave her a neck rub and she melted, having to resist the urge to throw herself at him.

During the late movie she fell asleep on Barry's shoulder. She pretended to stay asleep while he gently lay her down. *Patient man*, she thought. He kissed her forehead and covered her with a blanket. Then Barry slipped silently out the door.

Chapter 18
The Dock

"Congratulations, Mr. Coben," Frank said, leaning his hands on John's worktable. "You have a chance for a new job. There's an opening back in the dock. We think you can do it, unless your hip gives you trouble."

"Dock?" John had never thought of changing jobs. The loading dock was considered the best job in the workshop. Only the smart ones got to work there. They got paid more and they often moved on to jobs in town. John knew who the dock workers were, since they hauled boxes in and out of the workshop area, but they didn't socialize with the other workers. The dock was like another world.

"Scott got a job at McKinley's grocery store. So you're up," Frank was giving John one of his rare smiles.

John knew it was an honor to be treated like a smart one, yet he felt a twinge of uncertainty. From where he sat now he could see Betsy and Lonnie working, and he could easily meet them at each break. The dock was far away at the other end of the warehouse. He hesitated.

"Me not know how."

"They'll show you what to do. You just do whatever they tell you."

"Me eat yunch wif Yonnie?" he asked. He had to see Lonnie and Betsy at lunch time, his favorite time of the day.

"Eat wherever you want. You can still see your friends at breaks." Frank crossed his arms impatiently. "Now come on. They want you to start today. This is a great opportunity." Frank motioned him up.

John stood up and waved to Betsy. She waved back. Her lip was swollen today and she looked awfully white. She told the supes she fell down, but John knew it was Richard. He followed Frank past the rows and rows of tables filled with workers. They looked up as he passed. Everyone would know he had a new job in the dock, an important job. They passed beneath the raised metal door and entered the cavernous dock that was half the size of the entire workshop. The walls were stacked with boxes, and workers were busy using tools and machines that John had never seen.

Frank led John to a small office at the back of the room and introduced him to Chuck, his new supe. Chuck was a tall, rough-looking man with the thickest arms John had ever seen. A tattoo of a heart with a snake around it showed beneath his rolled up T-shirt sleeve.

"So you're going to work back here, now," Chuck said revealing a large gap between his front teeth. His face was chiseled and he reminded John of *The Rifleman*. His deep-set eyes probed John as he spoke. "It's hard work, but you look strong. I expect my workers to follow orders and do their best. Can you do that?"

"Yep." John tapped his chest. "Me good wo'ka'."

"That's a good attitude," Chuck said, picking at his teeth with a toothpick. "Attitude is important."

Chuck led John to where a man leaned against a walker with a flat metal plate sticking out at the bottom. John had seen these pass through the workshop loaded with boxes, delivering supplies to work stations.

"Do you know Skip?" Chuck asked.

"Nope. Me Don." John stuck out his hand.

Skip crammed his hands into his pockets.

"Shake his hand, Skip," Chuck ordered.

Reluctantly, Skip gave John's hand a quick shake.

"Skip's not too talkative," Chuck said, "but he knows his job. He's gonna teach you what to do. You're gonna be his right hand man loading and unloading trucks. Just follow him and do what he tells you."

"This is a hand truck," Skip said, patting the handle. He lifted a box, set it on the silver plate, then pointed to the next box. "You put that one on."

John lifted the box up. It was heavy and he could barely swing it into place before dropping it on the top of the other box.

"Careful!" Skip snapped.

"You'll break your back lifting that way." Chuck said, and showed John how to squat, then lift. "Use your legs, like this, John."

John tried another box, squatting the way Chuck showed him. It was easier. His hip hurt a little, but he didn't say anything.

Chuck was watching and nodded approvingly. "You'll do fine. I'll check on you in a bit." He and Frank walked away leaving John alone with Skip.

Skip pointed to the next box. When it was in place on the stack, Skip pushed down on the handle and the boxes leaned back against the metal frame. He motioned for John to follow him, and wheeled the load toward a huge door at the far end of the dock.

Using his foot to set the hand truck upright again, Skip pointed to a red button on the wall. "Push it," he commanded.

When John pushed the button, the whole side of the building began to move. John jumped backward, startled. An immense door cranked upward revealing the gaping back of a truck nestled right up to the dock. Warm air rushed in from outside.

Another worker appeared and laid a wide plank down across the gap from the dock to the truck. Skip wheeled the boxes over the makeshift bridge and into the opening of the truck. The hollow rolling sound of the hand truck wheels and Skip's footsteps echoed inside the truck.

Skip motioned for John to come inside. John tested the bridge with his foot before hurrying across it. He helped Skip unload the boxes, then Skip let John wheel the hand truck back into the warehouse. They picked up more boxes and loaded them all into the truck.

For the rest of the morning, John helped Skip load and unload boxes from the trucks that came and went. When a truck pulled away, John got to push the button to close the door. Each time the door opened, a blast of warm sea air swept over John's sweating body. John wiped his forehead, feeling tired but happy. He was doing real work now. A man's work.

At the lunch bell, exhausted and hungry, John made his way to the eating tables and sat between Betsy and Lonnie.

"You like the new job?" Betsy asked.

"Ha'd wo'k. Me tiyed," he answered. He swiped his forehead to show her how hard he had worked.

"That's nice," she said, placing her arm around his shoulder affectionately.

John put his hand around her waist and kissed her cheek.

"Not here, John," she said, but she was smiling.

"How you yip?" he asked, pointing to her swollen mouth.

She pulled her lower lip out so he could see the cut.

"You teo Miwie?" John asked. He was worried because Betsy was coming to work hurt more and more often.

"No. Richard say don't tell no one. But I tell you." Betsy paused with downcast eyes and lowered her voice. "If I tell you somethin' else, you promise not to tell?"

"Me not teo." John crossed his heart.

"Richard hurt me someplace else, too," she whispered. "Told me not to tell or he punishes me. Promise you won't tell?" She glanced around to make sure no supes were watching.

"Me pwomise. Hope ta die, stick a needo in my eye." John leaned close.

"He hurt me here." She pointed quickly between her legs, glancing around again for a supe.

"Ouch." John knew girls didn't have much down there, but getting hit between the legs must hurt them just as much as boys.

"How come hit you de'e'?" John wondered.

"Not hit me." She looked away. "You know, do that nasty thing."

John wasn't sure what the nasty thing was, but he pretended he did. "Oh."

"He says I be bad sometimes. Do bad things. He punishes me." Tears spilled out of Betsy's eyes and onto her cheeks. John brushed them away.

"Me sowy, Bessy. You okay?" He put his arm around her.

"I be sore. Don't want him to do it again."

"You yive wif me?"

"Yeah!"

"Us git mawied?"

"Okay." She kissed his cheek. He would have to ask Sarah again if Betsy could live with them and how to get married.

"Fa' out! Us yive my woom." He gave her five. "Yonnie, okay Bessy yive ou' woom?"

Lonnie nodded.

Betsy smiled and leaned her head against his shoulder. John couldn't think of anything else to say. He hated Richard more than anyone in the world, even more than Ricky. He wanted to beat him up. But every time he told Betsy to tell a supe, she said Richard would beat her if she told.

So John didn't tell either.

All afternoon he lifted boxes on and off the hand truck, and in and out of delivery trucks. He was tired and his hip ached, but he learned how to lift by turning slightly to the side so his good leg took most of the weight. At afternoon break, John hurried from the dock to the cafeteria to meet Betsy and to let her feel his muscles. He was pretty sure his arms were already getting thicker.

As he limped toward the cafeteria he saw Ricky being wrestled to the ground by Randy and Frank at the dummy table. Another supe was helping a new worker stand up. Her chair lay back on the floor. Ricky must have pushed her over.

John shook his head. "Bad Wicky," he mumbled to himself.

Ricky kicked and fought the supes, screaming out an amazing array of cuss words. When the supes dragged him into the time-out room, the swearing was muffled somewhat, but Ricky banged and kicked on the door. Some workers stopped momentarily to stare at the time-out room, but the break-time chatter grew louder and Ricky's cries were drowned out as workers streamed to the cafeteria.

Laurie-the-Greeter walked past the time-out room on her way to her break. John heard her cry out above the din, "I see water! There's water in there!"

John couldn't stay away. He took Betsy's hand and pushed his way through the crowd to see what Ricky had done this time. From under the time-out room door, a stream of yellow water flowed. Ricky was peeing just like he had done at Sarah's house.

One supe ran for the mop while Randy pulled some chairs out of the way of the stream. He yelled at everyone to go back to the cafeteria or they would miss their breaks.

Just as John turned to leave, Laurie-the-Greeter yelled again. "Ooo! What's that?" Beneath the door they saw Ricky's fingers dart out, pushing a sticky brown substance under the door.

"That's poop!" Laurie-the-Greeter cried. She raised her hands and ran through the workshop aisles shouting, "Poop! Poop! Under the door!"

The next day and the next, Ricky had to stay home from work. Sarah had to come in to work out a plan with Ken before Ricky could come back to the workshop. John was glad Ricky was being punished. He was bad. Very bad.

Although John liked his new job in the dock, he missed being on the workshop floor. From the dock he couldn't run and look if he heard an uproar. Just yesterday he had missed seeing Sally choke on a wadded-up envelope. And he had been inside a big truck when someone pulled the fire alarm. Chuck made the dock workers leave the building through the open dock door rather than going out the green workshop door like everyone else.

But for the most part, John felt proud to be working on the dock. The work was more interesting than the assembly line. Even Skip wasn't so bad once John got used to him. He didn't say much and he was kind of grumpy, but he sometimes did things that surprised John. John had told him he liked music, so one day Skip brought his harmonica. He slipped it out of his pocket and waved it in front of John.

"What dat?"

"It's a harmonica, stupid." Skip slid it back and forth on his mouth making sweet sounds.

"You good."

"Here." He handed it to John. "You try it."

"Me?" Carefully, John held it to his lips and blew. No matter where he moved it, music came out. Skip let him keep it the rest of the day and play it whenever he had a chance.

John tried hard to fit in with the dock workers. He laughed at their jokes, even though he didn't understand them. A few times he took the cigarettes they offered and pretended to smoke, sucking the smoke into his mouth and then letting it out. He didn't like the taste, though, and the smoke made him cough. He practiced holding the cigarette like they did, tapping the ashes on the edge of a box. He never got the hang of it and decided he didn't want to smoke after all.

At the end of the week, Skip invited him to eat lunch with them at the table near Chuck's office. In this small break area there was a tiny refrigerator and a sink, and the dock workers could get free coffee from the percolator.

John felt torn. He knew Betsy and Lonnie were waiting for him, but he badly wanted to be with the smart ones, too. He decided to eat lunch quickly in the dock, then hurry out to visit his friends.

All through lunch he sat on a folding chair eating as fast as he could. He listened to the smart ones talk. He tried to understand what they were talking about, but they talked about their friends, their families, places they liked to go. As soon as he stuffed the last bite of cookie into his mouth, John stood up.

"See ya yata," he mumbled through the remnants of his cookie.

"Where ya going', John?" one of the workers asked. "Aren't you havin' fun?"

John stopped. "Me goin' ... out de'e." He pointed to the workshop.

"You like them weirdoes better 'n us?" Skip asked.

He didn't dare say yes. He paused. "Me go bafwoom."

Hurrying away, he heard them all laugh.

The following week, John spent more and more of his breaks and lunches in the dock, rushing out to the workshop for the last few minutes to see Lonnie and Betsy. He didn't even have time to go to the bathroom and sometimes he had to leave the dock between breaks to go. Chuck didn't like that.

When Betsy asked him where he was, he told her he couldn't leave the dock. He told her that Skip made him eat with them. He felt bad about fibbing, but he couldn't tell her how much he liked listening to their stories and feeling like a smart one. Soon he started to remember the people the dock workers mentioned in their stories, like Skip's brother who was a lawyer and put people in jail, and Jerry's sister who just had a baby.

The Thursday of his second week in the dock, when John hustled to the cafeteria after eating lunch, he found Betsy still at the table with her head lying on her arms. Lonnie sat beside her, finger flicking and chewing his tongue noisily.

"What w'ong, Bessy?" John asked. "You sick t'day?"

She raised her head. "Yeah. I don't feel good." The circles under her eyes were very dark next to her ashen skin.

"Wicha'd hu't you 'gin?"

She nodded. "Don't tell. He'll beat me," she whispered. She closed her eyes. John had never seen her look so sick.

"Me teo Miwie you sick. Hu ca' docto'."

"No. Not the doctor," Betsy said weakly. She didn't even open her eyes.

John felt uneasy. He wanted her to go to the doctor and get some medicine to make her well, but he didn't want to tell on her, either. He had promised.

"Bessy, you feo my a'm?" John held his arm up and squeezed his fist like Popeye. This time she didn't answer. John put his hand on her back and patted it. He looked around for a supe, wondering what he could tell them without breaking his promise.

Millie caught John's eye from across the room and hurried over. She put her arm around Betsy and lifted her face up. "Betsy, you look terrible. Come with me to the infirmary. I'm going to call home."

"No! Don't call home. I'm all right." Betsy sat up unsteadily.

"You're pale as a ghost! Tell you what, I'll just have Nancy check your temperature. Come on, let me help you." Millie lifted her to her feet and this time Betsy didn't protest. She hadn't eaten her lunch, so John stuffed it into the bag and followed them to the sick room.

Millie helped Betsy lay down on the cot and Nancy stuck a thermometer in her mouth.

"John, could I talk to you for a minute?" Millie asked.

She took him into the hall. "Do you know what's wrong with Betsy? She has gotten worse every day."

"Hu sick."

"I know, but why?"

John looked at his feet and shrugged. "Me not say. You git docto?"

"Yes, I am going to call the doctor. I've tried talking to her foster parents but all I get are excuses. And she clearly is afraid to tell me what's going on. If you think of anything else she has told you, anything that has happened to her that might make her sick, would you tell me? It's important."

"Okay." John opened his mouth to say more, but Nancy called Millie back to the infirmary.

"Look at this," she said, showing Millie the thermometer.

"Oh, my God," Millie exclaimed.

The bell rang. Millie sent John back to the dock, assuring him that she would take care of Betsy.

As he worked, John tried to sneak over to peek into the workshop, but they were so busy with incoming trucks that he couldn't get away until break time. When the afternoon break buzzer rang, he hurried out to find Betsy, searching their usual places. She wasn't there.

Finally, he found Frank. "Whe'e Bessy?"

"She wasn't feeling well."

"Hu in sick woom?"

"No, actually she went to the hospital," he said.

"Hospito?"

"Yeah. But don't worry. The doctors will take care of her. I'm sure she'll feel better soon."

"Hu go ambliance?"

"Nancy took her. Ken didn't want to raise a ruckus."

"Me go! Me ca' Sawah, go hospito!"

"No, you can't go. Just go on back to work now. Everything will be all right."

John couldn't concentrate on work. He tried to picture Betsy lying in the hospital with tubes sticking out of her arms and nose. He had never been to a real hospital, but he had seen them on TV. Hospitals had lots of doctors and doctors could fix people. She'd be all right now, he told himself.

Skip yelled at him, breaking him out of his inside world. "John! What are you doin' staring into space like a weirdo? Get to work."

Carefully, John cut open a box of supplies with the little knife they called an X-Acto blade. Skip had shown him how to hold the blade pointing away from his body, in case it ever slipped. It glided smoothly along the taped seam and the box opened like magic.

Just as John pulled the plastic bubble wrap out and squeezed a bubble between his fingers to hear it pop, Millie ran into the dock area. John was surprised to see her back here. He stuffed the bubble packing into an empty box to play with later.

"Hi, Miwie. Bessy at hospito'."

"I know. I need to talk to you, John. Would you come back to my office please?"

John shook his head. "Me wo'k. Skip be mad."

"I already spoke to Chuck. You're excused from work for a little bit. It's important. I need to ask you some questions about Betsy."

John closed the little knife and slipped it into his pocket. He followed Millie to her office.

She pulled a chair out for John to sit on. "Do you like coffee?"

"Yep," he lied. He drank the coffee when he was with smart ones, but the taste made his mouth foul.

She poured some coffee into a Styrofoam cup. "Do you like it black?"

"Yep. Bwack." John felt like a grown-up just holding it.

Millie shut her office door, then sat down in a swivel chair. She scooted it close to John and leaned forward.

"John?" she said softly, "I need to know what happened to Betsy."

He watched the steam rise from the coffee, his stomach churning with emotion.

"How did she get hurt, John?"

He tried to take a sip of coffee, but it burned his lips.

"For Betsy's sake, the doctors need to know what happened so they can help her. You want to help her, don't you?"

"Yep." He had been afraid to tell on Betsy, but now he was afraid not to. He squirmed.

"I'm not going to beat around the bush, John. Every time we call to see why she has a new bruise, her parents say she fell down the stairs, or bumped herself on something, or ran into a doorknob. But we think Betsy has been badly abused. Beaten up by her foster parents. The doctors say there are too many injuries on her body for them to be accidents."

Millie paused. Her brow was deeply creased and she searched John's eyes. He kept silent.

"Did she run into a doorknob? Is that why her stomach hurts and she won't eat?"

"No." John hesitated. His mind was swirling now. He thought of his promise to Betsy not to tell, then he thought of Betsy lying in a hospital bed.

"What did she tell you? We can guess most of it even if you don't tell us. If she's been hurt by her foster parents we can keep them from hurting her again. You want to help keep her safe, don't you? It's okay to break a promise, John, to help Betsy get well."

John whispered, "Wicha'd ... him hu't hu."

"Richard. Her foster father?"

"Yep. Hu not s'pose ta teo. Wicha'd beat hu up."

"That's what we thought. Don't worry. It's good to tell when you're helping someone." Millie patted his knee. "How did he hurt her?"

"Him hit hu in 'tomach." John showed Millie with his fist. "An' face, and a'm."

"He hits her. What else, John? You're doing great. You're helping Betsy by telling us."

"Him hu't hu udduh pwaces."

"Like?"

With a trembling finger John pointed between his legs. "He'e." He hung his head. He had broken his promise.

Millie shut her eyes for a moment and touched his arm before she spoke. "Oh, God. I was afraid of that."

"Bessy be mad, me teo."

"Being mad is not as bad as being sick." Millie gave him a hug. "John, you did the right thing. You helped Betsy."

～

John couldn't sleep. He sat up and searched the wall with his hand until he found the light switch. Every time he closed his eyes, he saw Betsy's pasty white face, then crazy Henry lying in blood, then a long procession of dead people's faces he had seen on TV. Millie had called Sarah that evening from the hospital to tell them Betsy was in intensive care. Sarah told John that meant she got the most doctors and nurses she could get. John figured that was good. She would be well soon. Sarah said she would be praying for her. John prayed, too. But he couldn't stop worrying.

Unable to sleep, John got up and padded into the kitchen, careful not to disturb Barry who was sleeping on the sofa. He rummaged quietly through the cupboards for something sweet to eat. He found a bag of baby candy bars for their lunches and some cookies in the shapes of animals. John took them back to his room.

He sat cross-legged on his bed and munched down several candy bars. He wished he could talk to Sarah right now, and he wished he had a picture of Betsy to look at. He would have to ask her for one when she came back to work.

John ripped open more candy bars, savoring each bite. One by one, he ate them all. He ate all the cookies, too. When everything was gone, he shoved the wrappers onto the floor and under his bed. He lay back, listening to the silence of the night. Even Ricky seemed to be sleeping soundly.

The next thing he knew, a white groping hand had slipped under the door of his bedroom and grabbed him. A scream caught in his throat.

"John, John! Wake up!" Barry said, shaking him. "You must have been dreaming. Looks like you had a party last night without me."

When John pried his eyes open, Barry was squatting beside his bed counting the little scraps that littered the floor.

"Geez, John," he said, gathering up the wrappers. "Twenty candy bars and a whole package of cookies? What possessed you?"

John sat up and rubbed his eyes. Why was Barry waking him up in the middle of the night? The motion of sitting up made his stomach reel. He flopped back down and groaned.

"You have to get up. You're late. You must not have heard my wakeup call. Lonnie is almost done eating, man. One more day of work after today and then the weekend. Hurry up, now."

John fumbled into his pants while queasy surges rocked his stomach. He pulled on his socks in his awkward way, his left foot bent behind him so he could reach it. His stomach churned more when he stumbled downstairs. Everyone else was finished eating breakfast.

"So you had a party by yourself last night. Hope you and yourself had fun," Barry joked.

"No pa'ty," John said, feeling burpy.

"Maybe you had your girl up there," Barry teased.

"Bessy in hospito'."

"Oh, yeah. Sorry."

John gulped. He didn't dare tell Barry how sick he felt.

"Hurry up, John. Good thing you guys made your lunches last night. Why don't you grab a piece of bread and an orange to eat for breakfast on the bus?"

Bile rose into John's throat at the thought of food. "Not hungwy," he said through clenched teeth.

"Not hungry? Not hungry?" Barry nudged John with his elbow and winked. "That's a first. So those candy bars didn't settle too well, huh? Bit off more than you could chew? Eyes bigger than your stomach? I could go on..."

John brushed past Barry to the kitchen. He opened the refrigerator and snatched his lunch sack. Even the sight of the Cheerios box made his stomach lurch.

"Don't forget to brush your teeth," Barry called. "You don't want to have to get dentures, have to take them out every night and set them in a glass."

John wished Barry would shut up. He wasn't usually this chatty. John went upstairs to the bathroom and shut the door. He swished the toothbrush around in his mouth then used the toilet.

The yellow bus had picked up everyone except Lonnie when John came down.

Barry waved John and Lonnie out the door to catch the white city bus. "Goodbye guys." He imitated John's guttural voice, "Goodbye, Bawy, have a nice day."

Usually John laughed when Barry mimicked his voice. Today, however, he waved him away. He didn't feel like kidding around.

"What, no 'Thanks for waking me up, Barry, otherwise I would have been late for work?'"

"No."

"Well, I'm insulted." Barry slammed the door in mock anger. John clutched his stomach and rushed to the end of the block to wait for the bus. He was puking behind a bush when Lonnie caught up with him.

Lonnie tisked his tongue, patted John on the head, and signed "sick." John nodded his thanks as he wiped his chin.

When the bus pulled up, they climbed on and moved to the back. The motion of the bus jerking forward sent another wave of nausea through John, but he held it in. When they arrived at the workshop, the warning bell had already rung and everyone was hurrying to their stations. John automatically searched the room for Betsy until he remembered she wasn't there. He hung up his coat, then looked around for somebody to ask about Betsy.

Millie waved to him from across the workshop and zigzagged toward him. "You look pale, John. Are you sick?"

"Me betta' now," he answered, pointing Lonnie to his worktable.

"Just to let you know, I called the hospital this morning. Betsy is still in intensive care."

"Dat good?" he asked.

"That means she's still very sick. They're running more tests."

"Oh." He figured tests were good. John didn't know what to say. His stomach was empty and he was getting a headache.

"You better get to work. It will keep your mind off Betsy." Millie patted him on the shoulder and walked away.

John didn't want to go back to the dock today. He wanted to talk to Lonnie and his other old friends. He walked slowly, stopping to wave at Lonnie on his way to the dock.

As the morning wore on John's headache grew worse. He couldn't concentrate. Everything seemed lopsided today.

Skip didn't usually say much unless John goofed up, so today was one of Skip's most talkative days. First, John dropped a box on his toe. He was sure he broke it, but Skip made him keep working. Then he accidentally bumped Skip's arm causing him to drop his cigarette down the drain hole. Skip cursed him.

When a whole stack of boxes slipped off the dolly that John was pushing, Skip yelled, "You jerk! Chuck oughta send you back on the floor with the other 'tardos."

Going back to the workshop floor sounded good to John today. Whenever Skip wasn't watching, John sneaked over to see if Betsy had come in yet.

After several of these side trips, Skip yelled, "What's a matter with you anyway?"

"Yookin' fo' Bessy," John said crossly.

"Your girlfriend? She's the one with the crooked face, right. Walks funny."

John growled. "Bessy pwetty."

"Oh, well, she's a 'tardo like you. Too ugly for me."

John started to protest, but he didn't have the strength to argue.

Skip lit a cigarette and talked with it hanging out the side of his mouth. "I ain't no retard. They put me here after I had my motorcycle accident." He touched a deep scar on his forehead. "I used to be smart. I had a good job workin' in the shipyard."

"Assident?" John had always wondered what those marks were on Skip's face.

Skip smiled. "Yeah, I used to ride real good. Did some racing. Now I can't even get a license." He blew smoke out his nose. The cigarette bobbed precariously on his lip.

"Me wan' dwive moto'cyco'," John said, revving his hands on imaginary handlebars.

"You? No way. You won't drive, you won't get married, you won't have no kids, you won't ever work no place but here, cause they don't want you out there." Skip pointed with his cigarette out the dock door. "Nobody wants to see weirdoes around."

John didn't like what Skip was saying and he didn't believe him. "No good! Me gwow up, me mawy Bessy!"

"Grow up? Look at yourself? You are grown up, you idiot. How old are you?"

"Uh ... fou'teen." John said the first big number that popped into his head.

"Fourteen, shit. You're probably thirty-five. You might as well accept it. This is as good as it's going to get. Nobody out there gives a shit about you. Or me." He stamped out the cigarette.

"No good, no good! Me, me twenty." He remembered hearing something about turning twenty at one time.

"Better get back to work." Skip nodded toward Chuck who was walking over from his office.

"What's the matter, boys?" Chuck asked.

"Nothin'." Skip picked up the fallen boxes and hefted them onto the dolly.

"Nufin'," John repeated. "Us wo'kin'." He paused, then told Chuck, "Bessy in hospito'. My gewfwend."

"I heard about that gal," Chuck said. "That's too bad she got beat up by her foster dad. How's she doing?"

"Tensib ca'e. Yots a docto's."

"Hm. That's too bad. Well, you guys get back to work. Only fifteen minutes 'til break."

When the break bell rang, John left the dolly in the middle of the aisle and darted out to find Millie. He found her talking to Ken and tapped her shoulder.

"Hi, John," she said, touching his arm gently.

"Bessy okay?"

"I just called again and they wouldn't give me much information over the phone. I think she's about the same." Millie didn't look very happy. She turned back to talk to Ken. John stood behind her to listen.

"The nurse told us they had talked to her foster mom last night, but that they hadn't come down to visit her at all. Then when they tried this morning there was no answer. She asked me if we had another phone number for them, or if we knew who Betsy's legal guardian was. I told her I'd check to see if we had any information. I couldn't find anything in her file."

"Well, as an adult she has no legal guardian unless someone has a court order for legal custody. Do they need permission for surgery or something?"

"I'm not sure. She wouldn't give me any medical information, just told me that she needed to locate the foster parents."

"Did you try their number again?"

"Yes. No answer when I tried, either."

"Maybe I'll run by their house on my way home," Ken said. He narrowed his eyes and his nostrils flared. "I'd like to give them a piece of my mind."

Ken squeezed John's shoulder. "I know this is tough on you, John. We're doing all we can and so are the doctors."

Millie followed Ken back to the offices.

Lonnie waited at their meeting post. He looked lonely standing there without Betsy. He giggled when he saw John and tried to tickle John's neck. But today Lonnie's silliness was not fun, only irritating. John pushed his hand away.

"Yonnie, Bessy in hospito'. Sick!"

Lonnie signed "sick," and tisked his tongue.

"Hu 'tensib ca'e. Dat good. Yots a docto's."

Lonnie nodded. He tried to tickle John's neck again.

"Me go toiwet," John said. He had needed to go for some time, but Skip called him a retard if he didn't go during breaks. After he finished, he stood in front of the bathroom mirror and talked to himself, practicing what he would say when Betsy came back to work. He kissed the mirror and practiced smiling. When he came out, the bell rang. He hadn't had a chance to talk to Lonnie or get a Coke. He had missed his whole break.

Sulking, John stomped back to the dock. He whipped the dolly around and jammed it under a pile of boxes like a spatula under pancakes. The more he worked, the madder he got. He didn't feel like working today. Barry woke him up late, he felt sick, and Skip called him retarded. And now he missed his break with Lonnie.

Most upsetting was Betsy's absence. John imagined marching into that hospital, hoisting Betsy to her feet and hauling her back to work. This was where she belonged and she wasn't here. Why did she have to get sick?

"John!" Skip's gruff voice broke through John's reverie. "John!"

He looked up.

"Stop talkin' to yourself and get to work! You expect me to do all the work by myself?" Skip shoved John hard enough that he staggered a few steps before catching his balance.

Stumbling always unnerved John. He glared at Skip, his vision blurring in anger.

Skip took his cigarette out of his mouth and flicked the ashes in John's direction. "Idiot," he sneered. "You belong in the loony bin."

That's what the basketball players had said at the park. John didn't know where the loony bin was, but he knew this was an insult. He lowered his head and charged. His head struck Skip in the stomach, thrusting him backwards. Skip hit the wall but didn't fall down. John was determined to knock him over. He charged again, flinging his arms around Skip's waist and tumbling them both into a mountain of empty boxes. John's knee struck something hard and pain shot through his leg. Somewhere in the cardboard cave of collapsed boxes, John lost his hold on Skip. He grabbed his own painful leg with one hand and groped around for Skip with the other. He wanted to punch Skip's fat mouth. But Skip was gone.

When the pain subsided a bit John, tried to crawl out. As he shoved one box away, another fell on top of him. Finally, he heaved a big one to the side to reveal Chuck marching toward him from the office. He looked piping mad. The other dock workers had gathered around, too. Everyone loved a fight.

Skip stood over John, clenching his fists and shouting, "Come here, you big fat asshole! You wanna fight, I'll give you a fight!" Skip had a bright red bump on his forehead next to his scar.

John sat back on his haunches to rub his leg, afraid he wouldn't be able to stand up.

Chuck grabbed John, wrenching him to his feet by his shirt collar, and nabbed Skip with his other hand. "What the hell is going on?" he demanded.

"He tackled me!" Skip yelled, giving John an evil stare.

"Him, him, him say bad tings," John said foggily.

"I just said the truth, you fucking idiot! You do belong in a loony bin!"

Chuck held them back from each other. "All right, all right. I don't know who said what first. I do know it takes two to fight. John's upset today because of his girlfriend, but that's no excuse for fighting. And Skip, you have a rude mouth. Both of you need to cut it out."

Skip muttered, "Fucking bastard."

John lurched toward him.

Chuck shouted, "Hey! That's enough now! You both need to cool off. Skip, go to my office. I'll deal with you in a minute!"

He pushed Skip away, then pulled John's face close to his. "Now listen, John. We put you back here because we thought you had a chance of succeeding …"

But John wasn't listening. He was watching Skip retreat toward the office. Behind Chuck's back, Skip spit at John and stuck out his middle finger.

Rage swelled up inside John like a balloon ready to pop. He lunged sideways, swinging his arm to get free of Chuck's hold. His fist accidentally clipped Chuck's jaw.

"Oops!" John covered his mouth. "Me sowy!"

Chuck snatched John's arms and twisted them behind his back. "Damn it! That's it. You're in time-out!"

"No! Me sowy! Not mean hit you!"

Chuck shuffled him out of the dock toward the workshop as John struggled desperately to get loose.

"No good! No time-out!" John cried. The time-out cubicle was for dummies, for bad boys, like Ricky.

"You earned it, you get it." Chuck dragged John down the main aisle past the staring eyes of the workers.

"Where you going, John?" Laurie-the-Greeter called.

John bowed his head and didn't answer. They rounded the corner to the dummy circle.

"He's going to time-out!" someone called.

"Uh-oh, he did a bad thing!" someone else cried. Their voices felt like spears.

By the time they reached time-out, John was quaking all over. Peter and Ricky sat at the dummy table with a few others. They all stopped and stared. Ricky smiled and silently formed his favorite words, "Muthafucka."

"No time-out!" John pleaded. "Me be betta'! No hit, no fight!"

Chuck pushed him toward the door. "Rules are rules. Ten minutes of time-out. Should be more than that for hitting a supe, but this is your first time, far as I know. While you're in there, think about your behavior."

John dropped to his knees, sliding out of Chuck's grip. He clutched Chuck's legs. "Pwease! Me be good now. Not fight. No time-out!" John felt his stomach gurgle up in his throat. He swallowed hard.

"Sorry, John. I hate to do this, but it's for your own good. When the timer goes off you can come back and talk to me."

Before John could protest again, Chuck scooted him on his knees through the door, pried his hands off his legs, and lifted him onto the blue matting that covered the floor and walls. The door slammed.

"See you in ten minutes." Chuck's voice was deadened by the heavy door.

The time-out room was silent. John beat the mat with both hands until his anger turned to despair and he lay his head down on his knees and wept. After several minutes, his sobbing slowed. Wiping his running nose and eyes, John sat upright. Slowly, the room began to sway as if he were riding over waves. John lay back on the mat forlornly, still snuffling. He stared at the cage-covered light bulb in the ceiling burning bare and hot, and he waited for the swaying to stop.

But instead, the room began to spin. Horrified, he found himself in Cadby. Moaning sounds grew louder by the second. The scent of urine and feces touched his nostrils. Naked inmates with hollow eyes swirled above him. They came closer and closer. Their hands reached out to him, fondled his face. He cringed and shut his eyes. The hands probed his body. Twisting onto his stomach he curled himself into a ball. Fingers inched down his back.

Panic seized him. John rose to his hands and knees. His breath came in quick gasps and his stomach surged. Unable to stop the anger, confusion, and worry, John's emotions gushed onto the mat in a vile river.

Chapter 19
Trouble

Sarah opened her car door for John and he slid into the front seat. "You're pale as a ghost, John. You must really be sick."

John reached over and punched her arm. "Punch Buggy," he said weakly.

Sarah rubbed his shoulder affectionately. "You don't have to keep playing Punch Buggy if you don't feel well, John." She regretted teaching him this childish game.

Ken followed them out of the workshop. "He threw up in the time-out room. I hope he'll feel better by tomorrow."

"Time-out? Why was he in time-out?" Sarah was puzzled. John had never been in trouble at the workshop before.

"I didn't get the whole story from Chuck," Ken replied, "Something about a fight in the dock."

"Skip say bad tings," John said. He leaned his head against the seatback and closed his eyes.

"Let's not worry about it now, John. Tell me later." She patted John's leg. She had never before seen John sick and she felt an unexpected urge to mother him. This novel impulse made her wonder, silently, whether she had a biological clock after all.

"Thanks for calling me, Ken," She said. "I'll call if he's not coming in tomorrow."

Ken shut the car door and Sarah pulled away. "I'm sorry you're sick, John. You can just rest this afternoon. Maybe you have the flu or something."

"Bessy in hospito'," John said, his head lolling toward Sarah.

"Yes, she's still in the hospital. I'm sure you're worried about that, too."

When they got home she put John on the couch with a pillow and light blanket, and brought him some hot tea.

"Just stay there and relax. I have some calls to make and will be working at the table if you need something." Sarah switched on the television for him.

She tried to call Barry to find out how John had seemed last night, but he wasn't home. Sarah took out the data notebook and checked Ricky's new behavior program chart to see if there was any progress. The incidents of outbursts and extreme behavior had diminished, but they were becoming more severe when they did occur. She plotted the graph and decided to implement the next step, which was a takedown procedure that would start as soon as they were trained. The director of the local boys' home had agreed to train her staff on the techniques of safe restraint. Sarah called him and set up the training for Saturday morning.

After a while she checked on John. He had fallen asleep. She turned down the TV. As she wrote instructions into the staff journal, she heard the front door creak. Jana shoved the front door open with her foot, carrying two bags of groceries. She was an hour early.

"Hi!" Jana called, then hushed herself when she saw John sleeping on the couch. "I saw your car out here. Is he sick?"

"I think so," Sarah whispered. "He was in time-out for fighting, totally out of character for him, and threw up in there. He must be really upset about Betsy being in the hospital. Or he's getting the flu."

"Poor guy." Jana backed through the café doors and Sarah heard her clanking around in the kitchen making too much noise to be just putting the groceries away.

"What are you doing in there?" Sarah called softly.

"I want to clean out this disgusting refrigerator before the guys get home," Jana answered. "It has been making my stomach turn."

"Wow, that's dedication," Sarah replied. She picked up the phone again. She needed to get hold of William today. Ricky had had a rough weekend with Gordy and Todd. There was a study she remembered William quoting in one of his lectures that she thought might give her some additional insight, but she couldn't remember what journal it was in. This was his usual office hour, so she rang William's office number.

"Hello, Dr. Montgomery here," he answered.

"Hi, William. It's Sarah."

"Hi."

When he didn't follow up his greeting with a question, Sarah continued. "I, uh, I was wondering if you remember the reference for a study you talked about in your Severe Disabilities seminar that explained a graduated punishment regime counterbalanced by an increasing reinforcement schedule. I want to cite that in my paper and make sure I have all the details for my program for Ricky."

"So Ricky is still there?" he asked. "I thought you were going to send him back."

"We talked about giving him one more month, remember?" Sarah wondered if he had someone in his office. He sounded distant.

"Oh, yes, I guess we did. You know, I don't remember that reference. It probably came out of the Abnormal Behavior journal. I'm sure you can find it."

"Well, uh, yes, I'm sure I can." This wasn't like him. In the past he had taken the time to look through old notes to find an article that would help her out. It sounded like he was putting her off.

"By the way, Sarah ..."

"Yes?"

"How is your writing coming? I'm looking at your file here and you were supposed to have your theoretical framework revisions to me three weeks ago. If you're going to stay on schedule, you should be starting the literature review and design chapters. Have you talked to Ernie yet? He can help you with the statistical analysis. You were planning to defend next March, right?"

Sarah was taken aback. He knew what they'd been going through with Ricky being lost and all his behavior problems. Her original plan had been March, and she knew she was behind, but she hadn't even finalized the methodology section. Everything kept changing.

"I haven't contacted Ernie, not yet. But I will as soon as I have time," she found her voice becoming vitriolic. "I'm working as fast as I can under the circumstances."

He didn't seem to notice. "That's good. Let me know if you need to revise your timelines. I'm going to be gone next spring and summer quarters to Vienna for my sabbatical so that would push off your defense 'til next Fall. Anything else?" His voice was curt.

"No, that's it. Thanks." Sarah hung up, once again disappointed in William's confusing mood swings. What happened? Was he getting pressure from somewhere to push her project through? That didn't make sense. Was another student in his office? Was he tired of dealing with this whole group home scene after the fiasco with the surveyors and the media attention? He had seemed so supportive just a couple of weeks ago.

"What's the matter?" Jana asked, popping her head through the café doors. "You sounded upset. Were you talking to William?"

"Yeah. He was acting kind of strange. I can't figure out what's going on." Sarah stared out the front window toward Mrs. Hanover's house.

"Strange, how?" Jana came and sat down across from her at the table, wiping her hands on a dishtowel.

"Just ... detached, not helpful. He treated me like any other student in one of his classes, I suppose. I expected ... well, more. He's been so supportive." She picked absently at a hangnail.

"Off and on," Jana reminded her. "I'm not that surprised that he's backing off."

"Why do you say that?"

"Oh, nothing." She seemed to change her mind and started to rise.

"Wait!" Sarah caught her arm. "Do you know something I should know?"

"Well, I don't want to be the one ..." Jana paused again.

"Tell me! I need to know what's going on." Sarah pulled Jana back into her chair.

Jana sighed and unconsciously lowered her voice. "Barry told me yesterday that he heard William has a new girlfriend, a first year doc student. Can't remember her name."

Sarah lowered her eyes. "Oh. That explains it."

"I think it was Cindy something."

"I don't know her. I set a boundary so he's moved on, I guess."

"I'm sorry, Sarah. I know he has been a good support to you. But you didn't want to get involved with him anyway, right?"

"Right. It's okay. I knew I was pretty much on my own when he didn't help during this whole Ricky ordeal. At least now I know why." Sarah swallowed the lump in her throat.

Jana squeezed Sarah's hand once more. "From what I gather, you're lucky, Sarah. His poor wife. I wonder if she knows about this latest one."

"I wonder, too. Maybe she has her own man on the side. I hope so," Sarah smirked. "I wouldn't get involved with a married man, you know that. It's just frustrating that he doesn't seem capable of maintaining a professional relationship with his students. Either he sleeps with them or cuts them loose."

"He's a reprobate." Jana headed back into the kitchen.

The phone rang. Sarah automatically picked it up.

"Hello?" she said, lost in thought.

"Hi, Sarah. It's Ken."

"Oh, hi, Ken. What's up? Did you find out what happened in the dock with John?"

"It's something else. The hospital called just now. I thought you'd want to know." He paused. "I thought you'd want to tell John yourself. Betsy didn't make it."

"What?" Sarah cupped her hand around the receiver and whispered, "She died?"

"Yes, I'm sorry. She passed away about an hour ago. Internal bleeding was all they told us. There's an all-points bulletin out for her foster father's arrest. We'll find out when the service will be and I'll let you know."

Sarah felt like a stone had landed on her heart. "Oh, Ken, this is terrible. How am I going to tell John?"

"I don't envy you, Sarah. Let me know if there's anything we can do." He hung up.

Sarah was deeply shaken. She slipped into the kitchen and whispered the news to Jana who almost dropped the dish she was holding.

"How are you going to tell John?" Jana wondered, wiping tears from her eyes with her dishtowel.

"I have no idea. I'm beginning to hate this job. I'll see if he's awake." She silently prayed, questioning how much she could take and why God allowed things like this to happen to innocent people. Then she asked for strength to get through what she had to do.

Slipping quietly into the dining room, she hesitated. John was sitting up watching the television. *Maybe I shouldn't tell him now,* she thought. Maybe she would tell him later, or tomorrow. She stopped, holding the moment of indecision like a bomb in her hands. Once she told him, everything would change for John. She decided to pull the pin, gently as she could. He was an adult. He needed to know before the others came home, and they were due in half an hour.

Sarah walked to the sofa, carefully pushed his legs over and sat down beside him. "How are you feeling, John?" she asked, rubbing his back.

"Betta'. Me good," he answered, smiling pathetically.

"I'm glad. Do you want some more tea?"

He nodded. Sarah brought him another cup of hot tea, postponing the dreaded task while she practiced what she would say. She sat down again and handed him the steaming cup.

"John, I'm afraid I have some bad news."

John looked at her expectantly, not understanding her subtle preparatory attempt.

"I have to tell you something that is going to make you sad. It makes me very sad, too."

His expression turned more serious. "What sad?"

"Betsy... she didn't get better, John. In fact, she passed away. Just now." Tears welled up in Sarah's eyes as she anticipated his reaction.

"Pass 'way?" John shook his head. "Bessy in hospito'. 'Tensib ca'e. Yots a docto's. Get betta', come back to wo'k. Us git mawied, yive he'e!"

Sarah put her hand on John's knee. "I'm sorry John, very very sorry. I know you cared for her so much. It's hard when we lose someone we love."

John shook off her hand. "Not yose Bessy! Hu come back!"

Sarah looked into John's agonized face. The message seemed to be getting through. "She's gone, John," she said softly.

He pushed her away and thrust the blanket off. "No! Bessy not gone, come back!" He stood up and backed away from Sarah. "No, you w'ong! Hu come back tomowow."

"I'm sorry, John," was all she could say.

John stomped up the stairs yelling, "No, Bessy not gone!" He slammed the wall with his fist rattling the house.

Sarah leaned her face into her hands and quietly wept for John.

Chapter 20

Death Bugs

Work was slow Friday. There was only one truck to load in the morning. Chuck made John work with Tony instead of Skip. John tried to stay out of Skip's way.

Before the morning break, John ended up in the bathroom at the same time as Lonnie. Lonnie wasn't allowed to go more than three times a day, so they were both excited when they unexpectedly found each other there. In adjoining stalls, they giggled and talked. Lonnie bent over until he could peek under, which made John laugh hysterically.

Finally, Lonnie's' new supe, Marcus, came to check on him. "Up to your old tricks, Lonnie?" Marcus asked. "You've been in here long enough. Finish up and come out. You have one minute."

When Marcus left, Lonnie and John guffawed. Lonnie flushed.

"You go?" John asked.

"Uh," Lonnie said.

"You wipe?"

Lonnie sireened playfully, "Aaahhhhhh!"

They emerged from their stalls and gave each other a high-five. "Be good, Yonnie," John warned. "No time-out."

Lonnie nodded and meandered out without washing his hands.

This was the only time during the day John forgot about Betsy. After the morning break Chuck called the dock workers to the back for a safety meeting. Several paint-spattered chairs were pulled together in a semi-circle. Safety meetings were held so Chuck could tell them about new rules, or about how someone got hurt so they would be more careful.

The chairs were already full when John got to the safety meeting. He pulled up a box to sit on. He tried hard to listen as Chuck rambled on about a new packaging machine they were getting, and how recently someone had almost cut his finger off using the box cutter, but John's eyes burned with fatigue. He leaned against the wall behind him. Slowly, his eyelids wavered.

He heard Chuck say a lot of tools were being lost lately, and they should be sure to... John didn't hear the rest.

The next thing he felt was a sharp jab. Without opening his eyes he brushed at the irritation to his shoulder. It shifted to his side.

"Git up, you lazy weirdo." Skip's voice was followed by a shove that sent John hurdling to the floor. He opened his eyes just in time to catch himself. Whipping around he saw Skip walking away, whistling. The chairs were all empty now.

"Hey!" he called scrambling to his feet.

A strong hand clamped John's shoulder. "You don't want to start another fight, now do you?" Chuck asked.

John shook his head.

"I told him to wake you but he pushed too hard. I'll talk to him."

John kicked at a scrap of paper.

"Just stay away from him for a few more days. Now go get your broom and start sweeping up. There's no truck due in for an hour." Chuck let go of John and followed after Skip.

John shuffled over to the tool closet and picked out his favorite broom. It had a short handle that fit him better than the others, and he had carved two rough circles on it with his box cutter to remind him of Betsy's letter "B".

As John pushed his broom across the cement floor, raising a bigger and bigger cloud of dust, he thought about Betsy and mumbled under his breath. "Bessy, you come back. You be okay." He remembered the words Sarah had spoken yesterday, *"Betsy passed away."* John wasn't sure what passed away meant, but he was sure it meant she was still sick.

The noon break bell rang. John lay his broom by the pile of dirt and limp-skipped toward the lockers. He grabbed his lunch and pushed through the crowd to find Lonnie. They sat in their usual spot, unconsciously leaving an empty place for Betsy. They didn't talk much.

When John got up to toss their sacks into the trash he noticed Millie standing with a group of supes near the door that led to the offices. She was talking and the other supes were leaning close to listen. Her eyes were red. John was drawn by Millie's anguished expression. As he crept closer, snatches of conversation became audible.

"... Autopsy last night ... massive internal injuries," Millie was saying. "... beaten repeatedly ... no one can find them ... disappeared."

John moved close, hiding behind a post.

"The sheriff went out to their house and it was all cleared out ..." Then her voice cracked. Tears flowed down her cheeks and she wiped her eyes. Ken put his arm around her. Another supe wiped her eyes, too. Frank shook his head and stared at the floor. One by one they walked away.

Something was terribly wrong. John clung to the post, trying not to be seen. He wasn't sure why his heart fluttered like he had been running. Millie drew a tissue from her pocket and dabbed at her eyes and nose. Then she spied John. Tears rolled down her cheeks as she walked toward him.

He instinctively drew back. Millie was going to tell him something he didn't want to hear.

"John? I just want to tell you how sorry I am about Betsy." Millie wiped her eyes.

"Bessy get betta," John said, backing up another step.

She took a deep breath. "Sarah told you last night, didn't she? There was nothing more the doctors could do. She was hurt too badly. I'm so sorry Betsy died."

The words struck him like a slap and he jerked. He knew what "died" meant. It meant they never came back, like Crazy Henry.

"No!" he shouted.

Millie looked confused. "I'm afraid so. I thought Sarah already told you. Betsy was too badly injured inside."

"No! Bessy 'tensib ca'e. Hu be okay!" His heartbeat drummed in his ears. Why was Millie saying this? That's not what Sarah said.

Millie stepped closer to him and tried to put her arm around his shoulder. "I wish you were right. We're going to miss her. Especially you, John. I know you were close. I'm really sorry."

"No good, no good!" John shouted and pulled back.

"I know it's hard to believe. I'm in shock myself."

The bell rang.

"Me go back wo'k. Bessy come. Hu be betta." John marched through the rows of tables toward the loading dock, the room swirling around him.

"Wait, John!" Millie called after him.

Even though he tried to crowd them out, Millie's words pounded up from his own feet with each step. "Betsy died, Betsy died, Betsy died."

John covered his ears with both hands to block the words. The rows of tables in front of him seemed endless. The floor was uneven. Chuck stood in the archway leading to the dock with his hands on his hips, watching John. If John could only make it to the dock, everything would be normal again.

He started to run, stopping short right in front of Chuck. He pulled his hands down expectantly. Chuck would tell him Betsy was okay.

"I'm sorry to hear about Betsy, John. What a shame. Do you want to take a break and sit down for a while?"

"No!" John screamed. "Bessy aw wight!"

"John, nobody is trying to hurt you. We feel bad, too. Why don't you sit down in my office until you feel better. It's always hard to understand when a friend dies."

John had to get out of this place. He spun around and bolted for the door.

"Where are you going?" Chuck bellowed behind him. "Come back here!"

John jogged toward the exit, zipping around tables until Frank stepped into his path and put his hand up, "Hey! Slow down there, pal."

John ducked into the next aisle. He wove around workers' chairs, stumbling over feet and table legs until he came to Clarence who completely blocked the aisle.

John pushed on Clarence's chair and screamed, "Move! Move!" but Clarence was planted like a tree in his path.

Glancing behind him, John saw Frank coming down the next row. More than anything, he didn't want to be caught. He dropped to his knees, dipped under the table and crawled around Clarence's legs. Then he jumped up again to run.

Just as he rounded the last corner that led to the exit, John tripped over the flap of an open box, falling onto his hands then his face.

Pain shot through his nose into his face and tears sprang into his eyes.

"Come on, John, let me see." Frank tugged on his wrists. John twisted away, gritting his teeth against the pain.

"What happened? Is he all right?" It was Millie's voice.

"Just a bloody nose, I think," said Frank.

Blood? John opened his eyes. His hands were red. He screamed and began to shake. He was going to die!

"It's okay, John, you're going to be fine," Millie soothed. "Lie back and we'll get a towel." She laid him back and helped him pinch his nose.

Within seconds someone tossed her a towel and she dabbed gently at his face. John flinched.

"Let's put ice on it." Millie soothed him with kind words, smoothing his hair with her hand while they waited for the ice. She placed the frozen bag on the towel and sat beside him while the cold slowly numbed the pain.

"He's out of control," John heard Frank say. "Yesterday and again today."

"Oh, Frank, mellow out," Millie retorted.

"Well, he should be consequated for running away. Maybe he needs time-out again."

"Shut up, Frank," she snapped. "He's upset about Betsy. Wouldn't you be?"

"You're reinforcing him," Frank said, his voice and footsteps retreating.

"John, I'm going to call Sarah and have her come and get you. I think you need a few days off." She readjusted the ice. "Just lay here until she comes. You'll be all right."

In a few minutes, Millie came back. "Are you feeling better yet, John?"

"Yep."

She helped him sit up and wiped his face and hands with the wet towel. John liked Millie. She was kind. She didn't usually lie to people.

"Miwie? His voice sounded like he had a cold.

"Yes, John?"

"Bessy dead?"

"Yes, she is, John."

"Hu come back wo'k?"

"No, John. She won't be back. I'm so, so sorry."

"Me, too." The pain from his face trickled down to his throat causing it to tighten in a burning knot.

∽

The following Saturday morning, John sat on the porch with Lonnie waiting for Sarah's punch buggy to pull up. She stepped out of the car wearing a long black skirt. John had never seen her in anything but jeans before. She was wearing make-up and her hair was tied up in a ribbon.

"You pwetty, Sawah," John said as she approached. Then he stood up and said, "Punch Buggy!" slugging her arm gently.

"You win, John. And thank you for the compliment. You look nice, too." Gordy had found a white shirt and black pants for John to wear, and even loaned John a tie.

"Is Lonnie coming with us?" she asked.

For the first time ever, John shook his head. "No. Me, you. Not Yonnie."

He was disappointed when Sarah swung by Barry's apartment to pick him up. Barry waited for them on the curb wearing a suit coat, another rarity. He carried an extra coat for John. John got out of the car briefly so Barry could crawl in the backseat.

As they drove, Sarah told Barry she had found a dentist who would make new teeth for Lonnie. John tried hard to imagine Lonnie with front teeth, but he couldn't.

"How did Ricky do at work this week?" Barry asked leaning forward to talk to Sarah between the bucket seats.

"He pulled someone's chair out from under them and swung at the supervisor a few times," Sarah answered.

"How long are they going to give us?" Barry asked.

"Ken said two weeks. Ricky has to improve significantly or he can't come back to the workshop." She worked the long stick and they sped up.

"Do you think the new procedure is going to work?" Barry asked.

"I hope so."

"Yeah, I can't wait to learn that take-down thing."

"Too bad we had to postpone our training today. I just wish I could find a reinforcer that works for him. That would help, too."

John wanted to talk to Sarah about the funeral, but she chatted with Barry all the way to the church. He stared out the window at the houses passing by, wondering what was going to happen at the church. John had never been to a funeral before—he'd only seen them on TV and they looked sad. Everyone wore black and cried.

When they arrived, Barry helped John slip on the suit jacket he had brought for John. Looking at his reflection in the car window, John smoothed his hair back while Barry fixed the collar and adjusted John's tie. Other people were also arriving, everyone wearing black.

Inside the vaulted sanctuary where John and the other guys went to church every week, an organ played church music. The last time he was here Betsy was with him. A sprinkling of people were seated in the pews, mostly clustered at the front. John recognized Millie's long hair at the end of one row sitting beside several workers from Cloverdale. Splashes of flowers adorned the altar and more rested precariously atop a long shiny box in front of the altar.

He tugged on Sarah's arm and pointed. "What dat?"

"Shh!" Sarah drew him into a seat. She whispered, "That's the casket, John."

John had seen coffins in scary movies, and usually they had a skeleton or Count Dracula inside.

"Dat Dwaclia's home... me see in movie."

"No, John. It's where they put someone's body when they die. Then they will bury the casket in the cemetery."

This was spooky. John shivered. He asked Sarah, "Who in de'e? Dead person?"

"Yes, John." She glanced at him sidelong. "Betsy. This is her funeral."

"Bessy?" In a scary coffin? John hadn't thought about anything like this. He didn't know a funeral would be scary.

The music stopped. Everyone was silent. Pastor Conley walked up to the pulpit. He prayed and then began to talk about Betsy. He talked about God and Jesus, and how Betsy had gone home to heaven. He said she was happy and well now and they would all see her again some day.

John leaned over and whispered to Sarah, "Me be good, go heaben, see Bessy."

Tears flowed down Sarah's cheeks as she nodded. Barry put his arm around Sarah. She dabbed at her eyes with a tissue then put on her sunglasses. John started to ask her why she was wearing sunglasses indoors when the music started again. This time everyone stood up and sang a song. Pastor Conley read something about weeping with those who weep, and about turning into dust. All around them, people sniffed. Laurie-the-Greeter wailed loudly. A woman John recognized from the church sang a song all by herself and then Pastor Conley prayed one more time.

When the organ began, everyone stood up. Row by row, the people ahead of them started moving in a line toward the front of the church. John thought it was strange because they usually left through the back.

When the man in the dark suit stood at the end of their row and nodded to them, Sarah whispered, "Do you want to go up and see Betsy?"

John perked up. "Bessy? Yep." He followed Sarah and Barry into the aisle. What would Betsy look like now, lying in that box?

They waited in line behind the slow procession. Nobody spoke. Women held tissues to their noses and wiped their eyes. Up ahead, John saw the casket. It shone, dark and smooth. When they got next to it, he noticed he could see himself in its black surface. He studied his reflection, slightly curved, and made a silly face at himself.

Barry nudged him and shook his head. John stepped forward, and suddenly, there was Betsy. She looked small lying in the long box, and nearly as white as the billowy lining. Her dark circles were gone and she had on a new dress. She lay very still, her eyes shut tightly. She looked so calm and quiet it seemed like she was sleeping. John snuck his hand into the casket and shook her arm.

"Bessy! Wake up!" he whispered. Her arm was cool and firm under his touch. With his other hand John reached in and touched Betsy's cheek like he used to do. She always blushed when he did that. Betsy's cheek was cold, too, and she didn't respond. He jerked his arm away. Staring at her face he realized it looked different, not like Betsy at all. This is what a dead person looked like. Why did Sarah make him come here? Repulsed and confused, John pushed past Sarah and ran out of the church.

Outside, the sun shone brightly. John blinked. He didn't know what to do. He stood amidst the quiet crowd and rubbed his hands on his pants, trying to get rid of the feeling of her dead skin. Nurse Julette had always told him people could catch sicknesses from each other from little bugs you couldn't see ... what if little death bugs had climbed onto him? What if he caught death from her? He stuck his hands in his pockets.

"There you are, John." Sarah said as she and Barry caught up with him.

"Need wash my han's." He pulled them out and showed her. "See deaf bugs?"

She raised her sunglasses. Her eyes were red. "No. No death bugs." She gave him a long hug and John leaned his head onto her shoulder, never wanting to move.

"Are you okay?" she whispered into his ear.

"Bessy dead," he answered as tears sprung to his eyes. Words he had been thinking for quite a while but had never said jumped out of his mouth. "You be my mama?"

Sarah patted him softly and cooed, "Yes, John. I'll take care of you. Let's go home."

She looped her arm through John's, her other arm through Barry's, and they walked like the Mod Squad to her punch buggy.

John wanted to punch her arm and say, "Punch Buggy," but he couldn't take his hands out of his pockets. She didn't say it either.

Chapter 21
Moment of Truth

On the drive home from the funeral Sarah had to admit she felt comforted to be in church, especially on such a sad occasion. She was reminded of her youth and her exuberance about her faith then. It seemed like a long time ago. When was the last time she had attended a service?

Barry sat next to her staring out the side window, lost in thought. Sarah turned the car radio on but the rock and roll music was out of sync with their moods. She switched it off again. Glancing at John in the rearview mirror she wondered for the hundredth time if her brother would have looked anything like John, if he had survived. Lost in thought, she wondered what John was thinking, how he felt. He finally seemed to understand that Betsy was gone. She doubted that he thought about his own mortality like she did. She had a sudden urge to call her mother, to tell her about John and Betsy and her angst over Ricky. Sarah knew she was trying to make up for what her mother had done to her brother through her work with the group home. If only she could talk to her mother about all this, maybe she could forgive her. What would her mother think of her endeavors? She wished she knew.

As they mounted the steps of the group home porch, Sarah patted John on the back. "I'm going to fix your favorite dinner, John, roast chicken with stuffing. You don't have to help today—you're off duty. Gordy and Todd are going to take you all to the park for some exercise first. Then we'll go out for ice cream after dinner."

"Me not hungwy," John said. He hurried to the main floor bathroom and Sarah heard the faucet turn on.

"Washing the death bugs off, I guess," Sarah murmured to Barry.

"I wish I could climb inside his head to see what he's thinking," Barry mused.

"I was just wishing the same thing." Sarah hung her purse on the hall tree.

John emerged from the bathroom and stomped straight up the stairs, saying he was going to bed.

Gordy almost crashed into John as he bounded down the steps. "I hate to spring this on you right now but you have to see something." Gordy's normally jovial expression was solemn.

"What is it?" Sarah asked wearily. Couldn't they have one afternoon without some kind of trauma?

"Not good. His worst yet," Gordy said. "You won't believe it unless you see it yourselves." He motioned for them to follow.

Sarah sighed.

As they passed John's bedroom door, they heard soft weeping inside. Sarah exchanged a sad glance with Barry.

Todd stood guard at the bathroom door, holding the handle. "We've got him trapped," Todd said looking stressed. They heard banging and then a crash coming from inside the bathroom.

"Oh, no," Sarah said, too drained to be panicked. "What's he done now?"

Gordy led them into Ricky's room. The window was shattered and the sun shone through outlining the jagged shards of glass still clinging to the window frame. The dresser was tipped over and clothes were strewn around the floor. Ricky's bed was stripped clean except for the puddle of urine in the center of the mattress.

Barry whistled. "Whoa! Looks like a hurricane blew through here."

"That's a good way to describe him," Gordy said. He lifted the corner of the mattress. "Look at this."

On the box spring lay a hammer, a screwdriver, a few butter knives, a chunk of broken glass.

"This is the one I had to wrestle out of his hand when he came at me with it," Gordy said. He picked up a large butcher knife from the floor and pointed it at them menacingly.

Sarah's covered her mouth in shock and whispered slowly, "Oh my God."

Barry swore under his breath.

"Did he hurt you?" Sarah asked, turning pale.

"No, he's fast, but I'm faster." Gordy flipped the knife in the air and caught it by the handle. They all stared at one another for a few stunned moments.

Finally, Sarah spoke what was on all of their minds. "What if one of the guys had come in here first? Someone could have been hurt ... or killed." The truth of this sunk in even as she voiced it.

Barry spat. "This isn't normal, even for these guys. He must be crazy or something."

"Or something." Sarah leaned against the wall, her knees weak. "Nothing has worked. He's only gotten worse. William always said there can be co-morbidity of mental illness with developmental disabilities ..." She was talking mostly to herself, rummaging through old class notes in her mind.

"Co-mor ... what?" Gordy asked.

"Oh, it just means two problems at the same time." She knew what she had to do and it pierced her. Taking several deep breaths to calm herself, Sarah set her feelings aside for later. Finally, conjuring up her flattest voice, she said, "That's it then. We have to send him back."

◈

Sarah and Barry helped Gordy clean up the mess in Ricky's room. They boarded up the shattered window, and flipped over the soiled mattress. Todd escorted Ricky back to his bedroom, leaving wet footprints down the hall carpet—he had peed all over the bathroom. Sarah sopped these up while the three men talked about how to secure Ricky's door from the outside. Gordy offered to run to the store for a padlock. Sarah hated to do that—they could shut her down for this, but since nothing better came to mind, she assented. What choice did she have? She stationed Todd outside Ricky's door.

While they waited for Gordy to get back, Sarah tried to call William. There was no answer at his home or his office. He was probably off gallivanting with his new lover somewhere. She hoped his wife was doing the same thing to him.

Gordy returned with a hasp and they screwed it to his door, securing it with the padlock. They hung the key at the top of the doorframe so it would be readily available in an emergency.

Sarah peeked in on John and she decided to let him sleep. He must be as exhausted as she was. Sarah asked Gordy and

Todd to take Lonnie, Mick and Peter to the park so she could figure out what to do.

When they were gone, Barry made coffee and Sarah rummaged around the kitchen for some chips. They sat down at the dining room table and Sarah cupped her coffee in her hands. She found herself staring blankly at the built-in cabinet.

"Is the coffee all right?" Barry asked, breaking her out of her pensiveness.

Sarah took a sip and gazed at Barry. "It's fine, Barry. I think I just need something else."

"A gin and tonic?" he smiled.

"That would be better," she acknowledged. Sarah was melancholy. Looking across the table at Barry, she realized he was her only friend. How would she have ever managed without him?

"What are you going to do?" he asked.

"I have to call Larkspur. See if they can take him as an emergency admission. William was right, damn it!"

"Do they do that?"

"I don't know. I hope to God they do ... what will we do with him if they don't?"

Barry raised an eyebrow and shrugged. "I'm fresh out of ideas, boss. Unless you want to drop him back off at that shack and let him fend for himself."

"Yeah, it makes me wonder why we searched so hard for him," she said, only half jesting.

She grabbed the phone book and flipped through the pages. Larkspur ... she never thought she'd be calling them again. When the operator answered, Sarah asked for any on-site supervisor. She got a woman named Christine.

"Christine," Sarah said, pretending she did this every day, "I'm Sarah Richardson, manager of the group home on Oak

Street. I need to make an emergency placement with you. He's an extreme danger to my other clients and my staff. I'd like to bring him over this afternoon."

"I'm sorry, Miss Richardson," Christine said. "There's a process that we have to follow. There has to be a team meeting between you and our intake coordinator and there's paperwork to complete. Then the admittance committee has to make a determination if this is the appropriate placement for him."

"But he's already lived at Larkspur, so that was done years ago." Sarah tried to remain calm, but she sensed her voice hardening.

"Yes, but if he has left, then he'll have to go through the process again to be readmitted. We can't do anything until Monday. Call back to set up a meeting with Sandra Bailey, the admittance supervisor."

This is an emergency," Sarah said, no longer trying to hide her anxiety. "He threatened our staff with a knife. He could have killed someone! You must have an emergency placement option. We can do the meetings and paperwork later. Right now, he's not safe to have in the community!" She wanted to bite her tongue after that popped out.

"I'm sorry, there's nothing I can do today. If you had called yesterday..."

"He didn't threaten us with a knife until today, ma'am!" She knew her sarcasm wouldn't help but she couldn't stop herself. Her hands began to shake.

There was a hesitation on the line.

Sarah jumped at it. "If you don't help me I'm going to call the police and put Ricky in jail. I'll contact the newspaper and let them know there's a dangerous Larkspur client in the community." Sarah was proud of herself for thinking of this trump card, knowing, of course, that this was the last thing they would ever want, or that she would ever do, for that matter.

"Can you hold?" The line went silent.

After several minutes Christine came back on the line. "All right. We can make an emergency thirty-day diagnostic placement. Bring him to the main office. Bring his paperwork. Someone will contact you for a meeting first thing Monday morning."

Sarah covered the phone and mouthed to Barry, "They're going to take him!" Then in her calmest voice she said, "All right, then. Thank you for your help."

She stared at the phone for a moment after she replaced the receiver. Her face fell. She had done it, the very thing she had despised and criticized her mother for doing; she had taken care of her big problem by putting him out of sight.

Barry put his hand on her shoulder. "You did the only thing you could do. He's not making it here."

Sarah looked at him sadly. "Do you really think so? Maybe later he could try again. Or maybe he could get on some medication."

"Yeah, maybe."

Sarah battled back the tears that stung her eyes. Barry came around the table and held her for several minutes. She leaned into his shoulder and they unconsciously swayed back and forth. They both knew Ricky would not be coming out again.

Just then there was a knock at the front door. Sarah and Barry quickly drew apart as if they had been caught doing something they shouldn't. Sarah flushed and hurried to open the door.

Mrs. Rockmont stood on the porch in a flowered sundress, newspaper in hand. Mrs. Hanover stood below her on the steps. She wore her gardening hat and gloves.

"Hello, again," Sarah said. Her heart was heavy and all she could think of was, *what now?* Barry came up alongside her. His presence bolstered her.

"Hello," Mrs. Rockmont said. She cleared her throat and glanced back at Mrs. Hanover, subtly motioning her up the steps. But Mrs. Hanover ignored her.

"How can I help you?" Sarah asked. "This isn't a very good time for us, actually Maybe you could come back another time."

"I, uh, we saw the paper this week, the article about the girl who died." Mrs. Rockmont held it up for Sarah to see. In the local crime section was a small article about Betsy's death by abuse and a request for help from the public in finding Richard.

"Oh, I hadn't seen this," Sarah said quietly. "She wasn't one of ours, but she was John's girlfriend. In fact, we just got back from the funeral."

"Terrible, terrible," shuddered Mrs. Rockmont. "This kind of thing should never happen."

Sarah gave Barry a sidelong look. What were they up to? He shrugged almost imperceptibly and put his hand reassuringly on her back.

"If you'll excuse us," Sarah started to say, but Mrs. Hanover stepped forward onto the porch and took over.

"What we want to say is that though we think these kids would be safer in a more protected place, we are very sorry for your troubles and that this sort of thing happens." Mrs. Hanover paused for several moments and looked down at her feet. When she began again her voice was edged with emotion. "I have a grandchild, Tony, who was abused by his father, that bastard. He's in prison now. He shook Tony so badly when he was four months old that he broke his neck. Tony is..." Her voice choked.

Mrs. Rockmont put her hand on Mrs. Hanover's arm. They all waited silently while she regained her composure.

"He's in a wheelchair. He can't speak or walk. He's six years old now and the doctors say he'll never be able to do anything for himself."

"I'm so sorry," Sarah said. She reached out and took Mrs. Hanover's hand. "I had a brother who was born disabled. He went to an institution and died there and I never knew him at all. That's why I'm doing this."

Mrs. Hanover hugged her as if Sarah was her long lost child. They both cried.

When she finally let go, Mrs. Hanover wiped her eyes with a tissue she had hidden in her sleeve. "So I want to tell you that we're dropping the lawsuit. You're welcome in our neighborhood. I'm sorry I've been, well, less than understanding."

Sarah smiled weakly. "You didn't know us and it's natural to feel afraid of people who are different. Thank you so much. We will try to be good neighbors."

At that moment they heard a crash from upstairs. Everyone glanced up and Barry turned and shot up the stairway.

"That's Ricky," Sarah said, laughing through her tears. "He's been having a bad day."

Mrs. Rockmont tenderly squeezed Sarah's arm. "You take care of these people. Let us know if there's anything we can do."

"Thank you again. Please feel free to come by and visit. You're welcome here anytime."

Mrs. Rockmont put her arm around Mrs. Hanover's waist as they ambled down the sidewalk.

Sarah shut the front door and scurried upstairs. Barry had opened Ricky's door and was righting the dresser Ricky had emptied and thrown to the floor. Ricky stood on a pile of bedding, naked and smiling. His spaghetti arms dangled at his side as he trembled in a spasmodic jerk that shook his whole body. Then he began to pee.

Chapter 22
Starlight

John slept for three hours after the funeral, waking up with his eyes crusty. He rubbed them open and found Lonnie sitting cross-legged on his bed knotting the new socks Sarah had bought him.

"Yonnie, what you do? No tie socks." John stretched and yawned. He glanced at the window. It was still light. What day was it? He couldn't remember at first, then scenes of the funeral came back to him; the church, Betsy in that box, the feel of her waxy skin.

He pouched out his lower lip and told Lonnie, "Bessy die, Yonnie. Me sad."

Lonnie tisked his tongue, shook his head and kept knotting socks.

John sat up. "Me hungwy. You hungwy?"

Lonnie nodded. John tried to unknot the socks but he only undid three before he broke a fingernail and tired of it.

Lonnie followed him downstairs where they found Sarah, Barry, Gordy and Todd sitting around the dining room table looking sullen. Sarah was on the phone, the curly cord stretched across the aisle.

"That's right, Jana," Sarah was saying into the phone. "There was nothing else we could do. I wanted you to know. See you Monday."

"Who dat?" John asked. He looked at all four of their serious faces. Something was happening, he could tell. Something bad.

"Oh, that was Jana," Sarah said. She turned back to the other counselors. "I'll take him. I have to fill out the paperwork."

"I'd like to go with you," Barry said. "You shouldn't have to do this alone."

"That would be helpful, thanks. Todd, would you pack a few of his clothes and I'll get the file from my office."

"No problem," Todd looked the saddest of everyone, his face scrunched up in a deep frown. "I'm really sorry, Sarah."

Sarah tried to smile. "Gordy, maybe you could take the guys to the store or something. That'll distract them while we're gone."

"Sure," Gordy stood up and draped his oversized arm over Lonnie's shoulder affectionately. Lonnie reached up and patted his cheek, barely able to reach it. John noticed again how tall Gordy was, even taller because of his puffy hair.

"What happen?" John asked. Somebody was going somewhere.

"Well," Sarah said haltingly, "Ricky is moving. This afternoon."

"Move? Whe'e?" John's heart quickened.

"We might as well tell him," Sarah said to the counselors. She turned to John. Her eyes were rimmed in red. "Ricky is moving back to Larkspur."

"Wicky go Ya'kspuh"?" John asked in disbelief.

"That's right." Sarah sighed. "He needs some time to learn to behave."

This wasn't sad news, it was great! John sandpapered his hands in glee and elbowed Lonnie. "Wicky go Ya'kspuh'! Cabby! Him bad!"

Lonnie copied John's sandpapering and giggled.

"I didn't say Cadby, John. Starlight, actually." Sarah stood up, picking up the coffee cups from the table.

John pictured the dayroom at Starlight. It seemed very far away now. He could imagine people sitting on the floor and lying across the furniture. He could hear Mamie thumping her head, see Jackie drooling on the couch sitting beside one of the girls, and picture someone twirling in the corner. And in his mind he saw Timmy twisting in his bean bag chair, mouthing words, his eyes searching for someone to talk to.

"Me go Sta'yight?" John asked, surprising himself.

"No, John, Ricky's going to Larkspur. You're staying here," she said and gave him a reassuring pat. "Don't worry."

"No, me bisit!"

Sarah paused. "I'm surprised you would ask. I thought you hated that place."

"Me, too, buddy," Barry said. He leaned back in his chair until it balanced on two legs and stretched his arms behind his head, yawning. "I've never heard you say anything nice about that rat hole."

Sarah frowned at Barry and mouthed something John couldn't catch.

"I mean that... place," Barry corrected himself.

"Me see Timmy, my fwend." John tapped his chest.

"If you really want to come," Sarah said, "I don't see any reason why you can't."

"Only that they might decide to keep you." Barry slugged John playfully, almost tipping his chair over backward.

John tried to punch Barry back. "No, me yive he'e, Sawah's."

"Don't tease him, Barry," Sarah said. "John, don't believe anything he says."

They smiled, so John smiled, too. But he felt odd inside, thinking about Starlight He was uneasy, and yearning to go, both at the same time.

~

Sarah's car eased up the cracked driveway that led through the open iron gates of Larkspur. She slipped into a parking spot in front of a stately brick building John knew to be Balhalla Hall. The late afternoon sun lit up the white columns and shuttered windows, now in need of paint. Stretching up the hill behind Balhalla, the grounds were covered with uncut lawns and magnificent maples. The dozen or so wards were spread over the campus like a convention of prisons.

Sarah turned off the engine and pulled the brake lever up. "Barry, would you stay here with Ricky while I check him in?"

Barry sat in the backseat next to Ricky. They were squished between books and papers that littered Sarah's car. "Sure thing," he said patting Ricky's leg. "I want to enjoy these last quality moments with Ricky. Don't want to leave anything unsaid."

"Yeah, I bet." Sarah glanced back at Barry then said to John, "Do you want to come in with me?"

"Yep." John tried to be brave, even though his insides felt squishy. A sense of dread flooded over John as he got out of the car. Misty memories of forgotten faces and the echo of whispering voices haunted him, raising the hair on his neck. He had the feeling he was being watched. He glanced around behind him.

They strode up the broad marble steps together and entered through tall double doors. The hall was white and empty and their footsteps echoed on the tile. Voices could be heard coming from somewhere unseen.

John lagged behind Sarah, studying the old-fashioned pictures of men on the walls who looked like presidents. He hadn't been to Balhalla for years, not since they brought him to the meeting. He remembered sitting at a long shiny table with people in suits all around him. They talked about him, about where he should live now. It was after that meeting that he moved from Moonbeam to Starlight.

Sarah stopped at an open window and put her arm on the high counter. John waited behind her.

"May I help you?" A white haired woman with a wrinkled face rose from her typewriter, and came to meet them at the counter.

"Yes. I'm admitting a client."

"Patient?"

"Yes, I suppose."

"New referral?"

"Returning."

The woman glanced at John over her glasses. "His name?"

Sarah looked back at John, "Oh, not him! This is John Coben. He's just visiting with me. The client, uh, patient is Ricky Carlton."

Sarah unzipped her backpack and pulled a large yellow envelope out. She set it on the counter. "Here is the paperwork."

"Where is the patient coming from, miss?" the woman asked, opening the envelope and glancing at the papers.

"He lives, lived in my Oak Street group home, the university research project. I cleared this through Christine."

"Where is the patient now?"

"Out in my car."

"I see." The woman selected a long form from under the counter and handed it to Sarah. "You'll have to fill this out."

Sarah wrote on the paper for quite a while and finally told the clerk she was finished. "There you go."

The woman came back again from her desk and adjusted her glasses. "All right. You may bring him in and I'll call an orderly."

"He's supposed to go to Starlight. I know where it is. Could I take him?" Sarah asked.

"What about him?" She nodded at John.

"He'll help me. He used to live there and I think he would like to visit his old friends, if it's all right."

"I don't see why not. I'll call and let them know you're coming."

"Thank you." Sarah walked away quickly, followed closely by John, who had to hop-skip to keep up with her.

Barry had moved to the driver's seat and he opened the car door when he saw them coming. Sarah wiped her forehead to let Barry know it was done.

"Did it go all right?" Barry asked.

"It went. This place gives me the creeps. But everything is set. They're expecting him. How was Ricky?"

"A perfect angel." Barry pulled Ricky out of the backseat by the arm.

Sarah opened the hood and lifted Ricky's bag out.

"You carry it, Ricky," Barry ordered.

Ricky only twitched his spaghetti arms.

"Let it go," Sarah said. "What's the point? He's someone else's job now."

"Someone else's headache, you mean."

John picked up the bag. "Me cawy."

Sarah and Barry led the way up the sloping path, both holding Ricky's arm. John tagged behind with his burden, stopping every little bit to switch hands. They passed Beacon Hall and Moonbeam. A few stray workers walked by, going on unknown errands. John said hi to each one, though he didn't recognize them.

Ricky was silent. His eyes darted about, taking in the scene. At one point, he jerked and pulled away from them, but Barry scrambled and caught him within a few stumbling steps.

When they all stopped to catch their breath, John surveyed the campus. Larkspur looked worse than he remembered. Grass pushed its way through cracks in the sidewalk, gray showed through in places on the white painted buildings, and the old stone fence by the cow pasture was nearly covered with blackberry vines. Among the railroad tracks beyond, high weeds poked up so that the tracks were barely visible. John still remembered when he was a little boy and a worker had crawled over that fence. The train had thrown him farther than two football fields, they said. They found him in several pieces.

"You know," Sarah said, puffing a little, "they put these institutions on hills in the old days so the bad humors would rise up and not infect the townspeople."

"What?" Barry sounded surprised.

"It's true. Spooky, huh?"

"Dark ages." He shook his head.

"Ready?" Sarah started up the hill again.

John picked up the suitcase and they trudged on. When they neared Starlight at the top of the hill, they passed a man in a hat standing near the path with his back to them. As they approached, he pulled the corner of his hat down over his face, turning slightly to look at them. Quickly, he looked away again.

John recognized him as Monte the Monster from the canteen. He always tried to cover the inside-out part of his face that was red and puffy.

"Hi, Monte," John called.

Monte glanced over again, covering his face with his hand. "Beautiful day," he replied.

"How you?"

"Just fine." Then quickly, Monte turned, pulled his hat down and rushed away.

"Poor guy," Sarah said, shaking her head. "He sounded intelligent, and he's trapped here because of a birth defect? How sad."

"Yep. Him sma't one."

"Can't they do something about that?" Barry asked.

Sarah shrugged. "I don't know. You'd think so."

John recognized Starlight before they arrived, with its red brick walls and high windows. Even the crack on the door glass was still there. Mamie had banged her head on it during one of her fits.

Sarah buzzed the doorbell and they waited. An orderly John didn't know unlocked the door. A sickly smell enveloped them, that mixture of cleaners and pee that John hadn't smelled since he left. Ricky stopped just inside the door and wouldn't move. Barry had to get behind him and push. As they walked slowly down the hall together, the noises from the dayroom grew louder—a television commercial, someone moaning, a rhythmic thumping sound. A worker shuffled past dragging a blanket and talking to himself.

John swallowed hard, wishing he hadn't come. They stopped at the nurse's office counter. John set the heavy suitcase down.

Cookie stood at the paper-strewn desk. She fingered a clipboard and stared into the dayroom through the large window.

"Excuse me," Sarah said softly.

Cookie looked over. "Well, hello again! Haven't seen you around here for awhile. You must be bringing Richard."

"That's right. He goes by Ricky."

Barry pushed Ricky forward.

"Hello, there. Aren't you a pretty one?" Cookie glanced past Ricky to John. "Well, if it ain't my old pal, Johnny Coben!"

She smiled and lumbered out to grab John in a bear hug. Cookie seemed bigger than ever, soft and spongy to hold. John laughed.

She pushed him back at arm's length and looked him over. "You moving back? Just couldn't take it out there?"

"No!" He pointed to Ricky. "Wicky stay."

"Just teasin'. I heard you were doin' good out there," Cookie gave John a pat on the butt. "You look good, Johnny. You've put on a few pounds. Eatin' well, huh?"

"Yep. You, too?" John pointed to her stomach.

She chuckled. "I'm doin'. And you need a haircut and a shave."

"He chose to let his hair grow out," Sarah noted. "Cookie, this is my associate, Barry."

"Nice to meet you." They shook hands.

Barry was quiet, folding his arms behind his back and peering curiously into the dayroom.

Cookie turned to Ricky again. "So you're gonna be staying with us, Ricky."

Ricky watched her, wide-eyed. Grunting sounds drifted in from the dayroom. Ricky glanced that direction and his face twitched.

"That's Paulie. He's having a bad day," Cookie said. "So, Sarah, tell me about Ricky. I know he used to be at Moonbeam."

Sarah handed her a copy of the paperwork. "He doesn't talk very much, at least not appropriately. But he swears like a sailor. There are some other behavior problems, too."

"There always are. Like what?"

Sarah drew another paper from her backpack. "I made you a list of things he does, things he doesn't like, and things he responds best to. I hope this will help."

Marley appeared through the door at the other end of the office. He nodded to them, then said to Cookie, "I cleaned that up. You want me to start showers? His teeth were still stained and he was as skinny as ever.

"Sure," Cookie answered. "We're gettin' a new one here, name's Ricky."

"Hmf." Marley slithered off without another word.

"So let's see what else he does." Cookie read through the list, "Throws things out windows, big and little things ... ain't no windows low enough for that here.

"And he turns over mattresses at night," Sarah said.

"We'll tie 'em down."

"And sometimes he's very non-compliant, won't do anything we say."

"Well, we'll fix that. Right, Johnny?" Cookie winked at him.

John fingered his crumpled ear. He pictured Cookie grabbing Ricky's ear and dragging him across the room. Yep, she could fix that.

"Him hit Yonnie, too," John added.

"There ain't no hittin' allowed, is there, Johnny?"

"Nope. Go Cabby," he said definitively.

"That's right. If they get aggressive and hurt somebody, they go to Cadby. That's why Johnny went there that one time."

"What?" Sarah sounded surprised.

"Yeah, Johnny had a little problem once, hit a tech in the back when his friend Lonnie got in trouble. She fell and got a concussion, so Johnny ended up in Cadby for a few days."

Just the thought of that day made John feel sick inside. Lonnie had been in a "no" mood because the tech wanted him to take a shower, and he had just taken one before she came on duty. But she wouldn't believe them. She dragged Lonnie into the shower, stripped off his clothes, and was testing the water when Lonnie hit her. John hadn't been able to stop him, and when she slipped and banged her head on the tile, John had panicked, afraid Lonnie would be sent to Cadby again. Lonnie had been there twice before and the third time meant a month in the pit. So when the tech woke up and started screaming at them, John told her that he had hit her. Lonnie hadn't said a word and John went to Cadby for three days.

Sarah stared at John. "I never knew that, John. No wonder you are so afraid of that place."

John opened his mouth to tell her what really happened, but Cookie broke in. "That cured him, though. Never hit a tech again."

John decided to wait until later to tell Sarah it wasn't his fault. Cookie wouldn't believe him anyway. Besides, he was anxious to see Timmy and the others before they had to leave.

"Cookie?"

"Yes, Johnny?" She pinched his cheeks. "You look so good, Johnny boy. I've missed you around here."

John stroked her cheeks in return. "Me miss you too, Cookie. Me bisit fwends?"

"Why, sure. You go ahead."

John moved into the dayroom and stood still for a minute, staring. This, John's home for so many years, now looked barren, like a place someone forgot to move into. Yet nothing had changed ... same few ragged pieces of furniture, same bare walls and glaring light bulbs, same people. But now they looked different to John. One worker spun in circles in the middle of the room, others wandered aimlessly or lay sprawled over the furniture and floor. Mamie sat in a corner, her blouse crookedly buttoned and hanging over her bare shoulder. At least she was dressed. She rocked slowly, thumping her head on the wall.

"Mamie! Cut that out!" Cookie yelled, even though she couldn't see Mamie from the office. Mamie stopped and hit her head with her fist instead.

Jackie, the irritating little man with the enormous dripping tongue, got up from his seat and stumbled toward John. He stood within inches of John's face, smiling broadly, his tongue hanging to his chin.

"Hi, John!" he said, patting John's arm affectionately. "I know you!"

"Hi, Dackie," John said. He patted Jackie's balding head. "How you?"

"Good!" Jackie dug into his pocket, staring open-mouthed at John. "I got money! Money in my pocket!" He pulled out a dime and held it up for John's admiration.

"Dat good, Dackie. Whe'e you git money?"

Jackie pointed vaguely toward the office with his middle finger. "Cookie give me money! Money in my pocket!"

"Dat nice, Dackie." John watched as Jackie put the dime back into his pocket and headed for the office, walking as if he were facing into a powerful wind.

John spotted someone familiar, but out of place. He stared, struggling to remember. Then he realized who it was. Rochelle!

She must have moved over from Moonbeam. Her hair was matted in back and her clothes hung loosely around her boney shoulders. When she glanced up at John through greasy wisps of hair, John could see her face twisted into an awkward expression. He waved half-heartedly. Her glance was fleeting and without recognition. She quickly hid her face with both hands.

John felt an emptiness in his gut now. He realized he had few friends here, except Timmy. John searched the room for Timmy's beanbag chair but it was gone. He walked back to the office to ask Cookie about Timmy. Jackie stood close to Sarah, staring at her breasts. Jackie liked girls. Sarah was talking to Jackie politely and he reached in his pocket and pulled out his dime.

"I got money!" he said to Sarah, shaking the dime in her face. "Money in my pocket!"

"That's great," Sarah said. "What are you going to spend it on?"

Jackie paused, unsure what to say, and stuffed it back in his pocket.

"He don't like to spend it," Cookie told Sarah. "He just likes to have money to hold on to. He's funny that way."

John approached Cookie and held up his hand to get her to stop talking about Jackie. "Cookie?"

"Yes, Johnny?"

"Me no find Timmy."

"Oh, Johnny. That's a sad case. He died shortly after you left. He fell out of his wheelchair and broke his neck. We never found out who forgot to fasten his straps. He's better off now. Couldn't move a muscle to wipe his own nose."

"Oh, my gosh!" Sarah exclaimed. "He was your friend, wasn't he John?"

John felt like someone had socked him in the stomach. He stepped back against the wall to keep from toppling. Timmy was dead, too? Crazy Henry, Betsy, and now Timmy. He should never have come back!

"It was a real shame," Cookie said. "I know you liked him, Johnny. You was the only one could understand his mushed-up speech. Maybe he just gave up when you left."

She paused. "Anyone else you want to ask about?"

John shook his head. There was no one left. He desperately needed to get out to where he could breathe. Tugging on Sarah's sleeve he said, "Yet's go. Me sick."

"Okay, John." She patted his hand and backed away from the dayroom entrance. "I guess we better get going, Cookie."

"Okay. Nice to see ya'll. Especially you, Johnny." Cookie pinched his cheek once more.

Sarah turned to Ricky, holding his hand in both of hers. "Ricky, this is your new home now."

"You already explained it to him three times," Barry whispered, pulling her by the arm.

"I know. I just have to do this," she whispered back, then turned to Ricky. " Ricky, I'm sorry to do this to you but if you work hard and learn to cooperate, maybe someday you can come back."

"Sarah is a worrier." Barry shrugged to Cookie, backing away.

"So you listen and do what they say, you hear?" Sarah's voice cracked on the last word. She hugged Ricky, but he didn't hug her back. Ricky just stared at Sarah, eyes wide, unsmiling.

"He'll be just fine. Don't worry," Cookie assured her. "We'll do our best."

"I'm sure," Barry murmured under his breath. Sarah poked him with her elbow.

Mamie started banging her head against the wall again. Cookie sighed and put her hands on her hips. "Excuse me. I gotta take care of her. You can just leave his things right there and we'll take care of 'em."

Cookie walked across the dayroom to Mamie, grabbed her face with both hands and yelled at her to stop.

"See? That's their best," Barry said to Sarah.

"Oh, Lord. I have to get out of here immediately or I won't be able to do it." Sarah turned to Ricky once more. "I wish you could understand. We just can't handle you right now ..."

Ricky only stared after them. Jackie stood next to Ricky trying to show Ricky his dime.

"He doesn't know the difference, Sarah." Barry gently snatched her arm. "One place to harass people is just as good as another."

"Bye, Ricky." Sarah waved and turned. Barry drew her down the hall. John stumbled after them, holding his stomach. He wished they would hurry. He gulped to hold the contents in.

"I just hate leaving him here, Barry," Sarah said. "How would you like to be dumped somewhere like this when you didn't even know why?"

Barry linked Sarah's arm in his. "I know, I know. It's hard. But it's the right thing to do, remember?" They walked swiftly down the hall.

John's thoughts whirled. Maybe even Ricky didn't deserve to live here where people slid out of their chairs and died, where they got their ears pulled and had to go to Cadby if their best friend accidentally hit someone. Maybe he should tell Sarah not to leave Ricky here after all.

He glanced back. Ricky stared after them, an evil look in his eyes. *Then again,* John thought, *if Ricky comes home, he might hurt Lonnie again.* John stumbled on, bent double with nausea.

When they got to the door, Sarah stopped. As the tech unlocked the door and held it open for them, they all turned to look back. Ricky had followed them half-way down the hall then stopped, uncertain.

"You stay here, Ricky." Barry called back. "We'll see ya later."

Ricky reached out as if to motion to them, then his hand jerked in a wild, meaningless gesture. He opened his mouth with a distorted grimace. His voice echoed down the hall in a last desperate call, "Muthafucka!"

Chapter 23

Secrets

Gordy and Todd insisted that Sarah leave the house when she returned from Larkspur. Gordy said she looked like death warmed over. A short drive later she and Barry sat at Rennie's in a booth by the window. She munched absently on her french fries, having finished off her burger.

"So you really think we did the right thing?" she finally asked Barry.

"Of course," Barry said. "What else could we do? He was going to hurt someone. He already hurt Lonnie. You are protecting the other guys, Sarah. That's what counts."

"That's what I need to focus on, the other guys," she acknowledged. She had been thinking mainly of the gnawing guilt she felt. "But Barry, what if you had to live there? Can you imagine being dropped off at a place like Starlight for reasons you don't understand and left with strangers? Who knows what they'll do to him when he acts up?"

"I hate to imagine. But then I can't imagine throwing a chair through the window, either, or collecting knives under my mattress to hurt people with." Barry smiled sympathetically and sipped his coffee.

"In my head I know you're right, but in my heart... I'm confused." She stared out the window.

"What could be confusing?" he asked. "It's clear cut. You made a decision based on the best available data in the interests of four other men who can't defend themselves. Simple."

Sarah felt a stab of defensiveness. "Simple for you, Mr. Science, but I'm talking about feeling like I've betrayed Ricky. Not just that, I failed him."

He snatched her hand and held it firmly in both hands. "I'd say Ricky failed you. Just because one guy couldn't cut it doesn't mean you failed. Far from it. Look how well the others are doing."

Sarah slumped back in her seat slipping her hand away. "But I feel so remorseful, or maybe disloyal. I feel like a traitor to him. I can't stop thinking of Ricky standing there in the hallway calling out to us to rescue him."

"And cursing us," he reminded her.

"And for some reason I keep imagining what my mom would say." She felt tears stinging her eyes and fought them off.

"What would she say?" Barry leaned forward on his elbows.

"I think she would ask me why I'm wasting my life. She would defend herself by saying they're better off being safe and with others of their kind."

"I bet she never visited an institution before she sent him there," Barry remarked. "She probably had no idea what kind of life she was sending him to."

"Probably not. But Dad said she visited him, so eventually she knew. Why didn't she take him out? I don't understand that."

"Maybe she felt it was too late. She just did what the doctor said she should do and didn't question it. Then she was married to your dad and you were born. It just wasn't done in those days."

"Yeah, it's interesting how people can't think outside the ethics of their own time."

"Not many of us are visionaries like you, Sarah."

Sarah blushed. "That's not what I meant."

"No, I mean it. You're definitely outside the norm." Barry smiled.

Sarah smiled back. "Hey, I'm not sure that's a compliment."

Barry tapped his fingers on the table, thinking. "It sounds to me like this is more about your brother and your mom than Ricky. Maybe you should call your dad again and talk to him about it. There might be something he hasn't told you that would make you feel better."

"Like what?" She was dubious.

"Like, uh, like her parents were so ashamed of her they forced her to give up the baby. I don't know. It's worth a try, though."

She picked at a hangnail then bit it off. Barry had a good point. How could a science guy be so insightful? "I'll think about it. I can't imagine Dad telling me anything that will make me feel better. He left her after twenty years of marriage, and disgustingly, for the proverbial younger woman. I have a hard time forgiving him for leaving her to die alone."

"Did he know she was sick when he left?"

"I don't know, actually. Maybe not. I always assumed he knew but maybe she didn't tell him. She didn't tell us a lot of things, as it turns out."

Barry checked his watch. "I better get going. I'm late in turning in my paper for my independent study. I just couldn't get it done with my other summer courses being so heavy. I've got to finish it before Fall quarter starts or I'll never be able to keep up."

"You're late because of me, aren't you? All our troubles and the extra time you've spent helping us out?"

"No worries. I'll get it done."

"What's your paper on?"

"Chlorofluorocarbons and the depletion of the ozone. There's some professor in California studying whether using certain kind of spray bottles harms the ozone layer in the atmosphere. I've been trying to get a copy of his latest paper."

"Wow, that sounds technical. I couldn't do what you do. My brain doesn't work that way."

"I couldn't do what you do!" Barry grabbed the bill off the table.

"No, let me get it. I was the one who needed a shoulder to cry on." Sarah tried to snatch the paper out of his hand but he was too quick for her.

"No biggie. Let me treat this time." He laughed. "I like cheap dates."

She kicked at him under the table. "See if I ever offer to pay again."

He started to stand up, then sat back down. "Hey, I heard William has a new love."

"Yeah, I know," Sarah pushed out her bottom lip, pretending to pout. "He evidently gave up on me."

"Yeah, you poor thing. Rejected by the guru for fresh meat."

"I hate it when guys say things like that." She grimaced in distaste.

"Sorry. Slipped out."

"Just don't forget that if not for him ..." Sarah started.

"If not for him I'd probably be working in the Student Union happily serving bagels."

"Just think of all the excitement you'd have missed; sitting in someone else's pee, waking up all night to wrestle a naked man into corners ..."

"Searching the bushes for him at all hours of the night, listening to Beatles concerts played on a suitcase guitar ..."

Sarah grinned. "And so much more."

They both laughed. Then Barry said seriously, "If not for the guru I never would have met you."

"I've thought about that, too." Sarah took his hand again and leaned forward. "I care about you, Barry, you know I do. You're a great friend and support. You don't know how much I appreciate all the extra time and help you've given me."

"That's because you're so cute."

She hesitated, afraid to say anything that might drive him away, but wanting to create the distance she needed right now. "I'm just, just so overwhelmed with everything that's going on in my life. I don't think I can manage more than a friendship right now. At a different time, after my dissertation."

"That's cool. I'll be here." His hand slipped away and he left, stopping to pay the bill at the cash register.

Sarah sat alone in the booth to finish her coffee. She had known for several months now how Barry felt about her. She cared about him deeply and she was attracted to his easy-going ways and warm smile. He had been a faithful friend, but when she finished her Ph.D. she'd be taking a university position God knows where. Barry was still in grad school and would have other plans for his career. Having a relationship was complicated, especially with all of her responsibilities at the group home and her dissertation yet to finish. Even though she longed for intimacy and ached for a man's touch, Sarah reluctantly pushed thoughts of romance with Barry aside.

Throughout the rest of the day Sarah thought about her conversation with Barry. At the grocery store where she picked up milk and bread, in the bike shop getting her tire repaired, and at the library where she stopped to photocopy yet another article on management of severe behavior problems, Sarah mulled over what he had said. He was willing to wait for her. Sorely tempted to throw herself into a sordid affair, she weighed the pros and cons of getting involved before her dissertation was finished. But she always came up with the same conclusion. Not now.

That evening while Sarah sat on her blanket-covered loveseat trying to read and fighting sleep, Barry called. He had gotten a good start on his paper and wondered if she wanted company.

His voice sounded so inviting on the phone Sarah couldn't say no. It had been awhile since she'd had anyone over and cleaning house was not her forte. She stuck the stray dishes into the sink, ran the overflowing garbage out to the dumpster, and piled up her loose papers. She heard his knock before she had finished picking up her dirty clothes.

Opening the door, she was happier than she expected to see Barry standing in the apartment hall holding his bike with one hand and clutching a small bunch of flowers with the other.

"Flowers? Oh, Barry, you shouldn't spend your money like that. I know how much you make, you know."

"I thought you could use some cheering up." He rolled his bike inside and propped it against the wall.

Sarah stuck the flowers into a jar with water and set them on the crumb-laden kitchen table.

"We could go to a movie or something," Barry offered.

"We could. Or we could save money and see what's on TV. I've got a couple of beers, I think."

Sarah opened the fridge door and peered at the pitifully empty shelves. "Actually, only one beer. I'll pour it for you."

"I'll share," he said following her into the galley kitchen. He opened a couple of cupboards until he found the glasses and pulled one out.

"Don't look too closely," Sarah said, backing him into the living room. "I can't remember when I last cleaned."

"You'd be disgusted if you saw my place," he said. "Guys never clean." He popped the top off the beer and poured some into the glass for her.

Sarah found a half-bag of slightly stale chips and poured them into a bowl. They sat on the only available seating, the loveseat. Feeling a little awkward after their conversation that afternoon Sarah leaned back against the cushioned arm so as not to touch him. She bent her legs up creating a wall between them.

"So, did you call your dad?" he asked taking a swig from the bottle.

"No, not yet. I'm thinking about what you said, though. I might call him tomorrow. It's late there."

"Yeah, I guess it is. But I've been thinking about this. If it was my brother I'd be curious about what happened to him. Your mom said he died, but what if he didn't and she just told you that?"

"What?" Sarah stared at him. "Why would she lie to me? Well, I guess she did already."

"So you wouldn't go looking for him."

"Why wouldn't she want me to look for him? That doesn't make sense." Sarah's heart began to race. She had never thought of this, a possible further deception by her mother.

"I don't know. Maybe she didn't want to burden you with him. She never told you about him to begin with. Maybe she thought he was dead. But maybe he wasn't."

"You mean she might have assumed he was dead because she had lost touch with him?"

"Who knows?"

"Why would you even think this?"

"I love mysteries. Read them whenever I can. Your dad is the only one who could answer these questions, though. Maybe she just wanted to protect you."

"Protect me? That's a crock. Protect herself is more like it. I just can't see her making that up, that he's dead."

Barry shrugged. "Even if he is dead, you might be able to find out what happened and where he's buried."

Sarah ran her fingers through her hair and thought for a moment. Clearly he either doubted her mom's story for some reason, or was just trying to splice together pieces that didn't fit; the logician in him. "That's a good point. I never thought of that. Isn't that weird? I never considered the possibility of visiting his grave, where ever that might be. But why do you doubt what she told me?"

"I don't know, just a hunch. Something about her story didn't add up for me. Too convenient, maybe. I'm probably way off base. Wouldn't it be nice to know, though?"

"All right, all right," Sarah laughed. "I'll call my dad and see if he knows something he's not telling me. You're pushy, you know that?"

"I like to think of it as insistent." Barry reached over and handed her the phone that sat on the table at his end of the loveseat. The cord stretched across his lap and he set the phone down between them. "I'll wait."

"Now? But he's asleep already."

"He might be, but wouldn't he be happy to hear from his beloved daughter whom he hasn't heard from since ..." He gave her a questioning look.

"Last winter. Granted, it's been awhile." She had to look up his number before she dialed.

Barry pointed toward the apartment hallway. "Do you want privacy?"

Sarah shook her head. "No, I want you to hear. Hello, Dad?"

Barry smiled. Sarah cocked the receiver slightly away from her ear and leaned toward Barry so he could hear. He leaned over so their hair was touching.

"Sarah?" Her dad's voice sounded sleepy.

"Did I wake you, Dad? Maybe I should call back another time."

"No, no, sweetheart. I was still reading. Just getting a little sleepy. How are you?"

"I'm fine. How are you and the family?"

"We're great. David's had the flu and has missed some baseball games, but otherwise everything is good. How's your project coming?" He was perking up.

"It's going okay. It's a lot of work. We've had a couple of set-backs, but I think it's going to work out. I'm shooting to finish in March, or maybe June."

"We're planning to come for your graduation, so let us know when. I'm so proud of you, darling. This is quite an accomplishment."

"Thanks." She thought about explaining what had happened with Ricky and William, but that wasn't the reason for the call. She glanced at Barry whose eyes stared at her from six inches away. He nodded.

"The reason for my call, Dad, is that I've been thinking about Mom and my brother. I have some questions for you."

Her dad was quiet for a moment. "All right, what is it? I don't know much, you know." *Is that disappointment in his voice?* she wondered.

"Well, I've been thinking. Mom told you that he died in the institution, right?"

"Yes. When you were a toddler."

"So he would have been a young child."

"I guess so. Six or seven, I suppose. He had a lot of medical problems that go with Down Syndrome. I don't know specifically what they were: something about his heart."

Barry whispered to her and she covered the phone with her hand. "Ask him what institution."

She uncovered the phone. "Do you know which institution he was in? Did you or I ever go with her to visit him?"

"No, we never went. She wouldn't let us. He was in the California state institution for the retarded in Fresno. She'd take the train down there by herself about once or twice a year. Then after you were born she stopped going. A couple of years later she told me he had died."

Barry nudged her again and she covered the phone. "Is he sure he died? Did they have a service or was there an obituary or anything?"

"Sarah?" her dad said, "Is someone else there?"

"Oh, sorry Dad. Yes, my, friend Barry is here. We've been talking about this and were just wondering what really happened."

"Is this someone I should know about?" he asked interestedly.

"Uh, well, he's a good friend." She felt her cheeks warming.

"All right. I won't pry."

Sarah repeated Barry's questions even though she thought them useless. "Are you sure he died? Did you go to a service, or see an obituary or a death certificate or anything?"

"Well, no." He hesitated again. "I guess I figured the state took care of everything. That is kind of strange, come to think of it. She didn't take those trips anymore so I never doubted it. Why do you ask?"

Barry urgently mouthed something to Sarah.

"Just a minute, Dad." She covered the phone.

Barry whispered, "Ask him if he could have possibly been transferred up here to Oregon."

"What?" Sarah didn't know where Barry was going with this. "Why would they do that?"

"So your mom could visit him up here instead of going to California."

This was a new thought to Sarah and she was caught off-guard. She stammered into the phone, "What, what if she had him transferred up to Oregon where she could more easily visit him?"

"Well, that's a thought," he answered, clearly puzzled. "I suppose it's possible. If she never told me I'd have no way of knowing, and she could have visited him without me suspecting. But why would she do that? Why would she tell me he died?"

"I don't know." Sarah's mind was swimming with alternatives. "I'm just thinking out loud. Maybe he came up here and that's why she stopped going to California. I'd sort of like to find out for sure what happened to him."

"Just in case," Barry whispered.

"In case what?" she asked him, covering the phone again.

"In case he's still alive and your mom didn't want you to find him."

She paused and repeated this into the phone.

"I never thought that much about it," her dad admitted. "Your mom didn't let me into that part of her life. In fact, she only told me what happened one time and then barely ever mentioned Jonathon again."

"Jonathon? That was his name?" Sarah caught her breath. Why had she never thought to ask his name?

"Yes. I thought you knew. I thought she told you everything before she died."

"No. Just that I had a brother who was retarded and that he died in the institution."

Barry tapped her leg. "What was his last name?"

Sarah looked at Barry questioningly as she asked, "So his last name was Stuart, Mom's maiden name?"

"Stuart? I'm not sure." Her dad paused. "Maybe. I never asked. What does it matter now?"

"I'm just curious. I might be able to find his grave. Could he have been named after his father?" Her heart began to race as she wondered where this might lead. "Who was the father? Do you know?"

"Oh, Sarah, sometimes there are things it's better not to know."

"Then you do know! Why didn't you tell me before?"

"Still trying to protect you, I guess. Sometimes I still think of you as my little girl. Yes, I do know. Your mom made me swear I'd never tell you."

"But why? Is it someone I know?"

"He was an older guy, a distant relative."

"A relative? Oh, yuk!"

"Your mom was under age, he was married. This guy would even show up at family reunions like nothing happened, with his wife and five children in tow. She pointed him out to me one time. She hated his guts, the slime ball, but she never told anyone else, as far as I know. Your mom tried to steer clear of him, but she couldn't be too obvious about it because she didn't want her parents to be suspicious."

"Oh, my gosh!" Sarah was suddenly angry at her mother all over again. "Dad, why would she sleep with a guy like that?'

"You're being awfully hard on her, Sarah. I... I don't think it was actually consensual."

Sarah drew her breath in sharply and barely squeaked out the question. "You mean ... he raped her?"

"Yeah, pretty sick, isn't it?"

"Oh, no! Poor Mom!" Sarah's stomach tightened into a ball, like a knife had been thrust into it.

Barry put his hand on the back of her neck and drew her close to him so that their heads touched. "I'm sorry, Sarah," he whispered. "I never would have tried to ..."

The painful lump in Sarah's throat prevented her from speaking.

"You're upset," her dad said. "I shouldn't have told you. In those days they just didn't talk about these things. She called it a family concern and took the shame on herself. I think she blamed herself somehow. He must have had a lot of control over her."

There was silence on the phone for a few seconds as Sarah regained her voice. "I feel awful. I wish I could take back all the things I said to her when she told me. I said mean things to her, Dad. I was so angry."

"I'm sure she understood, sweetie. She should have told you herself years before. One more thing."

"There's more?" Sarah was incredulous. She wiped her eyes and nose with her sleeve, shaking.

"To be perfectly honest, you do know him. He was your great-uncle Stan, your grandma's brother."

"Great-uncle Stan? Oh, not him." Stan had been one of Sarah's favorites, especially attentive to her when she saw him, although rarely. He died the year before her mom of a sudden heart attack. She began to weep.

Barry put his arm around her and pulled her to his chest, patting her arm and smoothing her hair. "I'm so sorry, Sarah," he whispered. "I never should have pushed you to do this."

She handed Barry the phone as she sobbed uncontrollably.

Hesitantly, Barry took the phone. "Uh, hello. This is Barry, Sarah's friend." He listened and then said, "Okay. I'll tell her." He hung up.

"Your dad says he'll call you tomorrow. And he's sorry. And he loves you." Barry rubbed her back until she finally leaned back away from him, wiping her eyes.

"I'm okay," she said sniffing. "It's good that he told me. It does explain things. Lots of things."

Barry rested his arm on the back of the sofa behind her.

"So that's the big family secret. Rape and incest, intrigue and sin. No wonder she was so ashamed. Maybe I can now stop being mad at Mom for things she obviously couldn't help."

"Her family probably would have blamed her in those days."

"Probably. And on top of that, the shame of having a retarded child. It must have been terrible for her. I can't imagine the pain she went through. No wonder she didn't want to talk about it with me. I would have asked questions she was too ashamed to tell me."

"Wow. You never know about people's lives, do you?" Barry shook his head, thinking.

They were silent for a few moments, then Barry asked, "So what was your great-uncle's name?"

"Stan. I thought you heard that."

"His last name."

"Oh, Cohen. Stanley Cohen. Suddenly, I hate him."

Barry's face scrunched up in thought. "So his name was Cohen. Stan Cohen."

"Right. So?"

"Your mom had a Jonathon Cohen and now we have a John Coben. Funny coincidence."

"Hmm. That is pretty weird." It struck her, what he might be getting at. "No, Barry, not our John. It can't be him. My brother died in California."

"It is weird, though," Barry said almost to himself.

"Yeah, weird." After several seconds Sarah found herself staring at the wall. "No. That just can't be."

"You're probably right. Too much of a coincidence." Barry set his empty beer bottle down on the coffee table.

"Yeah. I think it's good for me to know the truth, finally. I just need some time to digest it."

"Maybe I should go." Barry started to stand up.

"Please don't. I'd like you to stay."

He sat down quickly. "If you insist. Anything on TV? Or maybe you want to talk some more."

"Not really. Enough drama for one night. Let's see what's on." Sarah switched on the television.

An old Carey Grant movie was on and they settled back to watch it. Sarah rubbed her tense shoulder with one hand. Her trapezius muscle felt like a rope under her skin. Barry noticed and offered to give her a neck rub. Sitting on the floor in front of him, with his strong hands working away the tension, she felt herself melt under his firm touch. She hadn't been so exhausted since the nights they spent searching for Ricky. When he stopped his massage, Sarah was so relaxed she was barely able to crawl back onto the loveseat.

Barry flopped a pillow onto his lap and drew her head down to rest there. He gently smoothed the hair away from her face sending a sensation of longing through Sarah's body that she had not felt for a long time. She glanced up at him about to say something but he shushed her and patted her arm. She fell asleep, the warmth of his presence soothing her soul.

Chapter 24
The Visit

A week later as Sarah was just leaving to head out for her morning run, the phone rang. It was Barry.

"Hey, I was thinking," he said instead of "hello."

"Uh oh," Sarah replied. "We're all in trouble now."

"Yeah, yeah, yeah," he acknowledged, getting back what he had previously dished out. "I was thinking that we should make a little trip up to Larkspur to visit Ricky. I bet he's missing us by now."

"Oh, I'm sure he is. And he thought he had it bad here," she remarked. "But I think you're just projecting. I think it's *you* who misses him, isn't it? Don't deny it."

"I can't get anything past you," Barry said, playing along. "I can't go another day without seeing his bright shiny face. I'm thinking of adopting him so I can see him all the time."

Sarah laughed. "You better board up your windows and hide the knives, then."

"Already done."

Sarah thought about Ricky standing forlornly in the hallway of Starlight staring after them. "I do feel sorry for him, though."

"Me, too. But not that sorry."

"So you really want to go? I wasn't planning to go until next month when I have to decide on our new subject."

"You're a glutton for punishment, you know that?"

"I need five clients for the funding."

"No need to explain. Hey! While we're there we can do some investigating."

Sarah's suspicions about the real reason for his call were confirmed. "Investigating what? To see if John Coben is Jonathon Cohen? I've thought about it and there's no way. Mom was secretive, but not malicious. How many John's must there be at Larkspur?"

"I think it's possible. You'll have to prove to me he's not the long lost brother you've been looking for. There's such a strong resemblance. He looks just like you."

"Hey! You better watch it, buster." Sarah said, mocking offense. There had been a definite change in their repartee since last Saturday night when they both ended up sleeping most of the night on her loveseat. She had awakened around 3:00 A.M. with Barry's arms wrapped around her and his head resting on her hip. The television was hissing after going off the air. When Sarah stirred, Barry wakened, too, apologizing and stumbling for the door. But Sarah had tossed him a pillow and blanket and staggered to her room to finish the night.

"Seriously, I don't think so, either, but they may be able to help you track him down and trace when he died and where he's buried. Maybe some weekend we could go down to California to find him."

Her voice softened. "Okay. I'll go with you. But I'm only doing this for you. I'm at peace with not knowing."

"Whatever you say, boss. Pick me up at 10:00 in front of the Baker Building."

Sarah smiled to herself as she hung up the receiver. Barry was holding back, but his intention toward her was clear. And her feelings of genuine admiration were growing into deep affection. She was losing the fight.

Sarah pulled her car to the curb and reached over to open the passenger door for Barry a few minutes after 10:00. He slid in and threw his backpack into the backseat.

"Got my paper turned in," Barry said. "Just in time to register for Fall classes. I have to take a class from Fitzgerald this term. Worst professor in the department. Last time I took a class from him all he did was read from the text."

"Too bad professors don't have to learn how to teach before they become professors," Sarah sympathized.

"There's no point in going to class. It kills me to pay that much when I could just read the book on my own."

"I hate that," Sarah said. "That's why I'm going to be such an excellent professor. I was a teacher first."

"No kidding. You *will* be a great professor—wish I had you for Atmospheric Chemistry."

"I bet you're looking forward to a break, even if it's only a couple of weeks. Are you going home to Santa Fe?" Sarah hadn't thought to ask before and he hadn't mentioned anything. She would need to find someone to do the overnight shift if he was leaving.

"I think so. My parents said they'll buy me a ticket. I should have mentioned that before, sorry. Maybe Todd would fill in for me."

"Todd may be leaving, too. But don't worry. I'll find someone. Or I'll sleep over myself." She turned onto the coastal highway and sped up. The top was down and the rushing air somehow freed Sarah's mind, as did the sight of the waves crashing against the rocks. Her curls swirled wildly around her head, sometimes blocking her vision. She swept them back, having to hold them out of her eyes with one hand.

"Need my cap?" Barry shouted, reaching back to pull a baseball cap out of his backpack.

"Okay, thanks." After she pressed the cap over her locks, she glanced at Barry and posed.

"You look gorgeous." He gave her a thumbs-up.

She shook her head and laughed. "You don't give up, do you?"

"Not really. Did I tell you how beautiful I think you are?" He gently pushed an unruly curl behind her ear.

Sarah smiled in spite of herself. "You're embarrassing me!"

"Good!" He leaned his head back onto his seat and reached both arms up into the wind. "I love summer!" he shouted.

Sarah agreed, "Me, too!"

When she turned into the Larkspur driveway and downshifted for the hill, they both sobered. Just passing through the iron gates felt like entering a prison. The trees seemed to lean ominously over the car along the one-lane drive.

"I almost forgot how much I hate coming here," she said. "It's creepy."

"It's like entering the Gates of Hell." Barry laughed Vincent Price-ishly.

Sarah crept up the drive and pulled up to Balhalla Hall. Jerking up the brake she said, "Do you think they'll actually give us any information? After all, why should they?"

"Because you're going to take another one of those guys off their hands. They need you."

"Well, yes."

"And because you're so charming and intelligent."

"Yeah, charm is important to them, I'm sure. Let's visit Ricky first. Then we can go by the main office to look at client files. They gave me the names of three possible clients when I phoned yesterday." She dug in her pocket for a folded piece of paper and handed it to Barry.

"There you go. One of these lucky men is going to be part of our little family."

They tromped up the hill to Starlight. Sarah rang the bell. The same greasy-looking tech opened the door for them. Sarah felt a bit sick as the wave of unpleasant scents wafted over them.

"We're here to see Ricky Carlton," she said, stepping inside before she lost her nerve.

"Ricky? Oh, yeah. He ain't here," the tech said. His face was acne scarred and his white uniform was wrinkled and dingy.

"We just left him here a week ago. Where is he?" she asked.

"That's a wild one, he is. He hit the night shift tech, Grady, and broke his jaw. He's in Cadby for awhile. Grady won't be back for a month."

Sarah felt slapped. "Oh, geez! I was afraid he might act out. Where is Cadby? Can we visit him there?"

Barry shifted uncomfortably and backed out the open door, tugging on her sleeve.

The tech stepped out with them and pointed down the hill. "It's that one. But they don't allow no visitors there. You'd have to have an order from above for that." He raised his eyes upward as if to imply God.

"Well, thanks anyway," Barry said. He led Sarah by the elbow back down the path.

"Oh, Barry! Damn it!" Sarah cried. "I never would have sent him there if I thought he'd be in Cadby inside a week!"

"I know. What a bummer! But sounds like he deserved it, hitting someone that hard."

"No one deserves Cadby, from what I've heard." She was angry at Ricky and angry at herself.

"If anyone does, it's Ricky. Maybe it will straighten him out."

"I doubt it. He won't even know why he's there."

"Well, maybe they'll medicate him now. That might help."

"That's probably the answer for Ricky, at least short term. He's got to get some control." Sarah was frustrated with herself and the system. "There just isn't enough research to support other methods yet. That's what some of William's research is about. Five or ten years from now we might know some better techniques and everything could be different." She tossed up a prayer for Ricky, realizing there was nothing she could do now.

They got directions for the Records Department from the elderly receptionist in the admittance office. Pushing open a heavy wooden door at the end of the paneled hallway, they entered a room with dozens of shelves of dusty files lining the walls. Sarah forced a smile as she approached the Records Clerk.

"Hi. I'm Sarah Richardson. I'm conducting experimental research for the university." She used her most professional voice, wishing she had worn something other than shorts and a tie-dyed T-shirt. "Perhaps you've heard about the group home I started this past year with five severely disabled men from Larkspur?"

The hook-nosed clerk looked at them over his half-glasses. "No."

Undeterred, she continued, "Well, I have permission to view files on these three clients." She handed him the list of prospective replacements for Ricky. "And this one, too. He's already in my group home." She wrote John's name at the bottom.

"She has clearance from the top," Barry added, glancing heavenward.

Sarah subtly kicked at Barry with her foot.

"Clearance papers," the clerk said, holding out his skeletal hand.

Luckily Sarah still had the paperwork signed by Dr. Balhalla in her backpack. She scrounged around in the bottom of the bag until she found the now-crumpled envelope. "Here you go."

The clerk adjusted his glasses and slowly unfolded the letter, reading it word for word. "This doesn't say anything about a records search." He lay it down on the desk.

"If I can't see their records I can't make a decision on their appropriateness for placement in my residential facility, now can I?" Sarah leaned forward, resting both hands on the desk, trying to sound forceful. "If you would like to call Mrs. Jacobson I'm sure she'll verify this."

He eyed Sarah once more, read the paper again, and shrugged. "What are the names again?"

The clerk led them to a small table at the back by a window. He pointed to two chairs that Sarah and Barry pulled over while he fetched the files. Sunlight reflected off the small cloud of dust that rose when he flopped the thick files down in front of them. Then he left them alone.

Scooting close together Sarah and Barry poured over John's bulging file first. She already had copies of his most recent reports, so they skipped these and started traveling back in time through the notations from John's life. Daily notes and short reports described routine exams, reports on illnesses, his chronic hip displacement, a resolved heart murmur. After skimming many pages of uneventful notes they ran across a report of the incident where John hit the tech, and his subsequent visit to Cadby. The note taker had questioned why John would show violence because it was out of character for him. No other incidents of this type were recorded.

John had moved from Moonbeam to Starlight in 1968, and from Beacon to Moonbeam before that. No explanations were given for these moves. He had attended school at Larkspur until he was thirteen when it was determined he would never read or count past ten. After that he had several campus jobs before ending up in the laundry room. Many reports mentioned John's love of playing imaginary games, and his best friend, Lonnie.

One supervisor had written about an entertainment program John put on for the staff and clients, dressing other residents up in makeshift costumes and using them as props in his performance, starring John, of course. This "patronizing act" was later reprimanded by the dean at the time. John was not allowed to perform anymore.

Sarah's and Barry's heads nearly touched as they skimmed through more documents and pointed out interesting tidbits to one another. They kept their voices low so the clerk wouldn't hear. Sarah could smell Barry's shampoo and the coffee on his breath. She found herself longing to touch him. While she was momentarily distracted by these thoughts, Barry suddenly stiffened and tapped the page.

"Here's something! A report of his transfer at age six from Mendelssohn Home for the Retarded. Where's that?"

Sarah shrugged. "Never heard of it."

They skimmed down the report, then turned the page. A stapled packet of handwritten notes, faded and sometimes illegible, was the last item in the file. It contained records of developmental milestones like when John spoke his first word, walked independently, and was toilet trained.

Sarah's heart thumped perceptibly as they turned over the last few pages. This was a record of the earliest part of John's life. If there was anything to Barry's hypothesis they would find it here. She hadn't seriously considered Barry's idea as plausible until she slowly flipped back each page of John's history. What if she found something that would change her life forever?

Barry turned to the last page. It was an admission form to Mendelssohn dated 1944. The return address indicated that Mendelssohn was in Fresno. Sarah's heart beat into her throat.

The writing was faint, written in pencil in a tight and delicate handwriting. The name of the infant being admitted was hard to read, but when Barry and Sarah bent close to the paper simultaneously, the writing was clear enough to make out.

"Johnathon," Sarah read quietly. "But it's spelled funny."

Barry pointed to the last name. "Look at that ... C-O-H-E-N."

They could both see the tightly constricted handwriting, the strokes of the "h" nearly touched at the bottom.

"Is that an 'h' or a 'b'?" Barry asked.

"Could be either one," Sarah whispered back, in shock. She flipped the last page over and stared at the admitting parent's name. Even though it appeared immature and rather shaky, there was no mistaking her mother's familiar signature.

Chapter 25
Mama

A week after the funeral, John and Lonnie got off the white bus at their usual bus stop. They walked home slowly, heedless of the hot sun beating on their backs. John missed Betsy every day. He kept looking at her empty chair whenever he had a chance to peer into the main workshop area, still surprised that she wasn't there. At lunch, he and Lonnie stood by the post where he first met Betsy and John cried. Millie gave him a big hug every time she saw him, and even Ken came by and patted him on the shoulder, telling John how sorry he was. Skip had been extra nice to John, which meant leaving him alone, and Chuck let him take an extra long break so he could be with Lonnie.

John held Lonnie's hand as they made their way home because he knew Lonnie was sad, too. They didn't speak. Opening the front door, he started to head upstairs to his room. He was exhausted and just wanted to lie down.

Unexpectedly, Sarah rushed over to him and swept him into her arms. "How are you doing, John?" she asked. Her voice sounded funny.

"Fine," he responded automatically. When she finally let go of him he could see that there were tears in her eyes. Sarah was sad, too. Everybody was sad. John just wanted to go to bed.

"I need you to do something, John," Sarah said. "We need something at the store and I need you to go with me."

"Me tiyed," he said, wiping his burning eyes.

"I bet you are." She smiled at him and squeezed his shoulder. "But this won't take long. We need to drive."

Reluctantly, John turned toward the door, wishing for once that Sarah would just leave him alone.

"We'll be back pretty soon, Jana," she called, donning her backpack.

Jana waved from the dining room where she was helping Peter set the table. "Take your time."

John punched Sarah's arm as soon as they stepped onto the porch. "Punch Buggy."

"You're too quick for me, John," she said, sounding like she had a cold.

They drove into town and Sarah parked near the water. Sailboats were lined up against long wooden sidewalks. They got out and John followed her along the walkway, passing several small shops. The water smelled funny here, like fish. Small waves lapped against the boats and the boardwalk, shimmering in the light of late summer. John heard the familiar calls of seagulls overhead and he watched them soaring in circles above the masts of the boats.

"What us buy?" he asked. They had never gone shopping down here before.

"Actually, I don't really need to buy anything. I need to talk to you." They turned in at a café overlooking the water. A waitress seated them and Sarah ordered cokes for both of them. John was surprised and pleased to have some special time just with Sarah.

After their cokes were served, Sarah drew some photos out of her pack. "I wanted to show you something," she said. Her voice was soft. She laid two pictures on the table. One was of a woman holding a young child with curly hair, and another was the same woman standing by the ocean, her hair blown by the wind.

"I have to tell you something about her," Sarah said pushing the photos close to John so he could see them.

John bent low, looking carefully at the pictures. Something was familiar about the woman. He studied her face. Finally he remembered.

"Dat Miss Wicha'dson," he said, tapping the picture. "Me know hu'."

Sarah stiffened and put her hand over her mouth. Her hand was shaking. "You know her?"

"Yep. My fwend. Bisit me, Beacon, Moonbeam."

Tears squirted from Sarah's eyes and she turned pale. "She visited you at Beacon? Here in Oregon?"

"No, Ya'kspuh'," John corrected her. He tapped the picture again. "Yep. Hu' my fwend. Not see fo' yong time. Whe'e hu go?"

Sarah didn't speak for several minutes as she buried her eyes in her napkin and wept. John patted her arm sympathetically.

"What w'ong, Sawah?" he asked over and over. "What w'ong? You no yike Miss Wicha'dson? What w'ong?"

Finally, Sarah's crying subsided. She snatched several napkins out of the napkin holder, blew her nose and dabbed at her eyes. "John?" Her voice sounded funnier still. "This is your mother, Miss Jane Richardson."

"Mama?" John bent over again to stare at the pictures. "Hu' my mama?"

Sarah nodded, still fighting the tears.

"No, hu' Miss Wicha'dson. Not mama."

"I know. I don't' know why she didn't tell you who she was. Sometimes people call their parents by their name instead of 'Mother' or 'Mom.'" Sarah shrugged. "But the important thing is, and I just found this out, she is your mother."

John was suddenly elated. "My mama! Whe'e mama now? Us bisit?"

Sarah looked down at the table and took a sip of her coke. "I'm sorry to tell you this, John, but she died four years ago. We can't visit her."

John stared at the pictures. His elation turned to sorrow. He touched the pictures, gently stroking Miss Richardson's face with his finger. "Hu' gone yong time ago? Hu dead, yike Bessy?"

"That's right. You haven't seen her for a long time, have you?"

He shook his head. "Nope." He hadn't even thought about her for years.

Sarah took his hand. "I have to tell you something else, though. And this is the good news."

John looked into her watery eyes. She was smiling now.

Sarah pointed to the picture of Miss Richardson holding the little girl. "This is your mother, and this little girl is me. That is my mama, too."

He scrunched up his eyebrows in confusion.

"I'm your sister, John." Sarah squeezed his hand and tears flowed freely down her cheeks once more. "You're my brother. This is our mother, both of us."

John didn't know what to say. He stared into Sarah's face, looked at mama's picture again, then at Sarah. For the first time he noticed a resemblance between Sarah and Mrs. Richardson. "Dis you mama?"

"Yes, it is."

"You my sisto'?" John could hardly believe what Sarah was saying. He never had a sister before.

"Yes, John. I'm your sister. You're my brother. We have the same mother. You're the answer to my prayers." She took his hand in both of hers. They were damp.

"Me hab sisto'! Sawah, you my sisto'!" He shook his head in wonder.

Sarah gazed steadily into his eyes, smiling and sniffing. John broke into a smile, too. He chuckled to himself. It was his dream come to life. A real mama and even a sister! Sarah grinned broadly, happier than John had seen her for a long time.

He laughed out loud and slapped his knee in the sheer pleasure of seeing her happy. Sarah began to snicker, too. John laughed harder, snorting loudly through his nose. Sarah cracked up, breaking into a full-throated guffaw. They were so loud that people in the coffee shop stopped to look at them. But they couldn't stop. They fed off one another, howling with joyful abandon until tears streaked their faces and John's sides hurt.

Between gasps for breath, John squeaked, "Me hab sisto'!" and burst into laughter again.

Sarah nodded through her chortling, doubling over and holding her stomach. "And I have a brother!"

༄

October 16
The gaily wrapped gift lay across John's lap, almost too big to hold. His enormous smile was contagious. Gingerly he touched the shiny paper.

"Open it!" Barry shouted. "Just rip it open!"

"Yeah, rip it," said Jackie. He had arrived three weeks ago and had already settled in. His tongue hung below his chin, a drip of saliva poised at the tip. He slurped it up and said, "Rip it, rip it!"

John looked up at Sarah. She stood behind the sofa, her hands leaning on Barry's shoulders. Her eyes glistened.

Slowly at first, then with gusto, John tore the bright paper off the package, revealing a cardboard box with a picture of a guitar on it. He sucked in air so fast everyone laughed.

"Guita'? Fo' my bi'fday?" He could hardly breathe.

Lonnie stopped his flicking and signed "guitar," then he sirened joyfully and sandpapered his hands.

Jackie jumped up and ran to John, leaning precariously over the gift box and drooling. "It's a guitar! It's a guitar! John got a guitar for his birthday!" A drip of saliva hit the box as Jackie danced around shaking his hands in excitement.

Mick sat on the sofa arm. He fingered the lucky rabbit's foot in his pocket that he used now instead of papers or pencils. Peter watched out of the corner of his eye from his rocking post at the front window.

Barry stood up and fished a jackknife out of his pocket. "I can't stand it. Here you go." He handed the knife to John.

Inch by inch John cut along the box seam, just like he had learned to do in the dock. He lifted the flaps of the box open. Inside was a golden guitar! The shiny wood facing shone so that John could see himself reflected in it. An intricate pattern of inlaid shells surrounded the hole beneath the strings. The neck was dark brown with silver strips. It was the most beautiful guitar John had ever seen.

He gazed up at Sarah. "Mine?" He wanted to make sure.

"Yes, John, it's yours. Happy birthday!"

John poised his hand over the strings, closed his eyes and strummed. The rich sound bathed his heart in comfort. Tears stung his eyes. His very own guitar! Then he leaned his head back and laughed, a full-bodied howl of pure delight. He and Lonnie gave each other high-fives, giggled, and tickled each other, then high-fived again.

"I'm glad you like it, John," Sarah said.

"Time to retire your suitcase, buddy," Barry added.

"Now we expect a concert, of course," Sarah said. "We'll give you a few minutes to practice. After we eat your cake, that is."

"Let's sing," Jana called from the dining room. She brought a flaming cake over to John and held it in front of him while they all sang "Happy Birthday." John stopped stroking the smooth curves of his guitar long enough to blow out the candles. Everyone clapped.

Jana took the cake back to the dining room table and cut pieces for everyone. "Come on up to the table," she called.

John set the guitar carefully back in its box and pulled Lonnie to the dining room by the hand. Barry set the timer. "I'll give you extra time to eat today, Lonnie, since it's John's birthday."

"Happy birthday, John," Jana said again as she handed him a piece of chocolate cake with ice cream.

Sarah sat down beside Mick to make sure he didn't snarf his whole piece of cake in a single bite. All she had to do now was say, "Just one, Mick," and he took one bite at a time.

Peter was seated at the end of the table so he wouldn't rub shoulders with anyone, though touching people didn't bother him as much as it used to. He flapped his hands between forkfuls and curiously studied the overhead light. Jackie sat on the other side of Sarah, talking constantly with his mouth full.

With every bite bits of cake peppered his shirt and pants. Sarah hadn't started working on Jackie's eating yet.

After cake, John retrieved his old suitcase and ceremoniously gave it to Lonnie. Then he gently picked up his new guitar. Barry offered to tune it for him. When John was ready, Barry put on a Beatles album. The music started. Barry turned it up loud.

John stood up with his knee on the sofa to balance the guitar. He strummed madly, gyrating his hips as best he could and bellowing pretend words along with the song. When the song was over everyone clapped and cheered.

Jana gathered up her things. "I better get going. See you tomorrow." She gave John a big hug and kiss on the cheek before she left.

Shortly after Jana left, Sarah said, "Bedtime, you guys. Tomorrow is a work day. Go on up and get ready for bed. Jackie, you need to shower tonight."

"Shower? Again? Not again! Please not again!" Jackie used this conversational opportunity to stand close to Sarah and stare at her breasts.

"Yes, every day here, Jackie."

"I didn't wet," he said, still staring at her chest.

"I know and that's great. But you have to shower anyway." She lifted his damp chin with one finger. "Can you please look at my face when we're talking?"

He did for a moment, then his eyes drifted downward again.

"He appreciates the finer things of life, Sarah," Barry joked.

"This will definitely have to be one of Jackie's goals," Sarah said, giving Barry a scolding look. "In fact this would be a good goal for all college boys."

"You mean college men," Barry corrected, laughing.

"No, I mean boys. Even men are boys when it comes to this." Sarah stood with her hands on her hips frowning at Barry, her head cocked to one side.

John shook his head. He didn't understand what they were talking about but he knew Sarah wasn't really mad at Barry. In fact, he could tell by the way they looked at each other that they were girlfriend and boyfriend now. He nodded for Lonnie to follow him up the stairs, carefully holding his guitar high overhead so it wouldn't hit the wall. He made Lonnie carry the box because he planned to put the guitar in it every night for safekeeping.

Once they were in their room John gave the guitar strings a few more sumptuous strums before he laid it gently inside its box and closed the flaps. He couldn't believe this was his very own guitar. He smiled to himself. He loved his life at Sarah's.

He and Lonnie got their pajamas on, used the bathroom, and climbed under the covers. Now that the nights were cooler, they no longer kept the window open. And with no Ricky to wake them, they all slept soundly.

John turned on his side so he could see Lonnie. "My bi'fday, Yonnie. Me git guita'! My best bi'fday eva!"

Lonnie nodded and smiled, reaching out to pretend to tickle John's neck, even though he was too far away to reach him.

"You my best fwend, Yonnie," John said.

Lonnie waved good night and turned over.

But John was too excited to sleep. He glanced over at his nightstand. Mama's old picture sat propped next to his lamp. An idea struck him.

Slipping down the stairs quietly, he peeked around the corner to see if anyone was still up. Barry and Sarah sat on the couch. The glow of the TV lit the room. They were kissing.

John tiptoed toward them until Barry suddenly looked up. "Hey John! I thought I heard something. You shouldn't sneak up on people like that."

"Sawah you gewfwend?" John asked, just to be sure.

"Yes, I think you could say that," Barry answered, tenderly touching Sarah's cheek.

"Sawah, you yove Bawy?"

"Well, yes, John. I guess I do love Barry, though I haven't actually told him that. Thanks for spoiling that moment for us." She smiled at Barry.

Barry laughed and kissed her cheek. "I guess I love you, too, sweetie pie."

She lightly punched Barry's leg. "And I love you, too, John."

"Me yove you," John said.

"Good night, John." Sarah snuggled up to Barry and lay her head on his shoulder.

"Sawah?"

She turned. "Yes, John?"

"You hab pictu'e, Sawah? Me need you pictu'e."

"A picture of me? I don't have any."

"I do," Barry said. He fished his wallet out of his back pocket and handed John a photo booth set of four small pictures. In one picture Barry and Sarah were making faces, then sticking out their tongues, then kissing. The last picture was Sarah alone, smiling shyly.

"Me hab?" John asked tapping the last photo.

"Well, I guess so," Barry sounded like he didn't really want to give it up.

"Tanks," John took the photo and backed away quickly before Barry changed his mind.

"Fine. You can have them." Barry shrugged and put his arm around Sarah again. "We'll just have to go and do that again."

"Sawah?"

"Yes, John?" She sounded a little impatient this time.

"Me hab mama pictu'e?"

"Oh, sure. It's in my backpack, I think." She got up and rummaged in her backpack until she found it and handed it to him.

John took it and studied it close to his face. That was Sarah's mama and his mama. Miss Richardson.

Sarah plopped down on the couch again and motioned John closer. She kissed her index finger and touched the finger to John's cheek. "Good night now."

John imitated this new kind of kissing and touched his finger to her forehead. "Night night," he said.

He plucked the scissors out of the junk drawer in the cabinet before limping back up to his room. Lonnie didn't move when he switched on the light. Sitting cross-legged on his bed, John picked up mama's picture in its battered frame and removed it. He crumpled it up and tossed it toward the trash basket. It was just an old magazine picture of a pretty girl that Cookie had let him cut out, anyway.

John cut apart the photo of Sarah and carefully positioned mama's and Sarah's pictures in the frame so he could see both their faces. Lying back on his pillow he set the picture where he would be able to see it when he first woke up. Leaning up on one elbow, he kissed his index finger and touched it to Sarah's lips then Mrs. Richardson's lips—mama's lips.

John switched off the light. "Night night, Sawah," he whispered. "Night night, mama."